The Finest Type of English Womanhood

The Finest Type of English Womanhood

Rachel Heath

HUTCHINSON

LONDON

Published by Hutchinson 2009

2 4 6 8 10 9 7 5 3 1

Copyright © Rachel Heath 2009

First published in Great Britain in 2009 by
Hutchinson
Random House, 20 Vauxhall Bridge Road,
London SW1V 2SA

www.rbooks.co.uk

Addresses for companies within The Random House Group Limited can be found at:
www.randomhouse.co.uk/offices.htm

The Random House Group Limited Reg. No. 954009

A CIP catalogue record for this book
is available from the British Library

ISBN 9780091925864 (Hardback)
ISBN 9780091925871 (Trade paperback)

The Random House Group Limited supports The Forest Stewardship
Council (FSC), the leading international forest certification organisation. All our
titles that are printed on Greenpeace approved FSC certified paper carry the FSC logo. Our
paper procurement policy can be found at www.rbooks.co.uk/environment

Mixed Sources
Product group from well-managed
forests and other controlled sources
www.fsc.org Cert no. TT-COC-2139
© 1996 Forest Stewardship Council
FSC

Typeset by
Palimpsest Book Production Limited, Grangemouth, Stirlingshire

Printed and bound in Great Britain by
Clays Ltd, St Ives plc

For my parents, Andrew and Judy

When down from the silken ladder he caught her
in his arms and further and further brought her . . .
till the carriage was everything.
And she smelt the black carriage, round which there lay
peril and hot pursuit
ready to spring
And she found it covered with cold like spray;
and the blackness and coldness were in her too.
Into her hood she crept away
and felt her hair like a friend still true,
and heard estrangedly a stranger say:
I'mherewithyou.

'The Abduction', Rainer Maria Rilke

'Generally speaking, for the whole of her life how was her health?'
'Excellent. She was one of the finest types of English womanhood,
   physically, mentally and morally.'

Mrs Daisy Ellen Gibson, during her cross-examination by Mr Roberts
KC at the trial of James Camb for the murder of Gay Gibson.

March 1948

My father was a man so skinny and weedy as to be rendered almost incapable of imposing himself on anyone or anything. He allowed his house, our home, to fall into a grievous state of creaking disrepair and the garden along with it; the long lawns, the rose garden, vegetable plots and orchard were always thick with weeds and brambles, but one summer holiday he did something strange and unexpected.

I watched him wordlessly from an upturned pot in the corner of the greenhouse. This greenhouse was large and derelict, it leant against the back of our house like a needy relative, both annoying and reassuring, and I had never seen him working in there before that summer, though I knew he kept a small collection of hand tools under a rotten bedding tray, and once in a while I had caught sight of him from between the branches of my tree house, standing with his arms limply by his sides, looking up through the broken panes at the pale grey sky above, appearing as confused and accidental as all the ruin around him.

But that summer was different, the Great Grafting Summer. It was one of the sort that childhood should be made up of; I was ten, I wore boys' shorts and vests, ran free and abandoned, shoeless, wild and neglected through our garden and the fields behind. But this event in the greenhouse interested me, something marvellous and queer was happening, something which promised unexpected hope. He was a quiet and shy man, uncomfortable around other people,

I

often prickly with me, but that summer he suffered my presence in the corner of the greenhouse, caught up as he was by the pleasure of unusual activity.

Grafting is a method of propagation, you join plant parts, so they will grow as one. For instance, you might propagate a cultivar that will not root well as cuttings or whose own root system is inadequate if, say, they do not have strong enough foundations. But look, I was ten, it was all much simpler then. My father had been given some new buds to graft onto the stems of the old brown rose trees which lined the front of our house.

I had never once seen the old rose trees flower. I can't imagine who had given him the new buds in the first place, he didn't have any friends, and neither he nor my mother mixed with anyone from the village. Some friendly soul perhaps had dropped by and left them with him, perhaps they'd taken pity on us, holed up at the end of that long drive in our damp, miserable and flowerless house. Either way, he dug up those long dormant rose trees from the front garden and then, painstakingly, grafted the new buds onto the old stems and then planted them back out again. My mother had come out from time to time to watch him, in her high heels, smoking a cigarette, aloof and sceptical.

'It'll never work,' she said. 'You can't put two plants together and believe they'll become one. It's impossible. These trees are old and dead, just like everything else around here.'

He ignored her and somewhat against the odds, I now realise, he proved her briefly but triumphantly wrong. The graft took and grew and we were treated to vast tumbrels of pink and yellow roses and I would skip past them touching their petals and glorying in their excessive sweetness. They were extravagant and short-lived, but I celebrated them every day that they bloomed, and one warm night, as they were coming to their end, I stole down to pick up a few of the fallen petals to keep as a reminder of that summer, when suddenly everything had seemed touched with the heady scent of hope.

This is how I think of my and Gay Gibson's stories, as a graft, good buds put on strong roots, two quite separate people, two stories, which have to be grafted together to make any blooming sense.

I have fetched Gay's diary out from its hiding place – wrapped up in my old cardigan and flung onto the top of the hotel wardrobe, aiming for it to land in the furthest, blackest corner. I had to climb up on the chest of drawers in my stockinged feet and catch it with the pointy edge of a coat hanger. Doubtless she'd have preferred that I keep it in my underwear drawer, somewhere feminine and secretive. I have the diary out now in front of me, I like reading it, she was my friend and I miss her. Though I have adopted a rather scattergun approach to it, valuing her dreaminess and strangeness, her intimacies, far over narrative chronology.

I've decided to stick in some cuttings from the newspapers, to put them into the final pages – is that a strange thing to do? Perhaps it's wrong. She hasn't stuck much else in here, no bus, train or ship tickets, no theatre programmes or notices. I'm sure, if I'd kept a diary, I would have hoarded souvenirs and glued them in, with little caption boxes below, carefully inked in each precious memory. But if I'd had anything to stick in from those years they would have been memorandums and leaflets, badly typed circulars to 'My Comrades' and pamphlets. How pointless that would be, made-up things, an imposition on my life – nothing to do with me anyway. Gay knew well enough, I suppose, that mine and hers was an internal world of diaries, silent fears and whispered asides, of the odd halting message delivered over a rackety telephone system.

I like the early sections of her diary, I can feel her straining for 'best handwriting', they give me an idea of what Gay might have been like if she'd never left Birkenhead; fun, game, a local beauty with thwarted ambitions. It makes me sad to think of what became of her, of how and why. Of course there's all the usual schoolgirl guff, but sometimes something comes swinging out of those pages, which show me just how ripe she was for the plucking, how easily bruised, how odd and excitable she was, I suppose. I know what they say in the newspapers, that she was an innocent who fell into the hands of James Camb, wicked deck steward aboard the *Durban Castle*, and that she fell victim to his most unnatural advances. Though everyone has loved making a 'mystery' of it all. Poor Gay. She deserves a better send-off than this. She would have adored all the press coverage of course, her picture on the front of the national papers and her name so much the centre of every conversation. Take this front-page article, cut out, by me, from the *Daily Mail* two days ago:

MURDER OF ACTRESS ON HIGH SEAS

It was a sultry night, even for the tropics. The 17,000-ton liner the *Durban Castle*, homeward-bound from South Africa was doing 18 knots through the shark-infested seas, 90 miles off the West African coast. Almost three o'clock in the morning — most of the passengers were asleep, their cabin portholes open. The nightwatch were up and awake. There had been a dance in the ballroom and the ship had been bright with music and happy people, but now all was quiet. Only the noise of the engines and the swish of the water against the sides of the ship. And then bells sounded in the first-class pantry; signal lights flickered outside the door of Cabin 126 — the cabin occupied by a beautiful British actress. So began the mystery of what happened to the 21-year-old Eileen Isobel Ronnie Gibson, known as Gay, star of the play *The Golden Boy*, returning home to England after a successful tour. Today in the Great Hall of Winchester, now being used as an assizes court, the prosecutor for the Crown alleged that the answer to the mystery was that she had been murdered in her cabin and flung through the porthole . . .'

Shark-infested waters! Oh, and also this one, yesterday, from the same paper, I have stuck it on the opposite page:

One outstanding feature of Gay Gibson's mental make-up emerges — she could not resist men.

But for the press and the barristers to know everything, the truth, they would need to see and understand the graft. For grafting to be successful the two parts must be compatible and each must be at the correct physiological stage and then that union must be kept moist until the wound has healed, namely it must be cared for. Gay and I don't meet until late in our stories, but when we do our readiness for one another is everything. I shall write it down here, my and Gay's stories, interweaving, fighting for air, pressed between the covers of her diary. I could start on the deck of that ship, us with salt in our hair, the muffled sounds of dancing, the heavy warm air and the sweet taste of rum on our lips, Gay waltzing in the arms of an elderly, slightly harassed-looking gentleman, winking at me over his shoulder, but it would not be enough, would not be sufficient. No, Gay and I start as different girls, hijacked only later by strange events and by our own indi-

5

vidual flaws. We both start as immature schoolgirls awaiting and longing for escape, more similar than either of us ever realised.

Let's start with me, Laura Trelling, as I was, only two years ago but still a long way from South Africa, a long way from ersatz Johannesburg, a long way from that dry, dry place. It is 1946 and I am standing in the dark hall of my parents' house in Sussex, pressing the telephone against my face, listening to Charlotte Locks – plump, popular and sexually active – issuing a reluctant invitation. I am seventeen.

PART ONE

One

'I'm holding a Bonfire Night party and we are a little low on gels—' Charlotte had been taking elocution lessons and was taking care to crisply e-nun-ci-ate each syllable – 'and as it happens, Laura, you are on my mother's list below the grocer's daughtah.'

I loved her la-di-da turn on the telephone because I knew how little she wanted to invite me, and how at odds her grand ways were with her clammy secret life. Charlotte had been seeing Roddy Bellows, a pale boy with a permanent look of sorrowful alarm on his face, all through our final term at school. She'd regularly climbed out of the dormitory window on Saturday nights and we had obediently gathered to watch her hare across the playing fields, nightdress flapping under the school pullover, her plump legs powering out into the fading summer sunshine and the waiting arms of Roddy Bellows. She was running towards adulthood. Roddy would wait for her under the hedgerow at the end of the fields, gripping a small bunch of wild flowers which the following morning would be laid out in a neat line on top of Charlotte's locker, their pale stems bruised and flattened.

'Thank you, Charlotte,' I said primly. 'I would love to attend your functshun.'

9

I had not seen Charlotte or any of my old school 'friends' since our final day some five months before. Mrs Frobisher's Academy was a very minor school, very small everything really, located in a seaside town, not far from where most of us lived. They offered us girls a sympathetic consolatory education, embarrassed when we had to endure the rigours of trigonometry and fractions as it was generally accepted that such dry, masculine abstracts would be totally useless to us in our careers as the wives of local doctors and dentists. Charlotte had admitted to 'concerns' about what prospects Roddy Bellows might have; he'd told her that he wanted to be a poet but she hadn't seen this as the romantic gesture it doubtless was, hadn't seen the wild flowers as hopeful proof of his sensitive nature, for Charlotte wasn't a romantic girl, no, indeed, she was practical to the point of ruthlessness. But Charlotte's assignations must have left some impression on us. We, these pallid, developing girls in our too-tight tunics who had grown up during the war – and who now found ourselves at the end of school just as the war had ended – had seen a future through her, had started to piece together what the form might be, what we might expect from our own Roddy Bellows who, according to Charlotte, would be out there, one for each of us hovering spectre-like in the unseen future, their wispy hands holding drooping cornflowers and gesturing to us to come, come, come under the hedgerow.

So, 5 November 1946, 6 p.m. for punch and finger snacks, fireworks at 8 p.m. followed by the promise of late dancing on the terrace. A party! I'd been invited! I wore my school uniform! It was a perfect example of how I was back then. Surely I must have known not to wear my uniform, and of course I did have other clothes (though most were too small or babyish for a girl of seventeen) and so I can't for the life of me understand why I put my school clothes on in the first place. I had failed to distinguish myself in any way at Mrs Frobisher's but I had tried over the years to make some improvements, to drown out the little girl brought up in that big, dark village house, the feral child allowed to run free through the fields, to pick fights with the village boys and to set intricate traps for the baby rabbits each spring. The Academy had spent years pressing home to me the advantages of keeping my shoes clean and my hair brushed, dawn and dusk. But I had been too easily distracted, by the oddest things, like the flickering light in the school bathroom, the backs of Violet Carruthers' knees (empty, pale and always visible), to pay proper attention to these lessons in self-improvement and presentation. There was much dormitory talk late at nights on presenting oneself. Charlotte, apparently, presented herself very well. 'Oh yes,' they'd nod into the darkness, 'Charlotte's charming.' 'But right now,' I'd say, joining in where I wasn't wanted, 'she's under a hedge being pressed into the mud by Roddy Bellows. That's not very charming, is it?' and they'd groan and say, 'Oh, you don't understand, Laura, you don't know how it is. You don't know anything about these things.'

Mrs Frobisher kept a series of jars on the low shelf in her class-room at the Academy, each housing a mutant frog in the various stages of its monstrous development. You could barely see them through the cloudy greenish liquid, but if you pressed your face right up it was possible to glimpse a creature with proper back legs but no arms, or to see the fleshy whiteness of an underbelly hove into view with arms held out and a tail behind. That was how I was that autumn after leaving the Academy; suspended and unformed with a slipping, sliding understanding of what was left and what right, what was right and what wrong.

*

I tried to fix a torch onto the handlebars of my bicycle with parcel string; it was cold and dark, one of those evenings when the air feels sharp and dangerous and, because the torch wouldn't sit properly, I was worried about cycling through Elms Wood and on to the next village without any light. I tried holding the torch between my teeth, but this made me dribble so I put it in my pocket instead and just concentrated very hard on not looking up, and cycled round past the village green and down the lane out of our village with my mouth closed because it hurt to breathe in too deeply. I knew that Elms Wood was my enemy and that I had to conquer it. I knew that once I had made it through the wood I would be safe and that the lane up to Upper Emiswick was quite steep but short, and then I would find a party, to which I had been miraculously invited, in full swing. Perhaps the ride through Elms Wood was more significant than Roddy Bellows, perhaps my fervent desire to attend a party was what gave me enough courage to steam through, my teeth gritted, my eyes fixed on the terrible darkness ahead of me, and the courage to do all that followed after.

A school hymn came into my head, the one that starts 'He who would valiant be', and I pounded on the pedals and by the time I got to 'let fancies flee away', I was halfway through the wood cutting a chase through the night air, giddy with relief and surprise at my own daring. I knew that some of the branches hung low and that when the path got narrower I was in danger of coming off, but felt gloriously invincible and kept going until suddenly I was back out into the open spaces and the lane that led to Upper Emiswick.

I wasn't certain that I would know where Charlotte's house was, even though I had picked up a lot of details about it from her at school. I knew that it was red-bricked and that her mother had won prizes for the beautiful garden, that her father hadn't joined up for 'specialist' reasons but that he had built a long curved driveway in front of the house because being in the motor trade he'd wanted to ensure there was ample parking space. I knew that everything was 'just so' in Charlotte's house and that her mother had wallpapered her bedroom, one Christmas holiday, in a paper chosen by Charlotte (cream with climbing roses) and that she had curtains to match. As I arrived in the village, I could see a string of pretty paper lanterns hung from some trees in the distance. I was very moth-like.

There was indeed a long driveway and even though the party was clearly being held at the back of the house, I felt too self-conscious to cycle up, so I got off and threw my bicycle into the hedge at the bottom. I was exhilarated, I suppose, from the ride and instead of going in through the front door I decided to push my way through a bush at the side of the house. It was a terrible prickly fight, getting through the bush, and when I finally emerged, triumphant, onto the terrace, somebody screamed in surprise, and because I was pretty pumped up after riding through the wood and everything I screamed too, because she gave me such a jump, and then a group of girls in dark coats, standing near me, started screaming too and Mr Locks came striding over shouting 'Ho there!' and things like that.

'It's me,' I told him, laughing, 'it's Laura Trelling.'

I could hear the girls in their coats tutting, as though it had all been some ghastly tomboy prank and then Charlotte came pounding across the terrace towards me.

'We're not at school now, Laura,' she hissed. 'You'd better jolly well shape up if you want to stay.'

A woman in a headscarf appeared behind Charlotte's shoulder, I imagined this to be her horticulturally superior mother.

'Are you the daughter of Mrs Trelling at the Grange?' she asked.

'Yes.'

She gave me a glassy smile and raised an eyebrow slightly, then put her arm through Charlotte's and they went off together, whispering things.

The group of girls on the terrace instinctively moved away from me, like a shoal of fish. They looked different. Within just a few months those previously inky creatures, with their passionate tears over hockey selection and wild delight in rice pudding, had metamorphosed into slender young women who wore lipstick and had considered opinions on the weather and what they, and their mothers, had considered appropriate footwear for this evening. ('Mummy said she thought court shoes would do, so long as I was careful to stay on the paths.' 'Oh *absolutely*, so did mine.') I pulled my coat firmly round me so they wouldn't notice I was in my uniform, but no one came and talked to me because they were still keeping to their discrete huddles and observing the petty laws of who was allowed to be friends with whom.

Roddy Bellows and some of his friends were standing near the bonfire, poking it with sticks and teasing each other with that forced awkwardness and parade of too-loud laughs that was meant to impress. The clouds were clearing and I looked up at the stars and I remember watching the sparks flying out the top of the bonfire, hopping from one foot to the other, standing in the shadow of the house.

'Here,' he said, and he pressed a cup into my hands and closed his fingers around mine, and then gave me that sideways look of his. 'It'll warm you up.'

It was so unexpected to be touched, to be given something. I looked up at this man, and he was a man, not a boy, standing in front of me, smiling, his face half hidden by the shadows. He was tall, his face long and pale, the collars of his coat upturned. I drank the punch obediently, it was warm and sickly, cloying. I could hear the shocking bangs and fizzes of the bonfire as I drank, but I was also aware of a new sound, of a terrible rushing noise in my head.

'Well, that's what I call an entrance.'

He took a step towards me, I shot a quick look at him and then away again, down at the cup, swirling the remains of the punch round and round. He leant over and picked a twig out of my hair.

'I didn't want to come through the house. I thought it might be wrong.' I wondered if I was shouting, I could have been, the roar of a river in my head was deafening.

'Quite. It's a bloody dire party. I think I'm meant to be playing with Charlotte, but she's ghastly, don't you think?'

'She's playing with Roddy Bellows anyway,' I told him quickly. 'They do it under the bushes.'

The man laughed and pulled a stupid face. I'd embarrassed him, perhaps he was not so old after all. Why was he talking to me? Why was he standing so close?

The light from the French windows behind lit up the back of his head and the few hairs which stood up at his crown. He caught me looking and ran his hand over to try and smooth them down. And I was looking. I was staring at him, he looked foreign, different. That was it, just different, in ways I couldn't immediately fathom. I knew that he was not one of the poor country boys with their creeping sexuality and overbearing fathers, who were routinely lined up in front of us at dancing classes, at the summer ball and now at Charlotte's house. He was too old, for starters, and I'd never seen him before. I knew odd, drifting and alarming details about the boys from the 'other school' because the girls pleasured themselves by circling around them and then, from time to time, taking quick diving pecks at their unsuspecting heads. I knew that Richard Hill collected dried flowers (whoever had he thought to tell that to?), that Joseph Clark had tried to touch Cynthia Lawn's breasts during the waltz and then hotly denied it afterwards, that the cross spotty boy, whose mother it was rumoured worked in a factory and whose father had died in the Far East, was going to Cambridge next autumn, and that Charlie — the one whose spine sticks out at the bottom, so it feels as if he's growing a tail — had an older brother who had fought, was handsome but already engaged to a French girl and that Charlie's mother was highly sceptical about this alliance. These boys were our shooting gallery of opportunity but not one of them, not even Richard Hill with his sad tired books of pressed rose petals, had ever shown even the slightest quiver of interest in me.

He was tall, this man standing in so close, and I could see curls of hair standing away from his head, he was looking right at me. I had no idea how old he was, his face was a strange grey in the half-light, but when he returned my gaze, he was unflinching and steady, his eyes wide and black, a streamer of yellow light from the house lying across his head. I could feel his look on my skin.

'I didn't mean "playing" in quite that way,' he said with a smile, and then I felt the shock of his touch again as he took my arm, meaning for me to move out of the shadows, and I did, allowing him to guide me across the terrace and down towards a little mossy wall which separated the house from the garden. We sat down, and I swung my feet casually against it.

'So . . . ?'

'Laura.'

'Laura, what are we going to do to keep ourselves entertained?'

'They're going to have fireworks. It's 5 November, you see, and after the fireworks there will be "late dancing on the terrace".'

'Right. Shall we get drunk then? And since you haven't asked, I'll tell you. My name is Paul Lovell and I'm the guest of honour,' he said, producing a hip flask from inside the folds of his overcoat. 'I brought my own – do you want some?'

I took it. The contents of the flask burnt my lips and fell hot and slick down my throat, the surprise of it momentarily deadening the noise inside my head, and when he took the flask back his hand brushed against my fingers and I felt a shiver of pleasure to see him drink from the flask, without wiping the neck clean first. I wanted to get drunk with him, though I don't think I'd ever been drunk before, I wanted to enjoy the evening by feeling light and heavy at the same time, I thought we might stumble and giggle through the rose beds and not give a damn about what anyone thought, I wanted us to be bound together by something that could set us apart from the others, I wanted very much for him not to wander away from me.

'Isn't this awful? These bloody awful people. Jesus, I can't believe this place. What's it called? Upper Earwig or something?'

'Upper Emiswick.'

'Christ, look at them. They don't have the first idea of what's going on out there, in the real world, do they? What are you doing here? You don't belong here.'

No, of course I didn't belong in Upper and Lower Emiswick. Of course I didn't.

'Do you live here then?'

'I live in Lower Emiswick.'

'Do you really, Lower Earwig?'

'Yes,' smiling at the popping of some inexplicable bubble, 'I really do.'

'You're really quite pretty when you smile, do you know that?'

'How can you tell? It's too dark.'

'Good point —' he was laughing — 'but all the same I suspect you're pretty in an odd sort of way, and probably much smarter than all of them.'

'Oh no,' I told him quickly, 'I'm really not at all. Have you been in the war then?'

I suspected that he had been somewhere muddy and horrific, challenging. I was not surprised that he should despise us, this perfect stranger. He was looking ahead of him, I could see those curls again caught in the light, he had what my mother would have called a 'good nose', he was frowning. He was, without doubt, quite the most handsome man I had ever seen.

'No. I'm a pacifist,' he said. 'Do you know what that means? The terrible thing is, I'm meant to be grateful for this party. I've come down from London to attend a party being held in my honour, which I really didn't want in the first place. My aunt asked the Lockses to have a party for me, she thought I might like to meet some young people, but look at them, I don't want them that *young*.' This amused him and he laughed, a quick, restless laugh, and took another swig from the hip flask. I pulled my coat more tightly around me, I wanted to tell him that yes, of course I knew what pacifist meant, but I didn't get the chance.

'I was in London, I had to come down specially. The whole thing is a farce really. I only came to please my aunt. Why do you suppose I did that?'

'You needn't have bothered. They'd have had the party anyway, even if you weren't here, because Charlotte likes to show off.' It

18

was the only thing I could think of to say, I didn't have an answer to his question.

Banging my feet against the wall, my hands stuck deep inside my overcoat pockets, one hand gripping the torch, the other wrapping the parcel string around my fingers, until I could feel it biting in quite hard.

'Show off?' He was looking at me. The garden was layered in light and darkness, the bonfire, the lights from the French windows behind us, the little paper lanterns, the girls huddled in dark coats, the occasional glare of a cigarette among the wet looming shadows of the bushes. The dangerous crisp air still circled me, I could feel it across my neck and in my hair.

'I wish it would snow. I'd love to see some snow.' He fished inside his coat pockets again. 'Here, look at this.'

Paul passed me a creased photograph, folded in two. I opened it up and turned around on the wall, almost lying down, to find the puddle of light behind us. It was a picture of a young boy wrapped in a coat and hat standing with his feet wide apart in the snow. He looked cold and startled and was staring up at the camera, unsmiling. A shadow reached across the ground towards him, stopping at his toes; it was the person taking the photograph, I knew that, but I still found it ominous and sinister. It made the boy look so vulnerable somehow.

'That's me. That's the last time I saw snow. I was nine when that was taken, it was my last winter in England. The following spring we went out to South Africa.' He leant across nearer to me, to study the photograph. I could feel his breath near my ear.

'You don't look very pleased about it. It might snow at Christmas, I suppose.' I sat up quickly, handing the photograph back to him. 'It's only snow. You think it's exciting when it first comes because it makes everything look different, but actually it's quite boring after a while. Not that different from rain really.'

'I thought it was a sweet picture. I thought if it snowed while I was over here I could get someone to take the same photograph of me now, standing like that, in the snow.'

'Why? What would be the point of that? Why are you carrying this photograph of you as a child about the place?'

I wasn't meaning to be rude. I was trying hard to make what I hoped might be appropriate conversation, but at the same time, I also couldn't, for the life of me, understand why anyone would do such a thing.

'I don't know,' he laughed, 'now you put it like that, I really don't know. You are a most uncompromising person, aren't you?'

And I could feel him looking at me again, then he took the photograph and ripped it firstly in two, and then into quarters, quickly forcing it into tiny pieces. When he'd finished he tossed it into the air, without much force, so it fell down on top of his shoe, like snowflakes in fact, and he had to kick the little pieces off him. I wanted very much to jump down off the wall and collect it all together again, to stuff them all back into his pocket, so he wouldn't regret meeting me. I must have moved a little because he grabbed my arm and said, 'No, leave it. Don't you see? You were right, I was being stupid and nostalgic. You know what, I rather think you've – what did you say your name was?'

'Laura, Laura Trelling.'

'Well, Laura Trelling, I rather think you've just saved me from myself. I only came over to you because I felt sorry for you, coming in like that and all those horrible girls being mean to you, but I'm glad I did. You're quite the most refreshing and unexpected person I've met in a long time, and I'd like to kiss you now, if it wouldn't irritate you too much.'

Unexpected, but not unwanted, and not even strange. The mossy wall, the soon-to-be-exploded fireworks, our damp coats, Paul leaning over to kiss me on the cheek. His lips near to mine, the strangeness of his skin, the sweet smell of alcohol. I wanted to touch his mouth with my fingers.

'You made a noise just then, when I kissed you. Don't worry, it was a nice sort of noise. It's reassuring to know you're human after all. God, I'm fed up,' reaching for my hand, which I gave to him, and which he thrust into his coat pocket. 'Look at these people. Don't you loathe obligations? When d'you think we'll be free of them?'

'I'm not obliged to anyone.'

'You are to me now, because I kissed you. You're obliged to cheer me up and to tell me when I'm being sentimental. I rather suspect you don't do silly sentiment, which is a good thing by the way even if you do seem a little lost. Do you feel drunk yet?'

'Not really.'

'Me neither. I wonder if I might be a bit lost too.'

I sat quite still, my hand curled up inside his pocket. I could feel his hand, on top of mine, it was quite warm, and also something else in the corner, a cigarette lighter perhaps? He thinks I am lost, he thinks I am uncompromising. I say this to myself, inside my head, slowly. Nobody, except perhaps a teacher, had ever passed comment on what sort of a person I was before, nobody had ever said 'you are like this' or 'you are like that'. And just as I was deciding whether I liked it or not, Paul leant over and kissed me again, fully and squarely on the lips this time, and then, instead of pulling back, he just stayed there, with his lips pressed against mine, and us both with our hands in his pocket.

*

21

Our kissing didn't last long because Mr Locks let off the first firework, and we both jumped up in guilt and surprise when a rocket whizzed into the sky and splattered a million different stars above us. Paul laughed and whispered, 'I thought they'd got the guns out,' into my ear.

It was an excellent display. There were lots of rockets and Catherine wheels lined up by the far fence, and Mr Locks raced back and forth lighting each one to time so that there was never a pause, never a time while we waited for the next one to go off. I was happy watching the rockets scream and wheel through the air, bang, bang, whoosh, bang, sizz. Everyone clapped and cheered each time, and this must have inspired Mr Locks to keep up his impressive pace. There were big cheers of 'bravo' at the end, and he took a funny bow by the bonfire even though he was clearly exhausted, and Charlotte rushed over and gave him a hug, which seemed to please him too. Then everyone turned round to come up by the terrace and I saw some people looking at Paul and me standing back there, all on our own. They walked past us and up the steps, and some boys helped Mrs Locks to move the tables to one side, while she set up the gramophone near the window so that we could dance. Then Charlotte came looming out of the shadows,

'You've got to dance with me, Paul. You're the important guest, and I'm the hostess,' clearly proud of how well her party was going. 'I've neglected you. Chronic of me. Should have looked after you better methinks,' she said looking me up and down.

'Oh,' he said, 'we're just off actually, Laura and I. But thank you, Charlotte, thank you for everything,' and he leant over and patted her shoulder.

Oh the joy of that moment! Charlotte's open mouth, her shock

and then her steely glare, nobody but nobody ever spoke to Charlotte Locks like that.

'Come on then, Laura,' he said loudly, grabbing my arm, and
pulling me along beside him, 'I'm going to walk you home.'

'But,' I gasped, 'but the party's not over yet, and you're the guest
of honour.'

'Don't care,' he whispered, still striding forth. 'Let's get out while
we can. The London train's already left so I might as well walk you
home. Come on, we'll go out the way you came in.'

And we marched across the lawn and up the steps and over
towards the bush. I have no idea whether everyone was watching
us, but in my mind they were, open-mouthed and silent as we forced
our way back through that bush at the side of the house.

*

We used my torch to find the bike at the bottom of the drive, and
Paul offered to wheel it along for me. I remember thinking how
strange and nice it was to have someone do something for you,
but half wishing that I was pushing the bicycle, it was mine after
all.

'So. Lala,' Paul said, as we turned down the dark lane, 'do they
call you that? Lala?'

'No.'

'Well, I will.'

'I don't think I'm a very Lala sort of person.' I flashed the torch
up to his face.

'Oh yes, I think you are. Lala.'

I wondered whether it was a good thing to be a Lala. I'd never
been considered interesting or entertaining enough for a nickname

before. Lala. I tried it out under my breath as we walked along, letting my tongue trip against my front teeth.

'Do you think we'll get into trouble? For leaving like that?'

But Paul didn't make small talk. He seemed so certain about things, so definite and absolute. I thought him both wonderful and embarrassing.

'We have to turn into Elms Wood at the bottom. I was quite frightened when I rode through here this evening.'

'Well, you won't be frightened now, will you? Here, hold my hand,' and he took the bike in one hand and held out his other to me, 'that's it, hold the torch up, Lala, so we can see where we're going.'

I slipped my hand into his, and he gripped it tightly as though it were he that was afraid. We walked into the darkness. The vaguest silvery fingers of moonlight slipped through the trees giving an unreal, shifting sense of dark and light. I felt queasy trying to follow the bouncing light of the torch.

'I just closed my eyes and pedalled like mad and hoped for the best.'

'Good girl. Brave Lala,' he said, and squeezed my hand even harder.

'Are you scared?'

He didn't answer. I pretended to trip a couple of times, just so I could, awkwardly I admit, throw the torchlight up towards his face, to see if I could tell what he was thinking. I was curious. I had never kissed a boy before. Never even come close. I'd thought that if it ever did happen, it would be the result of some messy, complicated misunderstanding, like in a Shakespeare comedy. I'd once, accidentally, kissed a teacher at school. He'd leant in towards me and without thinking I'd turned up towards him and kissed him on the mouth. He'd explained, afterwards, that he thought he'd seen a dirty mark on my face and was just checking before he ordered me out of the room to clean it off. Now I wondered what sort of kiss Paul had meant it to be. Charlotte had told us that she opened her mouth when she kissed Roddy and we'd all practised kissing our pillows, lying flat on our stomachs and pressing our faces into the starchy pillowslips, mouths wide open, like so many goldfish. Was I supposed to have opened my mouth when Paul had kissed my cheek, might it be a sign of supplication and readiness?

'You're so serious.'

'So are you.'

'Well, this is a serious matter.'

He was teasing me.

'How can you be friends with those people?'

'They're not really friends. I just went to school with them.'

I stopped short of telling him that I didn't have any friends. That I was, by my own reckoning, a backward girl of seventeen who had lived her life so far in the murky half-light of a cold home and a provincial boarding school. A girl who at this very moment was taking great gulps of the wintry wooded air, half wanting to skip away from him and escape the terrible noises in my head, to be able to stand up straight and talk out loud to myself about all the things that mattered to me when I lived alone in the pale blue spaces that were my life.

We picked our way carefully along the path. He was having some trouble with the bicycle and I offered to take it from him, but he refused.

'So Charlotte does it under the bushes, does she?'

'With Roddy Bellows.'

'I bet her mother doesn't know.'

He shook his head and gave a long, low whistle.

'Are there wolves in this wood, Lala?' Letting the bicycle fall to the ground, he swung me round in front of him. 'May I?' and he started to undo the buttons of my coat. 'I thought so,' he laughed, holding the coat open and looking at my tunic, 'you are priceless!'

'I don't know why I put it on. I wasn't really thinking.'

'I think you look marvellous.' He said these things so easily, standing in front of me, barring my way up the path. 'You're so unaffected. I don't think I've ever met anyone quite like you before. How old are you?'

We were in the middle of the wood, at the darkest part where there was already a tightness underfoot because the pine needles on the ground had started to freeze; there was no sky above us, no horizon, only the snap of our voices in the chilly blackness. I shone the torch up towards the linking branches above our heads, and could see the pale mist of my breath caught in the light.

'I have left school. I just put this on for some reason. I don't have many clothes. I just wasn't thinking very straight.'

He held up his hand, giving the impression of reaching out for something in the air, just the edge of his wrist and the cuff of his coat caught the beam of the torch. There was a decision in the air, perhaps it was this that Paul had been reaching for.

He moved – yes, I'm sure it was this way, I am sure that it was him that moved – into the light of the torch, lowering his hand now, and standing in the full glare of the beam. He was completely still just looking straight down the light towards me. There was a flicker of hesitation on his face, quickly replaced by the slightest hint of warning in his eyes and then, lastly, affection and self-indulgence. He moved across the frosted pathway towards me, reached for the torch and, taking it, he dropped it to the ground. I couldn't see his face though I knew it was coming closer, could smell the air of him as he took my face in his cold, hungry hands.

When he stopped, when we stopped, he was laughing. I could feel his chest moving against my coat and his mouth in my hair.

'I'm only kissing you, Laura,' he said, 'you don't need to be so frightened. Here, I'll get the torch now.'

'I'm not frightened, but I've never kissed anyone before,' I said, and I clenched my hands up in my coat pocket. I might even have shouted it out above the deafening roar in my head.

'Really?' He shone the light on me now. 'Well, I hope it was all right. Come on, let's get you home.'

He was impatient, artless even, keen to move on, but I could not move. I stood in the heart of Elms Wood, the rushing noise in my head getting louder and louder still, filled with the distinct, chemical understanding that all the irrelevant details of my tiny life were swirling in front of me, like dust motes in the air or like waves around the head of a drowning woman, and that everything, in one burning moment, had changed, irredeemably, for ever. It was as simple as that.

Paul was further up the path, leaning on the bicycle, calling to me over his shoulder.

'Hurry up, for God's sake. It's freezing out here.'

Gay's Diary
This is my diary. Very private. For my eyes only.

2 October 1943

I've decided to keep this diary because I've had a very interesting sixteen years so far, and I'm worried that when I'm older I will forget all the interesting things I have seen and done. Someone will want to write a book or a magazine piece about me, and they'll ask me to tell them all about my life and then I won't be able to remember anything. Of course, I'll say things like 'Me? Who wants to know about little old me?' and then this handsome reporter (sensitive and funny, like James Stewart) will say, 'But, Miss Gibson, you must know that the whole world is crying out to hear your story – please tell us.' And I shall be in Hollywood then, lying on a white sofa, wearing a fluffy white jacket and little shoes, and I'll bend down towards this writer person, who will be sitting on the floor, and say, 'Oh very well then. Now let me see, where shall I begin?'

And then what if I really don't know where to begin, because I just can't quite remember what's happened? And the public, those that read movie magazines anyway, will already know most things about me – the pictures I've starred in, the leading men I've had dinner with – will have seen the photographs of my last visit back to Birkenhead (waving from a train carriage) and being greeted by ecstatic crowds. So they'll need something else, won't they?

Also, I've no one here who really understands me and sometimes I have so many things going round and round in my head that I think I'll burst if I can't get them out somehow.

So here goes, and I'll try to keep it brief. The first thing to know is that I am a daughter of the Great British Empire. I was born in Jamalpur, India, during the monsoon. I don't remember much about this of course, though Mother says I was a beautiful baby with a shock of red hair, and the midwife when she saw me cried out something in her language and hugged Mother telling her she'd been delivered of an angel, but Mother says all she could think of right then was the noise the rain was making on the roof. I can't remember much about India. Sometimes I think I do, but Mother says this is just me dramatising. I tell her, 'No. I can remember a room with mud on the floor,' and she says, 'We never had mud on the floor, Eileen! We left India when you were four months old. How could you remember anything?' But I'm sure I can remember this muddy floor, and white sheets hanging on a line outside the window, blowing in a breeze. And other things too. I don't see why I shouldn't be able to remember things from when I was a baby.

I've just been downstairs to find Mother and to ask her to tell me something about Jamalpur that I can write in here. She said, 'Your father worked for the East India Railway as a blacksmith and when it rained it rained and when it was hot it was hot,' and then Father came into the kitchen and said, 'We saved many souls in Jamalpur, Eileen. During our time there the Baptist ministry grew tenfold.'

It was a mistake to go downstairs because now Father wants me to sing for him at the piano. He said, 'You can leave your auto-biography till later, miss. Come and practise.' This daily practising is becoming embarrassing because if anyone calls round while I'm singing, Father just leaves them outside on the step until I've finished, he won't let me be interrupted, and then when they're finally allowed in, they look a bit cross and look at me as if it's all my fault and not Father's at all. Last night one of father's friends from the chapel came round (he waited a full ten minutes on the step) and when he came in, I could see him scowling at me and he came striding in the room and he says, 'You all set to go to the secretarial college then, Eileen? When do you finish at school?' and I said, 'Oh no, sir, I'm going on the stage. I'm going to be an actress,' and he didn't like that one bit.

15 October 1943

Margaret and Lauren told me they thought I was a big-head and that all the girls were talking about me because I'd been seen down the shops on Saturday wearing a fur coat. 'So what?' I said to them. 'I do own a fur coat,' and they called me a liar and said I'd borrowed my mother's and I told them, 'My mother wouldn't be seen dead in a fur coat. It's mine.' Then Margaret said if I did own a fur coat, could she borrow it at the weekend? And I said yes of course she could, and then we agreed we'd walk home together, which we did, holding hands, and chatting about things. I told her about how my father had bought me the coat when we'd come back from Persia to see me through the winter, because I'd had malaria. And she said, 'Why aren't you dead then?' and I told her that not everyone died from malaria, and she thought that was interesting. She said, 'I really didn't know that, Eileen.' Then she said, 'You're different to how you used to be – before you went away, I mean,' and I asked her what she meant and she said, 'Well, you're all grown up. My mother says you won't be long in Birkenhead. Not now you've seen the world.' She's going to come round on Friday to borrow the coat.

Mother doesn't like this new house. She thinks we're getting above ourselves, living here without a rent book. Mother still walks to the old shops, she says she'd rather stand in line with familiar faces than go to the shops just round the corner. She makes a great scene about going out too, telling us both that we'll have to wait for our tea tonight, because she's got to walk all the way down to the butcher before he closes and it's a good mile there and back. Father gets this glint in his eye when she says this, but he doesn't rise to it, doesn't say, 'There's another butcher round the corner, dear, go there,' which is what I'm screaming out to say. He sits down and says, 'Well, not to worry, Daisy. Eileen and I can wait a while longer.' I think it's a silly state of affairs, so yesterday I said, 'Why don't we get a servant, Mother? To save you the fetching and carrying,' and Father laughed but Mother went bright red and looked like she might hit me. 'Listen to you,' she said, 'swanning about this house like you've not got a care in the world, while I work my fingers to the bone. You should be helping me out. You're the daughter. A servant indeed! Who do you think we are?' and I genuinely was trying to be helpful and I said, 'Well, we used to have servants in Persia,' and she slammed her housekeeping book down on the table and stormed out the house, banging the front door after her. I opened the kitchen window and yelled out at her, 'There's a butcher's only five minutes away!' but Father came after me, and told me I should know better than shouting out the window and I was to let Mother be.

She has hung up the curtains from our old house, though they are much too short. Father told Mother that he thought she might enjoy being able to do the house up as she'd like, but she said she didn't like one bit, it would be a waste of money and effort, when what was wrong with our old house anyway? On the day we moved in she stood in the hall with her arms crossed and said to him, 'This is a haughty house, Joseph Gibson.' I quite like the house and I've told all the girls that we've moved into Banbury Road and that we have an apple tree out the back, and a proper garden path with a black gate at the end of it.

Father doesn't care about carpets and curtains and such things, he told us that he'd worked hard and was pleased to have such a big house to show for it and Mother said, 'Are you telling me we lived in all those "forren" places just for this?' and then Father looked all serious and told her to remember all the work they had done spreading the word of Christ to the dark sides of the world, and she couldn't think of anything to say to that.

So that's us then, the Gibson family reluctantly going up in the world.

When we first came back, none of the girls at school were interested in hearing about Persia but I let it be known that I can now horse-ride and that in the summer I used to take my bedclothes outside and sleep under the date palms and that I'd played a lot of golf. I'm not like Mother, I'm not going to pretend that we're still like the little people, grateful to be living in these tight streets without a thought of what might be out in the world. I couldn't be like Mother and pretend we're just as we were before. Look at her, she's travelled all over the world – when we went out to Masjid-i-Suleiman she organised everything. Just her and me on the train, on the SS *Marco Polo*, then in the car from Damascus to Beirut, in the coach and then the train to Basra, and yet you'd think she'd never been further than the end of our street. I don't understand it.

There isn't much I miss about Persia because I was pretty bored most of the time. I suppose I miss the servants, even though they were a nuisance because they had no idea of cleanliness, and I liked the horse-riding and badminton at the club, even though I wasn't very good at it.

I miss Seda. I think about her a lot. She promised to write to me when she left to go to Tehran for the hot weather, but she never did. I don't know why and now if she does write then I won't get her letter because she can't know where we are. When I first met her I was surprised that she could speak English and ride and swim and things. I thought she'd be different because of her being Armenian and everything, but really she was just like me. She liked the pictures too. And she was funny. She had this funny way of frowning just before she was going to tell a joke, as if she already knew how funny it was and it was driving her crazy not being able to wait until the end. She was a really fast swimmer too, she could beat me and her brothers, and when she rode she was completely fearless. I'd like to be more like Seda. When I'm at school sometimes I pretend I am her, as I walk down the corridor, and I find I walk quicker, I feel stronger and I wave to people.

I asked Father if he could ask the Anglo-Iranian Oil Company to send her address, so I could write to her, but he said that would be impossible and I wasn't to ask again. He said, 'You know, Eileen, when we travel we must learn to travel light,' and I asked him what he meant and he said, 'Well, can you imagine Seda here? Going to Birkenhead Secondary for Girls? No, well, that's what I mean by travelling light. Leave her behind, she's not part of your life here.' I started to say that I didn't want her to come here and live with me, I just wanted to write her a letter, but he wouldn't let me finish, he just said, 'We're in Birkenhead now, Eileen, remember that.'

Then Mother came up to my room that evening and said, 'Father says you were asking after Seda again.' And I told her I just wanted

33

to write her a letter because she'd gone to Tehran and never written like she said she would and Mother went over and stood by the window and said, 'Did you ever wonder why she didn't write, Eileen?' and I didn't answer her. Then she looked over at me and said, 'We didn't tell you the truth. She didn't go to Tehran for the hot weather, she went because her parents wanted to get her away from you.'

I called her a liar and a couple of other bad things and she came over and slapped me hard across the face. 'Stop it, Eileen, stop it!' she shouted at me. 'Why don't you listen to what I'm saying? They thought you were unnatural. They asked to be moved, they told us they thought you were crowding her, her and her brothers, always going round there, asking for things. It wasn't proper, they said you were unnatural.'

We were both crying now and she tried to hug me, but I wouldn't let her. I hate her. How dare she make these things up. She's jealous of me. She's old and stupid and ugly and she hates me because I'm not any of those things.

2 *November 1943*

I've decided to change my name. There's not a single actress called Eileen that I can think of – and Margaret can't think of one either. I think it's an ugly, common name. Father is organising dances with Mr Chalmers in aid of the Birkenhead Red Cross and St John's Ambulance Brigade Prisoner-of-War Fund and their committee is called the Top Hat's Gay Dancing Company and that made me think of Gay. Gay Gibson. On first impression, clean and cheerful – but then when seen in a theatrical programme or spelt out in lights above Shaftesbury Avenue, it's got the glamour of a leading lady. Gay Gibson. I love it.

Talking of Mr Chalmers, he came round this evening to see Father, and he had to wait outside again. And when I was standing by the piano, trying to keep up with Father's piano playing, I could see him staring in the window at me. He had his whole body pressed up against the glass of the window, so that his hat was knocked back on his head a little. And I was singing 'Ave Maria', and I looked over at him, and he raised his hand a little, and waggled his fingers at me.

I stopped singing and said to Father, 'Mr Chalmers is outside,' but Father didn't stop playing, didn't even look up, he just said, 'He can wait.' And off we went again. Well, I found it difficult to concentrate, knowing Mr Chalmers was there, looking so peculiar and all, and then when he came in, and Father went off to get his chapel and Red Cross papers, Mr Chalmers came over and stood very close to me.

'That was lovely singing, Eileen,' he said. 'You look quite out of breath.'

And I was, I suppose, because my chest had that tight feeling and I was trying to catch my breath still, by leaning on the piano.

'Do you need some water, dear?' he asked, and then he reached out and put his hand on my back.

Well, I shook my head because I couldn't talk yet, and he took my arm and ran his finger up the inside part, following the line of the vein, up into my neck. And he had this funny look on his face, and I was still trying to catch my breath so I just smiled at him and then, the dirty old dog, he looked down at my titties – and he didn't even try to pretend that he wasn't! Then he goes, 'If there's ever anything you need, Eileen, you'll remember Uncle Charlie, won't you? I can get things, you know, I know people in Liverpool, who can get things, and really, I won't charge much,' and he's still holding my arm, and then he goes, 'That was a joke,' because I didn't laugh, I suppose, so I nod at him because I'm still not able to talk properly yet. 'You're going blue here,' he says and he runs his finger across my lips. When Father came back into the room, he turned round quick enough and said, 'Oh, Joe, I was just worried about Eileen. She seems a little out of breath,' and Father said, 'Oh, she'll be fine. Her chest gets a little tight sometimes.'

When Mr Chalmers left he called through to the kitchen from the hall, 'Goodbye, beautiful,' and I said, 'Goodbye, Mr Chalmers,' just about as sweetly as I could manage. Isn't that just hilariously funny?

6 November 1943

They're auditioning for the pantomime at the Liverpool Empire. Mr Chalmers saw the advertisement in the local paper, and brought it round to show me. 'I'm going up for it,' I told him and I cut it out with Mother's kitchen scissors and put it up on the shelf above the cooking range. He said he'd thought of me when he'd seen it.

9 November 1943

There's been a lot of fuss and trouble about the pantomime. Yesterday, Mother saw the clipping and showed it to Father, who came over all serious and said, didn't I know that there would be 'professional theatre people' going up for these parts. And I said, I thought of myself as a professional theatre person and that I wasn't exactly imagining I would be a PRINCIPAL. I told him that Mr Chalmers had brought it round and that it had all been his suggestion and Father says to her, 'Well, if Charles is involved?'

This evening I went round to the Chalmers house after tea. His wife opened the door and looked me up and down and I said I'd got a message for Charles from Father and she held out her hand for it, but I said I had to tell him in person. So she doesn't invite me in or anything, just shouts down the hallway, 'Charlie, it's that Gibson girl for you!' and then he comes beetling up the hallway like a man possessed. Sheet white he was, and he looked dead silly because he'd still got his napkin tucked in his shirt, and food round his mouth. And he said to his wife, 'I'll deal with this,' and she goes off shooing the children back to the table who have come out to have a look too, and then he comes outside and pulls the front door closed after him.

'Well, Eileen, this is a surprise,' he says under his breath, and looking up and down the street.

'You've got to tell Father that you'll take me to the Liverpool Empire on Wednesday,' I tell him.

And he's wiping the food from his mouth.

'Oh I have, have I?'

'You said I was to tell you if I ever wanted anything.'

'Now hang on a minute,' he goes, 'I meant stockings and chocolate and the like, I'm not a bloody taxi service.'

'They'll let me do it if I go with you, I know they will. You can wait for me and then bring me back.'

And he's closed his front door and is standing shivering on the doorstep but he's looking at me like he did that time at the piano and he goes, 'Well, I suppose I could if you ask nicely, Eileen, like a good girl.'

So I says, 'Please, Mr Chalmers, would you take me to the Empire on Wednesday?' all eyes and smiles, because I'm guessing this is what he wants and then he sort of taps me on the bum with this big grin on his face and says, 'Since you asked so nicely, yes I will. I'll do whatever you want, Eileen,' and I says, 'Pick me up from the corner of Argyll Street on Wednesday then. Noon.' And I walked off then, and didn't look back.

17 November 1943

I got a part! The man there was nice, and he said my singing and dancing were very impressive. I'm to be in the chorus. The man, Lionel something, said he would be looking to me to keep the chorus under control and in line, as I'm going to be the oldest one. Am so happy. It felt really good to be up there on the stage. Charles sat at the back and said I'd done really well, he said I looked a million dollars. On the way back we shared a bar of chocolate he'd got. He said he was really proud of me, and even thanked me for letting him come and share in this exciting moment. He thinks I'm going to be really famous and then he looks all upset and wants to know whether I'll remember him when I'm famous. I told him I would, I'm not going to be like that, and I told him all about you, diary, and said I write down most everything I can so I don't forget things. Then he goes, 'Am I in your diary, Gay?' which made me laugh, and I refused to tell him, saying it was a secret and all, and I still didn't tell him even when he tickled me so hard.

Two

The morning after Charlotte's party Paul came back to the Grange, and when I saw him from my bedroom window, marching across the lawn, his red scarf flying in the wind like a warning flag, I grabbed my coat and bolted out the door to cut him off before he came too close.

'Shouldn't we do this properly?' he asked, grabbing my arm. 'I'd rather. I don't want us to go behind their backs.'

'But I haven't said anything to them.' I was trying to walk away through the long grass. 'I'll show you around the village if you like.'

Paul came after me, the bottom of his trousers already sopping wet.

'Bugger the village, Lala. Bugger it.'

He was casting his eye around, quickly taking in the house and the grounds, drinking in the turreted rooftops and mullioned windows, the heavy overgrown hedges that tumbled around the bottom edge of the garden threatening to overrun the five wizened fruit trees which Pa still called 'my orchard', though they were black from aphids and their meagre fruit was never picked but left to rot on the ground. I don't think the Grange looked deprived and forbidding to him, he was smiling.

'Quite a place you live in, Lala,' he said quietly.

'Was. It was my father's father's father's or something, but it's falling down now. The windows are all rotten and the roof leaks and you can't heat any of it, and this winter if we want hot water we've got to boil it up in the kitchen because all the pipes are broken. I hate it.' I was gabbling.

'Yes.' He looked at me carefully. 'Yes, it is a bit creepy, I suppose. Come on, we might as well look around, seeing as I'm here. I didn't go back to London, you see, I rather found I wanted to see you again.' He looked bemused for a moment, astonished at himself. 'You look quite different in the daylight, you know.'

So did he. The night before he had been a shadowy figure of promise and surprise, his face caught in the light and then plunged into darkness, fireworks had danced in his eyes, and his hands had been streaked with moonlight. I hadn't slept for the whole of the previous night, I had been reliving every moment of the night before, pacing my bedroom, intent on remembering every detail, every incident, ensuring I had it all in the correct order. I was sure that it would be important. I hadn't been mooning about the room, dancing on the rug and hugging a pillow to me, I had been very concentrated and serious about it, demanding perfect recall. That morning I sneaked around him, still staring, pleased to see that he looked younger, his face longer and kinder than I had remembered, his hair more mouse than dark with soft babyish curls around the temples and along the neck of his red pullover. I took in his large pale blue eyes, his long striding legs, his sudden, whipping laugh and tried too hard to satisfy this curious enthusiasm for the potting sheds, the derelict stables and the marshy, slippery banks of the pond where he delighted in wading through the reeds, looking for nests. I wanted, very much, to please him.

I showed him my old tree house and told him about the roman numerals I had etched into the floor with Pa's letter opener.

'Let's see,' he said, and pulled himself up the trunk, pulling bits of bark off with him.

'What were you counting?' he called down, squatting on the planks, reaching out his arm to steady his balance.

'The years until I was sixteen.'

'Poor Lala.' He poked his head out and pulled a face. 'Poor Lala. Gosh, you can see for miles up here.' I saw him scanning the back of the house and those nasty uptight little gorse bushes that ran alongside the path to the kitchen doors. 'I don't suppose it could come quick enough. Typical of the idle aristocracy really, all this. They plunder the land for centuries on end, nothing more than a bunch of bandits, and then they let it all fall apart. Why don't they *do* something? My father would turn this place around in no time. How can they bear to let it all collapse around their ears?'

He jumped down then, and got to his feet with a look of modest triumph on his face.

'Didn't think I'd make that,' he told me, rubbing the green stains from his coat. 'Shall we go in then? Say hello? I'm rather curious. Oh, and Lala, thank you for showing me your tree house,' and he laughed, and swung his arm across my shoulders.

He showed no sign of feeling anxious or nervous. He strode into the drawing room, wet trousers flapping around his ankles, with a steady smile and his hand outstretched. Ma and Pa were sitting in their wing-backed chairs, each nursing a pre-lunch whisky. Ma was flicking through one of her fashion magazines and tutting in disapproval while Pa was keeping time to the ticking clock by tapping his foot against the fender. They looked up in surprise and I, always the coward, hung back behind Paul.

'Hello, Mr and Mrs Trelling. I'm Paul Lovell, a friend of Laura's,' he said, just like that.

They rose to the moment in a way that made me almost proud of them. Pa insisted Paul sit down and take a drink with them and there was a bit of fuss about trying to find him a clean glass; one was found on the sideboard and I saw my father pull his shirt out of his trousers and whizz it around the inside of the glass when he thought no one was looking.

'How intriguing!' Ma said, leaning forward. 'Wherever did you meet?'

'At Charlotte Locks' party,' Paul said, smiling over at me and nestling down into the red sofa, crossing one leg over the other. He tugged at his trousers. 'Sorry. Got rather wet. Beautiful garden though, Mrs Trelling.'

Ma took the compliment with a gracious bowing of her head.

'Yes, we're frightfully lucky to have it.'

'This is a lovely room.'

'Thank you, Paul,' she purred. I could not see her behind the wings of her chair, I could only see her legs in their black trousers crossed in front of her, and then see her recrossing them again, slowly, and her hand smoothing down the leg to her ankle.

Nobody told him that it was the only liveable room in the house, and the reason it was full of paintings and heavy blocks of ancient furniture was because Pa periodically dragged another piece in to save it from early destruction by damp and woodworm. He'd shoved the sideboard from the dining room up against the wall, beside the bureau, saying it could stay there until he found a better place for it. You had to thread your way very carefully through that room, following a well-beaten path towards the sofa and their chairs arranged around the fire. It had the appearance of a well-heeled antique shop, of the sort that suggested these were all dearly beloved pieces, which just happened to be for sale, and perhaps you might like to wander around and find something you could love and the vulgar matter of pricing could be dealt with later. The curtains, a heavy, faded tapestry which, when drawn, showed the Battle of Hastings (arrow in the eye and all), were usually left open, despite the draught, because they had started to crumble around the edges, to shed a skin of dust and decay.

'Did you show him my orchard, Laura?' Pa positioned himself in front of the fire, clasping his hands behind his back in a way that perhaps he remembered his father doing on such occasions.

'Yes.'

'Was the party *fun*?' Ma asked him.

'Not bad. Jolly good fireworks. Laura was by far the best thing there though.'

He was being gallant. I was still standing, leaning against the sideboard and trying to look at ease. Trying to appear as though this was not only a perfectly normal course of events for me, but also for my parents.

'Ah yes,' said Pa, nodding at me.

Ma leant forward in her chair. I saw her raise her eyebrows and tilt her chin at Paul.

'I used to *love* parties,' she said, expansively.

*

Ma, by her own account, had been quite the party girl in her day. If she was to be believed, her entire youth had been spent in a constant whirl of tennis parties, shooting parties and debutante balls.

'Such giddy times!' she liked to tell me. 'I was always in demand.'

There was more than a hint of accusation in these stories. I spent my school holidays drifting from room to room, rearranging the furniture in my bedroom, drawing patterns on the windowpanes, or on Mondays, when Mrs Humber came in, I'd join her in the kitchen, and she'd push some peas to be podded or dough to be kneaded towards me with an apologetic half-shrug, and silently get on with her own work.

My mother would hunt me down, wherever I was.

'When I was your age, boys were fighting over who would partner me at tennis.' ('What, at *twelve*?' I should have said, but I didn't, instead I obediently hung my head in shame.)

There was something intriguing about this life she spelt out. The afternoons were always sunlit and full of poetry, of illicit whispers and secret messages, of starched linen, ice-cold lemonade and adoring, witty suitors. There was Archie McKenzie, a tall boy with estates in the Highlands and a degree from Oxford. He sent Mother letters in Latin, which she, with her meagre education, couldn't hope to decode but she felt that if she had then perhaps she might now be dressed in the best McKenzie tartan and making brief, flowery visits to her grateful tenants in their peaty crofts. Who else? A second cousin whom she always referred to as 'that ravishing boy who was to become one of the best on Harley Street' – and then she'd add by way of an explanation 'his parents always ate their bananas with knives and forks' – and who had wide tanned arms and a marvellous opening serve. There was a whole family of boys, falling out of their trousers and off their hunting horses at the sight of her in a black coat and white jodhpurs and who considered it a matter of family honour that they take it in turns to offer them-selves for dancing at the hunt ball.

'Ah, yes,' she would finish, 'but that was back then. Before I met your father and he brought me here. Before we became *reclusive*.'

She liked to let the word roll around her mouth.

'And how did you meet Pa?' Because there was a time when I was interested. 'Did you meet him at a party? Did Pa play tennis?'

I wanted to hear how my thin, nervous pa might have come leaping over the net towards her, sending the other suitors spinning in his wake, and how he must have swept her up into his bendy arms. But there was no 'ravishing' for Pa, no pride in his superior scholarship or his family's brilliant way with fruit — no, her face clouded over, blighted by the memory of this crushing misjudgement.

'No, he *never* played tennis,' she'd say, as though this represented all that was so very small, so very meagre about Pa.

'A smashing girl,' Pa had murmured, when I'd asked him, and then he'd looked sad and overwhelmed, 'raven-haired.'

So then I wondered whether perhaps it was just possible that Pa had won her hand because, well, he'd *asked*, hadn't he?

My mother had given birth to me in a kind of mindless fury. She liked to steal up to the nursery when I was very small, holed up in two rooms with a succession of surprised and intimidated governesses and tell me of the extraordinary events of my becoming. Extraordinary to her, I should add. She'd married my little pa, and moved into the Grange, his family home, straight after their honeymoon on the French Riviera. When she'd arrived, sunned and singing from the late nights in the grand hotel, Granny Plum and Grandpa had met her in the stony hall.

'And Granny Plum said, "Talk about putting the cat among the pigeons."'

Ma would be leaning against the wall, looking down at me,

sitting at some small wooden desk empty save a line of blue and red pencils, and the governess sitting obediently in a far corner, waiting to begin her lesson.

'What did she mean? Did she think you'd eat them?'

She'd been twenty years old, flushed with social success, delighted finally to have a ring on her finger and a house in the country to go to for the summer. She had trunks full of the finest Parisian dresses, little boxes lined in satin and fur, small delicately coloured bottles of scent and special married lady undergarments, bought by her aunt, and still wrapped in pink tissue paper. My father existed in a state of mild confusion, benign and adoring, he'd endured their honeymoon abroad – too hot, too French, too expensive – and had been grateful to return to his cool, hollow family home.

Ma can't imagine what she is doing in this musty damp house, with the lumpy bed and no heating to speak of. She decides to hate it. She lies in bed in the mornings and calls complaints through to her husband in his dressing room. She hates the curtains, the floors, the stairs, she hates the view from the windows, she hates the smell. She really hates the smell. 'What is that?' she'd say, crinkling up her pretty nose during tea in the drawing room, 'Whatever is that awful smell?'

She wants to invite people down to the Grange for parties. She imagines that she will fill the house with light and laughter, that she will be an exemplary hostess and that young men will ask her to dance out into the night, across the terrace and down the lawns and will whisper in her ear, 'If only I'd found you first.' But Granny and Grandpa Plum are not keen on parties, they are country folk whose concerns are only the management of their estate and preserving the memory of their two dead sons, killed not many years before in France. They are a puritanical couple, hard and

46

uncompromising, who believed their sons' sacrifice for king and country was noble and proper but who indulge their grief with uncompromising hardship and misery. My mother is the daughter of an optimistic industrialist, and she is used to the modern world, to shiny machines and brand-new cutlery, and is certain that everything can be refreshed, changed and thrown about. She does not understand the empty corridors of their grief, their insistence on eating only very small amounts of unsavoury foods, for she is a young woman with appetites.

'I never thought we'd stay here, you see, Laura, I thought we'd live somewhere else.' When she told me these stories I must have been only six or seven years old and so she is still hanging onto the memories of her youth, still cherishing the spoilt, modern girl she was, but over the years that girl has slipped from my mother's fingers, has spiralled away over the pointy chimneys of the Grange.

'Why didn't you?' I am a most obedient child, and though I know the answer I still ask the question, my body already charged with hot spots of guilt and fear.

'Because I had you. Quite unexpectedly of course. I didn't even know how babies were made, I didn't know that what your father did to me in the bedroom was—'

Then one out of three of the governesses would cough from her corner. She would be one of the kinder, plainer types who was only recently employed and who probably liked me, though I was stupid and plain, and who might have felt sorry for me, or for my mother.

'Mrs Trelling,' she might say, 'I'm about to begin Laura's lesson,' or if she were really brave (and perhaps had sad, thwarted stories of her own to tell), 'I don't think this is something for the child to hear.' Though my mother would bat away her objections as she might a particularly insistent fly.

'Nonsense, one's never to young to hear about a woman's lot in life. It's better she knows this than her ABCs. Learning never did me any good. We have no power, Laura, not over our bodies, our minds or our lives. Now that's an important lesson for you to learn, my girl. Don't fill your head with silly nonsense because your life will amount to nothing, you will amount to nothing.'

Then the governess might come over, and take my mother in her arms and escort her from the schoolroom or nursery or wherever we were. I know I scrutinised her from a distance, with a child's obsessive eye. 'She's a very complex person,' my father liked to say. I'm sure he rocked me in my crib to the rhythm of that sentence, crooned it gently, while he held me in his arms, laying his small, sad hand across my purple face, my baby-black hair, trying to ease out the creases in my tiny, bewildered being. Sometimes it would be 'artistic' or 'highly strung' and I remember 'special' making a pleading appearance for a few years, when I turned ten. There was a time when I gratefully sucked at this idea of my mother's uniqueness, as hungry for a reason as a baby for its mother's milk. But all the time my father was gently imploring me to be kind to her, inside I knew the truth. I knew it wasn't special to take to your bed complaining of headaches for weeks at a time or artistic to scratch away at the edges of our lives, I knew that she had no control over her life or her body, and that neither did I.

By the time Paul arrived at the Grange, she had become vindictive and drunk. The courses of grief, which ran through that house, grey and swirling and unstoppable, and which had taken my father as their birthright and then slowly seduced my mother to their chilly grip, were still only lapping at my feet. Though I knew them, and I knew I must escape them, I could not judge how much of their coldness were already within me; I fancied not much, I trusted I could be warmed up, but mostly I knew I must escape.

*

In the drawing room the effort of entertaining our unexpected guest was beginning to tell. My father was shuffling from foot to foot, his hands now stuck deep into his pockets, his face frozen with the fixed, alarmed smile of the very shy, baring his teeth slightly in the effort to appear jovial.

'You'd better be getting back,' I said to Paul.

'Right.' He struggled to his feet. 'Thanks for the drink. Lovely to meet you both.'

'You must come to lunch,' Ma declared. 'Tomorrow.'

Pa convulsed with a tingling kind of shudder.

'Well, that would be lovely, but I'm afraid I have an appointment in Oxford tomorrow. I could come back next week though, next Thursday perhaps?'

He was so well brought up. So violently normal. Ma bowed her head in regal assent.

I walked with him out of the house, and down to the iron gate. We walked in silence, our feet crunching on the frozen gravel, I could feel a chilly breeze around my neck, and I wondered whether Paul could feel it too.

'That seemed to go all right,' he said when we reached the gate. 'I have to say I've never been in such a place as this. It's all pretty ghastly, isn't it?'

'Will you come back for lunch?'

'I think I'd better, Lala. You rather need saving really, don't you?' And he looked confused again, and shook his head, as though he

49

still didn't know what it was which drew him to me. He pulled me towards him and we kissed, though fleetingly this time, the lightest brush of his lips against mine and across my cheek.

'Please come.' My words reached through the cold bars of the black gates towards him. He took them and smiled.

'Yes, I'll come back. Don't you worry,' he said, walking away, and then turned back and gave me a cheery, incongruous, wave.

*

An urgent message was sent immediately to Mrs Humber. Ma wrote a note, which she gave to me and told me to cycle down to her cottage and make sure I gave it to her personally, mind, I was absolutely not to slip it under the door.

I watched Mrs Humber carefully as she read it. She was leaning against the low front door of her cottage, smoking a cigarette. I knew that she had a husband and children, but was still unprepared for the gaggle of boys whose faces were pressed against the upstairs windows; they were sticking their tongues out at me, and laughing. My goodness, I thought, she's the old woman who lives in a shoe.

'A luncheon party?' she said, sceptical, taking a draw of her cigarette.

'Yes.'

'How many?'

'Four.'

'*Seven* people in all then?'

'No. I mean one extra person. Four in all.'

'Oh,' she said. 'Tell her she'll be lucky to have a pheasant for next Thursday, but I'll be up in the morning.'

'Thank you, Mrs Humber.' I was trying to ignore the shouts from

50

the upstairs windows, which had now been opened. She nodded, and then gave in, unable to resist.

'What's going on then?'

Turning my bicycle round, I called airily over my shoulder, 'Oh, it's a friend of mine, Mrs Humber. He's coming for lunch,' and then cycled away, holding my head up high, feeling the wind smarting against my recently kissed cheeks.

*

We didn't have pheasant, of course, but Mrs Humber brought a chicken with her. I watched her walk up the driveway, holding it by the legs, the neck hanging down near her knees. She slapped it on the table in the kitchen.

'Nothing wrong with a bit of curried chicken, Laura.'

We were to have the best tablecloth, Granny Plum's table napkins and the dinner service from the cellar. I was charged with fetching it up and then with rinsing the dust and grime off the plates at the big stone sink in the kitchen.

'Do you think it's too cold in there, Mrs H?' My mother was sitting at the kitchen table, drumming her fingers on the tabletop. 'Do we need a fire?'

'I'm not sure the chimney's clear, Mrs Trelling.'

'No, well, quite. Coats on for luncheon then, I think. The devil's in the detail, Laura, the detail.'

'Yes, Ma.'

When I'd finished washing the dishes, I dried them and laid them out on the table. I was worried about Pa and went looking for him. He was in the gunroom, laying his father's shotgun collection out on wobbly trestle tables.

'Everything all right, Pa?'

He didn't turn round to look at me, his hands were shaking and I noticed he was wearing his tweed jacket and matching trousers, which normally only made an appearance on Christmas Day.

'You look smart,' I told his skinny, bent back.

Ma got dressed up for the event too. She wore a blue woollen suit, which was a bit furry around the elbows but was beautifully off set by a heavy cream silk blouse, with flowing, falling collars which spread out across the jacket. She wore her best brooch on the lapel; a shooting comet studded with diamonds and sapphires. I wore an old, slightly too short cotton dress flecked with green and brown – army colours – and over the top a fawn jumper, with a lively pattern across my breasts and green buttons at the neck, of the sort favoured by five-year-olds. I was in camouflage.

Ma waited nervously in the hall for Paul to arrive. I felt queasy with unease just watching her. She paced the carpet in the hall, smoking a cigarette and kneading her toe into the permanent hillock in the hall rug, which no one had ever been able to iron out.

'Can't understand why this doesn't stay down. What are you doing, Laura, moping in the shadows?'

'I'm not moping.'

She took another drag and flicked the ash onto the offending rise in the rug.

'What time did he say he'd be here?'

'I don't think we agreed a time. What time do people normally come for lunch?'

I couldn't account for why Ma was so anxious, nor even for why she had so spontaneously invited him in the first place. Perhaps it was a throwback to a time when one issued invitations to young men with wet trousers, or perhaps she believed that he was coming to court her, I wouldn't have put it past her.

Paul arrived striding into the hall, smiling confidently into our pale, apprehensive faces. Ma told me to take his coat and when he passed it to me, he winked and whispered, 'I told you I'd be back,' and as I turned to put it on the chair, I quickly buried my face into it, inhaling the intoxicating blend of smells that made up Paul; early winter frost, mothballs, the slightest whiff of tobacco and a sweet, lemony smell that I couldn't quite place but suspected might be a perfume, his aunt's perhaps? Pa surprised us by shuffling over at some speed and slapping Paul on the back.

'Come to the gunroom, old boy,' he shouted too loudly. 'Lots of lovely shooters. Come and take a look.'

They were in there for an age. Ma and I stood awkwardly in the drawing room. She was pacing around the bit of carpet in front of the fire, knocking back a huge tumbler of gin.

'He's going to ruin everything,' she told me. 'Whatever are they doing in there?'

After the second glass I was dispatched to find them. Paul and Pa were standing side by side looking at the guns,

'That's a shotgun 3422, you'll notice it has a double barrel,' Pa was mumbling. Paul saw me in the doorway and smiled. He rolled his eyes. It was affection, not disrespect, but there was something different about him. He looked restive, not frightened exactly, but more boyish than I'd remembered, more vulnerable.

'Ma wonders whether you'd like to come and have a drink now. Before lunch,' I said.

'Righto,' said Pa.

There wasn't a starter. We went straight into the curried chicken with boiled potatoes. I think the chicken was a little underdone, because I could see streaks of blood on mine and had to heap lots of the sauce on top. We didn't wear our coats, but we should have because the dining-room chairs were damp and I could feel a wetness sneaking into my dress during lunch. Pa sat at one end of the worm-raddled table and Ma at the other, with Paul and I facing each other in the middle. The room was dark because the shutters were stuck and neither Mrs Humber nor I had been able to force them open, despite repeated attempts with a chisel, but the table was, finally, balanced.

'I read a most amusing thing in the paper the other day,' my mother said. 'Every man secretly wishes himself to be the only child of a widow. Do you think that's true, Paul?'

Paul was trying to be suave. He laughed and let his head bob about a bit and grinned at her pretending he understood the joke, but he was flummoxed, I could tell.

'Well, I'm an only child,' he said, lamely, 'but not of a widow.'

'Ah, yes,' said Ma, as if he'd said something very important and profound. 'I'm reminded of the words of that great poet Samuel Taylor Coleridge. Are you familiar with his work, Paul?'

Paul said that he was not, and she went on trying to quote some pieces of poetry, but forgetting them and getting herself in a muddle and then getting cross with Pa and I because we had no idea what she was talking about and couldn't swoop in and quote the lines perfectly. Paul saved us by pitching in with what he must have thought his most winning line in conversation.

'Have I told you, Mrs Trelling, that I live in South Africa?'

But if Paul thought that would inspire a long list of questions about himself, he was mistaken.

'You look perfectly English to me. Didn't you have a cousin in the Cape once, Jocelyn?'

'Malaysia.'

'Of course, I remember meeting the most exotic man from India once. I couldn't have been . . .'

And on and on it went. I had to pick up the plates between courses and collect the apple pie, which Mrs Humber had left on the kitchen table. Ma told me to serve it out, and I was nervous because I wasn't sure how to judge the size of the portions, I gave Paul too much and he had trouble finishing it. By pudding we had fallen into a terrified silence, and I was racing the final piece of pastry around my plate with the fork, desperate to see it gone. Pa was looking down at his plate, trying to appear benign, and Ma, the worse for the drink, had slipped into a brooding sulk. She kept shooting beady and vindictive looks at Paul.

'Would you like to come for a walk?' I asked him, cramming the final piece into my mouth and pushing my chair back.

'Yes.' He got to his feet too quickly and then remembered himself. 'Thank you for the delicious lunch, Mrs Trelling. Thank you.'

She looked at him contemptuously.

'You lie. You're lying,' she whispered.

'Off we go then,' I said brightly.

We were drunk with relief. We both bounded out of the house, barely managing to catch our breath, and he followed me as I pelted across the fields behind the house, only stopping when I knew the Grange was out of sight. I sunk down into the grass, grabbing fistfuls of the cold, wet blades in my hands. Paul collapsed beside me.

'Bloody hell,' he said.

'I know, I know.'

'Every man secretly wishes himself to be the only child of a widow. What was all that about?' He leant over on top of me and pinned my hands back into the grass.

'Nothing, nothing, nothing.' I shook my head from side to side.

His face was close to mine and I could smell the sweet wine and curdling curry on his breath.

'I've missed you this week, Laura Trelling. I kept thinking about you, I don't know why. You've got under my skin, how did you do that?' and he was trying to be light about it, but I could tell he meant it.

'We fell in love in Elms Wood,' I whisper, 'I remember the moment it happened.'

'We've got to get you out of here,' he said, now pressing his entire weight on top of me. 'I think I'd better marry you,' and he started kissing me, surprising me by sticking his tongue in my mouth and licking the backs of my teeth.

This was Paul Lovell's gift to me, offered with neither hesitation nor humour. I clutch at this memory, of us shivering in the long November grass, the knees of his trousers soaked through, a damp chill crawling up my spine, the heat of his breath on my neck.

'I can't leave you here with parents like that. You'll grow old and queer and smell of old ladies' things within a year.'

'I will not smell of old ladies.'

'You will too, mothballs, lavender bags and invalid food. So what do you think, Laura Trelling, shall we be married? Can you take the risk? I will if you will. We don't have much time though, you need to decide quickly.'

I am a fish in a fast, unfamiliar river, caught in the cold brackish water and streaming through rippling light, catching glimpses of the smooth dark pebbles below. Soft, wide-eyed and fluid. My innocent mouth wide open promising, just as Charlotte had taught us, sweet and happy relief.

'Yes, yes. I'll take the risk. We shall.'

23 January 1944

I'm going to kill myself. Lionel rang today and offered me a part in
a new play. I didn't get to the telephone in time because I was upstairs
when it rang, but I came running down quick enough when I heard
her saying, 'How nice of you to think of Eileen ... yes, Gay ... but
I'm afraid she'll be unable to perform in your theatre piece as she is
shortly to be attending secretarial school.' Mum looks stupid when
she talks on the telephone because she always holds it a long way
from her ear. I've shown her a thousand times how to do it, I've said
to her, it's not going to burn you, you have seen a telephone before,
haven't you, but she won't listen. She also talks in this dumb way,
'How nice of you to think of Eileen,' as if Lionel were asking me on
a bleeding picnic. She saw me hurtling down the stairs so she hung
up pretty quick, and scuttled away into the kitchen.

'It was only chorus and non-speaking work, Eileen,' she says,
throwing flour on the table and grabbing hold of her pin and refusing
to look at me.

'What? I want it, Mother, I want to do it.'

'I told you that you looked silly during *Babes in the Wood*, didn't I?
You were much too tall for the chorus.' And she's kneading the
bread now, turning it round and round on the table, getting flour
all over the place.

'That's because they were children, Mother, they were bloody
babes, weren't they? Children from the local stage school. I was
supposed to be taller than them. I had responsibility for them.'

'Watch your language, Eileen. Well, it didn't look right. You elbowing your way to the front of the line, and kicking so high and singing so loud, when you were standing there with little children.'

Father won't listen to me, he says I'm to do what she says and go to secretarial school. 'Get some qualifications under your belt, girl,' he says, 'then see if you can get work. Besides, there's plenty more things to worry about,' and he shakes out the newspaper. 'Look at this.'

War. War. War. It's all anyone ever talks about. War, rations and bombs. I think I'll go mad if I have to stay here any longer.

'Cheer up. Come and sing some Noël Coward for your old man at the piano.' He doesn't see that it is a nasty thing to be standing at the piano singing for my father when I've been on the stage at the Liverpool Empire and had my name in a theatrical programme.

February 1944

How would Sir like his coffee? Would Sir like to put his dirty, dirty naughty hands up my skirt while I take dictation? Is Sir aware that he keeps looking at my breasts while I'm doing Sir's filing? Does he like to see the rosy buds of my nipples moving up and down as I bring Sir his afternoon tea, with one, oh go on then, Gay, why not, it's been a long week, yes, let's have two of the arrowroot biscuits seeing as it's a Friday. Does Sir's wife know that Sir likes to sit on my desk in the mornings and lean in close pretending he's interested in the mail? I will not be a secretary after I've done this course, not for anything, not for the bloody war that's for certain. Endless pointlessness. All the paper depresses me. Curling up at the edges and smudged with ink and dust and bits of people's things and the clunk-clunk of a hundred girls on typewriters, their tongues stuck between their teeth. Eugh.

Went to the pictures with Maureen, Glenda and Lucy to see Judy Garland and Van Heflin in *Presenting Lily Mars*. Maureen wanted to wait and go and see *Shadow of a Doubt* because now she's engaged she likes to think of herself as a serious person but we said we thought it looked too boring. I know she's older but honestly to listen to her go on you'd think she'd been married and divorced at least twice. Afterwards she made a great play of showing off her new compact and lipstick and asking us if we wanted to go down the Kingsland on Borough Road at the weekend. Well, Lucy said pretty quick that her mum wouldn't let her go until she was eighteen because, she says, you get some pretty loose types going down there. So Maureen says, it's because some of the GIs come over from Liverpool proper to dance there. So then Lucy goes all silly and pretends to faint, and says how she wishes she could come, and Glenda says quickly, 'Your mam won't let you and neither will Gay's, so that'll just be you and me, Maureen. What shall we wear?'

And then Maureen says, 'Anyway, don't you have someone to meet on Saturday nights, Gay? Cos from what I hear, you do.'

And I wanted to ask them whether they ever feel like they fall in love every day. Because I feel that I do. Sometimes it's just a fella on the bus, or someone I pass on the street and he might look at me and me at him, just for a second, as we're passing on the Borough Road or somewhere, and I want to stop and I want him to kiss me right then and there on the pavement. I want him to grab me and kiss me and hurt me as we go crashing down onto the pavement. I can't help it. I want strangers to touch me.

They all looked at me when Maureen said that and one of them, I forget who, giggled a bit. Like they'd all been talking about me. What do they know, what do I care anyway? Me and Charles

Chalmers down the backstreets, him pressing me up against the wall and going on and on like he does. I don't think they know that. I don't understand the half of what he says, I don't much care. I don't want him to love me, but I get this feeling that I like the brickwork in my back, and the dark night and the air-raid signals going off. I can close my eyes, I can pretend anything I want to then. I feel alive even if it is just me and Chalmers and him with his hands down his trousers.

It was quite a good film. But at least Lily Mars got the understudy part to begin with, so that she could then step out on opening night when the leading lady falls sick. I've not even got as far as that. I bet if I'd done Lionel's play someone would have spotted me in the chorus and made me a star. I can sing just as well as Judy Garland any day.

10 March 1944

As we were walking home Father said that if the secretarial thing wasn't working out and as I only had a little while until I'd be eighteen and doing National Service, why didn't I try out nursing, like Mum had done? I didn't know what to say to him. Hadn't he seen me up there, wowing the benefactors of the St John's Ambulance Brigade Charity Night just the night before? I told him I'd think about it, and then I said, I'm not like Daisy, you know, I've been places, we've been places, I can't pretend I'm like her, and he said he knew that. But I don't think he does, not really. I don't sleep much at the moment. I've put my little travelling clock under the pile of dirty clothes in the bottom of my wardrobe so I don't have to see how long the night is.

Am writing this in the dispensary at the Walton Hospital. I hide in here as much as I can. I'd rather be a secretary any day. The hospital disinfectant has brought me out in a nasty purple rash – all over my hands and up my arms. I feel like weeping every time I look at it. I can't believe the things they want us to do, emptying out bedpans, dressing wounds, making beds with turning corners, plumping pillows. It's disgusting. And all these pale, sick men in their pyjamas. Everyone calls them 'our heroes' but you've never seen less heroic-looking men in your life. They're all lost to themselves. Some of them call out for their mothers in the night and then piss themselves. I know I should be kind to them, and it isn't that I've got anything against them personally, but I SHOULDN'T BE HERE. This is a horrible mistake. I tried telling Sister that the other day, but she's one of those sour, puckered-up women who don't listen properly. I said to her, 'I'm not sure I'm really cut out for this, you know,' and she said, 'Nonsense, you'll soon get used to it, Nurse. These people need our help.'

'Well, yes, I do know that, but not *my* help. I'm not meant to be here, you see. I'm an actress.'

'So you're the flame-haired nurse who sings in the dispensary, are you? I've had reports on you. If I ever catch you in there, my girl, I'll beat you for a week. Now go along to Ward 4, there's a bedpan needs emptying.'

The girls here are nice and friendly and none of them as squeamish as me. They're all so pleased with their uniforms and little hats and capes. They parade about in them outside the front of the Walton, showing off their trim little uniforms. I don't think it much of a uniform.

I've been thinking that I ought to try and finish it with Charlie, but it's strange because it wasn't as if we'd ever properly started, and he isn't taking no for an answer. I told him, as nice as I could, that I just thought I'd had enough of going down the back alleys with him, that some of the girls had said something about it, but he said I was a 'stuck-up bitch' and a 'whore'. He went a bit mad and started going on about all the things he'd done for me! He calmed down in the end and then he goes, 'You're the kind of girl that drives a man crazy, and no good can come of that, Gay Gibson,' as though everything were all my fault.

Everyone thinks I'm a good-time girl without a thought in my head. But I'm not. I have strange dreams. I dream about falling through golden hoops into the blackness. I dream about my body, about missing bits, or about my legs crumbling like old biscuits when someone touches them. I think I might be going mad. I think I might be dying inside my uniform. I don't eat much any more. Today I took the surgical scissors and I thought about what it would be like if I made some marks on my arms with them. Just to see what it would look like. I'm so white. My chest hurts and I can feel every hair on my head burning me from the outside in.

Three

Here we come. The stranger newly-weds, running down Baker Street, holding hands and falling over ourselves with joy. Paul is dressed in a smart charcoal suit, with a waistcoat and shining white shirt. Over one arm is his overcoat, which he took off when he came into the registry office, and in that hand a suitcase, while the other arm is spread wide across the pavement holding me at the end of it.

I prance along beside him. He looks different because he's been to the barber that morning, and the barber has taken his job seriously and cut off those curls and greased down his hair with pomade. Paul seems quite pleased with this look, and he glances over once or twice to catch sight of himself in the shop windows. Or perhaps he is looking at the two of us, to see what we look like now we're officially a lawful couple. I am very gay. I am wearing a dear little green dress with matching coat and pillbox hat. I am wearing make-up, stolen from my mother's dressing table, and the purple colours she favours are designed for older and darker skin and it lends me, on closer scrutiny, a slightly bruised look, but I'm laughing and smiling, enjoying the effort of keeping up with Paul's impressive pace as we barrel down Baker Street, forcing the other people to jump out of the way of our speeding expression of joy.

'Hey,' one man calls out as we rocket past him. Paul shouts back, 'We've just got married,' but we don't stop, don't turn round to see him waving his fist at us.

I need to stop. The new bra I bought from a boutique is too large for me and the wires are chafing uncomfortably against my skin. I am also having some trouble with my shoes, which are not designed for pounding down pavements at electric speed. Paul is very solicitous. Though I don't tell him about the bra, just that my toes are cramped and blistered and I need to take a breather. He has got down on his knees and eased my foot out of the shoe. He rubs my foot. He gazes up at me adoringly. This is a good start, I think, we are the very picture of elegant young love.

*

We were running towards a guest house off Baker Street where we stayed for one night before travelling to Southampton to catch the steamer for Cape Town. Paul had wired his parents to arrange my passage and had then made the date at the registry office. He explained that he didn't have much of his holiday allowance left, and could only stretch to the one day in London, because he'd used the last of his pocket money to get married.

Number 6 Woolbridge Gardens was one of those tall white buildings, with empty windows and scruffy pillars out the front, a small plaque was fixed to the front door, which simply said 'Guest House', as though to assure you it was not in disguise as something else.

Madame Dupont was the landlady, and when she met us in the hallway, her feet planted squarely on the red-and-black tiles and surrounded by dark green plants in copper pots, we made a great play of showing her my new slippery wedding ring. She hugged me to her and kissed me on both cheeks.

'Congratulations,' she said, eyeing Paul beadily.

She was a large woman, her body crammed into a tight black skirt and blouse, and her clothes looked as though they might give up and fly off at any moment. Her black hair was beautifully coiffured into an elaborate chignon and I was entranced by its bobbing sheen as I followed her up the narrow staircase.

'You have just the one case?' Madame Dupont said to me on the first-floor landing, clutching at the gold pendant she was wearing around her neck. I sensed she wanted to delay us for some reason. 'It is a long way up, *non*?' She blew out her cheeks and raised her pencilled eyebrows. 'You are tired perhaps?' Then without waiting for a reply, she looked about her with distaste.

'It is very English?' she asked Paul, gesturing to the florid carpet. 'You would not have this in France, I think.'

'Probably not,' agreed Paul, as though he were an expert on French interiors. This made me laugh and I had to look down at my shoes, to suppress my giggles.

'Your room is at the top. You would rather go down and have some tea perhaps?'

'No, really, we're marvellous.'

'Your friend, she says you have no wedding gifts to bring with you? That there will be no party?'

'No.'

'A shame. For a young woman about to start her life. A great shame.'

Reluctantly, she started on the second staircase, and when we were at the top of the house she unlocked the door to our attic bedroom. It was a small brown room built into the eaves of the building, with a tiny window which looked out over the backs of the neighbouring houses, a bed and a wardrobe, one corner of which had been sawn off so it could fit under the sloping ceiling.

'You are disappointed, I suppose?' she asked me, leaning heavily against the door frame and scrutinising my face.

'No. Not at all. I love it.'

And I did.

'*Alors*. Good. *Diner* is at six o'clock, in half an hour. Do not be late please.'

'Right.' Paul wandered over to look out of the window, throwing his suitcase on to the bed. Madame Dupont stayed there, looking at the two of us.

'Thank you, madame.' Paul did not turn round from the window when he said this, he did not sound grateful, he sounded extremely cross.

Madame sighed philosophically, tapping the pendant against her giant cleavage, looking at Paul's back, and then with surprising agility she grabbed my arm, her long finger nails biting into my flesh, and pulled me closer to her. She smelt foreign and expensive, mature.

'*Courage, mademoiselle, courage,*' she whispered in my ear, and then with one last consolatory squeeze of my arm, she left.

I sat on the edge of the candlewick bedspread. Paul was struggling to open the window, he was leaning his shoulder against it, trying to push it up.

'It'll be cold, won't it, with the window open, I mean?'

He was still pressed against the window, his suit jacket riding up over his shoulders, his head turned away from me, frantic now to open the window.

'The sash has probably swollen, the windows at home do, I mean, they get damp in them and then the wood all swells up, so the

66

windows don't open.' I was speaking quickly, annoyed at the light, awkward sound of my own voice. 'I think you have to shave the window down with a special kind of tool, you know, to rub the frames down, so that they fit together properly, because then they'll work again.'

'What the fuck are you talking about?' This stranger, my husband, turned round, flecks of spittle on the sides of his plump lips.

*

It had appealed to Paul, the idea of stealing me away, however willing an abductee I was. I had told him that they would never let me marry him. The truth is I hadn't wanted Paul to know how very casual they could be with me, how little they cared. I knew he had gathered enough evidence from his two visits to convince himself that I needed saving, but some strange pride stopped me from allowing him to ask them, I didn't want him to see me through their eyes, as eminently disposable, unlovable. So the very next day after the lunch, we hatched a plan. We took a walk to the local church; it was raining and we'd had to walk fast, brushing against the low stone wall which circled the graveyard. Paul's curls flattened in the rain, he had turned up the collar of his coat to stop the drips from the yew trees.

'They'll never agree. I know they won't.'

'Then we'll just have to whisk you away, won't we?' he'd said, smiling at me. 'I've got a return ticket though, you know that?'

Of course, he didn't live here, he was on a visit to the old country, a holiday. I did know that.

'Oh.'

'Let's do it, Lala. We should get married in London and then we'll catch a Union Castle steamer back home at the end of December. I can wire home and get them to arrange your passage. Do you want to? It'll be an adventure.'

What had I imagined? Little bride in Upper Emiswick? Certainly not. I'd imagined a flat in London, with a tiny kitchen and pretty curtains, Paul going out to work each day, to some unknowably important job and coming home each night smelling of the city streets and pressing me against the door of our purple bedroom. But if this was the plan, the adventure, then I could see there was little point arguing about it, I was hardly in a position to do that.

'Yes, all right,' I'd said.

And then he'd picked me up in his arms and said, 'Good. I want this more than anything. I feel safe with you, Laura Trelling. You've no idea how extraordinary you are. I know this is fast, but if you feel the same as I do, then it can't be quick enough, can it?' and then he'd kissed me and allowed his hands to undo the buttons of my coat and roam across my hot, tight body while my toes curled inside my damp shoes. After that Paul had only come to the Grange one more time. A week later, he'd come down to see his aunt and he drove over to see us in his aunt's new car, honking on the horn and beaming with pride. 'Fancy a ride, Laura?' he'd shouted above the noise of the engine. 'She's speedy.'

'Oh, Paul,' my mother had gasped, coming out to see what all the noise was about, 'what a beauty. Wait, I'll get my hat.'

She sat beside him in the front, while I huddled in the back seat wrapped up in his aunt's picnic blankets.

'The drive out to Lem Dipping is most agreeable,' Ma told him.

He drove very carefully and diligently, there was little sign of the speed he promised me, as we crawled through the lanes, under the bare branches of the winter trees.

'How about you drive for a bit, Mrs Trelling?'

'Oh, I couldn't,' she said, 'I might crash it.'

Though she clambered quickly enough into the driving seat, and concentrated hard on following Paul's instructions. She kept grabbing his arm when she thought she might lose control, and he had to lean over across her and take the wheel with a laughing smile. He'd stayed for tea that day, and Ma, a little giddy from the drive, had suggested we all play charades. I said quickly, 'Paul doesn't like that sort of thing, and neither do we, Ma, in case you've forgotten,' but she ignored me. I had to endure an awful afternoon watching Ma trying to act out 'The Lady of Shalott' and then see her laughing throatily and whispering drunkenly in Paul's ear, while my father hobbled about, stiff with clumsy shame, pretending to be Little Miss Muffet. Then Paul had decided, impulsively, bizarrely, to see whether he couldn't just fix up the roof of the potting shed. He said he'd been looking at it from the drawing-room window all afternoon and it was driving him mad. I found him a hammer and some nails, and watched him, wearing his scarf, from the safe distance of the frozen and disused vegetable patch, watched him in the fading light, banging and swearing and failing to make any progress. When he'd admitted defeat, I said to him, 'Don't come here again. You don't like it, I'll come to you,' and he'd smiled and sucked on his sore thumb. 'I'm going to arrange everything, Lala, don't you worry. Meet me at Paddington registry office on 30 December at four o'clock. It's all arranged, you need to bring a witness, can you do that?'

For the record, just so this is quite clear, I didn't during the weeks that followed question why Paul might want to marry me, not once, I trusted that he felt the same way I did. But I knew that I couldn't get to London on my own, I needed to enlist some help and I needed a witness.

I chose the Bathurst sisters, two spinsters who lived in the village. Cissy and Bibi Bathurst had come to the village two summers ago and had rented the damp, pinched cottage next to the church. People were modestly kind to them because they had no money and had to make their own clothes out of the scraps of material and cast-offs which sympathetic villagers left for them. Everyone knew that their father had been very rich, and that they had lived in a grand house in London, but that their father had died in a bombing raid which had devastated their house, and that far from profiting from his death, they had instead inherited his apparently substantial and hitherto unknown debts. By last spring, the strains of giddy jazz music had started wafting out of the cottage windows, and Bibi Bathurst was spotted sitting in their front garden in a bathing suit, smoking cigarettes and wearing red lipstick. Then the sisters found, according to Mrs Humber, that the charitable drops of vegetables and old curtains on the doorstep had started to dry up. It was at this point that my mother had taken them up and started inviting them over for a drink every so often. They suffered my mother's moods and vindictiveness in return for her sherry and a change of scene. The Bathurst sisters were my mother's only social life.

'Oh, but they are so entertaining,' she would say, 'we're social outcasts, one and all!'

They could only have been in their late twenties or early thirties but the silent, villagey, expectation was that they be grateful, middle-aged and entirely without hope. But the Bathurst sisters were refusing to comply; they gave off the whiff of something different, something rebellious and cosmopolitan. This is why I chose them.

Bibi wanted to know why my parents had refused us; she was sceptical, cynical, smoking cigarette after cigarette, puffing the smoke out the tiny sunken window in their kitchen. I told her we hadn't exactly asked them, so they hadn't exactly refused us. She wanted to know why. She wasn't scandalised, she was too sophisticated for that, she was just idly curious.

'We're going to South Africa,' I told her, sipping tea from one of their chipped brown cups, 'it's where he's from.'

'Well, that's all well and good but you ought to have the courtesy of letting your parents know that at least,' she'd said drily. 'We'll get you on that train, Laura, we'll find the money for you, but it does seem a little *rude* just running off like this, don't you think?'

'Oh, but how lusciously romantic, Laura!' said Cissy, beaming at me. Cissy wrote poetry, she thought it was all wildly exciting and sensitive stuff. Cissy's name didn't suit her at all, she didn't have Bibi's fine upturned nose or elegant cheekbones, she looked, it was widely supposed, like her father: clunky and morose, like a horse, a farm horse.

'Tosh,' Bibi had said, lighting another cigarette and throwing the match over her shoulder. 'There's nothing romantic about this, is there, Laura? She's brokered a deal, Cissy, any fool can see that.' Cissy's wide blue eyes had filled with tears, and she'd dabbed at them with the edge of her pleated skirt.

'Oh no,' I'd told them, shocked. 'I am in love, Bibi. I'm very much in love.'

'You?' she'd snorted. 'Her daughter? An apple never falls far from its tree, Laura, remember that.'

In the end Bibi had marched me up to the Grange, all wrapped up in her man's coat and old hat. She'd stormed into the drawing room and said, 'Laura has something to tell you both,' and I'd stammered about on the edges of the room, useless and pitiful.

'Paul has asked me, and I've said yes, he's asked me to marry him and to go to South Africa, I mean to Johannesburg, with him, you see.'

My mother stood with her back to me, pretending to examine the china shepherdesses on the mantelpiece. I could see her long finger curling across the edges of their perfect pleated pale blue skirts and their tiny fragile white legs and little black shoes. In the club in Johannesburg they mixed a special drink, a cocktail, I'm not sure what the ingredients were, vodka and something red. The red part was slowly dripped in, just a few drops at a time, falling gracefully through the viscous liquid, swirling down the long glass until eventually a mass built up and the vodka surrendered itself. It was called a Blood Shot. The first time I saw the barman mix it, I was instantly reminded of my mother's back in the drawing room at home and of her fingers clenching the shepherdesses' legs.

My father had burst into tears, then and there, sunk his head into his hands and wept bitter, bitter tears.

Ma spun round, her face contorted by shock and chilly rage.

'But you hardly know him,' she spat out. 'Why should you be able to leave here, and go off with him? Why? Why does he want to marry *you*, Laura?'

And then everyone had looked at me, and I'd shrugged and resisted the urge to say, 'Because he definitely doesn't want to marry *you*, Mother,' and said, 'He loves me and I love him,' instead. Besides, it was love, it was all for love as far as I could see, and even though I was not an expert in it and didn't really know how to judge it, raised as I was in this damp, secretive house, Paul was affection, he was love, he was all I'd ever dreamt of having.

★

Cissy had insisted on taking me to London, she had a friend who lived in Ealing and she'd agreed to put us up for a few days. I didn't want her to, I would have rather gone on my own. It was the way she went on, whispering about people who could marry us in the dead of night, clearly believing that Paul and I would be wearing cloaks and veils and arriving on horseback. I thought her envious and sentimental, I wasn't sure what we would find to talk about together. I didn't want to share the details with Cissy, I didn't trust her, but she had a friend in Ealing who was prepared to put us up for the night, so I was rather stuck with her, and she had agreed, rather too earnestly for my liking, to be my witness.

Pa had driven us both to the station to catch the milk train. He drove very slowly saying it was because he was worried about the ice and the dark, but he wasn't, he was torn up inside about my going away, but he couldn't find a way to express it. Cissy sat in the back of the car munching on mints and endlessly checking and rechecking the contents of her carpet bag.

'Take care, old girl,' Pa said on the platform, huge hot tears rolled down on to his scarf. 'Write me if you need help,' and he pressed an envelope stuffed with money into my hand. 'Don't tell your mother.'

I hugged him. 'I'm sorry, Pa, I'm sorry about all this.'

'Now, now.' He'd quickly pushed me back from him and nodded admiringly at me and turned to leave. I'd watched him making his careful, stepping way back across the silent platform to the car. He was so wary of imagined dangers – he'd brought an umbrella with him, and he thwacked it into each puddle, ensuring it wasn't disguised as black ice. He hadn't looked back.

Cissy's 'friend' was called Mrs Granger. She lived with her crippled husband in a tiny basement flat on a road off Ealing Common.

My heart sank as I bumped my suitcase down the outside steps, amazed at the sight of dustbins crowded around the front door. This was my first time in London. When the train had pulled into Waterloo, I was wide-eyed with exultation. I loved the soot and dirt, the ecstatic whooshing of the steam trains, and the people. So many people. Cissy grabbed my hand as we clambered off the train, and kept waving at porters in the hope of finding someone to carry our luggage. I only had the one suitcase. Typically, I had been quite at a loss to know what to bring. I didn't seem to *own* anything.

'We can manage them, Cissy.' I was impatient with her.

'No. We must get a porter,' she said. 'We can, now you've got—' and she nodded at my coat pocket, where I'd put the envelope of money, 'and a taxi, thank goodness.'

She was surprisingly confident. The country mouse had come home. She was very firm with the porter, quick to urge me to find money to tip him and very strident in giving our driver the exact directions to Mrs Granger's house. She relished pointing places out to me.

'We used to go shopping in that department store. Do you see it? Isn't it heavenly?' and she opened the window and stuck her head outside the better to smell the air. The driver complained, so she had to close it again.

'Isn't this thrilling, Laura?' she said, sitting back beside me and clutching at my hand.

Mrs Granger invited us into her dark little sitting room, and told us to sit down. There was lace everywhere. It covered every available tabletop, ran along the backs of the chairs and down the sides, it even dripped over the edge of the mantelpiece. She was a small, pert woman with a fast mouth, who was clearly very pleased to see Cissy.

'Oh, let me look at you!' How long has it been? How is Beatrice? Is she well? Would you like tea? It's Laura, isn't it? Tea? Mr Granger has the bedroom at the back, so don't go wandering in there, dear. That wouldn't do at all, would it, Cissy?'

Cissy agreed that it wouldn't do at all. She had been so puffed up in the taxi, so full of the pleasures of London air, but now at Mrs Granger's she started to deflate again, to sink back into herself, her long face pulled irretrievably downwards. Mrs Granger bustled about in her kitchen, making tea and calling messages through to her husband about our arrival, and what we were wearing and how pretty Cissy looked, while Cissy and I sat side by side on the sofa.

'Is there a telephone here?' I whispered to Cissy. She shrugged her shoulders in reply. I wanted to telephone Paul. He'd given me the number of where he'd be staying and had said I was to call him as soon as I got to London. It was very short and perfunctory note, but he had signed it '*Yours, everlasting in love*', which had pleased me no end. Mrs Granger came in with the tea tray, also covered in lace.

'I understand congratulations are due, Laura,' she said, placing it down carefully in front of us. 'Nothing like a wedding to cheer up the winter months.'

'Thank you,' I said, trying to look decent and modest.

'Not everyone can have the church wedding, you know, dear. You're not to worry about it. People get married in all manners of ways nowadays. It pays to be open-minded.'

I didn't call Paul that evening. Mrs Granger practically locked us in to her sitting room, plying us with tea and sandwiches, made with stale bread and served on tiny doll-sized plates. She talked a great deal about her husband and his condition. She told me how she had worked for Cissy and her family before their 'troubles', and how good they had been to her, and how she had always vowed to pay them back in some way and how pleased she had been when she'd received Cissy's letter about me, because it meant that she could at long last be of some help to this noble and unfairly blighted family.

Cissy and I were to share her bedroom as she had made herself a little bed on the floor in Mr Granger's room.

'Was she some sort of domestic then?' I asked Cissy, as we undressed.

She was uncurling her hair, which she always wore in a tight bun.

'She worked for my father,' she said, shaking her head so that all the hairpins went flying across the room. 'Talked him to death I should think,' and we both started giggling and got down on all fours to pick up the pins.

Later, when we lay side by side in the dark, my legs twisted around the outside of the blankets for fear of touching hers, she asked me, 'Have you and Paul ever, I mean, are you in trouble, Laura?'

I swear to God, I had no idea what she was talking about.

'No Cissy, I'm not in trouble,' I whispered back.

'Good, because there are ways of getting around that, you know.'

'Yes. Goodnight, Cissy.'

'Let's go out tomorrow, Laura. Can we? Let's go and buy your things in town.'

*

Cissy proved to be a devil at shopping. She had the long, lazy eye of the envious. She insisted that the assistants bring out drawer after drawer of gloves, and she would finger them carefully and then send them back and ask to see the ones with three buttons at the wrist instead of two.

'We need to find you something for your honeymoon,' she said, over coffee. She'd greedily ordered us both the lemon cake *and* the hazelnut parfaits. 'You must try these, Laura. We used to have them all the time. They're delicious.'

I was aware of how peculiar we both looked. How underdressed we were. I imagined that people were staring at us. Staring at Cissy with her long mournful face stuffed with cake, the icing smeared around the outside of her mouth. She said we were only to shop at the best places. That Harrods would have a 'colonies' shopping list and that Simpson's on the Strand was the best place, in her opinion, for sensible underwear. The cafe was heavy with second-hand air, cigarette smoke, wet coats and steaming pots of tea.

'I don't have that much money, Cissy.'

'But your father –' she said, reaching out for another parfait. My God, she must have been starving.

'I don't want to waste it all on clothes.'

'But it's not a waste, Laura, these are essentials.'

'How come you're such an expert suddenly?' I snapped at her. She looked terribly hurt and cast her eyes downwards, grabbing some more cake. I could see her cheeks wobbling.

'I'm just trying to be of some help,' she murmured. 'I've done my best to help you and Paul, haven't I?'

I thought she might start to cry. There was a telephone in the cafe so I excused myself and went to call Paul and the operator took such a long time putting me through that when I heard his voice, I nearly cried from relief.

'Where are you?' I leant my head against the wooden booth.

'Staying with a friend. How was your journey?'

He was being oddly formal.

'Pa cried when he said goodbye. He gave me some money.'

'Good old Jocelyn. Is Cissy with you?'

'Yes. She's trying to spend all the money on cakes and underwear.'

He laughed.

'Can't you meet us for lunch? We're staying with an awful old woman who talks all the time and her house smells. I need to see you.'

'Not much longer. I've got everything arranged. Have you asked Cissy to be your witness?'

'Yes. She's gone a bit mad actually. I think London's gone to her head.'

'Good girl.'

I didn't know whether he meant Cissy or me.

'I'll meet you at Paddington registry office at four on Monday Can you remember that?' he said, and I heard someone laughing in the background.

'Yes, of course. Who's that laughing?'

'It's no one. Chin up, Lala. Not much longer.' And then the operator came on the line and asked if we'd finished, and Paul said yes we had, a little too quickly for my liking.

'You've got to put this weather out of your mind,' the shop assistant in Harrods told us, 'I know it's hard, but you have to imagine just how hot it will be in South Africa.'

'She's getting married on Monday,' Cissy told him.

'Really?' He wheeled round and looked me up and down. 'Registry office, is it?'

He looked like an unusually spry goose. His white hair was greased

78

back and his chest was puffed up inside his uniform. He looked as though he could become very argumentative at the slightest provocation.

'Yes.'

'Then we need to find you something for that as well, don't we?'

Cissy was having a lovely time. She'd positioned herself on a gilt chair, with a plush plum-coloured cushion, just outside the changing rooms. She kept looking at herself in the full-length mirror, turning her head from side to side and giving herself silly little smiles.

The assistant produced armfuls of clothes for me to try on. They were horrible. Lady's linen safari jacket, check. Tennis dress, check. Simple evening gown with matching shoes, check. The whole thing was ludicrous and the prices extortionate. I was pricked with fear and inadequacy. I was overwhelmed by the fact that nobody sensible seemed to be in charge, that Cissy fancied herself to be in charge but she was deranged, and I'd never get out of the changing room alive because the assistant would peck at my arms and flap his huge wings at me.

'Cissy,' I whispered from behind the curtain. '*Cissy, I can't buy all this. I haven't the money. We have to go.*'

Mrs Granger saved the day. When we got back to her flat, empty-handed and Cissy in tears complaining about how I'd let her down and she should have known better than to take such an ungrateful girl to such a serious place, she patted our heads and made us tea. She said there was a boutique on the high street which was very fairly priced and she was sure I'd be able to pick up all I needed there.

'You don't have to buy everything now, dear. There'll be shops over there, won't there?'

On the night before my wedding Mrs Granger taught me how to smoke. Cissy had been unravelling all day, had behaved appallingly in Lillian's Boutique, complaining about the quality and quantity of the stock and was refusing to talk to me. She'd sat, ostentatiously, with her back to me all afternoon and after supper she went off to the bedroom, so Mrs Granger asked me if I'd care to join her in a smoke. She showed me how to hold it properly, between the two fingers, not the finger and thumb, and how to draw in the correct quantity of smoke in one breath. She was a good teacher.

'Doesn't that feel nice now?' she asked me, settling her head back against the lace. 'Now you'll always have the smokes, won't you? Even when you're far away from your loved ones, there'll always be something you can rely on.'

Mrs Granger knew, the goose assistant at Harrods knew, even Cissy in her over-imaginative madness knew; the great event that was awaiting me was not my marriage but the going away, the going abroad.

I can look at myself as if from a platform raised above Mrs Granger's sitting room — the top of my young head, the back of my hair unbrushed. Had I packed a hairbrush? A simple skirt of blue serge cotton, that same fawn jumper with the green buttons, my right eye running with tears because the smoke weaves up my face as I don't yet know to hold it away from my nose, hunched shoulders because of the anxiety of not knowing when to flick the ash from the top of the cigarette. Beside me, on the stained brown sofa, packages of clothes bought from Lillian's Boutique still wrapped in their trademark green tissue paper. I am watching Mrs Granger eagerly, copying her movements. I am ignoring Cissy's low moans from the bedroom, the fading evening light, the sooty vapours from the coal fire, the damp patches on the walls and the swirling brown wallpaper. I know nothing.

*

Paul was still struggling with the window, and I was still fingering the pale green bedspread.

'We're both tired,' I said quietly and Paul turned round to look at me. He was studying me carefully, in a way I found uncomfortable, but I met his gaze. It occurred to me then, for the first time, that perhaps, just perhaps, Paul was on the run from something too.

'Oh poor Laura.' He came over and sat beside me on the bed, taking my hand in his and kissed me softly on the cheek. The relief was almost overwhelming, a colourful cascade all over my body, I turned my face towards his, relishing his kisses.

'I wasn't angry with you, Lala. I've been an idiot, that's all. There's this meeting I'm supposed to go to this evening and I'd completely forgotten about it. I should go and say goodbye to some people, before we go home. I'm sorry.'

And I said what I thought any wife should or might say: 'Of course you must go to your meeting. I'll come with you if you like.' So keen was I to behave appropriately, I quite missed the mention of 'home'. Had I caught that I like to think I might have questioned it. But I didn't, so that was that.

Firstly we went down for dinner in Madame Dupont's warm and cabbage-steamy dining room. She must have told them about us, because the other four diners, all men, got to their feet and clapped when we walked in. Madame Dupont came bustling in and gave us all brown bottles of beer and slapped me playfully on the bottom.

She made some reference to my still wearing the same clothes, which I didn't fully understand, so I just smiled at her.

It was a perfect night. In view of this being a celebration Madame Dupont has ordered her 'travelling gentlemen' to pull the tables together so we could sit at one long table. Her gentlemen were all of a certain age with weary, creased faces and badly pressed suits. They did as she told them, and she sat at the head of the table, passing down mutton soup, and winking at me. We were warm with comradeship. Paul sat next to me, with one hand on my thigh, looking flushed and pleased. He laughed at some light-hearted teasing, but was civil in answering their questions, he said how glad he was to celebrate his marriage with them, how much he admired the common man. I was very proud of him, nothing was expected of me, I was just the recipient of these gentlemen's tender stares and smiles. One of them went up to his room and brought down a couple more bottles of beer, which he poured out into glasses, another toast was made, and they all raised their glasses to me and Paul and we blushed and grinned, downing those warm, burping bubbles in one go.

*

The meeting was in a damp Victorian hall, a bus ride away. I stared out of the window of the bus, at the damaged streets, the house shells, the crumbling city, the people rushing along the pavements; everything looked in ruin, like a mouthful of bad teeth. In the hall there was a huge banner strung across the front of a stage. It said: 'THE STRUGGLE AGAINST FASCISM IS THE STRUGGLE FOR SOCIALISM' in bright red letters.

'Whatever does it mean?' I whispered to Paul, as we sat down on two small wooden chairs, but he ignored me, the meeting had already started.

There were three men sitting on chairs beneath the banner, looking a little lost on the vast stage, and another man stood at the front, waving papers around while he spoke. I tried to listen to him. He was talking about Churchill and Germany, about how the Labour Party won't get it wrong, and then went on to say a great deal about how governments always insist that it is the 'propertyless poor' who are asked to give their lives during a war. Then one of the other men came shuffling forward in an old woollen waistcoat and everyone was very pleased to see him and he got a huge roar of approval before he even uttered a word.

'When the war started,' he shouted at us, tipping his hat onto the back of his head, 'the only attitude the workers could adopt if they wanted to free themselves from the horrors of both war and peace, was to organise together for the purpose of establishing a system of society in which the wealth of the world will be commonly owned by all the people of the world.'

There were only two ceiling lights in the hall and it was dark and I began to feel sleepy. I could not concentrate on the man with the waistcoat. I allowed my head to loll against Paul's shoulder a little, and drifted off, dreaming about Paul at the Grange, him running down the driveway, his cheeks red and smarting from the sharp winter frost, his face lit by the moon, an eerie wild look on his face.

Paul woke me gently by touching my face and kissing it.

'Time to go sleepyhead.'

The sound of chairs being scraped across the floor, the muttering of voices, small laughter and coughing.

'Is it finished?'

'Yes. You did jolly well to stay awake as long as you did.'

'Do you need to say goodbye to people?' I was sitting up now, rubbing my eyes a little, aware of a small stab of pain in my shoulder. 'Before we go?'

'No, that's all right. I don't know anyone here. Let's go back to Madame's, shall we?'

'I thought we came so you could say goodbye to your friends?'

Paul looked about him, careful to ensure nobody was listening to us, to me.

'It's not quite like that, Lala,' he said with a small, pained smile.

'Then why was it so important we come? I thought you had people you wanted to say goodbye to?'

'Yes, well, that's all done now. Come on, they'll be locking up the hall in a minute.'

It was raining when we came out, and as we didn't have an umbrella, we huddled together, pressed against an empty shopfront, waiting for our bus.

'Did you enjoy it?' I asked him, pleased to be feeling the cold drops of rain on my sleep-fuddled face.

'Enjoy it? It wasn't a night at the theatre, Laura. I'm not sure that enjoyment is really the point of political meetings.'

'What is the point then? Everyone seemed to enjoy the shouty fellow in the funny red waistcoat, didn't they?'

'They just agreed with what he said, that's all. I wouldn't worry about it too much, old thing, it's not something I expect you to do. That's not why I'm with you — why I married you — you're separate to all this.'

And then, though we were standing on the pavement, I felt unsteady as if everything was at risk, as though we were standing on very fine sand, the kind that shifts and slips under your feet, so you can hardly balance, and which makes you feel that for all the effort you put in, you really don't travel very far. The sort which at the slightest breeze blows up in your face and stings your eyes.

'But I don't want to be separate,' I told him, 'I want to do everything with you.'

But he didn't hear me, he had stepped out, frowning and impatient, into the rain, looking up and down the dark wet street for our bus.

Gay's Diary

December 1945, London

Poor diary, I've neglected you something rotten. As it happens, I got a bit fed up with myself droning on in here about silly things which ought not to have mattered a jot. What a schoolgirl I was, moaning all the time and carrying on. Well, there will be no more of that. I feel a different person now, I feel as though I am among my own people and just really so very much older. I can hardly bear to read back over the earlier pages in this diary!

I finally left Birkenhead, as quick as I could, and joined up with the ATS – that's the Auxiliary Territorial Service to you. I was billeted to Hampstead, which was fun but there were lots of girls there who were a bit of a pain, loud types with accents and daddies in the Admiralty and so forth. Diary, I put you away for a while then. I thought one of them might get a hold of it, for a laugh, and read it out loud like they did with Camilla's diary, and everyone thought it was funny, but actually she hadn't even written anything interesting. Just about how she was missing mummy and wondering whether Sparks was all right because she missed him so much and loved him most truly, and of course everyone thought that Sparks must be a boy, but it turned out to be a horse. They were a bit like that, and I didn't want them reading this because my life has not been one of true love for a horse.

'Oh it's only a jape, Gay' they'd have said, laughing and polishing their spectacles, and then what would they have thought reading about Charles Chalmers and so on? 'Oh we're not snobs here,' they kept saying, 'intellectual activity is more important than accents or background Gay. Being a good soldier and all that.'

I thought so much about leaving Birkenhead, and getting on, but it was odd when it actually happened. Not that I dwelt on it much, that would have been stupid. Quite babyish they were, mostly. There were a lot of cross-country runs too, which I could have done without. And, truth be told, I felt lonely for a long time, I didn't know where to put myself with all these girls, nattering about rubbish. 'Who's been corrupted then?' one of the girls asked when we were moved to a transit camp, rumour had it that we were to be sent out to India, there wasn't much to do, we were just waiting for orders which never came. 'Who has been corrupted?'

And I didn't know what they meant at first, but then I understood what she meant. 'Is it corrupt?' I asked, and they all laughed like I was being naughty. And I felt a sort of falling away then, something falling away inside of me because I had been corrupted. But then I thought you don't always know how or what you are, like you think you are in control but then you realise you aren't, not by a long chalk – like with Charles. And it made me queasy for a bit but then I thought that I have to make it up as I go along, if I want to get anywhere, and I do, so to hell with being corrupted, that's what I think.

And NO MATTER. Last month I auditioned and was accepted for Stars in Battledress!

Everyone knows more than me here. I mean this is to be expected, some of them have been doing tours with Stars in Battledress for years and years, all through the war. They are very experienced actors, and I have a lot to learn from them. I know that, but I still don't like being the new girl, the ignorant one. It doesn't seem right. I won't have any of their practical jokes, they can keep them to themselves and I think they know that. I don't know why I'm being so difficult, this is everything to me. Stars in Battledress! I wrote and told Father about my audition and he wrote back saying he was proud of all he was sure I would achieve in helping with the war effort. He said everyone back home was very interested in Stars in Battledress and they kept asking him whether I had met anyone famous yet. Father said that Maureen is doing her National Service at a transit depot near Chichester. Hah!

Wilfred says we're to travel across to France in those flat-bottomed landing craft. He and Stan both say they're going to be really sick. Wilfred wears silk shirts and has had his private's uniform cut for him on Savile Row. He says there's no point us pretending we're common soldiers and he doesn't see why we should have to dress like them either. Nobody in Stars has their hair the regulation length and Stan says when he first met Colonel Black, at his audition, he'd jumped up and saluted him and Black had laughed and shook his hand and said, 'We don't bother too much with all that here.' When I did my audition all Black said to me was, 'That's lovely, dear. Now remember to take a housekeeper with you when you go, won't you? You'd be amazed how quickly the boys seem to lose their buttons.'

I'm the only girl in our troup. There's me, Wilfred, Stan and Binnie doing all six parts between us. It doesn't seem to bother the others much that we're not so well organised. We're fast becoming firm friends.

January 1946, London
I rang the *Stage* to ask them if they'd be interested in running a piece on our tour – perhaps as a diary written by me, like this one

— and I spoke to this very rude man on the other end who said, 'Isn't Charlie Chester in SIB? Have you ever worked with Charlie?' and I told him that no, I had not yet had that pleasure, and he said, 'Well then, we're not interested, dear,' and I said, 'We are currently rehearsing *The Man with a Load of Mischief* by Ashley Dukes. We're going out to France and Germany,' and he said, 'Is Charlie Chester in it?' and I said, 'NO he is NOT,' and he said, 'Then we're still not interested,' so I put the phone down on him.

Feel a bit of a chump about it all, because I'd already told Wilfred this idea and he'd laughed at me and said, 'Good golly, Gay, why don't you just take out a huge advertisement for yourself, and be done with it?' and I'd told him that they were very interested actually. Perhaps he'll forget about it. I like Wilfred though. He's very posh, he knows the right way to say and do things, but he's friendly with it and he never looks down on me, though sometimes he mimics the way I talk. I said to him, 'I don't talk funny. I'm from Birkenhead not Liverpool. I don't have an accent. I used to live in Persia,' but he thought that was hilariously funny and he pretended to gag me with his purple scarf saying, 'You talk too much, Gay Gibson, far too much, you might be beautiful but damn you're excitable.'

Wilfred went to Oxford or Cambridge, I forget which. When the war started he said he couldn't join up quick enough. He thinks the war's a hoot. I've never heard anyone talk about it like this before. I told him where I come from it's all food queues and missing sons and sick boys in hospitals and bombs and he said, 'Poor you. Well, now you're going to have some fun, aren't you?'

January 1946, France

We have driven such long distances, and worked so hard I have hardly had a moment to write anything down. Everything is grey here and whipped by rain and wind and mud, and though the war is officially 'over' you wouldn't know it. I can't believe this war really ended, I think it just wore itself out. Looking around here, it's like the ground is exhausted, it couldn't take it any more. The play is going down well and I am in love. I fell in love.

The first time I see him he is sitting by the trucks talking to a friend of his in French, they are both looking up and gesturing me to come and sit down with them. Pierre points to the biscuit tin in my hand and asks me what it's for, I tell him it's for me to wash my hair in and he puts his hand in my hair. That was it, and now there's this thing that races and races and races. If I close my eyes I can see him now, in front of me, beside me, touching me.

When we're rehearsing I can hear him singing, little snatches of him here and there, across the broken sky, singing while he works. I'm rehearsing with Wilfred and Stan, we are going through our lines, but I can hear him nearby singing. We make love in the back of his scenery van. He says he wants to look after me, he asks if I am sick. I don't think the others trust me now, but I don't care. Pierre doesn't care, he just shrugs his shoulders and tells me to stay with him in the van, he says I don't have to go back to them, not ever, not if I don't want to. Pierre wants all this to be over, so he can go back home. He lives in a village in south-west France, he says he's pleased to have work driving our scenery van because it's better than soldier work. I take him tea made with my teabags, he doesn't smile when I give it him, he doesn't even look at me.

Am having trouble with my breathing, my chest is tight and small.

Have been feeling dizzy and light for days. I am struggling for air. I can feel everything, everything, as though it's a part of me. I think I know the refugees and the people we see on the road, think I know them in their grey overcoats and battered hats. Everything is broken up and chaotic here, the roads are all covered in rubble and it feels as though the whole world is here, picking over the rubbish and kicking back stones with their feet. Soldiers are drunk and wild with relief. I went and stood in the shelter near to Pierre, then I went out into the rain and stood in it. He didn't come after me, but when he gave me my cup back he told me to stay in the barracks for the night, otherwise he thinks I will get a chill and die.

Being in love doesn't feel like I thought it would. I think I'd do anything for Pierre. I think I'd kill myself if he wanted me to. Anything.

January 1946

Wilfred wanted to talk to me about Pierre today, he wanted to know what I knew about him. He said he was strange and that he never washes and that is why he smells so bad. He said Pierre reminded him of a bear he once saw in Moscow, it was kept in chains by big men with sticks and made to dance through the streets. Wilfred doesn't like Pierre, he says he's damaged and I should stay away from him. I don't care, I like him damaged and dirty. I love his wordlessness, I love that sometimes I have to wind down the windows of the van because he smells so strong,

Wilfred says he has to go away for a bit, he has to go meet someone but he won't tell me who. He says he'll make his own way to our next performance site, but he's worried about going and leaving me because of Pierre.

I sat up in the front of the van. He was tired and I thought he might crash. When I said this to him he just shrugged and said, 'What would it matter if I did?' He cheered up a bit and sang me French songs. He said I was beautiful and sweet and he wished he'd met me before all this. He said he didn't want to know anything about me, he just wanted to drive and sing. The road was slow and bumpy, and it was a cold, wet morning. Progress was slow. We kept being stopped and when someone pounded on the window, Pierre would wind it down but wouldn't look at the soldier who was talking to him. We smoked cigarettes. I gave him four packets because I have so many, but he didn't thank me, just put them down on the seat between us.

Where we performed was an old munitions factory. Wilfred is back, with a sausage and more cigarettes. The factory must have only been recently abandoned by the Nazis because there were still caps and cups and things left hanging around. The men sat on the old machinery and some climbed up and hung off the rafters. When there was no more space they stuck their heads through the broken windows to watch. I enjoyed it. I could feel their eyes on me, all of them. We got drunk after the show, on some vodka Wilfred had taken off some Poles further down the road, and I said to him, don't you love it here? It's like we're a ray of sunshine in this bleak and broken place, I love the mud and the cold and the broken-up buildings. Wilfred said I needed my head checking. No, I said, don't you love it? Driving on to the fields and the men all wrapped up against the rain and them all sitting out just to watch our play? Didn't he feel important and vital? And he said, no, he just feels cold and hungry most of the time. 'Gay,' he said, 'Gay, you've got to calm down. You're making yourself sick, you're crazy,' he says and gives me a hug. 'Nice girls from Birkenhead don't roll in the mud with weird French drivers, do they?

You're a sauce and you can't deny it. That's what you love, your queer Frenchman, not the place.'

When we were in the back of his van last night, lying in among the ropes, props and tools, I felt happy and as if I was home. With him. After we'd made love Pierre took my hand and pressed the burning end of his cigarette into it. I didn't move, though I felt the white heat of the pain. I didn't scream or anything. Afterwards he took me outside and broke up the ice in the bucket and stuck my hand in the ice. Then he wrapped it in bandages. The pain was wonderful and terrible. I liked it. It felt real. I'd like him to do it again.

When Wilfred saw my hand today he asked what had happened and I told him. He said, 'I told you so, he's a fruitcake.' He doesn't understand. I liked it. I wanted him to do it. He wanted to make his mark on me, I want all his marks on me. Wilfred gave me a hug. 'Don't be mad about him, Gay,' he said, 'he'll soon be off. He doesn't like you so much, you know. Everything is bad and wrong here, that's all. He's had a hard time. You can tell by looking at him. He's probably married. Don't let him hurt you again.'

Had a letter from Mother, she's back home now but Father has gone out to Durban in South Africa for work. She says she's going to wait for me 'in this blasted house on Banbury Road' until I find out when I'm going to be demobbed, so we can make plans. I can't go back to her again, not now. I showed the letter to Wilfred, and he said he thought I should think about going. What's left behind for you in Liverpool anyway? He said he knew some people out there, he could put me in touch with them, they could get me work in the theatres if I wanted, he said he could arrange some things for me, he said he'd only ask a couple of things in return.

Wilfred's taken to asking me questions all the time. He wants to know, do I think I could sleep with anyone? Could I sleep with them for information, say? I told him he doesn't understand it properly, it's not about the sex or the 'sleeping with' as he likes to say, that's not the important thing.

March 1946, Berlin

Pierre left us at the border. He had orders to go back to the coast and pick up another touring party, said he wasn't going to Berlin. He was pleased, he didn't want to see Berlin. He didn't cry. He told me not to cry and he took me in his arms and held me so tight I thought I might burst. I didn't want your hugs. I wanted you to hurt me again, I asked you if you wanted to but when I said this, you started to cry and you squeezed my hand and shook your head and then walked away back through the green trucks and the mud and the holes in the road, back past the empty spindly trees with no leaves, crying and shaking your head. I wanted to run after you and I tried to, I shouted something out, something mad and crazy and loud, and Wilfred had to come after me and drag me into the jeep. He gave me vodka, though it was breakfast time. Sleep, Gay, put your head on my lap and sleep, all this will pass, he said, and he stroked my head. My hair.

Berlin

It's all broken here, into tiny pieces, rubble. People are hungry and the buildings are falling apart, the ground is bad. I'm staying with a family who haven't eaten for days. I took food from the camp kitchen, stuffed it down the front of my battledress and when I got back I let it spill out over their table and they looked at me and burst into tears and then fell to eating it straight away. The mother kept pushing more and more of the food on her daughter, piling up bits of bread and sausage in front of her.

I told Wilfred this, I said it had made me cry. He hugged me but was stern. 'They were fascists, Gay, remember that, every last one of them, they don't deserve our sympathy.' That little girl wasn't a fascist, I said to him, she was just a hungry kid. 'The fascists don't mind if their children starve, Gay,' he said. Wilfred wants to know if I'm going to go out to Durban. He's quite insistent about it. He says I should make a clean break of it. I've told him I want to do another tour, before I'm demobbed, that being an actress is very important to me, I need to get all the experience I can. He wants me to go to Oxford with him when we go back. He says, 'We'll get drunk on black-market champagne and swim in the river.' He's got some acquaintance there he wants me to meet, some professor, will I come and have tea with them both, he thinks I will like this man, he says he's got interests in South Africa.

I can hardly think about this future, but everyone else is. I met a girl from Birkenhead after the show tonight, she's out here working for the Red Cross. She said she loved the show and wanted to know if I was homesick. She wanted to talk about home. She wondered if we knew any of the same people. She says street names to herself as she falls asleep, just to comfort herself. Laird Street, Park Road West, Borough Street, Arrowe Park, like that, then she said, Where did you live?' and I told her and she said, 'Oh, I'll add on Banbury Road if you like,' and I told her she could do what she liked and that I didn't much care. I didn't want to go back. She said she hated it here and wanted to go home. She didn't think they should let girls out here, she said it wasn't safe for us, she didn't mind working at home but it was different here because it was foreign. I told her I liked it. I liked feeling unsafe.

I told Wilfred I missed Pierre, in a funny way, because he didn't talk to me so much. Wilfred says I'm to stick with him from now on, he's going to look after me. Have got that tight feeling inside again, trying to breathe more slowly and have been lying down for most of the day. Hate that feeling, the feeling when there is no air in me, when I can't quite grab as much as I need, but I keep grabbing anyway, gulp after gulp, without stopping.

PART TWO

Four

This is why a person might write a diary, I suppose, so they can remember what they didn't used to know. I had found an atlas at the Grange, it was ancient and damp, and some of the pages had stuck together, but I had very deliberately run my finger down the sides of those thick brittle pages to find a map of Southern Africa. Only in that atlas, old and heavy with frayed binding and mottled pages, the place was pink and this had comforted me. I had traced my finger along the Indian Ocean and across somewhere called Zulu and up towards Johannesburg, a tiny, smart-looking dot on the map. Next to the shaded pink areas was the word 'Colony'. And then I had smiled to myself and nodded, and felt proud, I had shaken the dust off my hands and put the atlas back on the shelf. 'Fine,' I'd said to myself, 'good, now I know where I'm going, the pink place.' I struggle now even to remember the extent of what I was ignorant of, how foolish and naive I was. I don't know what I thought, I thought it might be like London or York perhaps, where we had once holidayed, going to visit my father's sister, and the dark walls of the city had seemed wet and all the people thin and cross. This was how I understood 'foreign' to be, a brief, fleeting sense of newness, though safe in the understanding that everything were all the same underneath.

Even as our little shuddery plane flew up from Cape Town, me holding Paul's hand and pressing my nose against the window, wondering at the brown and red earth and the high mountains down below, and scudded over the sprawling mass of flat Johannesburg, I still didn't really know that anything would be different, and besides, my mind was on other things, things to do with Paul and me and this strange new state of 'marriage'. In fact, what I was mostly thinking about, or trying to understand, was sex.

*

Our crossing had, largely, been a successful one. I had spent eager hungry hours leaning against the ship's railings, watching the changeable sea rise and turn against the horizon, sometimes fitful and choppy then, days later, pure and lush and serene. I loved its vast open expanse, its sense of purpose and endless promise. I adored the humming steamer, its light fittings, the smooth wooden handrails and the piles of tidy deckchairs. I was afloat with sensual pleasures, pinged by the sea's spray on my face; I felt agonisingly alive, to everything. I was excited, girlish, at the prospect of being alone with Paul for so long, for had not desire trailed us through the frozen branches of Elms Wood and then circled us in the long wet grass behind the Grange? I was confident about being with Paul, and even though the kisses on the bottom bunk were plenty pleasurable in themselves, and I gamely slid about beneath him, my eyes closed, reaching for parts of his body so that he would know that the thought of it — whatever it may be — did not revolt me, these kisses resolutely refused to develop into anything else. He would stop our kissing, and stand up. Adjust his shirt, and tell me he had arranged to meet someone or other in the Dome Over Saloon for a drink, and did I want to accompany him?

'There are people on this boat,' he'd say, putting on his shoes, 'who have no idea where they're going or what they're going to find when they get there.' He was trying to help them by answering their questions. 'And what questions they have, Laura, you'd never believe it,' brushing his hair in the mirror. 'Where will Evelyn buy her groceries? What sort of trouble will we have with the natives? In your opinion, Mr Lovell, is it a good place to start a family?'

He'd laugh at this and shake his head a little, then bend down and kiss my forehead and tell me not to wait up for him.

If I hadn't trusted the certainty of our love, I might have thought that he was trying to avoid me. I'd wait for the door to bang shut and lie curled up in the hot, narrow bed saying his name to myself, alarmed at how creased and messy I became at the thought of him. I couldn't understand why Paul wanted to muddy this time with the petty concerns of our fellow travellers.

I believed in Paul's version of events, in his world view. He was, I found out, a great believer in simplicity. He thought life could be straightforward and controllable, which was why he'd married me as he did, on a whim. It was intended, he'd wanted to and so he had. It was that simple to him. He told me this, sitting on the deck during the first week, his shirtsleeves rolled up to his elbows, his arms turning brown in the sun, his eyes closed. How refreshing it all was, after those creaky corridors and hidden miseries of home. He fairly opened up in the sunshine, his arms behind his head, a solid relaxed smile on his lips and I leant back too, with my arms behind my head, and practised the same smile, wishing that Charlotte Locks could see me now.

My marriage had preceded even me to Johannesburg, for before our ship had docked in Cape Town, we had been announced in the 'People In and Out of Town' section of the *Daily Express; 'Mr P. Lovell, only son of Mr and Mrs Lovell of Tenth Avenue, Greenside, arrives in the* Stirling Castle *in Cape Town on Friday, after a short visit to England. He returns with Mrs P. Lovell (née Trelling) after a short holiday trip overseas.'*

I struggled to see myself in this paragraph when (the real) Mrs Lovell fetched it out, within the first hour of our arrival, from behind the glass doors of her bureau to show me. I looked up at her in confusion. Why was she showing me this? Who was this Mrs P. Lovell who had returned with Mr P. Lovell? My eyes drifted across the other notices – *'Dr and Mrs Glackly of Hillbrow are going to Cape Town for a short stay. They are not at home . . . Mr Patrick Tosworth from Liverpool has arrived in Johannesburg on business. He is staying at the Carlton Hotel.'* Who were these people who so brazenly announced their holiday plans in the newspaper?

I handed the clipping back to Paul's mother, my hands were clumsy and slightly swollen, and I looked at her in the cool shadows of her dining room and wondered whether I could ask her about marital relations and whether she might be able to advise me on what exactly marital relations were.

'We'll keep this for your family scrapbook, shall we?' Bridget Lovell said firmly. 'You don't want to be careless with your memories, Laura,' and she struggled a little with the saying of my name, the very fact of it caught in her protuding teeth, and I realised that, of course, I could not ask her such a thing.

*

We came tumbling up the Lovells' short and immaculate drive, surely looking to all the world as free and aimless as two feathered dandelion seeds caught in a warm breeze.

The house was white, low and squat with a veranda, or *stoep* as I would learn to call it, which stretched across the front of the house and round to one side. The garden was small and yellow-dry, the sitting room where we sat awkwardly that first evening, dark and low. It was an unwelcoming and unforgiving house, it had no stories to tell and no interest in any stories a visitor might wish to share, it wasn't in the business of harbouring family secrets, there were no telltale stains or damaged plasterwork, no surprising corners or uneven steps. This house was as unimaginative and economical as its address suggested – 50 Tenth Avenue, Greenside. It was a series of rooms arranged over two floors, all of which were regularly scrubbed with soap and a wire brush and each as bereft of charm as the next. There were shutters on the outside of each of the windows which could have been pretty but they had been painted an unattractive brown and they made the house appear as though it were permanently frowning, and if you stood on the front lawn and looked up at this house it would insolently stare down at you, defiant in its emptiness.

Bridget and Robert Lovell did not come out to greet us; when the taxi stopped Paul jumped out, and rushed inside without waiting for me. I was hot and dusty, my mind trying to catch up with the sights I had seen coming in from the landing strip, the dusty roads, the black people carrying things on their heads, a wild dog barking at us, all the long straight streets we'd driven down, with their dizzying array of identical houses. I climbed out of the taxi, my legs sticking to the seat, leaving warm red patches on the backs of my legs.

'Well, well. Is this her then?' I heard a voice say, and looking up towards the house, squinting slightly in the bright light, I could see three figures standing in the doorway.

I walked towards them, feeling the strange dry and springy grass under my feet, still with my hand shielding my eyes. When I reached the door, I saw their faces in the shade and offered Robert Lovell my hand. He took it and held it tightly, a little too tightly, 'I'm Robert Lovell, your new father-in-law.'

'Come on inside,' Bridget had shouted. 'Come on in. Robert will get the luggage.'

As we sat in their sitting room, I quickly took in the two sofas, upholstered in a desolate pale blue, and one armchair, the few bits of cheap furniture which littered the corners of the room and the polished parquet flooring gleaming beneath our feet. It felt very empty. It suddenly struck me as extraordinary to be here, looking at these strangers while they scrutinised me. I could feel sweaty patches on the backs of my knees. I closed my eyes briefly, and was greeted with an image of Mrs Frobisher staring over her desk at me, her spectacles steamed up and shouting, 'Laura Lovell! Please pay attention. Stop daydreaming. One day these lessons in Home Economics will be useful to you.' I quickly opened them again.

'I'll get you both a drink,' Bridget was saying, standing in front of us, wringing her hands with what I took to be nervous excitement. 'What'll you have? Lemonade? Tea?'

'Sit down, Mum, we're fine. We had something on the plane from Cape Town. Really, please, sit down.'

I smiled up at her, in wedded agreement. It was cool in there, at least.

'Water? Juice? Something stronger? Oh, it's so good to have you back, Paul,' she beamed.

Mr Lovell came in and headed for a drinks trolley, his shoes clicking on the floor.

'What is it then, Laura? Gin, is it?' He didn't wait for a response. He set four glasses out and started pouring strong portions of gin into them. 'Where's Mary? MARY,' he shouted. A door banged open a few rooms away, and shuffling steps came nearer and nearer until the door opened.

'We need ice, Mary. The ice bucket is empty,' Robert said, without turning round.

Mary crossed the room to fetch the bucket, smiling at Paul, who jumped up to greet her.

'Hello, Mary, I brought you a present back from England. You'll never guess what it is.'

'Welcome home, Master Paul,' she said thickly, smiling at him. She was a small, stout woman wearing carpet slippers and a cloth tied across her head. I wasn't sure whether I should introduce myself or not, I didn't know whether it was proper, seeing as she was black, and a maid. So I waited for her to look at me, but she didn't, she just picked up the ice bucket and left the room.

'Well, how is the mother country, Paul?' Robert asked, handing out the glasses of warm gin, 'Tell us what you got up to.'

He settled himself down in the armchair opposite me, crossing one leg over the other.

'Well,' Paul said, loyally, 'I got married.'

On first inspection I couldn't see Paul in either of his parents. I suppose I had imagined that they would look alike, and that I would immediately warm to them on that basis, if I'd thought about them at all, which I hadn't. Robert was shorter than Paul, who must have got his height from Bridget, but he was powerful. When he sat down on his chair, I could see the thigh muscles straining and bulging against his trouser legs and because Robert wore his shirtsleeves rolled up above the elbow, exposing broad tanned forearms, it was possible to follow those sinewy muscles up over his level shoulders and into that thick ham-like neck. I thought he looked old-fashioned and rough, despite the gleaming Brylcreemed hair and the parting aggressively etched into his scalp. He looked like what my mother called a 'spiv'. Though she used this word liberally to describe any man she considered lower class and unnecessarily confident. I was disorientated by his combination of coiled strength and drawing-room civility. He was looking at me over the rim of his glass, he must have seen me staring at him, and when I met his gaze he widened his brown eyes slightly, with a quick challenging flash, as though he thought there might be a secret between us.

Bridget hadn't been able to sit down. She stood in the middle of the room, her huge pale hands clasped in front of her, beaming at Paul. Her mouth was overcrowded with teeth, like so many eager matrons at the front of a food queue, and when she turned to smile at me I half feared they were going to fall out of her mouth and onto the floor in a terrible clattering torrent, a pearl necklace unexpectedly snapping, and that we'd all have to get down on our hands and knees and help her pick them up. She was a tall woman, plain, with missionary hair done up in a bun; everything about her looked long, her legs, her hands, she had an angular body with a little bump of a stomach pushing against her sensible dress. I felt suddenly quite sick. I took a large gulp of the warm gin, which made me shudder even more.

Paul, sitting beside me, was smiling at them both.

'Aunt Gloria sent you both her love. She gave me some things for you, English things, they're in the trunk.'

'That was nice of her.'

'She thinks we need her charity, does she?' Robert was frowning, but still trying to smile, 'You told her, I trust, that we don't actually live in a jungle?'

Paul laughed. 'No of course not. I told her we fight snakes on a daily basis and wear vine leaves for best. Oh, sorry, Laura, I forgot to mention that to you too.'

And the three of them laughed and looked at me. I smiled back, not getting the joke, thinking that everything was suddenly alarming, being here, looking at them looking at me.

'She's only meaning to be kind,' Bridget said, wringing her hands. 'Did you meet Gloria, Laura? You live near her, I understand, I mean you *used* to live near her?'

'No, sadly I didn't have that pleasure,' I said loudly, sounding alarmingly like my mother. 'Everything happened in a bit of a rush really.'

'Ah yes.' Robert shifted in his chair, leaning back and running one hand across his polished head. He smiled at me. 'Ah yes, Paul does rather tend to rush at things, I'm afraid.'

Paul was looking down at his glass; he prodded an ice cube with his finger. Robert and Bridget stared at me. We sat in silence.

I asked if I could go and have a wash, maybe change out of my travelling clothes – not because I wanted to particularly, I just wanted to get away from Robert Lovell's dark eyes and out of that sitting room – and Bridget told me to follow her. She opened the door to the study under the stairs and apologised for not having a proper spare room, but she said she hoped I would be comfortable and that I was to use the closet in the downstairs lavatory to hang up my clothes. Paul had nervously tailed us.

'Mother! She can't sleep in here.'

Then Mr Lovell came in and we all stood staring at a camp bed stuck against the far wall, opposite his desk.

'She'll sleep upstairs with me,' Paul said, reddening.

'Do you like this cushion, Laura?' Bridget leant down and picked up a pink heart-shaped cushion, with a lace trim, which was balanced on the pillow. 'I made it for you.'

'Thank you.' I turned it over in my hands, not knowing what to say. I looked to Paul but he didn't say anything.

'Well, that's sorted then,' Robert said, grinning at me. 'Paul, bring in her cases and let the poor girl get some rest. More drinks for us, I think.'

I stood alone in the room, just looking at the camp bed, squatting disconsolately in the corner of this tiny room, turning that cushion round and round in my hands.

'God, look, sorry.' Paul came in with a suitcase, and closed the door behind him. He was grinning at me. 'It's quite funny really, isn't it? Must be a bit of a shock for them, that's all. They'll soon get used to it.'

'I don't think it's funny at all. They know we're married, don't they?'

'Yes, of course. We'll sort it out tomorrow.'

'They don't like me, do they?'

'They don't even know you, Lala. Look, have a wash and a nap or something. Dad wants to take me round to the Beresfords', they're having a party, just for a quick drink, and to say hello to everyone. We'll be back for dinner. It'll give you some quiet time.'

'I'm not tired, I'll come with you.'

'No, really, I don't think you should. They think you're going to rest, and that's why they suggested we go now. We'll only be an hour tops.'

108

'I never said I was tired. I said I wanted to wash. I don't want any quiet time. I want to go to the Beresfords'.' I was trying to sound emphatic, but there was an edgy, nervous trill to my voice.

'Laura, not now. I'll see you later,' and he kissed me quickly and left the room without looking back. I heard their voices in the hallway, Robert's cough, some quickly hushed laughter. 'Bye-bye, dear, we won't be long,' Bridget called out, and then the front door closed and there was a far-off sound of a car starting and driving away and then silence.

*

The heart-shaped cushion had *Sweetheart* embroidered in pale pink across its centre. I looked at this for some time, then I took off my shoes and rubbed my feet. Sweetheart? Lying down and staring up at the whitewashed ceiling I could feel the familiar rise and fall of the ship beneath me, as though I were adrift in the ocean on this tiny bed, rising up against stormy waves, careering off across the sea with only a lace-trimmed pillow for comfort or help. A clock chimed in an upstairs room.

How had I allowed myself to be left behind? I'd been too easy, too pliable. Paul should have stuck up for me; how was it possible that I'd thrown in my lot with him, so willingly, so readily, to come all this way and find myself alone again? I should never have agreed to sleep in here. I'd thought that as a married woman I would be awarded a different status, and with that status, I hoped, more asser-tion and worldliness. Robert and Bridget should have shrunk back with gratitude and admiration that I'd come to their home. What had I done, coming to this house of strangers without a thought? Perhaps they still would, I was being silly, I was overreacting. I'm tired, I told myself, there's a lot to take in. Everything will be fine.

I wandered over to Robert's desk, which was empty save a sheet of immaculate cream blotting paper and a photograph inside a silver frame. I picked it up. The photograph was of Paul and Bridget sitting by the side of a swimming pool. They were both in bathing suits, laughing into the camera; Paul must have been sixteen or younger, his young body glistened with water and he had his arm slung around his mother's shoulders. I was rather shocked by its nakedness and intimacy and put it down quickly, with a thud, deciding that I probably had just enough time to have a look upstairs before they came back from their party.

In the hallway copper bed-warming pans hung on the wall, together with a couple of bad paintings of English country scenes, haymakers and carts and such things. A narrow staircase led up to a tight landing off which were just two doors. I opened one of them and found myself in Mr and Mrs Lovell's bedroom. They had twin beds with matching eiderdowns, a simple brown wooden chair in one corner and over by the window was Mrs Lovell's dressing table, which had lots of photographs slid into the sides of the mirror. The dressing table was a little corner of emotional indulgence. All of Lovell human life was there; portraits of Paul as a very young child taken in a studio, his hair a mop of golden curls and his pudgy face unsmiling; the Lovell's wedding day, a riot of lace, parasols and make-do suits; Paul sitting on the back of a horse looking smug and pleased with himself; Paul in a school uniform holding up a piece of paper; Robert Lovell standing on the veranda of this house, in an open-necked shirt and holding boy-Paul's hand and laughing.

I sat down on the stool next to the dressing table to get a better look at the photographs and, perhaps, to try one of these drawers. I was picking up one of Mrs Lovell's ivory-backed hairbrushes – I think I had a mind to brush my hair – when I glanced into the mirror in front of me and then screamed, dropping the hairbrush onto the glass top. Mary was standing behind me, so close that I could feel her legs gently nudging against my back.

'Oh Mary!' I said, holding my hand against my heart. 'You gave me such a shock.'

I looked up at her face in the mirror, and she looked straight back at me, her eyes caught in the fading evening light. I had never been so close to a black person before.

'Not your room, Miss,' she said, reaching out her hand to return Mrs Lovell's hairbrush to its proper place.

'Yes, of course, I know. Sorry.'

'Um-hmm.'

I stood up and moved around to the side of the table. She wasn't looking at me, she was checking the dressing table, checking that everything was in its proper place, that everything was there.

'Must have got a bit lost.'

'Um-hmm.' She was still refusing to look at me. 'I heard a noise.'

I looked at her heavy hands, touching everything on the table, stroking the backs of the hairbrushes and allowing a finger to run along the top of Mrs Lovell's leather jewellery case. She could have been anything between twenty-five and fifty-five.

'A noise?'

'Yes, something breaking.'

'I don't know anything about that. I came upstairs because I couldn't find my own hairbrush, you see. I wanted to brush up before they came back,' and, as authoritatively as I could, I turned on my heel to walk out but when I was by the door I heard a strange gurgling noise and, turning back, saw Mary standing with her hands on her hips. She was laughing at me.

'Welcome to the Union,' she said, with a wide crooked smile. 'Welcome to South Africa, Mrs Lovell,' and then she turned back to the table, still laughing.

*

When I woke the first morning, my head was spinning and throbbing, and I couldn't remember where I was. It had been a hot night, a muggy airless heat, and I'd longed for a sea breeze to cool me. Paul had kissed me awkwardly in the hall and followed his parents up the stairs, and I'd been able to hear them above me. I'd tried to imagine Bridget and Robert lying in their twin beds with matching counterpanes and their whispered conversation. I wondered whether his Brylcreemed hair left a shine of grease on the pillowslip, and whether Bridget had to change it each evening, and whether every time he put his head on the pillow, she felt her stomach tighten and had to grit her many teeth together. I had dreamt of pigeons and cats.

Slowly it came back to me, as I lay in my bed, staring at the edges of Robert's desk. I was in Johannesburg, I was inside that neat little dot, with Paul, at his parents' house. I said 'Johannesburg' over and over under my breath trying to make it familiar but it quickly became 'Joanna's turd' and so I stopped. The air felt thick and tense. Opening the windows of the study, I leant out between the bars gulping in the dry arid air, wondering why they had bars on the windows, was it to keep strangers out or to keep me in? I didn't like them. I wanted cool English summer rain to fall on the roses so I could lick the drops from the petals. The yellow grass looked scratchy and sour, the flower beds parched and the earth all broken up into crazy-paving pieces. This place was making me dizzy and sick but I told myself sternly, as I pulled on my other cotton dress and ran my fingers through my straggly hair, I must concentrate hard on being a good guest, a capable adult, a decent wife and a respectable daughter-in-law.

At breakfast though I had trouble sitting upright, I had to hold onto the sides of the table. The dining room was small and table oversized, and there wasn't much room to pull your chair out. I felt as though I had to breathe in all the time, and I wondered why they didn't open a window. Outside the sky was a deep blue, and strong slants of sun fell across the table.

'Where's the nearest water?' I said, to no one in particular.

'You want a drink?' Paul was half out of his seat.

'She doesn't mean that.' Robert Lovell grinned at me from the top of the table. 'No water here, darling. No river, no lake, no sea for four hundred miles. Only gold,' and stamped his foot down on the ground, 'a mile beneath our feet. Gold and plenty of it.'

Robert looked different, all dressed up to go to work, for he was something of a dandy when he went to the office, favouring pinstriped suits with checked waistcoats and vibrant-coloured hand-kerchiefs, ironed socks and tall starched collars on his shirts. I thought he looked like a villain. He raised his glass of orange juice to me and drank it down in one.

'I looked Southern Africa up on a *map*,' I said defiantly. 'It was pink.'

Robert and Bridget looked at me, in silence, then at one another for a moment and then away again. Robert was smiling.

'There are plenty of things to do here, dear,' Bridget said even-tually, pouring me a coffee and passing it up the table. 'Lovely shops, hotels and plenty of cinemas. They're building lots of factories now and everyone says new people from Europe are coming off the boats every day, it's very exciting. It's a big place, Johannesburg, you've not come anywhere backward, I can promise you that.'

'How old are you, Laura?' Robert didn't look at me, he was busy peeling an orange. I could smell its citrusy bite.

'Bob!' Bridget laughed. 'You can't ask her that.'

But now they were both looking at me, expectant, I looked over at Paul, but he was studying the newspaper, pretending he couldn't hear us. He still looked a bit sleepy and unkempt.

'I'm seventeen, Mr Lovell.'

'Oh dear,' said Bridget, in spite of herself and then hastily shooting a look at Paul, 'I mean, how brave of you to do all this when you're so young.'

Robert looked pleased with this information; he nodded slowly, smug. Then he turned toward Paul.

'So you didn't get to Russia then, Paul? On your trip abroad? Visit the comrades?'

'You know perfectly well I'm not a communist, Dad,' Paul said evenly, without looking up from his paper.

'Ah yes, of course, socialist, is it? Is that the right word?'

'Yes, that's it,' Paul replied in the same flat voice.

'Just stayed in Sussex with Gloria, did you? Meeting Lisa and all that?'

'Her name, as you well know, is Laura. I went to London a bit too. Have you seen this? Did you read this article on Malan?'

'London, ah yes.' Robert shifted slightly in his chair and pretended to cough, to hide his pleasure. 'What does your new wife think about all this then? Malan makes a lot of sense, Paul. During the war they relaxed everything, even the pass laws, and look what happened. Suddenly all the Kaffirs are forming together in trade unions. Things will have to sharpen up a bit, the war's over now, we don't need any more of that liberal shit.' Robert spoke forcefully, but not with any passion, he was watching Paul carefully, goading him. 'I heard at work, there are some Kaffirs who want to organise a squatters movement! Can you believe that, Paul? They want to get rid of the pass laws, Paul, live where they want to, go where they want. How about that, Paul? You might have squatters up from Orlando, camping out at the bottom of our drive. You'd like that, I suppose.'

'What are pass laws? What are squatters?' I asked Paul, but he didn't look up at me. Nor at his father, though I could see the tips of Paul's ears had gone red. I wondered at Robert using his name so much when he spoke, like a playground bully, as though his name was in itself ridiculous.

'Let's not talk politics now,' Bridget said briskly, banging the coffee pot down on the table. 'Whatever will Laura think of us, it's breakfast time!' and she made an odd noise, a too loud, insincere attempt at polite laughter. 'Robert, you should be off, you'll be late.'

Robert wiped his face with a napkin and stood up, pushing his chair noisily against the wall.

'Didn't you know Greg Croker's son? He's just joined the company, Paul, did I tell you?'

'Richard? I thought he'd planned on going to Rhodesia?'

'Decided against it, got himself a good job, joined the capitalists instead. There might be an opening at work for you, Paul, I could have a word?'

But Paul was back in the newspaper, ignoring him, and Robert stood at the end of the table for a moment, contemplating his son's downturned head. Then suddenly he threw his napkin down the table, it blurred past me like a blue bird and landed with a thump on Paul's newspaper. Paul looked up at him then, his face quite blank, but empty with effort. It must have taken some restraint on both their parts not to say or do more.

'Right, well, have a good day, all,' Robert said. 'You all right, Lisa? You look a bit peaky.'

When he'd gone, Bridget started tidying up the breakfast table. She was smiling intently at me.

'Would you like to go into town today, Laura? Stuttafords first of all, and then perhaps lunch at the Carlton as a special treat, and you might like to see the Eskom building too, twenty-one storeys it is, Laura, the tallest in Johannesburg.'

'Oh thank you, Mrs Lovell, but perhaps not today,' I said rather weakly, looking at Robert's napkin in the middle of the table, placed there by Paul with contemptuous precision. 'I don't feel very well. I think I might need a day or two to get used to things. It is rather hot.'

Paul looked at me over the top of the newspaper. He was frowning.

'You can't sit around here all day though, Lala. I want to show you things, but I haven't got lots of time. I will need to start doing my own things soon, you know.'

I didn't ask him what his 'own things' might mean, but Bridget knew because she started gathering up the breakfast things with renewed vigour, banging the plates together and tossing knives across the table with those practical hands of hers.

'Paul,' she warned, without looking at him, 'Paul, I don't want any of that talk now.'

I wanted to get out of that small, tight room and went into the garden, hoping Paul would follow me. It was only a small plot, marked out by a low white wall at the bottom and a small driveway to the front and side. There were other, identical, houses on each side and opposite. The garden was full of strange noises and insects; I saw lizards sunbathing on the stones next to the rose bed, a party of red ants crawling up the step to the stoep and a strange bird strutted across the lawn, ominously sleek and dark. I sat down in a heap on the scratchy grass, feeling the hot sun burning my upper arms, thoughts like thunderclouds crashed inside my head, heavy and cumbersome and out of reach. Bridget followed me out into the garden.

'Are you all right, dear?' She prodded me with the tip of her shoe.

'Oh yes.' I found a quick smile to flash at her. 'Just sunbathing, trying to shake off this silly headache. It's so hot. It's glorious, such a marvellous place for a holiday, isn't it? And when I think of the wind and rain back home . . .'

'Yes. You've left all that behind you now, haven't you? Coming out here, well, it's a big thing to do, isn't it? You must be—' But she couldn't bring herself to finish her sentence, so she bent down and offered her hand and pulled me to my feet. 'There now, that's better, isn't it? Shoulders back, head high, all that sort of thing.'

Five

During the first week people were brought to the house to meet and view me. I found it shocking and surprising, I was so unused to even the *idea* of polite society. I couldn't understand their interest in me or why they were bothering to visit. Paul would disappear during these morning and teatime visits, and I would be left alone with Bridget, pulling my dress down over my knees, pulling my schoolgirl socks up and fiddling with hairgrips, trying to smile at them but all the time wondering why they were bothering.

The visitors were all middle-aged women, frumpy and doughy, wearing hot-looking suits, gloves and small hats set at a jaunty angle with little green flyaway feathers hovering over their ears. I was sat on one side of the sitting room and they were arranged opposite me on the pale blue sofas. Conversation wasn't easy, I couldn't think of anything to say to them. Bridget must have hoped that if she embraced this situation, me and Paul, as normal and satisfactory then others would too, but they didn't, they peered at me across the room and asked Bridget questions. She told them I was finding the 'adjustment' difficult, that I was suffering with headaches and she thought I had a little altitude sickness, that I was struggling with the thin Johannesburg air. Then they crossed their arms across their dependable bosoms, pursed their lips and nodded. One of them suggested I eat mashed potato, she said it would be the best way to fight off this sickness, I was to eat at least two bowls of mashed potato a day.

'Of course,' another said, 'there's all types coming here now, I see new faces every day. It's very hard to keep up nowadays, one simply has no idea who *anyone* is.'

And they all looked across the room at me, hostile and suspicious, and Bridget leapt to her feet and asked if anyone would like more tea. The sun would be beating down outside and we were all crammed in that carbolically clean room, wafts of disinfectant mingling with the smells of baking, and I felt myself sway with boredom and uncertainty on my chair. They revelled in Bridget's discomfort and embarrassment, they drank her tea and wolfed down her sticky scones only to trudge down the driveway muttering to one another, throwing quick furtive looks back at Bridget standing on the stoep gamely waving them off. They sensed a scandal and they weren't going to be bought off so easily. Bridget would return and shoot little looks at me while she called for Mary to come and gather up the cups and saucers.

In that first week Bridget and I were invited to a Ladies' Luncheon at the country club, an invitation which appalled and thrilled her in equal measure. 'It's quite an honour, Laura,' she told me, her watery eyes wide and unblinking, 'we're not members or anything. Isn't that kind of Mrs Waterback? So very kind.'

This was my first outing. We drove to the club, side by side in Bridget's car, in absolute silence. I balled my hands up tight in my lap, staring out the window, taking in all the tall trees and heavy verdant bushes, the maids in uniform carrying towels and laundry on their heads, a dog barking, cars, the walls surrounding identical houses and up above the high round sun turning everything brown and dry. The club was a large sprawling building set in pretty gardens. I followed Bridget down its long corridors towards the dining room, intimidated by the rows of photographs of their successful polo teams and by the serious expressions of all those men in blazers and matching ties. Bridget and I were sat at a table together, and she was so very nervous and apprehensive, so very concerned that I would behave appropriately in such auspicious company, that I lost all confidence and could barely eat the little morsels of fish put in front of me, let alone make polite conversation with the terrifying array of mature, battle-worn ladies at our table. She put on a good show, Bridget, though it was obvious that none of this was any more fun for her than it was for me. They were a little snooty and cool with her, I thought, patronising.

'Where did you say your son was working, Mrs Lovell?'

'Oh, he's just back from overseas, he's not working yet.'

'Not working! You'd better see to that, hadn't you? Don't want him lying around cluttering the place up, do we?' And they all laughed.

'He's got interests,' I said, wanting to come to his defence. The ladies looked at me, frowning.

'Now where did you say you're from?' an ancient woman with brown wrinkled skin and magenta lipstick sitting next to me asked, craning forward and offering me her ear. 'Talk into this one. It's the only one that works.'

'Sussex,' I shouted loudly into it.

'That's no good at all,' she declared, 'this isn't Sussex, you know, or Kent or Mayfair or any of those sorts of places,' as though they represented all my foolish girlish indulgences, and as if I wasn't slowly becoming aware of that fact. 'I don't know half the people in this room any more, we're overrun with strangers. Rosemary! Rosemary, I said, we're overrun with strangers. Who are they all? Common as muck most of them,' and she glared at Bridget who stiffened and blushed and looked down at her plate.

'They're all new people, Lady McIntyre, off the boats,' said Rosemary with a forced smile, before quickly adding, 'Not Mrs Lovell though, she's been here for years,' and everyone turned to look at her, as though surprised by this information. 'But she's not a member here, are you, Mrs Lovell?' and Bridget was forced to agree that, indeed, she was not.

'I'm looking forward to seeing Johannesburg,' I said loudly, 'It seems a very interesting place. I do want to find out about everything, about pass laws and squatters and all that.' I didn't know what these things meant of course, but I knew from Robert's conversation at the breakfast table that they might be somehow relevant to general conversation, might show just how enthusiastic I hoped to be about their city.

I heard Bridget breathe in sharply. I looked at her, staring at me, her mouth slowly forming a silent 'No'.

Lady McIntyre snorted. '*Very interesting* it is not, young girl. This is a fast, tough and vulgar place. You need to be one step ahead of it always, otherwise it'll get you and drag you down and don't you forget it. It's a mining town, built for commerce and exploitation. I've been here years and I've seen them come and go, believe you me,' and she turned and poked me in the arm with a fingernail. 'The ground is poisoned, love has no place in this town and I'll charge you not to forget that.'

I looked into her dark blue old-lady's eyes; they were steely and uncompromising. There was a silence at the table for a moment, and then Rosemary started asking questions, in a bright, breezy voice, about the upcoming tennis tournament and did anyone know whether they'd sorted out the pairings for the bridge club.

*

'It was awful, Paul, they all stared at me and they weren't very friendly. They said you weren't to lie about the place cluttering things up. I don't want to go again – can't you stop your mother from doing all these things? I can't think of anything to say to them, and they can't think of anything to say to me either.'

He and I were sitting out on the stoep, it was morning but already hot, I was listening to the disconcerting and, to my mind, hysterical whirring of the hidden insects in the garden, but trying to listen to Paul too. I was pleased to have Paul to myself. He had a habit of disappearing upstairs to his room leaving me aimlessly wandering about the house trying to avoid Bridget and Mary, particularly Mary who I couldn't get used to at all. I was forever seeing a triangle of pink out of the corner of my eye, the edge of her skirt sliding past an open door, she seemed always to be in the shadows. All attempts at conversation on my part – Have you worked here long? Do you have any family, Mary? – had fallen on mute and stony ground. If I tiptoed up the stairs and knocked on Paul's door, he'd stick his head out and say crossly, 'What is it, darling? What's the matter?'

Paul had made a list of places he thought I might like to go and things he thought I ought to see.

'You should visit all the places on the Reef, Lala' he said, chewing the end of his pencil and looking through his papers. 'There'll be some eye-opening places for you there. Perhaps we should start at the Public Library though, with the African Museum and a very good exhibition on the first floor of the geological history of Southern Africa.'

'Will it just be me and you, Paul?'

'What? Yes, I should think so, Lala, unless you want to invite someone else?'

I blinked at him across the sunny veranda. He wasn't looking at me and I didn't know whether he was joking or not. My arms were sunburnt already, and I found the air thick and difficult. The stone slabs on the stoep were burning hot under my feet, despite being shaded by a vine. Everything seemed quiet and blank. Paul was wearing a bright white shirt, it looked dazzlingly clean.

Our trips, that first week, were formal and well organised but with a tiresomely educational bent. Paul was quite adamant that we stick to his list, and I was just grateful to be on my own with him. We visited the Johannesburg Art Gallery in Joubert Park, where we ambled slowly through the empty rooms looking at the Pre-Raphaelite collection until Paul declared them 'bourgeois and boring', so we came back home early, surprising Mary and Bridget who had taken the opportunity to clean my room, thoroughly.

'You don't seem to have many things,' Bridget had said, doing that hand-wringing thing and nodding her head towards the closet in the downstairs bathroom where my few dresses were hanging. 'Are you having more sent over?'

'No,' I told her, leaning against the door frame, sticky with sweat and the taste of town on my skin, 'I don't have many things.'

We both of us looked at the neatly made camp bed with its perfect hospital corners, and then at my suitcase stowed by the door. What did she expect? That I would have put my family photographs on Robert's desk or lined a thousand pairs of shoes under the window, arranged hatboxes next to the filing cabinet? Bridget had narrowed her eyes a little at me. 'Oh? Well, we'll have to see whether we can sort you out, won't we?'

Paul took me to view the 'new buildings' in the city centre, off we went traipsing down the hot streets arm in arm. 'This is the Anstey building', that the 'Anglo-American Corporation building' and this 'the Astor building' – 'Aren't they tall, Lala? Don't you think them impossibly grand?' Oh, how it went on, the Chrysler building, the Chamber of Mines building, the Municipal Cooling Towers, huge great structures built with American steel, rising high above us, angles of glass and brick, throwing everyone below into canyoned darkness.

I found Johannesburg unsettling and uncomfortable, though I didn't tell Paul how frightened I was of all those foreign and black people on the streets, the strange smells and slow traffic, and there was always so much noise and dust. How could Paul see this place as anything more civilised than a frontier town? The Central Business District made me nervous, the skyscrapers and covered walkways; I couldn't see any greenery, there were no trees or open spaces, just high-reaching buildings and people jostling along the pavements, looking resolute. The wide raised roads from the northern suburbs fell down towards central Johannesburg, rocks by the side of the road, and any countryside looked untamed and wiry, bristling with dry grasses and flat spiky bushes. I liked the Carlton Hotel though, where we stopped one afternoon for tea and lemonade, it was reassuringly European. I liked the shuttered French windows and doors opening on to balconettes and the wrought-iron balustrades on the lower floors. Inside it was cool and cavernous and we sat on wicker chairs and sipped at the frothing lemonade served to us in silver cups, starched linen napkins draped over our knees. Though even the Carlton had been extended and modernised before the war, with three new storeys added.

'Goodness, why do they have to make everything so large, Paul?'

'Expansion, Laura, growth. Everything is possible here, it could be a marvellous place, the new world, everything is possible here.' He didn't look at me when he said it, he waved his hands around and looked straight ahead of him, smiling broadly.

'Paul, I do want you to tell me things. Tell me about what you want to do, tell me about the pass laws and the squatters. Please.'

And he'd frowned at me. 'Yes, yes, I will one day. But not here, Laura. Now, would you like some more lemonade?'

'Lady McIntyre said the place was overrun with foreigners, coming off the boats. Is that true?'

'I think,' he said slowly, looking at me with suspicion, 'that Smuts is encouraging white Europeans to come to the country, yes. Why are you asking these things?'

'Well, that's nice, isn't it? Because there are a lot of black faces here, aren't there? It probably needs more white people to make it a bit more civilised.' I was rather proud of this pronouncement, and looked at him triumphantly.

'Laura,' he said, looking cross, 'you don't know what you're talking about. Let's do this later. I'll order you some more of those sand-wiches if you like. You seemed to like the last lot.'

I missed Paul and I felt the need to touch him whenever an opportunity presented itself. I would reach over and tap his knee, or put my hand on his shoulder. Since we'd arrived at his parents' house I'd found him increasingly distant. I tried talking to him, but he was impatient with my questions and I worried that he thought me needy.

'Do you think they like me, your parents?' I'd say, trying to keep up with him, walking so fast down Eloff Street. 'I mean, is every-thing all right, do you think?'

'What? Yes, of course – Mum loves showing you off to everyone. You're doing very well. Now, Eloff Street is one of the earliest streets in Johannesburg, it's named after the government surveyor who laid out the first streets in the city.'

'Oh, I see. It's just, I was wondering, do you think we should do something about the bedrooms now? It's a bit odd, isn't it? My sleeping downstairs and everything?'

'Give it time, Laura. It'll all be fine. Everyone just has to get used to one another, I mean we do too, don't we? It's strange having you here, even for me, we just need to adjust to things a bit. Now come on, I want to show you Markham's mistake, and its four-faced clock dial.'

'But you don't regret it, do you, Paul?'

'No of course I don't, Laura' and he smiled at me, but he looked tired and annoyed. 'Now, are we going on?' and he was off, walking fast, holding his hand out behind him for me to catch a hold of.

He seemed very keen to educate me, but always about things I wasn't interested in, like who had built which skyscraper, he wouldn't tell me about his 'interests'. Mostly, though, I wanted the Paul I'd met in Elms Wood back. In the afternoons he'd disappear upstairs to his bedroom, and Bridget, not knowing what to do with me, sent me for lie-downs in my room, shooing me out of the sun and into the study. After our conversation in the Carlton Hotel Paul started to leave copies of the *Rand Daily Mail* for me to read while I rested in the afternoons, but the paper made me dizzy from all the foreign words and names – D. F. Malan, the Purified Nazi Party, Hertzog, Jan Smuts. I thought it an awful, mean little news-paper with scant news that I could comprehend; it was all articles on the sizes of oranges or the condition of the native bread or pieces declaring the state's firmest intention to enquire into 'citrus wastage'. I couldn't even understand the advertisements, 'Impala — the superfine mealie available from all grocers.' I tried reading the classifieds but there was no comfort to be found there. They advertised dairy cows, farm machinery and tea rooms. The whole paper stank of misery, austerity and farming. I told Paul to stop giving it to me, I told him I couldn't understand it.

'It's good for you to read it. It'll give you an idea of the place.'

'Well, I don't like it. I don't understand it, it's all about sanitary conditions.'

'No, Lala,' he said, looking cross with me, 'this paper is our liberal conscience. You have a lot to learn.'

'Then teach me, please. Tell me what you are up to.'

But again he gave me that clouded uncertain look, as though he thought I was testing him in some way.

One afternoon Paul came in and found me crying. 'Lala, you're crying, what is it?' But he didn't put his arms around me, he just sat on the corner of his father's desk, looking amused.

'I don't know,' I told him, wiping my face with Bridget's heart-shaped pillow. 'I'm trying really hard, but it just feels so strange here.'

'You'll get used to it — you're homesick, that's all,' and then he did sit down and put an awkward hand on my leg. 'I did tell you it'd be different, didn't I?'

'No you didn't, you didn't say anything about it at all. I've never been anywhere before.' I noticed that Paul's curls had started to grow back behind his ears; I reached out and touched them, turning his hair between my fingers.

'What are you doing?' he laughed.

'When are we going home, Paul?'

'But you haven't seen everything yet.'

'I don't want to see everything, I just want to go home and for us to find a flat in London and—'

'Oh come on,' he said, standing up, 'you're just being silly now. This isn't like you, Laura. What about that grand adventure we were on? You've got to give it time, that's all. Can you do that for me?' He looked down his 'good' nose at me, his blue eyes meeting mine, smiling slightly.

'Yes,' I said, not wanting him to be cross with me, but not really knowing or understanding what it was that I was agreeing to.

*

After all the excitement of meeting Paul and going to London and then on the steamer, it was strange having nothing to do. The Lovells were not like my parents, they wanted to be busy. They thought that doing nothing was wasteful, sinful even. Bridget's main activity seemed to revolve around cleaning. She would stand over Mary while she polished the floor, talking to her in wavy, incomplete sentences, pacing the sitting room and moving cushions, running a damp cloth over the already immaculate tabletops, stopping by windows and rushing off to get a bottle of vinegar to wipe away an imagined smear on the pane. She made lists too, long elaborate lists of food to be bought, chores to be done. I wanted to say to her, 'Stop cleaning your house. Why are you cleaning this house when it's already clean? Stop it.'

She had strong opinions on cleaning fluids and the best way to stop the ants getting in the house. I could hear her in the kitchen droning on to Mary and hear Mary's grunts in reply. My mother didn't have opinions on cleaning fluids, she never cleaned, she had no compulsion to try and control her environment. Bridget, though, rarely sat down, and I never quite knew where to put myself if Paul and I were there, back from one of our hot unsatisfactory trips, and if he'd gone upstairs to his room telling me he'd see me later, that he had 'things to do'. Bridget would be walking about the house, moving newspapers and arranging shoes in the hallway. I seemed always to be in the way, hovering nearby, purposeless. Bridget would smile at me anxiously and ask if I thought I needed a lie-down. 'Oh no,' I'd say, 'I've just had one actually,' and she would stare at me for a while with her watery apologetic eyes and then say something strange and disjointed such as, 'Of course, I never had a daughter,' and I would blink back at her bewildered, and then Bridget would wring her hands and say, 'I must go and talk to Mary about the flowers in the hall,' and stride off towards the kitchen. I would wander out to sit in the garden on one of the deckchairs, and close my eyes and try to look at ease.

There was always another sudden burst of activity before Robert came home at six o'clock, as though Bridget, had spent her day idly painting her toenails a deep cerise and talking on the phone, as though she thought she were about to be caught out. It was very odd, I thought. She'd say, 'Look at the time,' and suddenly rush about the house, rearranging the perfect cushions, or, 'Oh goodness, Robert will be back in a minute. Whatever will he think of me?' and she'd cast her eye around for some terrible indication of her laziness, and light upon a dropped petal on the hall table and snap it up. I dreaded Robert coming home. For all that it was disorientating and boring during the day, in the evenings the air palpably thickened and tensed with ripples of dissatisfaction.

On the occasions when Bridget did speak directly to me there was a sense of attempted purpose about the conversation, one which I could never quite fathom, and I knew my answers to be insubstantial, as though I were feeling my way through a dark room but wanting to be polite, trying not to bump into the furniture or grab on to a stranger's arm.

One afternoon Bridget came sidling into the study, where I was lying on the bed staring up at the ceiling. It was the afternoon in fact of the trip to the Municipal Cooling Towers – no wonder I had taken to my bed. We had driven down the long straight road, the sun in our eyes, Paul talking on and on about cooling towers, and my wanting to ask him whether there wasn't somewhere spacious and peaceful we could go, somewhere green and not so dusty, not so made-up. Bridget sat on the edge of the bed, cramming her hands between her bony knees.

'Are there more of you at home, Laura?' she said. The shutters were half closed and she sat in strips of light. I sat up and pulled my knees up against my chest and arched my neck, to try and alleviate the pain in my head.

'Sorry?'

'I didn't mean to disturb,' she said, looking about the room. 'I was just wondering whether there are more of you at home. Whether you have any brothers or sisters?'

'No, Bridget, no, there's just me.'

'But you're not there now, are you?'

'No, no, I'm here now.'

'Your parents must be missing you very much then? If they've no one else?'

'Yes, I suppose they are.'

'Do they have a telephone?'

'Do they—? Yes, in the hall. It's in their hall.'

'It is possible to book overseas telephone calls, you know, or else perhaps we could arrange to send them a telegram?'

'That's very kind of you, yes, we could do that.'

'I was wondering whether perhaps I should contact them? I wonder what they must think of us, bringing you all the way over here.' She looked at me then, her eyes narrowing slightly.

'I'm sure they think you are a very generous host,' I said slowly.

She was impatient with my answer but smiled at me and pulled a little at her dress, and folded her large hands in her lap.

'I didn't mean that, Laura. You see, it is a very difficult situation, isn't it? I mean, they, I know they met Paul — did they meet Paul?'

'Of course. They loved Paul, they adored him actually. To tell you the truth, Bridget, I think if they'd had a son, they'd have liked one just like Paul.'

I was smiling at her, hoping this was the correct answer, the one she was looking for. She smiled back at me but frowned a little. Her skin was dry, and so was her hair, I could see little pops of blood blisters on her face, I imagined that she tried to clean them off every night.

'They approved then? Of the two of you getting married?'

'Of course, they were thrilled,' I told her confidently. 'Excuse me, Bridget, I'm sorry, but I'm very tired. It was very hot in town and Paul wanted us to see the towers and the Old Market building. It was very crowded too and I could feel the dust in the back of my throat all the time.'

'Yes, I do see,' she said, looking down at me. 'Yes, that must have been difficult for you.'

*

Robert Lovell was, unsurprisingly, less circumspect in his dealings with me, but again he seemed always to be intimating at something that I didn't fully comprehend or understand, all conversations were an expression of his power, and I, foolish girl in my inappropriate clothes, didn't see why he felt the need to let me know things about him, about his wife and son.

He came back from work one morning, unexpectedly, swinging his briefcase in front of him as he crossed the lawn towards me. I was lying on the grass, wearing one of Bridget's straw hats, reading one of the six books in the house, *The Woman's Own Practical Guide to Housekeeping*. I had read the chapter on Pickling and Preserving three times already. I hadn't heard the car, or him, and was surprised to hear his voice.

'Hello there,' he said. I rolled over and saw his spotless black shoes beside me, glistening in the sun.

The hat had a wide brim, and even when I looked up, it was difficult to see his face.

'I left some papers behind, thought I'd come and get them. What are you reading?' and he bent down and took the book out of my hands. Turning it over he read the title and then looked at the page. '"In September, when there is an abundance of autumn fruits we find it an ideal time to consider ways of preserving apples." Is Bridget in?'

'She's gone to the shops with Paul.'

'Poor Paul, bag man for the morning then. How long have you been here on your own?'

I sat up, hastily pulling my dress down over my knees. I wondered whether I should stand up, but Robert sat down beside me instead. He hitched his trousers up when he sat, showing his ankle socks and legs. Then he took off his suit jacket and put it down carefully on the grass beside us, he was wearing flashy green cufflinks.

'You shouldn't ought to have to wear a suit like that for work here, should you? I mean, it must be so hot. There should be a different uniform,' I said, looking at his jacket next to me. I was nervous, gabbling, I didn't want to have an intimate moment with my new father-in-law. He ran his hand across his head and laughed, insincerely.

'I've been wanting to talk to you, Laura,' he said eventually. 'About Paul.' He glanced over at me. 'Has he any plans?'

'How do you mean?'

Robert coughed, and then smiled to himself. 'For work. Has he thought about what he wants to do? There's an opening at the firm, only a junior clerk's position, but it is a decent enough starting wage.'

I looked at him, and he stared back at me, raising his eyebrows slightly and trying to smile, trying very hard to be polite. It wasn't coming easy to him; for all that he was sitting down on the grass and pretending to be friendly, I still found him laced with menace. I fancied that I could see unloving ladies in dark dresses and sporting Christian gentlemen, with sharp moustaches and shiny-topped canes, move through him and throw shadows across his class-bound soul. I suspected that this conversation had been arranged by him and Bridget, that it was a set-up, that I was being set up.

'We haven't really talked about it, Mr Lovell. I don't know how long we're going to be here, you see. We might be going back to London soon, Paul might not think it worth getting a job here.'

I could feel his eyes on me again; confident on being alone, I had undone a couple of buttons on the front of my dress and I wondered whether he could see my breasts, I wanted to do them up again but without drawing his attention to them. I pulled my knees up instead and tried to pull the dress down so that if he moved he wouldn't be able to see my knickers.

'I'll be honest with you, Laura,' he said, stretching his powerful short legs out in front of him and leaning his head back into the sun. 'I'm not entirely clear why you married Paul, neither is Bridget. She wouldn't come out and say it of course, she's too kind for that. Isn't she? Don't you think Bridget kind?'

'Oh yes, Mr Lovell, very kind.'

'And, well, kind people can sometimes be taken advantage of, can't they?'

'I suppose so, yes.'

Robert sat up again then, and smoothed down his trouser legs. 'Well? You and Paul?'

'Why we married, you mean? We fell in love, Mr Lovell.'

He laughed then, and leant towards me and pushed the rim of Bridget's hat back off my face and cupped his strong hand around my chin. His touch was gentle, but it was deliberate and threatening. He leant in close and I could smell his aftershave – for one chilling moment I thought he meant to kiss me.

'I'm not a fool, Laura,' he said, looking at me straight with his black eyes. And then just as quickly as he'd grabbed my face he got up and brushed the grass of his trouser legs and said in a cheerful loud voice, 'I'll pick up those papers and be off then. Have a good day. When I'm back I'll be quizzing you on the best way of making crab apple jelly.'

He picked up his briefcase, I could still feel the shock of his fingers on my chin. 'Oh, and do call me Bob, I feel like a headmaster when you call me Mr Lovell.'

And then he strode away back up to the house. I lay down again and closed my eyes; I didn't open them until I heard his car starting and was confident that he had driven away.

When Paul came back from the shops he ran across the garden towards me; he was carrying a brown paper parcel under his arm.

'How are you?' he said, flopping down beside me, smiling. 'We bought you a present.'

My first. I tore at the paper and pulled out a scarlet bathing costume and held it up.

'Your father was here, Paul, he was rather strange and horrid. He wanted me to talk to you about an "opening" at his firm.'

'Good God, poor Laura.' Paul smiled at me. 'I like you in that hat. We should go up to the club and have a swim. I want to see you in that bathing costume.'

He circled my ankle with his hand, allowing his fingers to tickle up my calf. I squirmed on the grass, hot and sticky, I could feel the damp patches under my arms, beads of sweat trickling down my neck, blinded by the hot sun on the yellow grass and by all that was not being said.

*

The evenings were excruciating. I was eager to please, but untutored in sunshine and happy families, and I assumed they were a happy family because they willingly spent so much time together, sitting on the chairs each evening, talking and playing, listening to the radio. I found it exhausting, all that smiling, while my body was prickly with sunburn and discomfort. They were always doing something too, with their hands, and I had nothing, so I just sat, trying to look at ease, willing the hours away.

'So,' Robert said one night, 'I understand Paul took you over to the Great Synagogue on Wolmarans Street this afternoon?'

'Yes. We've seen a lot of buildings.'

'How fascinating. Paul's keen to keep in with the radical Jews, you know. Paul, how about you take your lady wife out to Jeppestown tomorrow, eh?'

'Oh, Robert,' Bridget flustered, 'of course he won't take her to such a place. What an idea. I thought we might go to Stuttafords on Friday, Laura? If you'd like to.'

'Thank you, that'd be lovely.'

Paul and Robert were playing draughts, and they were very serious about it, they were ferociously, intensely competitive. That evening, sat either side of a little table which was brought out for the matches, they were playing a particularly close game. Bridget sat in the corner opposite me, near the radio, and sewing some monstrous dress, she caught my eye and smiled.

'The draughts was all good clean fun until Paul started looking like he might beat Robert. Then things got serious.'

'I'm still ahead,' Robert said, without looking up. 'I'm still quite a few games ahead.'

Paul laughed. 'He actually keeps a running score, Laura, from every time we've played over the last, what is it, Dad, ten, twelve years? Can you believe that?'

'He writes it down in a little black book he keeps in his desk,' Bridget chimed in and she and Paul looked at one another and laughed. Robert, smiling during their teasing, was bent over the board, his tongue stuck between his teeth. He was considering his next move very carefully.

'Well then,' I said, trying to join in the fun, 'I don't think I'll learn to play, it all sounds rather frightening.'

'Paul didn't tell you about this competition then?' Bridget held her sewing up to the light and peered at it; she had pins in the corner of her mouth.

'No.'

'Oh.' She sounded disappointed. 'Perhaps he thought it might scare you off us?'

Robert let out a low groan. Paul had made some devastating move and was gleefully collecting Robert's black counters.

'You're a little rusty, old man.'

'We'll see, we'll see.' He leant back in his chair, smiling at Paul. 'Well, Laura, what sort of thing did he tell you then?'

'Oh goodness,' I said, smiling stiffly at him. 'Just the usual, I suppose.' I couldn't very well have said, nothing, he told me absolutely nothing about you whatsoever.

'He must have told you something.' Robert was looking at Paul, who was grinning as he elaborately piled up the counters one by one on the side of the table. 'Though I don't suppose it is the usual way to seduce a girl, by talking about your parents.'

'Seduce!' Bridget was embarrassed and she shot a quick look at me, shaking her head slightly. 'Really, Robert.'

'Look at that, Dad, quite a pile I've got here.' Paul looked very pleased with himself, excited even; he picked up the pile of counters and let them drop slowly out of his fingers into a neat column.

'Yes, I can count thank you, Paul. No, I think seductions are best done by giving a very good account of yourself. You might even risk bending the truth a little. Isn't that the way these things usually work, Paul?'

'Hmm. What things?'

Then Bridget leant over and turned the wireless up so the sound became quite distorted and the room was filled with big-band music and a man's voice, made indistinct and hysterical by the volume, telling us our evening's entertainment 'has been brought to us courtesy of SABC English Radio'.

'Turn that bloody thing down, woman. We're trying to play.'

'Well, play then,' she said crossly, biting through the thread with a quick snap of her many teeth.

*

Was it that night that I saw it for the first time? Sitting on the scratchy chair, my head throbbing and my arms burnt and blistered from the sun. I think it might have been. The loud radio, Robert's careful questions and Bridget's nervousness; it hit me like a blast of cold air: Bridget and Robert were frightened of Paul. The 'unsaid' in that house was all to do with Paul, and me of course in some small way, so they circled us, Robert more than Bridget, trying to find things out. There was history, complicated family history, and I was not fit to navigate it with any ease or success. I was sickly, dizzy and homesick, made insecure by Paul's distance, by how shadowy he had become — I needed to know about his 'interests', what he did in his bedroom each day — and by Robert and Bridget, by the way the ground beneath my feet seemed always to be spinning. It was as if the Lovells were waiting for something, biding their time, trying to be hospitable, waiting for all things to be made clear, but they were not patient people, they could not wait for long, and wasn't I there, sitting awkwardly on their chairs, smiling gauchely and fiddling with my clothes? They had no reason to be frightened of me.

Six

Bridget and I walked down Commissioner Street, past the Corner House and towards Stuttafords. Our progress was slow as the pavements were busy with people, women with bags and small children getting under their feet, black people doing menial work or leaning against the shopfronts looking at us, and the roads full of cars barely moving, honking their horns, stuck in an endless traffic jam. 'They're going to have to sort these roads out,' she said to me, shaking her head a little. 'It's become ridiculous.'

It was hot. I wanted to be on my own, I didn't want to be out with Bridget and her anxiety, the way she looked at everything and everyone twice, anticipating rejection. The trip seemed to be very arduous for her. When she thought I wasn't looking she would pull a handkerchief out from her sleeve and wipe it across her brow, and rest her face in it for a second, so she looked as though she were crying. I was tired with how effortful Bridget found me. I imagined that she woke up every morning, stretched and smiled to herself that all was in order in her universe, the house remarkably clean, Paul home and Robert happy, until the terrible memory of Laura Trelling overcame her, Laura Trelling in the study, wandering about the house, not answering questions properly. Then I thought she probably said a prayer to herself, like Mrs Frobisher had done before she ate her breakfast, and asked the Lord to send her the strength to deal with this particular burden. Bridget has brought an extensive list with her, she had shown it to me when we'd been sitting side by side in the tram car, careering down towards 'town'. There were a great deal of crossings-out and question marks on the list, and then quite a few arrows pointing over to a box which had 'Ask Laura' written in it. I traced the arrows back to the list, they started next to such entries as 'Table napkins?' and 'Dinner service?' and 'Household essentials'.

'Where did you live before here, Mrs Lovell?' I asked her as we made our slow progress towards Stuttafords.

'Manchester. Robert and I are both from Manchester. Do you know it?' and she looked suddenly hopeful, stopping in the middle of the pavement and peering at me. The buildings seemed so large and tall above us, so much glass and iron, it felt claustrophobic and dark down below.

'No, I don't. Do you like it here?'

A woman pushed past me, knocking me slightly, and then turned to apologise.

'Do I like it?' Bridget said frowning. 'Well, yes I suppose I do. We went to Cape Town once, and it was nicer there, we'd be there if it wasn't for Robert's work. It was − well − fresher, I suppose. Not that I'm not grateful, oh no, Robert has worked very hard to provide for us all. We both come from quite humble beginnings, Laura, not that you could tell that now of course.'

'But, I mean, do you think you're going to live here for ever, Mrs Lovell? Could you bear to? I'm sure I couldn't.'

Bridget got her handkerchief out again and patted her cheeks.

'Come on, Laura, we must get going. What are we doing hanging about talking on the pavements?'

Stuttafords was large and fancied itself as very grand. There were vast wooden fans hanging from the ceilings, and glass cases, and wooden tables with things laid out on them. Bridget breathed in when she entered, and her anxiety all but trebled. She played nervously with her list, looking up every so often and smiling at people walking past. I felt sticky and hungry; I wondered whether Bridget had written 'Have lunch' on her list.

'Now then,' she said, running her hand across a bolt of linen laid out on the cutting table in the haberdashery department. 'We could make bed sheets, napkins and pillowslips out of this, we wouldn't need too much yardage because if we were efficient we could use every last scrap, couldn't we?'

Bridget was talking loudly, aware that she was being listened to by the shop assistant. She was trying to impress with her brisk talk and no-nonsense manner, showing off her older, superior womanly ways. She and the assistant smiled at one another oozing complacency and skill and the assistant, with her plum-coloured hair and horn-rimmed spectacles, moved closer towards us, poised for the kill.

'Are we setting up home then?' she said smoothly, reaching for the tape measure hung around her neck.

'We certainly are!' Bridget said brightly to the assistant. 'They're going to be finding themselves a little bungalow very soon, aren't you, Laura? Just as soon as my boy finds the job which best suits his talents.'

'We are?' It came out quickly, unstoppable, with a gasp of laughter.

Bridget and the assistant looked over at me, Bridget's eyes wide; she took two quick steps towards me and grabbed my elbow, steering me towards the wall, away from the assistant.

'Robert talked to you, about finding Paul work,' she said accusingly, 'I know he did.'

She was angry, still holding on to my elbow, shaking it a little.

'We thought marrying you, for whatever reason that happened,' she said quickly, in hushed tones, 'was a sign of him *changing*, of him growing up. That's what we hoped, Laura, that's what we believed.'

Bridget was wearing an amber necklace; unusually for her it was large and showy, the beads a deep, soupy orange, it jumped a little against her neck as she spoke. A dry wispy hair had fallen from her bun, down against her neck and over the necklace.

'Bridget,' I said quietly, 'Bridget, I don't know about any of this. I don't know what we're going to do. We haven't talked about it.'

'You haven't talked about it?' she echoed, shooting out quick side-to-side glances across the shop. 'You love him though, don't you? That's what you told Robert.'

'Yes, yes I do. I don't understand this, Bridget, I don't understand what you're talking about,' and I pulled my elbow away from her. Her hand stayed in mid-air where it had been until, finally, it fell limply by her side. She coughed, scooped up the errant strand of hair and tucked it back into her bun. She tried to smile at me; her front teeth were quite discoloured this close up.

'No, no, of course you don't. Perhaps Paul hasn't been quite as completely honest as he might have been. That's what Robert thinks.'

'About what?' I said it, though I didn't want to. I didn't want Bridget telling me things about Paul, it felt wrong. She looked me up and down, and gave me another of her toothy smiles, her eyes frightened.

'Oh, I don't know. About himself, about his prospects, dear. That he isn't — wasn't — really in a position to marry.'

'He saved me,' I said bravely.

'He saved you? Oh my dear girl, oh dear.'

'We are married, Bridget, properly married. You shouldn't have put me in the downstairs room. It was wrong, I think it was just Robert trying to have a go at Paul, that's what I think. He never takes him seriously, does he? Mr Lovell won't even take our marriage seriously, the way he always pretends to get my name wrong.' Bridget looked panicky and hot, she couldn't look me in the eye. 'You went along with it because you didn't know any other way, perhaps you didn't really think we were married? I want to be a proper wife to Paul, I want to help him with his interests.'

'With his—? Oh Laura.' She looked at me then, with compassion and confusion. 'Let's not talk about it any more, dear, let's go and look at dressmaking materials, shall we? You need some more things, dear, you really can't keep going with what you have,' and in an attempt to sweep all that had happened aside, she linked her arm through mine. It felt awkward and strange, but I didn't pull away, instead I followed her through and pretended to summon an enthusiasm for the 'pretty pale green' and the 'candy-stripe blue'.

Back at the house, I went to find Paul. He wasn't in his bedroom, or the garden or anywhere I could see. Mary wasn't in the house either but I needed to avoid Bridget so I told her I was going to lie down. I closed the shutters on the windows and lay down in the darkness. I wanted to think things through but I couldn't, I was too hot and murky, still feeling the history of Bridget's sudden grip on my elbow.

I must have dozed off because the sound of Bridget's and Paul's voices came to me as though they were in my dream. They must have been outside the window, on the stoep, they were whispering, and I couldn't hear every word, but snatches came sailing in through the shuttered windows and into my sleeping head.

'I've just checked on her. She's asleep. Where were you today? Have the two of you had a row?' That was Bridget, she was being insistent. 'Poor child she's miles away from home. I know she's—' Her voice dipped.

'She's fine,' Paul said crossly. I could imagine him scowling at his mother.

'Put that paper down, young man, I'm talking to you. We can't ignore all this much longer, I've given her plenty of opportunity to tell me, but she hasn't. We need to find her a doctor and get things sorted out. It's irresponsible of you to carry on like this. How pregnant is she? Do you know?'

I could hear the scraping of chairs, perhaps Paul was standing up or his mother was dragging a chair over to sit with him.

'What?' He was laughing. 'She's not pregnant, Mum.'

'But, Paul, I just assumed, we both did — because of you getting married so quickly, and her having these headaches and lying down all the time.'

'Well, you assumed wrong.' He sounded amused.

Then why on earth did you marry her? You had no business doing that, not the way things are.'

Then I could only hear the hushed tones of whispering, and couldn't catch what either of them said. Wide awake now I crept over towards the window, pressing my ear against the shutters, straining to listen. Overhearing them had given me an odd, hollow feeling inside, like the barrel of a drum, skin stretched tight across the top, taut with anticipation.

'But this puts things in a totally different light,' Bridget was saying, sounding cross. 'Oh Paul!' and I imagined her scuffing the top of his head in irritation, and I wanted very much for him to stand up and tell her he was a grown man now and could she and Dad please stop treating him as though he were just some useless, wayward boy. But he didn't, of course.

'What were you thinking?'

I heard Paul give a low, painful moan, and then Bridget hushing him.

'Have you told her all about, well, *you*? Whatever will your father say?'

'I don't care what he says. You just jumped to the wrong conclusion. That's not my fault, is it? It doesn't change anything.'

'But it does, Paul, it changes everything. You've got some questions to answer now. Oh Paul, whatever have you done?' and then I couldn't catch what was being said as they were whispering again, but I knew that I had to get out there, sharpish.

They both reddened when I emerged, and I made a great play of rubbing my eyes and yawning as I walked over towards Paul, my bare feet slapping quietly against the stone floor.

'Have I slept long?'

'Not really, darling.' His voice was surprisingly tender.

'I'll fetch you some lemonade.' Bridget jumped up too quickly, and she gave me a steely look. She was trying to work out how much I might have heard, her face was pale and blank. She didn't move off to get the lemonade though, she stood there, stolid and stubborn, glaring at me.

'Thank you, Bridget,' I said. 'Lemonade would be nice.'

Everything seemed still and shining, Bridget, Paul in his chair smiling at me, the way the sun bounced off the ground. Eventually Bridget left, looking at us both over her shoulder.

'Right,' I said, slipping into Bridget's vacated chair and smiling back at Paul, 'I think it's time we shared a bedroom, don't you? It was your father, playing a trick on us. I'm sure it was. I told your mother that's what I thought. That he doesn't want to take us seriously. He's always goading you, getting at you.'

'I don't think it's quite that bad,' he said, with that suspicious look again. 'You're exaggerating, Laura, but,' and then he smiled at me, 'I do like this new assertive you. So yes, we'll do as you say,' and he leant back with hands behind his head and grinned at me.

Nobody said anything when I followed Paul up the stairs that night. Robert was on the tiny landing and a smirk played around his mouth as we edged past him, but he kept quiet.

It was a terrible squeeze though, Paul and I in his childhood bed, and the floor covered with his maps and old school cricket bats, his sweaty socks rolled up in the corners of the room. And me, in that bed in my nightgown, squeezed against the cold white wall, still waiting for Paul to touch me properly, in the way I thought he should, in the way I sensed could happen, as though I were liquid in a bowl, splashing against the sides, waiting for him to take me, to make sense of this endless, dizzying longing. But he just lay beside me, allowing his legs to hang out of the bed, occasionally throwing an arm across my waist where it lay, heavy and certain, making the backs of my knees tingle and I had to screw my eyes up very tight. If he fell asleep first I would allow myself to run my fingers through his hair, or to touch his chest, sometimes slipping a hand inside his pyjama top, feeling his soft and surprisingly hairless chest and stomach, soft, yielding. Sometimes Paul would frown or slap my hand away, though he were asleep, or sometimes he would smile and laugh. I would lay my head on his stomach, so I could hear his beating heart late at night.

Gay's Diary

Tuesday, September 1946, Wales

Stan and Wilfred had to carry me up the stairs to my room last night. They said I passed out in the minibus on the way back from the performance at the depot. I can't remember much about it. I remember the party in the officers' mess and how we all got high. Wilfred said I vomited in the bus, all over his best silk shirt. He said if he didn't love me so much he'd hate me. I told him I'd wash it for him. How the bus lurched, this way and that, and how it was dark outside, and I wanted to be rattled and to lie on the wooden floor and roll and roll against the seats. Wilfred said he knew people like me, he wanted me to meet them. 'They're people who live a vital life, people who want to make a difference,' he said.

Wilfred keeps talking to me, on and on, whether we're stoned or sober. He sits next to me on the bus to the depots or the transit camps, his arm across the back of the seat. I lean my face against the windows, I can't keep up. I don't follow him, I say to him, 'Stop, Wilfred, I don't know what you're saying,' and he laughs and kisses me on the neck.

October 1946, Wales

Wilfred can't wait for his demob. He says he's going to go in his suit and find a flat in Soho. He says he thinks he'll find work at the BBC because they're going to start transmission again soon, now the war's officially over. We've taken to drinking gin straight from the bottle to keep us warm. Stan gets it from somewhere, we don't know where. Wilfred says the black market in the Black Mountains must be blacker than black and he thinks it's paraffin we're drinking, but he only says this to tease Stan, he doesn't care what it is so long as it keeps us warm. 'What about you, Gay,' Wilfred says, 'what are you going to do?'

I don't know what to do. I need to work, I need to keep doing this. I won't let it all stop in some blasted rainy Welsh depot, me and the troupe and four engineers sitting in their mess looking tired and unshaven, and asking us in the interval if the play is over yet, because they'd quite like to get drinking now.

Have got that tight feeling inside again. Tried breathing more slowly and have been lying in bed most of the day. Hate the feeling that there is no air in me. Can't quite grab as much as I need. Wilfred came round with some drink, said he had to dodge my landlady. He said did I know my face and mouth were blue? Was I cold? He'd brought me an extra blanket too. He said he'd climb in with me if I liked, try to keep me warm. He says, 'Let's go to Oxford next week. You know that man I mentioned? He's well connected, Gay, he'll be able to get you work out in South Africa if you go. He knows all the theatre people, all the radio people. You'll just have to do one thing for him in return, it sounds like a good deal to me.'

I'll go. Wilfred's right, there's nothing for me here. I want to get out of the rain and the cold. I'll go with Mother, and follow up those contacts. I can't sleep well. My head is turning all the time, the sheets are damp and scratchy. I think I might have lice.

Seven

Paul started attending political meetings in the evenings; a car would arrive at the bottom of the drive after dinner, and he'd trot off down to it, waving to me.

'Left us again, has he?' Robert would say, sauntering across the room to sit next to me, pressing his thigh up against mine. 'What do they talk about, do you think? Him and the Kaffirs?'

'He's meeting with socialists not niggers.'

Robert liked this very much. 'Oh, do you think so? One and the same in this country, darling.'

'Can't I come with you?' I said to Paul. 'It's awful here without you. I want to know what you're doing, share it with you.'

But he wouldn't let me. He said he was going to places that wouldn't be safe, they were political meetings and the less I knew about them the better.

'But, Paul, they're circling me all the time, asking questions, wanting to know things. I don't know what to say to them. They won't talk to you so they take it out on me, you don't know what it's like.'

'Whatever are you talking about, Lala?' Paul said frowning, as closed to me as the shutters in the study, heavy, solid, only allowing the tiniest rays of light to sidle through and fall at odd angles. 'Don't start on at me, Laura. I couldn't bear it if you did, not you as well as them,' and he looked suddenly tearful. 'Nobody understands.'

'Oh no, darling,' I told him, declaring my loyalties, 'I'm not, I'm not. It's just your father is getting very grumpy about it, about everything. He doesn't like me one bit.'

'Bugger him, what does he know?'

'Did you see these people before me?'

'Before England? Yes, of course. Don't worry about it, Lala, It's got nothing to do with you or with us.'

He meant it kindly, but Paul had become permanently sulky and difficult, removed, as though fading in the sunshine like one of his newspapers, viewing me with such suspicion whenever I asked him questions. I was alarmed by the change in him; I tried every way I could think of to bind him in with me, to wind myself around him. I did try to talk to him too. I said, 'It must be strange for you, being here with your parents and me,' and then left a space unfilled, for him, but he never answered as I thought he should. Paul would look at me with his head on one side and say, 'Lala, what a funny thing to say,' like that.

I asked him over and over to explain the politics which were so important to him, until finally one afternoon he must have tired of my nagging, and he took me upstairs and pulled a box out from under our bed, and handed me a fistful of pamphlets. They were badly printed on yellow paper and had such titles as 'Africans Claims in South Africa' and 'Workers Solidarity Across the Coloured Line' and 'What does the Atlantic Charter mean?'. I tried reading one of them: redistribution of land, collective bargaining, universal suffrage, pan-African meetings, the Youth African National

Congress. It could have been double Dutch, or indeed Afrikaans to me, I had no idea what any of this meant. Paul squatted on the floor, rocking back on his heels.

'It's complicated, Lala. I'm not sure you'd really understand,' he said, eyeing me carefully,

'Tell me, Paul. I want to do this with you. I'm on your side.'

He sighed.

'All right, Lala. What do you know of the history of Southern Africa?'

'That it was a colony,' I said, remembering with relief the book from the Grange.

'Good girl. That's right. South Africa was firstly a Dutch colony and then an English one. Did you learn about the Boer Wars at school?'

'No, we didn't do wars really,' I told him, 'we did domestic science and a little bit about the Chartists.'

He frowned. 'The Chartists? Right, well, I'll find you some books then. Let's just do the here and now, shall we, otherwise we'll be here all day. There are different groups in South Africa. Roughly, the black native African,' he counted them off on his fingers, 'next, the Afrikaner — we might call them the Nationalists — then, well, various others, I suppose, the Malay Indians in the Cape and other Aziatic Indians in Natal, and then the white European population. Smuts is in control of the government, he mostly represents the white Europeans, and in opposition is Malan, and his Nationalists, he represents the Afrikaner interests.'

I nodded. 'Who represents the Kaffir interests?'

'I don't like the term Kaffir, Laura. It's an insulting word, please stop using it. Nobody — well, not at government level. The whites in this country have always been in control, since they arrived here, but now the blacks are trying to organise themselves in resistance to that authority. The blacks have no vote in this country, Laura, they have no or very little opportunity to own property, and they must each have a pass if they wish to travel freely around their own cities. A pass to show where they work, and to allow access. Now a new group called the ANC Youth League are forming, they are more interested in collective positive action, there are many radical young men, who want to crush the oppressive structures which govern this country. And you know why it is important that action is taken soon? Because there will be an election in 1948, and if Malan wins, if the Nationalists win, then they will introduce laws which they are writing now, oppressive laws, against freedom, against universal sufferage. They are creating a social blueprint for this country, which is contrary to everything we stand for, everything I stand for.'

'Golly.' It had been a long speech, and I'd been listening hard, or trying to. 'So what are you doing about it?'

'What am I doing about it?' He looked uneasy for a moment, and then stood up. He looked down at me, his hands folded behind his back. 'Well, working against those forces, trying to create a better society, more freedom, equality, to free the black African from his chains of oppression, to free the workers, to incite a revolution.'

'You're a hero?' It was an innocent question, but I meant it sincerely. Looking up at him, so powerful, so masculine. His intent was to free people from oppression, to work on the side of goodness. Even I with my sketchy understanding of the larger world could see that. 'The fight against fascism is the fight for socialism,' I said.

'Aha, of course, you did your bit on our wedding night, didn't you?' and he started to laugh and knelt down, grabbing at my ankle.

'Thank you, madam, for your services to socialism,' and he pulled me down onto the floor, his grinning face close to mine. And I dropped the pamphlet from my fingers and laced my hands behind his neck, trying to draw him closer to me on the floor, opening my legs, wanting to feel his skin slacken against mine. I grasped at his body, I wouldn't let it go, eyes shut, mouth open, hungry for Paul, feeling the weight of his legs on top of mine, brave and eager, mindless, certain.

'Don't ask me any questions, Lala, and don't believe anything my parents tell you,' he said into my neck. 'I do want to be a hero, yes, darling, I do.'

On the evenings when he came back from his meetings, long after I'd gone to sleep, he would climb into the bed and then he would curl his body around mine and hold me in his arms. He smelt different those nights — of sweat, and bad wine and petrol.

*

Robert was stirred by my lack of concern, by my lack of complaint.

'Why don't you stop him going?' he asked me one Wednesday night. We were alone, sitting outside in the dark, because he'd said it was too hot to sit inside. Bridget had dashed round to a friend who was ill, taking small pots of cold chicken soup with her. I was nervous of being on my own with Robert and had volunteered to accompany Bridget, but she'd said she thought her friend might be contagious and it was better if I didn't risk it. She patted my arm in the hall. 'Don't worry, dear. Bob's bark is worse than his bite.'

'Why should I stop him?' I said quickly, knowing I sounded childish. 'It's very important to him, what he is doing is very important.'

153

Robert had brought a paraffin lamp outside, and it cast a strange bluish light over his face. Robert had the ability to sit very still, unnervingly still, for such a powerful, compact man.

'I blame the university,' he said quietly, 'should have sent him off to work straight away, but Bridget insisted he go to Wits. It was going to be improving for him apparently. I only let him explore this interest because I'm so grateful he *has* an interest.'

I shrugged. 'I don't understand what you mean.' I was being defiant now. 'I don't know why you talk about him in this way, to be honest, Mr Lovell. I don't think I see him as you do.'

'Want a cigarette?' Robert produced a packet. 'I only do this when Bridge is out. She disapproves.'

I hadn't had one since that night at Mrs Granger's, but I took one from him and when I leant forward to light it from his match, my cheek brushed against his hand. I inhaled and coughed a little. Robert, surprisingly, didn't laugh at me.

'All right? Been a while, has it?'

We sat in silence, smoking. Mrs Granger was right, it was comforting.

'Do you like it here, Laura? How long has it been now, three weeks?' He pursed his lips and blew out a train of beautiful blue smoke rings.

'That's clever.'

Holes of wispy smoke trailed across the top of the paraffin lamp and then slowly dissolved.

'Picked it up in the factories when I was a boy.' He was speaking softly, and I had trouble catching what he said. 'What does your father do, Laura?'

'He looks after the land.'

Robert snorted. 'His or someone else's?'

'His.'

'I thought as much. You haven't answered my question: do you like it here?'

'You and Mrs Lovell have been very kind.'

'I take it that's a no then. We were surprised when we received Paul's telegram. About you.'

'Yes, you must have been.'

'Very surprised. We assumed you must be pregnant.'

'Yes, Paul told me. Are you expecting an apology?'

He laughed, a deep shuddering sort of laugh.

'Not from you, darling, no, but now I understand you're not, it does change things rather, you can appreciate that.'

'Why does it?'

Robert was sitting with his legs wide apart, as though inviting inspection. It disturbed me, his legs stretched out towards mine, splayed apart with powerful insolence. I was even more disturbed by the way my eyes kept being drawn, through the shadows, towards his crotch, I don't know why, I had to concentrate very hard on looking away, but I thought he knew every time I looked. I thought perhaps he was smiling to himself about this, slowly, confidently, licking his lips. I had trouble focusing on our conversation, my body was hurting from sunburn, I felt shivery and cold like you do when your body is too hot. The cigarette was making me light-headed, I could feel all the hairs on my arms. I tried to listen to Robert's dark, quiet voice without looking over at him.

'Because it means you are not Paul's accident any more, you are on purpose. You can't both go on living in my house for ever, you know. Bridget thinks I should wait it out, she thinks that Paul will realise his responsibilities soon enough and start to behave in a more mature fashion. She says marrying you was the first responsible thing he's done, but I'm not so sure. He's alwasy been useless, even as a lad, a bloody grasshopper.'

'I don't understand.'

'Don't give me that,' and he leant towards me in the warm darkness, and I wondered whether he was going to touch me, I wondered whether I wanted him to touch me. 'You're playing with the grownups now, darling. Stop saying you don't understand all the time. Can't you see? Paul's useless, totally useless. It pains me to say it about my own son, but there it is. You do see that?'

'No, not really, Mr Lovell. I love Paul and he loves me, and well—' I could feel the end of the cigarette burning towards my fingers; I wasn't sure whether to toss it on the ground or not. I flicked it instead, with surprising force, and it wheeled in the air above us until it put itself out and fell to the ground. I felt oddly triumphant at this unexpected dramatic success. 'And I don't think he's useless, I think he's a hero.'

Robert snorted again and sat back in his chair. I could just see him running his hand across his head, and again my eyes flicked across the space between his legs.

'What am I getting out of having you two here? Don't you ever wonder that, Laura? Why should I put up with you two as house guests? Do you think it's worth it for me, just to have your pretty face sitting at my breakfast table, lying out in my garden in your swimsuit?'

I didn't answer him.

'Don't you ask him the question a wife ought to, Laura? When are we going to have a house of our own, dear? A proper-sized bed? How long are you planning on staying with your parents for? When are you going to get a job?' He said all this, in a high, whining plaintive voice, needy and girlish, grasping. I found it offensive. 'I'm not going to provide for you two, Laura, you should know that. I don't look after the land, you know, I work. Proper work for a salary I deserve, a salary for me and Bridget to enjoy now our son is grown up and married.'

A car turned into the drive, and the light from the headlamps ran across us as it turned the corner.

'Cat's home,' Robert said, closing his legs and grinding his cigarette out underfoot.

*

Robert played it perfectly, of course, every time. That night when Paul came tiptoeing into our bedroom, dusty and dirty with dark rings under his eyes, I was waiting for him. I leapt out of the bed and jumped up, wrapping my legs around him and burrowing my face deep into his neck.

'Don't do it again,' I said, 'don't leave me again.'

'Hey,' he said, and set me down on the floor. 'What's the matter? Too hot to sleep?' But he sighed when he said it and plonked himself down on the bed to take off his boots.

'I don't think I can do this much longer, your father hates me.'

'Of course he doesn't.'

'He says we can't go on living in his house,' I blurted out, 'and he was horrible about you. He said you were useless.'

Paul took my hands and laid us both down on the bed. I looked at him, opening and closing my eyes, willing myself to see and remember the Paul I'd met in Sussex.

'Poor Lala,' Paul said softly, 'don't listen to him. He's just taking all this out on you. I'm sorry, I should have looked after you better.'

'That's what Charlotte Locks said to you, at the bonfire party. He's taking all what out on me?'

'Did she? You do remember the funniest things, Lala,' and he looked pleased about this. He ran his fingers across my face. 'It's late. Let's sleep, we'll talk it through in the morning. There's history, that's all, between me and Dad.'

'What kind of history? It's to do with the politics, isn't it?'

'Not now, Laura, in the morning.'

'Were you sent away to England?'

'Sent away?' He lay the flat of his palm against my cheek, pressing it slightly. Then he removed it and rolled over on his back and yawned, started undoing his shirt buttons. 'I suppose I sort of was.'

'Well, how am I a part of all this? Did you bring me back here as some sort of trophy? To annoy your father?'

I was watching his fingers undoing the buttons, sneaking a look at his flat, hairless stomach, waiting for the moment when the shirt would be undone and the flaps of the shirt would fall open.

'Lala, how can you think such a thing?' he said, without much feeling. 'Of course I didn't, of course not. I love you, darling,' sitting up and reaching under the pillow for his pyjamas, 'I love you, darling, I love you,' and he kissed me on the forehead, slowly and tenderly.

'We have to leave here, Paul, as soon as we can. How long is this holiday going to last?'

'I told you, we'll talk in the morning. I'm just going to change downstairs in the bathroom.'

'If you want to stay a month longer or so, why don't you get a job, Paul? Anything will do, just to get us out of here. We could rent an apartment. You could do anything, couldn't you, and you'd still have time for the politics, Paul? Paul?'

But he'd gone, back down the stairs taking his pyjamas with him, leaving me alone, curled up on our chaste single bed with all my unanswered questions spiralling through the air above my head like so many cigarette butts.

ʌ

And so it stayed. Paul going to his meetings more and more regularly and for longer amounts of time. My watching him walk down the drive, with a canvas bag slung over his shoulder, with neither a whimper nor a murmur. And then, when I could no longer see the tail lights of the car he had hopped into, I would return to the living room, where Robert and Bridget would glare at me with burning, manifest hostility.

I decided that they blamed me for being so obliging and submissive to Paul; they wanted me to create the fuss they couldn't bring themselves to make. I saw them as being sticky and compromised by their love for Paul. Bridget might have spent nights crying herself to sleep because her son, a boy so full of talent and natural intelligence, so like his father, had turned out to want something more than a bungalow in Richmond and a commute into the Central Business District each morning. Yet she remained optimistic about him, in love with him, wilfully so, like an abandoned pet who repeatedly returns to the empty family home, scratching on the back door in the hope that this time it will miraculously open. Robert prided himself on being more of a realist, but he, I could see, was stymied, stuck with Paul as a son, and for all his talk to me of his uselessness, he never once broached this with Paul. Robert circled him carefully, needling him sometimes but avoiding a full confrontation. On the nights Paul was home, Robert lit up a little, was the first to bring out the draughts or to suggest the two of them go out for a drink or swing by the Beresfords' house where he knew they were having a party or suggest that he and Paul might plan a fishing or camping trip soon.

But I thought they had no such compunction in their feelings towards me. I was sure that Robert saw me as a living reminder of Paul's 'waywardness', his 'impulsive uselessness'. If I hadn't existed then they might have tried to bury their better selves in the belief that his political dalliances were mere youthful folly, but I was there week in and week out, eating their food, sitting on their son's bed or prowling the garden perimeters. I knew their thoughts, and I knew them to be wrong. I thought them sinister and unknowing, incapable of knowledge or insight. What did they know? Nothing, nothing, nothing. They were parents, like my parents, only motivated by self-interest, cold, selfish, incapable of empathy, only wanting the best for themselves. Paul would prove them wrong, I knew he would, just as I had proved my parents wrong. Hadn't they thought me a drifting irritating creature, unattractive and unlovable – and hadn't I shown them that I wasn't?

Of course, my very presence continued to invite questions and suspicions, which Robert refused to be shamefaced about; when for instance they had friends round for drinks, Robert would wave towards me standing in the far corner of the sitting room, looking down at my feet.

'Have you met Louise?' he'd ask the room.

'I thought she was Laura,' someone would say, quickly and entertainingly, a show-off; a man in a blazer with shiny buttons, jangling his loose change in his pocket.

'Oh yes, of course, of course,' and Robert's eyes would gleam and flash at me. 'Such a surprising guest, don't you think?'

And I would look around the room, at the faces of all these strangers, who had been fashioned by this place; unsympathetic, venal and frightened. Dry, red and coarse faces, trying too hard. They were all convinced their maids were stealing from them or that the gardener meant to murder them late one night in their beds. They complained bitterly about their servants, but I could tell they had come to Johannesburg to start anew, to become masters in a new society. And what a place it was as I had seen it, with those hot blank streets in the city centre, the high buildings and wooden verandas, and the blinds pulled to the ground when it was hot so you walked through a suffocating canvas tunnel, the symmetrical suburban roads, the smell of the foreign and of fear. I stood against the wall, my fists clenched, still feeling the brush of Paul's lips against mine as we'd kissed goodbye. I would put up with it, with all the insults and unhappiness, with Robert's bullying, because I believed it would end eventually and we would leave all this behind, like a bad, inky memory and we would return to a place rich in history, where things were old and constant and where their frightened and victorious frontier mentality had no place. Just as soon as Paul had done what he needed to do.

Gay's Diary

I want to ask Wilfred and the Professor, do they think they'd be who they were without all this? I mean without these rooms, and Oxford, and the Professor's velvet throws over his chairs, and the piles of books and all that. I can't ask though, I can't get the words out in the right order. For all they spend the evening talking in red-wine voices about politics and the war and how the world has changed, they still look so comfortable and at ease.

The Professor is younger than I thought he would be, very pale and thin. He wore a dressing gown all evening, with nothing on underneath, I mean nothing AT ALL, I know, I SAW.

I've had fantasies all night, about being locked up in the Professor's rooms, like the princess in the tower. Drifting naked from room to room, hair falling down my back, pressing my face against the windows, showing my breasts, hearing the flip-flap of my naked feet on the Professor's thick rugs. Rolling about in front of his coal fire, laughing, pouring glass after glass of his champagne down my throat, twirling the edges of his dressing-gown cord between my toes. These rooms smell of men. Musty and closed-down, of cigar smoke and learning.

Wilfred is different here. He sat on the edge of his chair all night, prodding his finger in the air when he spoke and the Professor listened to him and nodded, tying and retying his dressing-gown cord, and laughing in a thin way, and Wilfred moved when I put my feet up on him, he frowned at me, as though I were irritating to him in some way. Well, he was irritating me!

I wouldn't be here with these two if I didn't think I was getting something out of it. They think they've caged me, that I don't know what they're talking about, but I don't care what they talk about. I just need the names and addresses of the people in South Africa, I need letters of recommendation, then I can get out of here.

It's so dark here, and cold and twisty, dirty.

This afternoon Wilfred went out to see somebody, it was raining and I didn't want to go with him. That left me and the Professor for a whole hour. He asks me question after question in his little lispy voice, I didn't answer most of them, I just shrug and play with my hair. He comes and sits next to me, and though I know he's a fruit, I can tell he wants to touch me. He's looking me up and down, licking his lips, and all I know is the rain outside and how green his rooms are, and how depressingly small everything is. He picks up my hand and holds it between his. 'I don't know where Wilfred found you, but I'm glad he did,' he says and he smiles at me. I let him hold my hand, I tell him, 'You know people in South Africa, don't you? People in the business, that's why I'm here, Professor, Wilfred told me you could help me out.'

'Oh yes, Gay,' he says, 'I can help you out. There's somebody I want you to meet, somebody is coming for tea tomorrow, and after that we can get you sorted out. How does that sound, dear?'

I tell him that sounds perfect, and I give his hand a little squeeze and he coughs and asks if he can touch my legs. Just like that, straight out with it, with a little, sorry smile. So I says he can do as he likes, I don't much care, it's only my body, my legs. And we sit like that for a while, him leaning down and running his fingers up and down my calves and sighing, like he might cry, and me staring out the window and racing the raindrops.

When Wilfred comes back, I tell him about this way the Professor looked at me, like he wanted to possess me but was repulsed too, and he laughs and says, 'But everyone looks at you like that, Gay. Don't you know that?'

Stupid bastard.

6 November 1946

He turns up late, this mystery visitor, which is just as well because I wasn't even up and dressed. I'd been lying in bed, sleeping sometimes and then other times wide awake, listening for sounds and turning my hands in the air in front of my face. I have lovely hands. Wilfred bangs on the door, 'For God's sake get up, Gay, Roy's visitor is here.'

I shout back to him that there was no need to be so crude.

I don't go straight into the study, I thought I'd make a bit of an entrance. I stand just the other side of the open door and look through the crack, and listen for a bit. I can't see much, just the stranger standing in the middle of the room, dripping wet all over the carpet, with his back to me. He says he was late because he had to catch a train from Sussex or some such place. Nobody wants to hear his stories. 'Now, young man,' the Professor says moving to stand in front of him, so I could see half his face, 'we have a girl here who is coming out your way soon and we rather thought we might give her something to bring out for you and your lot.'

'I'm going back soon,' he says, brushing the rain off his coat.

'Yes, I heard. December, isn't it? Well, that's a little early for us, we haven't gathered all the information yet, so we're going to give the package to her and then she'll meet up with you when she arrives in June. Were you followed here?' The Professor is enjoying himself.

The stranger looks over his shoulder, and I thought he was looking straight through the door at me, like he knew I was there. I breathe in tight, and lean against the wall.

'No,' he says, 'No, I don't think so.'

Well, I go in then. I fling the door back and stride in, in my black high heels and the silk dress I got from that family in Berlin, and they all look at me.

The stranger. He is wearing a red jumper, he looks healthy. I can't help but stare at him, as he is staring at me. I think of all those crooked teeth, and unshaven men, and the grey skies and the grey-green coats, of all that rubble and the smell and the lice and the bricks in the roads, and the children with hollowed-out eyes and Pierre on top of me in the van and the fires you could see through the windows of ruined buildings and the smell of the oilskins and the smell of the damp and the men and the cold air in Wales and my not being able to breathe, and the tightness in my chest and all that, I think about all that, looking at the stranger.

He is in red. The room is a dark green, and the clouds are heavy outside, and the Professor so pale and Wilfred suddenly so under-nourished and scratchy, and there is this stranger in a red jumper and white teeth and light curling hair.

'Hello,' he says.

'Hello,' I say.

And the Professor tells us all to sit down, but Wilfred doesn't, he is pacing about the place looking worried.

'So you weren't followed then?' the Professor says. And the stranger looks over at me and says, 'No, I didn't come straight from London, I took a detour. I met a girl. I don't see that anyone would want to follow me. I thought I'd have things to do over here, but nobody has given me instructions.' Then they talk on and on about this package, which I don't much care about.

The stranger doesn't stay long, and I follow him out of the Professor's rooms, I don't know why. I am drunk, we've had some champagne. I follow him down the little stone stairs, and out onto the dark street. He looks about him, as though unsure which way to go. It is cold outside.

'I'm jealous of this girl you met,' I tell him, coming up next to him in the street. He looks surprised. He says, 'She's a schoolgirl. She's nothing to do with this.'

I want to tell him I'm nothing to do with this either. I want him to have made a detour for me, I want him to sit in someone's house and say, 'I met a girl.' I want his story to be about me, all about me. Like a need in me.

'A schoolgirl? What's she like?'

He considers this for a moment, and then he says, 'I don't know her that well. Pure, honest, unusually so. The strangest thing is I don't seem able to stop thinking about her. There's something about her, I think she needs help.'

'You make her sound so small.'

And he laughs. 'Yes, she is, I think she is a small person.'

And then we both laugh, and I say, 'Are you going to save her then?'

'Do you think I should?'

'Well, someone in this bloody world could do with being saved, couldn't they?'

'Do you want me to?' And he's looking at me, in the street light, and I'm looking back at him.

'Yes, I want you to save the schoolgirl.'

'I could, couldn't I? Perhaps I will.' And then I lean in and kiss him on the cheek, and he smells of lemons. 'Do it for me,' I say.

And he blinks and looks at me, and holds his hand over the bit of the cheek where I've kissed him.

May 1947, Birkenhead

Mother found this diary the other day as we were packing up our things. She said she'd buy me a new one if I liked, seeing as this one was so battered and dirty, but I told her no, I liked this one, I just hadn't written in it much recently. She said, 'Well, keep it normal, Eileen, what you had to eat and where you went. That sort of thing. Life's getting back to normal now, isn't it? Don't want you getting sick again, we're getting away from it all, Eileen, that's all gone now. It'll make you laugh I shouldn't wonder to read that book when you're older and run off your feet with children and the like.'

She's going down to pay the rest on our tickets tomorrow. They're laying on loads of ships at the moment because everyone's wanting to escape Europe, she says. We're to travel in 'austerity conditions' because they haven't refitted the old troop ships yet. She talks of South Africa like it's the promised land. She stole a magazine from the dentist's this week, she wanted to show me this big advertisement about emigrating to South Africa. It was all blue skies and bright sunshine and happy children playing in a perfect garden. She says we'll be rich there. She says we might even have a servant again, and when she says this she is trying to persuade me, is pleading with me, and I want to tell her, I don't give a stuff about servants any more, and can't she see that?

Wilfred brought up the package this weekend. He's at the BBC now. He was very formal, awkward in the pub, looking about him like he had a bad smell under his nose.

'You're all set for the off then?' he said, sipping from his pint and not looking at me.

'Oh yes,' I told him, 'I'm going to take the place by storm. I've got the contacts now, I'm going to have them all,' and I laughed, but he looked at me, worried.

'Take it easy, Gay, won't you? Take it easy,' and he sort of smiled at me, for the first time.

'No,' I told him, picking up the package off the seat, and standing up and putting my fur coat on. 'No, I fucking well won't. See you, Wilfred.'

Gay uses a variety of pens in her diary, more often that not it is a pencil, especially in the French sections, and the words have become blurred, smudged with the sleeve of her battledress I imagine, and some of the writing is difficult to read, as though it were written in the back of a moving van. It smells too, the diary, I hadn't realised this before.

I have something else to stick in the diary now, a note that has been slipped under my door. It appeared just now, I could hear footsteps on the landing outside my room, and then a triangle of white appeared under the door. I didn't move, I couldn't, and then the steps fell away again.

I knew who it was. I heard him last night, as I was coming out of my arsenic-coloured room for dinner. I heard his voice, and I froze, half in and half out of my door, key in hand, evening bag on arm. It came from further down the narrow timbered corridor, from round the corner – at a rough guess he would have been standing on the step by the bathroom – and though I couldn't see him, I knew immediately it was Mike Abel.

What to do? Slipping back into my dark room, not daring even to peek up the corridor, I pressed the door closed and leant against it. His voice is thick with cigarettes smoked in Johannesburg's high, thin air, it rumbles with waves of false bonhomie – part South African and part cockney – fulsome, ersatz and clumsy. Just the sound of him made me jump, the way his voice filled the pink-carpeted twisting landing, booming below the low beams, as though he and the South African sun were here, intent on finding and bleaching out all the history and secrets of this most English of hotels.

I was sweating like a truant, even though all he'd said was, 'This is us, number fourteen, I've found the blardy room here.' It was a shock to hear him like that. The Norman Mead is filling up with ghosts from my past, the witnesses have arrived, storming along the corridors with their new, specially bought suitcases stuffed full of oranges, eager faces, shiny with unnatural suntan and excitement at being 'overseas' on official business. 'Ah yes,' they'd have told their friends, 'I'm off to England in March. I'm to be a witness at the trial for that poor dead girl. You know, Gay Gibson, the one who was murdered by the deck steward? I knew her well, intimately, such a tragedy, a beautiful girl.'

His note says:

Laura, I know you're in there. We need to meet before the trial starts, this is URGENT. There is something we need to discuss. Meet me at 6 P.M. in the hotel bar.

  Yours, Mike Abel

  PS Have they found the diary?

I may go, I may not. I haven't decided yet. He'll want to talk about the time he had sex with Gay in his car, at that party, when she went blue, cold and breathless. He'll want to tell me that now he's here with his wife he can't possibly say that, in front of her, in front of the court and will I agree not to mention it too. Not to mention how her hand was stuck to the window, and him with his bottom in the air, and her with her legs all up against the dashboard, and how he called me over, and we had to sit her up and bang her on her back, and how he forgot to pull his trousers up until later.

He'll say, 'I want to help this James Camb fellow out, because I bet that's what happened with him, I mean, I'm sure Gay died making love to him, but I just can't say it, you do understand that, Laura, don't you?' and he'll give me his greedy salesman smile, urging me to wash all his sins away.

Eight

Paul and I had the use of Bridget's car for the day and we were going out, just the two of us, for one entire long, hot, glorious day alone. I wasn't going to let anybody or anything spoil it, I had even smiled nicely at Robert when he said, 'What a surprising treat to have you at breakfast, Paul,' and said, 'Yes, isn't it?' in the lightest, airiest way I could manage.

We agreed that we would start with a swim at the club, and I slipped into the front seat beside him with my unused scarlet bathing costume wrapped up in one of Bridget's bath towels, and he beamed at me. We reversed slowly down the drive.

'God, I'm glad to be getting out of here,' I told him, winding down the window a little. We turned left out of the drive and went slowly down Tenth Avenue. 'This road is so straight.' I was slunk down in my seat looking out of the window at the rows of bungalows and houses in their perfectly measured-out plots of land, 'Everything is so well apportioned.'

'Not everything, Lala, not nearly everything. There are nearly a million people in Joburg, one half black the other half white, both living in fear of each other.'

We paused at a junction, I could see two white-blonde children playing in their front garden. Their mother standing on the porch in a dark blue housecoat holding the garden hose and firing jets of water at her yelping children who ran through the arc of water, screaming and shouting. Paul looked over and raised his hand out of the window, the mother waved back.

'Do you know her?'

'Of course, we know everyone around here. She's Afrikaans though, so Mum and Dad don't want to mix with her. Everyone likes to keep it tight here.' Paul turned to me. 'Let's not go to the country club, I can't stand the place. We'll head up towards Melville instead and take a walk on the koppies.'

'Yes, if you'd like to.' I wasn't happy that our plans had been changed so soon, and I had no idea what the koppies were, but didn't like to say so.

We purred along. The sun was overhead and my senses were filled with dust and Paul and the waxy smell of Bridget's car. Paul was humming to himself. Everything was going to be all right after all, we'd just needed to get away from Bridget and Robert and their house, and be on our own for a bit. I should have stored up all the educational trips for now, instead of wasting them on the first week, but now we'd be together again, and remember who we were when we were together. Now, in the sunshine, I could see that the gardens were well tended and the houses pretty. I began to like the tree-lined avenues with their low white walls and patched grassy verges. We passed mimosa and blue gum trees, azalea bushes, and huge clumps of bougainvillea spreading out across the low walls (though at the time I couldn't have told you their names, that came later).

'Are you happy, Laura?'

'Yes, I like this. I just like being with you.'

We parked the car on the side of the road, where small, irregular hills covered in long coarse yellow grass rose up beside us, dotted with small, wiry trees and shrubs.

'Are you sure we can walk here?' I asked Paul, climbing out of the car. 'It looks a bit wild.'

'It *is* wild, Laura, come on.'

Paul took my hand and led me through the tall grasses, presumably towards the bottom slopes of the hill. I could feel hard knobbly earth underfoot and wiry grass or thistles scratching at my ankles.

'Isn't there a path?'

'Come *on*.'

We came out of the longer grasses and started to walk up the gentler slopes, easier now on shorter grass, sometimes scrambling over small rocks and stones, kicking up red dust behind us.

'There's an old prehistoric settlement up here, Lala, Iron Age or Stone Age or something. We'll head for there. You all right? We go this way now, no more uphill walking.'

He was excited and proud, he waved his arms about. 'Isn't it beautiful, Laura?'

I was hot and breathless. We snaked our way through harsh scrubland, avoiding the bushes overladen with startling thorns, crushing underfoot small purple and white flowers which grew in clumps between the rocks. Everything was still and dry, the sky an unrelenting blue. We walked across long flat rocks, I could feel the heat of them burning through the bottom of my shoes, and back into longer grasses. Strange plants grew all around us; the bare silver-green branches of small desiccated trees reached across our horizon, beside us the knobbly dry land would sometimes erupt with strange growth, blackened stumps with tufts of coarse leaves but at the tip of each a delicate mauve flower hanging off the top.

'Whatever are these?' I crouched down, grateful for the rest. 'You wouldn't think that anything so beautiful could grow out of something so ugly.'

Paul wasn't listening, he was looking about him.

'Can't remember where we go now.'

'Are we lost?'

'You must be tired. Let's take a break.'

He found a long flat rock covered in crumbling yellow lichen for us to sit on and when I sat I could see my ankles were covered in tiny scratches and grazes, a little pearl of blood had started to form out the corner of one of them. I wiped it away and licked my finger clean, it had the same metal taste as the silver spoons at the Grange. I could feel the sun bearing down on the back of my head.

'Mum will be cross with me for bringing you here,' Paul said, putting his arm around my waist. 'She thinks you need only see Commissioner Street and—'

'Stuttafords and the Carlton Hotel, as a special treat.'

Paul laughed and pulled me closer to him. I leant my head against his shoulder. I could feel the heat of him through his shirt, but then worried that I would feel hot and clammy to him, so sat up again. I was wearing one of the three dresses I had brought with me, a rather matronly green dress with emerald-coloured buttons and a pleated skirt, which had appeared the height of sophistication in Lillian's Boutique with Mrs Granger. Now the skirt was sprayed with marks left by the dry red dust and the hem had started to come undone. I swiped at the dust marks. Perhaps we really were lost, perhaps Paul had brought us somewhere unsafe, and I had followed him without a thought.

'I've missed you,' I said lightly. 'Lots of things have happened, haven't they?'

'Yes, it must seem like that to you.'

'I was just wondering what our plans might be?'

'Our plans?' Paul removed his arm from around my waist, he leant down and picked up a long stick. He started prodding at the ground in front of us, sending up little sprays of red dust. I noticed then what unusually small ears he had.

'Yes, I think we should make some, don't you? I mean, it's been interesting here and everything, but I was just wondering what we thought we might do next? Where we're going to live?'

He didn't look at me, he was digging little lines and pathways through the red dust, then he started to draw spiral shapes, lines turning in and in on themselves.

'Fossils,' he said, 'ammonites.'

My hair was sticky against my scalp. I pulled it back behind my ears, thick with drying sweat. I bent down to wipe my face clean on my skirt.

'Your parents don't want us to stay with them, Paul.' There, I'd said it. 'I think we should go somewhere else. I think we should go home. I'm not sure how much longer I can do this, we've been here nearly four weeks. Your father hates me, he resents me. They don't want us in their house.'

'They *do* want us there. They're not cruel people, just small-minded.' He sounded affectionate and fatalistic. He looked over and smiled at me. 'Not that different from your parents, really.'

'No,' I said emphatically, 'my mother is cruel, definitely cruel.'

And Paul laughed, and carried on drawing his fossils in the earth; there was a crowd of them now, laid out in front of us, swirling at our feet.

'They won't kick us out, Laura, if that's what you're worrying about. They're good people.'

'It's not that, Paul, it's the way they talk about things, and how they pick on me, and how they never say anything to you but always to me. I think we should go, we won't survive unless we go.'

There must have been a sliver of steel in my voice, a cold grain-iness, because Paul responded quickly and defensively.

'Where is it *exactly* you want to go?'

Why had I said this about our survival? When had I begun to think about our marriage in these terms? From its impulsive origins perhaps, back at the Grange when Paul Lovell had said he'd better rescue me? When I'd feared that perhaps he might just put on his winter coat and trudge down the drive, shaking off the memory of me like a tune in his head he needed to be rid of? Or later, when we'd arrived at the Lovells' house and they'd been so sceptical about us, so disappointed in Paul?

'Laura, what is it you want exactly?' Paul was trying to keep his voice even and low.

I leant forward and grabbed the other end of the stick he was holding. I wanted him to stop drawing those endless spirals. He didn't let go but pulled on his end. I stood up and using both hands started to pull, feeling the stumps at its edges digging into my hands, and the dry red dust from its tip.

'What are you doing?' Paul laughed, his face turned up towards me and the sun. He started to pull again on the stick and I tried to dig my feet in behind one of the stones.

'I will not live here,' I shouted at him. 'I will not live here, Paul Lovell, and have you ignore me and leave me with your parents. You're supposed to be in charge. I don't like it here. I don't like the things your parents say about you. I will not sleep in that bed with you and not do . . . do . . . the things we're meant to do. The things that Charlotte Locks and Roddy Bellows did behind the bushes.'

Paul laughed even louder, as though he thought it all a marvellous game, and with one sudden strong pull from him, I lost my balance and came crashing down on the ground before him, falling on my knees and hands into the dust. Paul leant forward and pulled me up to sitting by my armpits so I was kneeling in front of him. He took my head in his hands, he pulled my face close to his. His blue eyes looked wide and his plump lips looked tight and white; there were beads of sweat on his forehead, lying in a line underneath his curls.

'Serves you right. Now listen up, Laura Lovell, You have to stop snivelling and complaining and screwing your little face up at the sunshine and at Johannesburg. You're lucky to be here – I saved you, didn't I? Have you forgotten that? You don't know the kind of pressure I'm under, this isn't easy for me either. Perhaps I shouldn't have brought you here, perhaps it was selfish of me. Do you think it was?'

'No.' I kept it short, sensing a threat, staring at his blue eyes.

'Good. Neither do I, because I met you and I loved you and I wanted to marry you. I never said it would be easy, I never told you that I had a job or anything like that. And you never *asked*, did you? So you can't pretend now that you did.'

He looked a bit unbalanced, I thought, vulnerable and angry. I could feel his hot hands around my face, a bit of white saliva had appeared at the corners of his mouth. I could feel his displeasure and disappointment, I didn't know what to say to him. Everything seemed so complicated somehow, I couldn't see or think straight.

'They thought I was pregnant, Paul, they thought I married you because I was pregnant. They want us to get a bungalow.' This last sentence came out in a wail of disappointment. The word 'bungalow' shot through the air between us, circling around those dry grasses and reverberating across the low hills.

Paul looked wildly at my face, his eyes flickering across it, as though he were seeing me for the first time, my eyes, my nose, my lips, the top of my head.

'I want to make a difference, Laura. I want to help. That's all. Is that too much to ask, to try and make a difference somewhere?'

I shook my head. My knees were hurting in the dust, I didn't want us to be arguing, I wasn't even sure what we were arguing about. He smiled then, all his anger gone in a moment.

'And as for Charlotte Locks and Roddy Bellows . . .' He slipped off the rock and onto the ground next to me, so we were both kneeling in the dust. Then he kissed me hard and angry on the mouth and pushed me down on the earth, onto his bed of ammonites, pinning my arms down by my sides, sitting across my stomach, frowning down at me lying in the dust.

And that was when we did it, for the first time in our married lives, down on that earth, the sun above, surrounded by rocks and thorny grasses, my knickers peeled and rolled onto one ankle, Paul with his shirt half undone, his eyes screwed closed, clutching at me, quick and ardent, intent on demonstrating something powerful to me, something masculine and capable. He pulled his shorts down below his knees, didn't look at me, but I didn't care. All I could think of was the strange sound of a bird in the sky and the smell of sweat on the dry, dry earth, and wondering if this was really what Charlotte had done, and surely not because wouldn't someone have known, wouldn't we have *seen* on her what had happened,

179

this altogether surprising thing, this extraordinary moment when Paul pulled my thighs apart, and quickly, so very quickly, entered me, with a low animal groan, and I didn't know whether to laugh or cry, because this was what I'd asked for, this was what I'd dreamt of since our honeymoon and during those long, hot nights in his single bed. This breathless moment of Paul inside me, and I could feel him in there, and then almost as soon as it had started it was over, and Paul looked at me then, his face red and amazed, that moment when he shuddered, like a man crying in a quiet place.

And though it were over almost as soon as it had started, I felt a creeping triumph about the whole business. Sitting beside him in his mother's car, my shoulders sore, knees bruised and burning and my thighs tight and stretched, I thought I had found a whole new set of muscles. I had this odd, odd feeling between my legs, as though I were both undone and refound. Paul was smiling, he kept looking over at me, he looked different, alive, pleased with himself.

'I wish we'd done it before, Paul, on the boat. Why didn't we?'

Paul frowned and I thought I had lost him, that he'd close down again, thinking I was criticising him. But instead his face softened.

'I held back rather, from you, from everything. It was stupid of me. You're right, Lala, about my father − he − he does affect me.' He looked relieved just to have said the words. 'He's so *critical*. I'm afraid, sometimes, that I am the person he thinks I am, that I'm useless. He makes me doubt myself − and he's such a strong man, a good man, such a *loving* father.' He shivered slightly on the seat next to me.

'Oh, darling,' I said, putting my hand on his knee. 'You're not useless. And anyway, you've got me now, and, well, I think you're wonderful.' I didn't say that in my opinion Robert was neither a good man nor a loving father. 'Besides, I think he's a bit frightened of you. He doesn't want to lose you, however much he teases you. He loves you.'

'Yes, I know, which makes it all the more wretched.' Paul started the car, and turned to me with sudden conviction. 'Lala, everything is going to be fine, I promise you,' and reaching over he kissed me and I could smell the heat of us on his shirt.

I wasn't shocked by the sex, I was fascinated. I wanted to do it again, more slowly this time, so I could keep up and concentrate on what was happening. What had happened?

'I have to take you back now though, I have to go somewhere.'

'Let me come with you, just once.'

He pulled a piece of hair from my face and tucked it behind my ear. He was thinking something through, and then, as I'd guessed he might, he made another of his impulsive decisions, I could see him warming up to it. He banged his palms on the steering wheel.

'Damn it. Why not?' And just as he'd realised we could and should have sex, he made another decision based on that same sudden surge of optimism and desire. 'Yes, damn it. You should come with me, of course you should, but no talking, no complaining and no bloody questions all the time.'

Nine

I had questions, of course, from the outset, but I did as Paul had told me and kept quiet. He said we were going to pick up a friend of his called Joseph; he was waiting for us on a street corner in Melville, leaning against a wall, reading a newspaper. Paul told me to jump in the back so they could sit up front together. Joseph didn't look very happy to see me there, he refused to get in the car, gesturing to Paul to come out and talk to him. I watched them from the back seat, Paul talking quickly and smiling widely, Joseph looking suspicious and clouded. He was slightly smaller than Paul, thin and dirty-looking, not looked-after; his face was sunburnt, which made him look pink and angry, his fair hair very short and aggressive. The hair on the back of Paul's head was sticking up, and I could see clumps of dust and dirt on his shirt collar. Paul put a hand on Joseph's shoulder, and leant in close and whispered something in his ear; eventually Joseph relented and they walked slowly towards the car.

'Laura, this is my friend Joseph,' Paul said getting in.

Joseph didn't say anything to me, he didn't even look at me, just nodded in my direction. I could tell from the back of his neck that he was a singularly intense individual; he sat ramrod straight and the fine neck bones stood proud, straining for perfection, a speckle of shaving rash peering round at me. Well, what did I care if he wanted to ignore me? I'd just made love to my husband for the first time.

Joseph lit a cigarette. We were heading north again, along a road lined with neat little houses, a poorer area but each of the houses had a porch and decorative ironwork across the front, and I could see fat white ladies sitting out with needlework on their knees, or rocking a baby in their arms. Paul stopped at a roadside cafe or an inn, I don't know what it was.

'She missed lunch,' he told Joseph, who didn't respond. Paul glanced over at me and winked. Joseph and I sat in the car in silence, until I said, 'Isn't it hot?' He swung round in his seat and looked at me, his face was thin and his mouth mean, he looked me up and down and I returned his stare, unblinking, and then he turned his back to me again. I willed Paul to be quick. When he came back he passed me a hot roll wrapped up in greasy paper and a bottle of pop, and he threw one in Joseph's lap too, and laughed at him.

'Bet you've not eaten for days, Joe.'

We carried on in silence. I don't know what was in that hot roll, some kind of porky mincemeat, I think, but it felt good. I hooked my feet up under me, and ate it so fast that globs of fatty gravy dribbled down my chin, dropping spots onto that green dress. Soon we were out bumping along an untarred road, ribboning under the huge sky. It must have been later in the afternoon than I'd realised; the sun had turned a reddy-yellow colour, and rising up against it, I suddenly saw blobs of red houses, clumped together, a haze of blue smoke spiralling up above the roofs. I'd never seen such a place before. It seemed a million miles away from the neat, perfect avenues of Greenside.

'Is that where we're going? What's it called?

'That's Sophiatown, Laura. Yes, that's where we're going.'

'But who lives there?'

'Everybody lives there,' said Joseph, tersely. 'Africans, Chinamen, Indians, the whole damn world. The whole damn world going to hell in a bucket of beer.'

'It's one of the few places where Africans can buy the freehold on their property, Lala, which is why everyone comes here. When they cleared the slum yards in Doornfontein a few years ago, lots of the Bantu came here, to find somewhere to live.'

'It's a racket.' Joseph wound down the window and flicked his cigarette butt out. 'Nobody needs a permit to live here so they come to Sophiatown. A lot of the stands here are owned by whites, but they don't live here, they just charge the rent. If you're native and own your own freehold, then you take in tenants to pay back the mortgage. So they build shacks in their backyards for letting. There can be as many as eight families living in one stand, and there might just be one tap, but nobody drinks the water because it's filthy.'

'It's a wonderful place, Laura, you'll see, but keep close to Joseph and me. We should go in quietly.'

I wasn't sure it sounded all that wonderful. Paul parked the car on what must have been the furthest corner of Sophiatown.

'We're going to walk from here,' he said, 'it's too conspicuous to drive right in.'

We walked five hundred yards up a dusty track; I wanted to hold Paul's hand, but thought it would be inappropriate to do so. We turned down a little alleyway, the houses were made of brick, but behind the low walls I could see shacks made of sheets and wood, zinc and rags. It was a stinking place. Paul and Joseph were immune to the powerful reek of the heavy air, but I had to pull the collar of my dress up around my nose. The place was teeming with people, in the yards, out on the streets, people cooking, talking, washing. Dogs ran towards us, followed by children with no shoes, but bright clothes. Nobody acknowledged us, but then nobody ignored us either. And there were people of all colours too, just as Joseph had promised. Chinese, Africans, mulattos even. I saw one Indian family sitting out in a yard handing round food between them, serving it up in bright red bowls, and everywhere the sound of music and singing, the banging of washtubs, a crying in the wind, footsteps running down dark alleyways, voices calling out to one another, the sound of someone playing a mouth organ, the stamping of feet, the crashing of bottles.

'It's here,' Joseph said, looking behind him. 'I'll knock.'

We stopped at a low brick house, with a red roof. The door was hanging off the frame and a piece of old cloth had been hung across the gap. Joseph knocked on the door and called through the gap. There was the sound of footsteps and the door opened a fraction. Two black men in suits and wide-brimmed hats passed by us in the alleyway, one of them whistled, or hissed at me through his teeth.

'Why did he do that?' I whispered to Paul.

'Shhh.'

'Aaaah, baas!' A woman's face smiled at us from behind the broken door, she had a mad, fixed grin. 'There ain' no people here for you, baas! Swear to the Lord. No people here for you.'

Joseph leant in closer to the door, and passed through a piece of paper. It was snatched out of his hand, and the door closed shut. We waited. Paul and Joseph looking down at their feet, not meeting each other's eye. I was hoping they'd made a mistake, and we'd be able to go back to the car and drive home. Paul looked ridiculously out of place in the shadows of that alleyway, in his open-necked shirt and shorts. He looked young and vulnerable, more nervous than I'd have liked.

The door opened a crack again, and the same woman appeared, but serious this time, no more grinning, no more 'baas!'.

'Who's she?' she said.

'My wife,' Paul told her, 'she's with me.'

'Hmmm.' The woman looked at me. 'You should know better than to be bringing your wife to a place like this,' and then she pulled the door open, kicking it back with her foot. She turned and walked down a dark corridor. 'Close it after you.'

'Come on.' Joseph went first and we filed in after him. We followed the woman to another door and when she opened it I was momentarily stunned by the bright lights in the room. The woman sat down at a little table in the corner which was covered with bottles of every size and shape. She looked up at the crumbling ceiling, humming to herself. There were three men in the room, two black and one white. They were sitting on an old couch, the bottom of which was falling through onto the floor. They looked up when we entered and stopped their conversation. I became aware of music coming through the far wall — it made the bottles of the table shake, the woman had to put her hand out to stop them. It was the craziest music you could imagine, wild thumping beats, and the sound of singing and shouting, rifts of unstoppable, wild playing. Someone had a trumpet, or something, the sound of it began to fill the room.

The white man on the couch got to his feet quickly and came over towards us, frowning. Joseph put his hand out but the man ignored it, rudely.

'Why are you here? Who sent you?' he whispered crossly. 'How did you know about this meeting?'

'They should sit down,' came a voice from the sofas, a rumbling warm voice. The white man frowned again and whispered something at Joseph, something I didn't catch, and then he looked at me.

'And who the hell are *you*?' he said.

'This is my wife. Sorry, there was a mix-up, she—' Paul said, but the man had obviously decided to make a fist of the situation, he seemed conscious of the men behind him on the sofas, who were staring at us. He smiled at me and shook my hand.

'That's marabi, comrade,' he said nodding to the wall. 'African jazz. There's a marabi party next door tonight.'

The woman whistled. 'Wilson "King Force" Silgee has come to Sophiatown,' she said softly, putting out her other hand to steady the bottles.

'Come in, come in,' the man said, smiling at me with false warmth, though I was already in. He looked around the room for somewhere to offer me to sit but all the chairs were taken. He was a small, wiry man with the keen, furtive look of a small dog, and he wore huge black spectacles on his thin face.

'Mother,' he said to the woman at the table, 'are there any more chairs?' She shook her head without looking over at him. One of the men on the couch said something to her I couldn't understand, and she then got slowly to her feet and left the room.

Paul and Joseph went over to the couch and introduced themselves. They sat down on the floor and looked up at the man in glasses, waiting for him to speak. I wanted to find somewhere discreet, so I leant against the wall near the table, I could feel the music then, drilling, thumping through the wall, bumping around my body. I could feel it throbbing between my legs. I didn't like this place, it felt dangerous and unknown. I hadn't liked him calling

187

me comrade, didn't like the fact that obviously Paul and Joseph were neither expected nor wanted at this meeting. The man in the glasses sat back down, smiled at everyone, and leant forward, putting his elbows on his knees and licking his lips.

'We've been discussing the importance of industrial legislation, particularly in the garment industry. I have been explaining to Mr Tengo and Dr Bitini our personal commitment to the emergent ANC Youth League. I have expressed the view that we feel it is both necessary and important that we work together towards our common goals.'

Mr Tengo and Dr Bitini exchanged a glance. One of them stretched out his legs and looked at Paul and Joseph sitting side by side on the floor.

'This is not a Sunday school,' he said, with a smile. 'These people should have chairs.'

'And,' the man in spectacles went on, 'I have reminded Dr Bitini that I feel the trade unions have a considerable role to play.'

'We are aware of your feelings, sir,' the other black man said, smiling softly. He was wearing a suit with a white shirt. 'We are all aware of your work and when my friend said you wanted a meeting, I said, "Yes, he is a friend of the African peoples, yes, I will meet with him."' He was smiling politely, but the air was thick with tension, tension in this room but with the sounds of wild dancing next door. 'But the European movements, even the SACP as it stands, do not have a place in the ANC Youth League.'

I can't imagine what I must have looked like, leaning up against the wall of that shack in my green dress, eyes wide and hair sticky and dusty. And though I knew this was an important meeting – that it was something powerful and relevant and important – I still had the guilty thought that Paul looked ridiculous. Diminished.

Sitting on the floor like that, at the feet of these men, getting his pale shorts even dirtier, nodding his head and smoothing down his hair with the palm of his hand. I tried to concentrate on their conversation but was distracted by those rhythmic beats in my back and my heart hammering inside my chest. I didn't understand what was being said, but I could feel the tension just as I could feel the music, like a current running through my body, charging it with little electric shocks. I didn't know what was happening to me, I was a different person. I wondered whether they could all tell. I blushed with shame at the certain thought that they knew I had just had sex, I suspected it was writ all over me, shining out of my face and my skin, as though I had been ripped open and they could all see inside of me, could poke about in there with their fingers. I crossed my legs, the throbbing had become disturbing.

'You will doubtless be aware,' Spectacles said, smiling back, 'that the SACP is not the movement it once was.'

'*You* will be aware that we believe we should be organising unions which are free of European leadership. Many people are in agreement with this.'

Bump, bump, bump. Where had Paul brought us? I had to put my palms flat against the wall, to centre myself a little. I wanted to leave, I wanted us both to leave and go far, far away from this place. I felt as unsteady as that time on the rainy pavement in London, as though the floor were rising up and falling away from me, nauseated with foreboding.

'Yes.' The spectacled man shifted slightly in his seat. 'We were not discussing "leadership" though, Dr Bitini, but collaboration.'

Dr Bitini stood up quickly, and looked about him. He smiled down at them all, and stretched his hands high above his head so his fingers brushed against the ceiling.

'How can we talk now, with this party next door? Eh?' He grinned at them. 'There is beer here on the table, and we sit down so seriously. Eh? Next door is the place to go, I think.'

*

Joseph and Paul agreed that it had been a very interesting and worthwhile meeting. They both thought that great risks had been taken in arranging such a meeting and they were sure something would come of it. Paul asked Joseph a few questions about the ANC Youth League. Paul, it seemed, was not as knowledgeable on these matters as Joseph, and though they were the same age he deferred to him every time. It seemed to have passed them both by that they had not been welcome at the meeting. Perhaps, though, this was how these things worked – what did I know?

'What did you think, Mrs Lovell?' Joseph asked.

It was dark now, and we were travelling slowly down unlit roads, the car's headlamps attracting huge, sleepy-looking insects which flew about in the rays of the lamps. I had almost run out of Sophiatown, and they had both had to walk quickly to catch up with me.

'I'm not sure what to make of anything,' I told him flatly. 'They didn't want us there, they didn't want any of us there.'

'Oh Lala,' Paul swivelled round in his seat briefly, 'was it all a bit shocking for you? At least now you've seen a little of the real Africa, haven't you? She insisted on coming, Joseph.' He was trying to be light-hearted, but he sounded disappointed.

'Yes, you said.' Joseph was lighting another cigarette, and his face glowed orange briefly. 'Something to write home about, eh?' and he threw the match out of the window.

'Can I have one?'

Joseph tossed his packet into the back of the car, quickly followed by the matches. I scrabbled down on the floor to find them. I lit a cigarette.

'How do I know you're not a journalist, Mrs Lovell? It wouldn't do to have the meeting written up anywhere, you know.'

Paul laughed nervously. 'She's not a journalist, I told you that, Joseph. She's just Laura, that's all, she's nobody. You're not going to tell anyone anything, are you, Laura?'

'It'd make a good story for the country club though, wouldn't it, Mrs Lovell? The evening I went to a shebeen in Sophiatown and met Africans and communists and trade unionists.' There was an unpleasant sneer to his voice.

'Well, to be honest, for all that it was a very good meeting like you say, I don't think it would make a good story at all. The ANC think this, the SAPC think that, you all talk in code, I couldn't understand a word of it. As for that music . . .'

Joseph laughed, and he looked over at Paul and laughed again.

'You're right,' he said, 'she's fine, she's nobody.'

*

It was late by the time we got back to the Lovells' house. Paul parked the car in the driveway. We didn't get out immediately, he drummed his fingers on the steering wheel.

'You asked to come,' he said eventually.

'I know.' He was disappointed in me. 'I did all right,' I said, 'I didn't make a fool of myself, or of you. I kept quiet.'

'I suppose you think I'm — I just hoped that—' But he didn't finish his sentence because I knelt up on the front seat, and took his face in my hands and kissed him hard. I took his hands and put them on me, I needed to have Paul again, to quell the sounds and the beats of the jazz vibrating inside my body and between my legs, to banish the sense of being unwelcome.

And that was the second time we did it, across Bridget's leather seats and me with my head uncomfortably wedged between the seat and the door, trying to take possession of Paul, trying not to be a nobody, urging us to belong, together.

Gay's Diary

Aboard the Carnarvon Castle *June 1947*

You'd never believe the sound two hundred children can make running on an uncarpeted deck day and night. It's horrendous. Running and pounding about the place, and nobody giving them a word or watching over them. I can't believe how many people they've crammed in here, but if the ship's decrepit so are its passengers – huddled together in our rationed coats and thread-bare stockings, pale pinched faces clouded over with bad memories, and seasick too, everyone vomiting over the ship's railings and wailing about how long the journey is taking. When we arrived in Biscay, I heard a man asking the Captain when we'd be reaching Cape Fred Astaire! I have no idea what he really meant, and neither did the Captain because he said, 'Just after Ginger Rogers Bay,' and then the Captain winked at me.

There's all sorts on this ship; Londoners, Liverpudlians, Irish and Jews. We had a party a few nights ago, out on the deck in our over-coats, and everyone got drunk and suddenly happy. Like we all knew we were going for a fresh start and people started telling stories about how they'd heard South Africa had done well out of the war, how manufacturing was up and production had boomed. How it was a civilised place, not like an African country at all, and how they'd heard that you could actually see oranges and lemons growing on the trees and fish leaping out of the waters.

Mother's struck up a friendship with another woman, who's going out with her little daughter to join her husband in Johannesburg.

'Oh, just like us then,' says Mother, and this woman laughed and said, 'Not quite, he doesn't know we're coming. He reckons he's seen the last of us, but he's got a daughter he's never met and I'm not letting him off that easy.'

The mystery package is wrapped up in my fur coat in the trunk. It's a big flat envelope addressed to Joseph someone or other c/o Witwatersrand University in Johannesburg. I haven't opened it.

Mother is driving me mad. She has these things she does, that I've never noticed before. She takes ages getting ready for bed, unbuttoning her dress and rearranging her slip. 'Just pull it off, woman,' I want to shout at her. I stare at her while she does it because I know she doesn't like it. Her body is so old. Just to look at it makes me faint. Her middle is all doughy and crumpled over, her breasts are huge and uncontrollable. I don't want to look like her. I'm going to take care of myself. Her shoulders hunch up when she's trying to get ready for bed, like they can't take my staring.

'Don't smoke in here, Eileen,' she says, 'I expressly forbid it.'

'Forbid all you like,' I tell her, 'I'll do as I please.'

Then she looks at me, all broken and unsure what to say or do with me.

'I thought it'd be nice for us, to have these two weeks together on the boat. Get to know each other again.'

I try to keep out of her way as much as I can. She wants me to get work as a secretary out there, she told me she's written to Father all about it.

'Oh no,' I tell her, 'not on your nelly. I'm going to be doing acting work there, Mother,' and she says, 'We don't want you getting ill, Eileen. Not like before. This is our new start, isn't it?' I tell her this isn't 'our' anything. She calls me 'cruel', she says she only wants what's best for me. She worries about me, she thinks I'm not like her. Too bloody right I'm not. She says to me the other night, 'I thought being in the army would change you, Eileen, help you to grow up and mature. Help you to understand about other people a bit more, see the world a bit differently.'

I ignore her, but I think of telling her that I don't want to see the world differently, I like it how I see it. I'm not going to grow old and fat like her, settle down and be quiet. Why should I? I think about telling her about Charles Chalmers or even Pierre or the leg-stroking Professor. I think I might tell her that my world is not like hers, that people are different around me, they want and need things from me, that usually I give it them too.

I sent a telegram to the one of the names the Professor gave me. I kept it short: '*Talented and experienced actress arriving in Durban shortly. Requires work. Will call on arrival. Gay Gibson.*'

Ten

How long might we have gone on like that? Paul, Robert, Bridget
and I holed up in their immaculate house and all three of us looking
to Paul to make a move, a declaration, but him upstairs in his
bedroom with the door closed and beetling off to meetings and
none of us, for whatever reason, telling him not to. Day after day,
sitting on the edge of the bed, turning the pages of the newspapers,
looking out the window at the hot sun beating down on us, the
garden getting drier, my throat stickier and my palms sweatier, and
then the weather slowly changing, the sun less hot, more clouds
in the sky, the first hint of rainfall.

I thought of my parents often, of them sitting in their cold,
damp house, deep in winter, crowding around the fire and my
mother snapping at my father about the pipes, or how noisy these
logs are, and did they *have* to wheeze and croak like that when they
were put on the flames? I wondered if they ever thought about
me, over here on the other side of the world, with three dresses
to my name, did they talk about me at all? Bridget had sent a
telegram, she had written it out painstakingly on the back of an
envelope and shown me. It said 'All well stop Am very happy stop

Will write soon stop Love Laura stop.' 'Will that do? Is there anything else you'd like to say?' and she'd peered at me. I'd told her no, I thought that just about summed it all up really. Then every week she would say, 'We haven't heard back from your parents, Laura,' and I'd shrug and smile and say that perhaps they were busy. I suspected that Bridget wanted to rope them in too, to our strange situation, she wanted them to arrive at the end of the drive and take me away, saying it had all been a terrible mistake, and they were awfully sorry for their daughter's behaviour, and frightfully apologetic for any inconvenience that had been caused. People didn't call round to see me any more, there were no more invitations to luncheon at the club. There was just me in this foreign land, trying to keep out of Bridget's way, clinging on to my husband, asking him insistent questions late into the night, trying to understand this land war, the dark names he used, where Orlando was, what the squatters were — I thought they literally squatted, down on their haunches in the middle of the road, looking defiant. And he became happy to tell me, pleased to speak into the warm night, whispering about the Youth ANC, who he said were a pressure group within the ANC, how he and other communists were trying to work with them, but they were resistant as they thought the communists 'fostered un-African interests' — he snorted at this. 'Do you,' I whispered, 'do that?' But he would ignore me and talk on instead about wanting to 'promote confrontation' with the authorities, about how important it was to politicise African opinion on 'bread and butter' issues. And I can't pretend that I understood it all, but I did love it when he spoke like this. Such long words, such a sense of purpose and direction, such understanding. It made me feel proud to be with him.

But of course something had to happen, something had to give and, unsurprisingly perhaps, it was the weak link in the chain, the person who had brought all of this about, Paul.

*

I was dreaming. I used to have vivid colourful dreams during that time, frequently starring Robert and Bridget, though they weren't in this because I remember exactly what I was dreaming about the night that Paul and Joseph appeared in the garden hurling things at my window, because I thought those thumping clods of earth were the footfalls of all the children I was looking after in a large house, not dissimilar to the Grange, only it wasn't the Grange because all the walls were painted a bright white, and outside the windows the sky was a deep blue and the house full of light, and children. I was in charge of these children, who were running about and screaming and shouting. The girls were wearing Victorian pinafores and boots and the boys were dressed in a uniform of tight jackets and breeches and they were all running pell-mell along the corridors with their arms stretched out behind them like little aeroplanes. I knew that they were looking for something, but I didn't know what and I stopped one of them, a little boy, and asked him what they were looking for, was it a thimble? and he stuck his tongue out at me and ran off, and I was running after him, even though I knew I was in charge, because I didn't know what they were looking for but I thought it was my business to know, and I was panicked by all this activity and the wildness of these children, clambering over the beds and skidding down the stairs two at a time, and so when the clods of earth started raining against my window, I thought it was the sound of a hundred feet hammering on wooden floors.

But then, slowly, I began to rise out of my dream, my heart still hammering with worry, and I heard a new sound, the sound of my name being called out in the night air, reedy and tuneful. Then another thump, against the window, definitely against the window. I climbed out of bed, still half asleep and drew back the curtains, I could discern three figures down below, dark shapes moving about in the flower beds.

It was Paul, I knew it, I knew it by the way he was bending down to collect the earth, his silhouette picked out by a high round yellow moon which threw enlarging shadows across the garden. My fingers fumbling on the catch, I opened the window a little, feeling the sweet night air sneak in and wrap itself around my midriff. I was still half with those curious children, and perhaps because of this, I smiled, suspecting that Paul was rewarding me with something impulsive and unexpected.

'Laura, Laura.'

'Hello.'

'Thank God, Laura, thank God. Come down, can you?'

'Whatever are you doing, Paul? Have you lost your key?'

'Yes, yes, darling, I have, that's right, come on down now, nice and quick. Come and open the kitchen door for us, can you? Don't wake anyone though, come on, I'll see you round the back.'

I grabbed Paul's dressing gown and, slipping it on, ran down the stairs in my bare feet, padded through the sitting and dining rooms and across to the kitchen at the back. I found the light and, putting it on, went over to do battle with the heavy bolts on the back door. I could hear a noise on the other side, someone groaning, and then another voice, telling him to hush. The bolts were stiff and sticky, and it took me a while to shift the top one back into its place.

'Hurry up, Laura, for God's sake, hurry up.'

'I'm trying.'

Eventually the bolt skidded into position and I opened the latch on the door. I'd only opened it a fraction when Paul came charging through, pushing me back against the wall. Joseph was with him, and he had a black man balanced half across his shoulders and half across his back, but he was much taller than Joseph and his calves and feet trailed along the floor as Joseph dragged him in. Joseph and Paul both had blood on their shirts, huge dirty crimson stains smeared across their tops and down on their trousers. I screamed. Paul had run through to the dining room and returned with a chair which he banged down in the middle of the kitchen.

'Put him on here, Joe,' he said, and then turning to me,' Now, Laura, can you go quietly, really quietly, and get us some bandages and hot water?'

'I don't know where the bandages are.' I was looking him up and down for signs of a wound.

'What? For God's sake, Laura, it's not me that's hurt,' and he left the kitchen again.

I stared at this man sitting on one of Bridget's best chairs. Joseph was trying to get him to lean backwards, but he kept sloping forwards, his arms wrapped around his middle.

'Help me,' Joseph looked up at me, 'take his shoulders and lean him back.'

I stepped forward gingerly, placing my hands on his shoulders. He groaned and I could feel in my fingers his urge to roll forward and buckle over, but I did as I'd been told and pulled him back. This time he stayed. Joseph was down on his knees, trying to prise the man's arms away from his middle, he leant in close and ripped at the man's shirt.

'Who is he? What's the matter with him?'

'He's been stabbed, badly, here, do you see?'

Joseph looked up at me then; there was something triumphant about the way he met my gaze, as though he were pleased to shock and scare me. Paul came back in then, carrying little white packets of bandages.

'Can we stop the bleeding, Joseph?'

'I don't know, I'm not a bloody doctor, Paul.'

'What shall we do? What do we do with these bandages then? Wrap them around or something?'

'How the hell do I know?'

'Jesus. Well, we should clean the wound, shouldn't we? First of all? Let's get some hot water and do that, I've got some gauze pads and some lint or something here.'

They were talking too fast, bent over that poor man's body, gazing at his wound and shaking their heads.

'We don't need hot water,' I said, surprised to hear myself speaking, 'just clean water. We'll use what's in the kettle, it'll already have been boiled. Get me a bowl, Paul.'

He looked at me with a relief bordering on gratitude.

'I knew you'd know what to do, Lala.'

Why? Whatever had happened to lead him to believe such a thing? Still, I took the bowl of water and opened the packets of sterilised bandages with my teeth. Joseph was holding up the flap of this man's filthy shirt, and underneath it was the gash of a knife wound, sliced through his skin, sluicing pink blood, like the juice of an overripe fig. I went down on my knees beside the chair, his head was lolling to one side but he met my eyes for a moment.

'This might hurt a bit, but I need to clean the wound. Then we'll get you to a hospital.'

'You'll need a needle and thread, ma'am.' His voice was deep and faraway-sounding, as though he were covered with a blanket. 'Fetch needle and thread, boil them clean. You must sew me up.'

'Oh, I couldn't do that!' I said skittishly, as though he'd just flirted with me and asked me to dance.

'I'll go,' Paul said.

Moses was a tall man, dark and shining in the kitchen light, with high cheekbones, deep eyes and a small beard. 'It's not that bad but it will bleed. I can talk you through what to do. I would do it but—' and he held up his right hand, which I could see was swollen and bruised, probably broken.

'No,' I said, dabbing at his wound with a sodden bandage. 'No, you must go to hospital. Where's the nearest one, Joseph?'

'Erm, well, I think there's a clinic in Orlando, but I'm not sure.'

'You must know where the nearest hospital is?'

'Well, not for him, no.'

'Non-European Hospital, part of the Johannesburg Hospital in Hillbrow,' the man said, ignoring Joseph, 'but I won't get there if you don't sew me up first,' and despite his grace and civility, I knew he was pleading with me. 'My name is Moses,' he said smiling, 'Moses Mvubelo.'

Paul came back in and he boiled the kettle on the electric stove. He fetched an enamel drinking cup out of the cupboard and dropped a sewing needle and some thick-looking yarn thread into it.

'I'll do it, Lala.'

'No thank you,' said Moses, smiling over at Paul, 'I would rather a woman.'

Joseph shot a look at Paul, and back at Moses. Joseph was frowning, he looked me up and down again, doubtful of my abilities. I looked back at Moses's side, my face close to his stomach, my elbows lightly brushing his thigh.

The blood was sticky and copious, it had drenched Moses's shirt and left trouser leg, it smelt warm and strong. The bandage was soon sodden, I looked about for something else, I didn't seem able to stem the flow.

When Paul brought the needle and thread over to me, laid out on a table napkin, his hands were shaking so much I thought he'd drop the needle on the floor and we'd have to start all over again. I took them from him and laid the napkin down on the floor beside me. Paul passed me a bottle of brandy.

'You must pour some of that drink on me,' Moses said, 'all over.'

'It'll hurt,' I said, though even as I said it, I knew he knew, and he smiled at me a little and said, 'Perhaps some for me first, eh?'

So Joseph held the bottle to his lips and then passed it to me. Moses smiled at me, giving me permission, a small but certain smile from inside his beard. I took the bottle and poured the brandy onto the wound, where I half expected it to sizzle and steam.

I don't know if you've ever tried sewing human flesh, but it's an extraordinarily difficult material to handle. Sinewy, tough and resistant. It wasn't much helped by the fact that my hands were shaking terribly and that Joseph and Paul were leaning in too close and audibly wincing each time I pulled the needle through.

I made a mistake by starting at one end of the gash – it had seemed the most logical thing to do – but by the time I'd got halfway along I realised my mistake because there were slack gapes forming where I hadn't lined the lips of the skin up properly. I couldn't see all that well either, the fumes of sweat, brandy, fear and panic were filling up the kitchen and making everything misty. I asked Paul to pass me some bandages, I thought I might cut them up and stuff them into the holes that had formed, to prevent infection I told myself, until Moses got to a hospital. I don't know what

I thought. I wanted to shout at Paul, to slap Joseph across his earnest face. I wanted someone adult and sensible to arrive and push me out of the way and get on with this terrible farcical job I'd been given. When Paul passed me the bandage, his hands were shaking too and his face was a terrible colour. He was crying. Why was he crying? He wasn't expected to play amateur surgeon, no one had supposed he might have superior embroidery skills simply because of his sex, had they?

In went the needle – not nearly sharp enough – through one side, pulling the yarn after it and then the effort to keep it straight, lining it up with the other side, trying to pull the skin closed, to ignore the pools of blood under the skin, the restraint of the blood which was no longer spilling over the sides.

There was a bang, as the kitchen door was flung open. We all leapt, I think, I don't know, I know I jumped to my feet, dropping the needle, so it hung on its thread off Moses's stomach, I might have screamed again even. It was Mary, in a dressing gown, she was holding a stick and frowning, framed in the doorway by the dark night sky.

'Mary,' Paul said, weakly. He threw his hands open, gesturing towards Moses.

Mary took a moment, narrowing her eyes. She didn't say anything, but I saw her eyes flicker from one of us to the next, taking in the needle and the napkin. Moses didn't look at her, he was looking down at his feet, but the rest of us did, as though expecting her to know what to do.

'I'm doing this,' I said, pointing to the needle. Mary sniffed, and walked over towards me, and resting her hands on her knees, she bent over to peer at Moses's stomach.

'Can you do it?' I wanted her to take the needle. My hands were covered in his blood, drying now, sticky and thick.

'You are doing it,' she said. 'Carry on.'

She lifted Moses's face up towards her and frowned at him. He smiled at her, and she made a 'tsk' noise. She stood beside me, watching.

'Well, carry on,' Joseph said, from the other side of the room. I glared at him.

In went the needle again, the yarn was shortening, will I reach the end, how awful to have to tie a knot and rethread the needle. I clamped the skin together, wondering whether I should abandon the neat stitching and make larger, bigger stitches, reaching across like spider's legs through his skin. My hands were still shaking, I had lost sensation in my fingertips from gripping the needle so hard, I thought I might cry. I could feel Mary behind me, watching. I pulled the yarn through, the skin obediently pull up into little pink and black peaks. I looked at Paul who was squatting down at my side, rocking on his feet, his arms wrapped around his knees; he returned my look, watery eyes pleading with me. I thought he wanted to put his arms around me, to lie down on the kitchen floor, wrapped around each other like the spoons in the drawer above our head, to close our eyes and will the world away. He smiled a little, and nodded, telling me to get back to work, so I did. Back in went the needle, clamp skin, pull through.

'Nearly done now,' I said loudly, mostly because I needed to say something to shift this block in my throat but also because I had to hear my own voice in that midnight kitchen.

'Thank you, Mrs Lovell,' Moses said above me.

'I don't think you'll be thanking me when you see what a mess I've made.' My voice sounded light and plastic, even to me. 'All done.' I pulled his shirt down over the wound. 'I don't think it'll last long though. A proper doctor will need to look at it soon, because it's not proper surgical thread, you see, and it will become infected.' I was talking to him as though he were a particularly slow child and I a capable no-nonsense matron. Moses listened and nodded, smiling wryly.

'Something has happened, Laura,' Paul said faintly, beside me. Moses placed his hand over his stomach and looked down at me.

'Thank you. You were very brave, Mrs Lovell.'

'So were you,' I said grudgingly.

'Moses Mvubelo, you must come with me now.' Mary stood with her legs wide apart in front of him. 'This kitchen is not tidy,' she added.

Nobody said anything, Moses got slowly to his feet, his face covered in pain, and Mary offered him her arm. They moved slowly over towards the door.

'Where are you taking him?' Joseph asked, stepping in their way. Mary stopped. I could only see the back of her head, but I knew how she was looking at him. Joseph stood to one side, and they went out the door, across the yard and into, I imagine, Mary's hut.

She was right, the kitchen was a mess. The three of us stood in bloodstained clothing, grouped around the empty chair, small puddles of blood on the floor, a pile of red bandages at its feet together with drops and pools of spilt brandy. I looked about me for something to clean it up with – there was a wrung-out dish-cloth balanced on the sink. I picked it up and squatted down to mop up what I could of the blood and brandy.

'What did you do, Paul?' The words came out carelessly, clear and pure like easily divided raindrops. As I spoke them, I imagined I could see them falling from my lips, down into the alcohol and smeary red marks on the Lovells' linoleum, wondering at how I knew, so certainly, that Moses having been stabbed in the stomach would be, had to be, somehow, Paul's fault.

I could hear Paul's crying, before I looked up. He was standing over by the sink.

'I don't know,' he said, looking down at me, gulping, clenching his hands in front of him. 'I . . . we . . . were in Sophiatown . . . we went for a drink . . . I think I . . . there was a fight . . . Moses got involved, he helped me out . . . he . . .' He was folding and refolding his hands, just like Bridget, panicked and frightened, he had to put one hand out to steady himself on the sink.

'You were taking – doing – radical action,' I said, moving my tongue around these uncomfortable and foreign words.

There was a low rasping noise from the other side of the kitchen. I looked over. Joseph, that noise was Joseph, laughing. He glanced down at me on the floor, stuck both his hands in his pocket.

'Sorry,' he said, not appearing apologetic at all. He took his hands out his pocket and crossed his arms, smirking. The extent of his dislike for me was palpable, I sensed he'd enjoyed this evening, the drama, the blood, the pain, the midnight rush from Sophiatown to here, Moses's groaning, Paul's panic and my flapping about on the linoleum trying to sew Moses's skin together.

'Pass me a bucket or something, I need to wring this cloth out.'

Nobody moved. Joseph stayed on his side of the room with his arms crossed and Paul banged his hand down on the draining board. He was being decisive, again.

'I have to go.' Paul's voice was low and intimate, he was taking deep, steadying breaths. 'I have to leave. It was an accident, Laura, a mistake, but I have to go away somewhere. I can't stay here now, it won't be safe for me.'

The kitchen door was still open, and there was the sound of voices raised in argument, Moses and Mary, I couldn't hear what they were saying but I could hear Mary's voice loud, strong and constant and Moses interjecting every so often.

'I'll come with you.' I sounded almost gay, confident, the words came so easily, such ready, obvious logic. Standing up, I walked over towards the sink, to wring the cloth out, to be near to him. 'I don't mind, what you're doing is important. I know that.'

'No, darling, no, you can't. I don't know where I'm going yet. You must stay here with Mum and Dad, you'll be safe here.'

You must stay here. With Mum and Dad. I am going away. I looked up into his frightened face and stared, and then a moment later, like a slap across the face, I could feel those drumbeats in my body, and I started to shout, pummelling him with my fists, shouting chaotic, filthy things. I threw punches and scratched his face. I was breathless and desperate, I could not be left alone here, I would not survive it, everything had become too out of reach, I was sinking down into this inhospitable land, I needed Paul to keep me up. Paul looked pale and astonished, his hands flew up in front of his face, and then quickly, feebly, pushed me away from him, back towards the chair in the room. I ran from the kitchen, pushing past Joseph who was open-mouthed with shock, and up the stairs to our bedroom.

Lying on the bed with my face pressed against the cold wall, I could hear muffled voices in the hallway and then Paul's steady deliberate steps up the stairs. He sat on the bed, but didn't touch me. I could feel the silence around us, his breathing, the smell of stale alcohol and fear, could hear him turning his knuckles around in his palm, there were bangs and pops in my head, the fireworks at Charlotte's party.

'I'm sorry,' he said. He leant over and planted a kiss on my head, he leant in close and allowed himself to linger in my hair. 'I do love you, Lala. I'm so sorry about everything. I will come back for you, I promise you that. The timing is bad for us, that's all, it always has been. You say you believe in our cause, our fight, then you must understand that I just can't stay now, not now.'

I could not turn to look at him, could not witness this abandonment, but I raised my hand to find his, so he knew that I was trying to understand, trying too to take a stand with him, side by side against his parents, against 'authority' – to be strong for these vague optimistic beliefs. I felt guilty about my display in the kitchen, oddly flattered that he called it 'our fight'.

'Are you going to save someone?' I mumbled into the pillow.

'Am I? I don't know, well, yes, yes that's it, Lala. The downtrodden, the oppressed. Now don't be self-pitying old thing, I'll be back soon.'

I felt his weight leave the bed and at once everything was light and empty and floating. I closed my eyes and felt myself turning round and round with dizzying speed. I crushed my face against the wall, tried to gulp in the musty air of the bedroom, I squirmed and flapped in the bed, opening and closing my mouth, the small dull fish pulled from the cool brown river and on to an impossible, inhospitable riverbank.

Eleven

Robert was sceptical. He poured me huge drinks, though it was early in the morning, narrowing his eyes as he passed them over, nearly neat gins, so strong that I ended up talking too fast, sounding and feeling unbalanced on the pale blue sofa.

'Exactly what happened?' he said, standing close to me, his legs wide apart. 'What did he say to you?'

'He had to go, he said he had to go,' I told them again. My eyes were red and scratchy, my words coming out in an incoherent, disjointed mess, spiralling across the room like bad knitting. 'He said he had to go somewhere, he had to go, he went.'

Bridget was sitting beside me. 'Did you have a row about something?' she asked, prodding my knee with her finger, and trying to smile encouragingly.

'What did he say exactly?' Robert was getting impatient. He turned to Bridget. 'It's a lovers' tiff, Bridge, he'll be back by tonight, tail between his legs.'

'Oh no,' I said, looking up at him, flushed, 'he won't. I promise you, he's really *gone*, gone.'

Robert and Bridget shot a look at each other then, Robert frowning slightly. What to tell them? How to explain it? How even to explain it to myself? I couldn't tell them about Moses, or this fight Paul had had in Sophiatown, not about Joseph or about the 'bread and butter' issues or anything. They would call the police, I knew they would, they would consider it their 'duty', they would say it was all a terrible mix-up, of course Paul must come home and sort it all out. I was still in my nightdress and as I sat there, gripping Robert's medicinal gin, I saw traces of blood around the wrist of my nightdress. I hastily folded the cuff over before either of them saw anything.

'You must have had a row,' Bridget said again, craning forward and showing me her teeth. 'What did you do wrong? When did you have this row?'

'What did I—? Well, we've been having it for a while.'

'Was it all a sham then, this marriage thing? Are you actually married?'

'Yes, Robert, yes, yes.' And I blushed from the lying and the grief. 'He said he had to get away, he's gone to Kenya or somewhere.' I didn't even know where Kenya was, I was hoping it would sound plausible.

'*Kenya?*' Robert and Bridget both said at once.

'Yes, oh, I don't know, does it matter? I don't know,' and then the gin-sodden tears started to fall and Robert raised his voice to me, impatiently.

'Let's go through it again, Laura, from the beginning. You met and fell in love, he brought you here and now *you've had a row and Paul has gone to Kenya?*' He spelt it out with incredulous emphasis, 'Is that right? Would you say that was the correct version of events?'

I nodded and snivelled, wishing I were wearing more than my nightgown. I held up my glass for more gin, unable to meet his disbelieving gaze.

'Well, I don't like to say I told you so, Bridget,' Robert said flatly, and then turned to me. 'I think you've had enough of that,' he said, taking the glass from me.

*

I sat in our bedroom, with the boxes of dusty pamphlets under the bed and all Paul's clothes still hanging in the wardrobe, sitting on our little bed, imagining I could hear Paul banging up the stairs, two at a time, bursting through the door and picking me up in his arms and kissing me. He would be joyful, energetic and amused to find me in such a mess. I am initially cross with him, he is contrite and understanding. He tells me he is sorry, he strokes my hair and whispers in my ear, 'I could never leave you, you're my Lala, how could I ever leave you now that I have found you?' But of course this didn't happen. I sat kicking my feet under the bed, looking about me, wide-eyed, feeling a nerve tinging in the back of my knees, sinking my head in my hands, a swirling mess of indignation and self-pity. I thought of those pale blue spaces I had lived in at the Grange and at school, the coldness of the dormitory floor, of the sound of my father coughing as he walked along a creaky corridor and the tapping of a branch against the schoolroom windowpane. I looked in the mirror propped up on Paul's chest of drawers, stared long and hard at myself, and tried speaking to myself in mature sentences. 'You are a married woman now, Laura,' I said. 'Things are different.' But all I could see was my schoolgirl face, surprisingly suntanned, streaked with tears and the skin around my mouth red raw and all bitten off.

*

Robert was downstairs, making phone calls. He was implacable, insincere, asking if they'd seen Paul, whether he'd come to their place last night. 'No, God no, nothing to worry about. Just trying to track the fellow down, that's all, you know how these youngsters can be. How's Marjorie? Good, we must all get together for drinks soon.' All that false heartiness and booming good cheer, and then the small dark silences between each telephone call, before, 'Yes, yes, Laura's still here, nothing to worry about. Suspect he's just had one too many, doesn't want to show his face for a bit. Naughty boy! But will you ask John if Paul's ever mentioned Kenya or Nairobi to him? Thank you, yes, I'll be here all day.'

After he had exhausted his address book, he called me back downstairs.

'Let's go through it again. Paul told you that he was going to Kenya?'

'Yes, I think so, yes, I think it was Kenya.'

Robert and Bridget sat side by side on the sofa, I stood in front of them. Bridget looked at me with pale watery eyes, her face looked all wrong and badly fitted together. The gin was lurching about inside my empty stomach, I was not sure how long I could keep this up. Bridget had a small plate of sandwiches in front of her, her dress was crumpled, a light smattering of crumbs across her breast; her skin looked old and powdery, folded-over with bitterness and effort.

'Who are these people he's been meeting, Laura?' Robert wanted to know. What the hell has he been up to?'

'I don't know, I don't know anything, I don't know what's happening, I don't understand this place.' I wailed at them, pulling at the sleeves of my nightdress, my bare feet, vulnerable, on the shining wooden floor.

'Go and get Mary, Bridget,' Robert said quietly.

He eyed me up and down. The French windows were behind me, and I wondered whether he could see everything through my pale, loose nightgown; his eyes were fixed on my breasts.

Bridget returned with Mary who stood just inside the door to the dining room. She took us all in with one broad sweeping gaze.

'Ah, Mary,' Robert said slowly. 'It seems Paul has gone off somewhere. Kenya, we think. Do you know anything about this? Did you hear or see anything?'

I had to look at her, I did, I had to plead with her as silently as possible. She met my gaze, I couldn't read her face.

'Master Paul?' she said slowly.

'Yes, come on, girl,' Robert said impatiently, 'do you know anything about it?'

'No, master,' she said, 'I don't know anything.'

He dismissed her with a wave of his hand.

'Well, well, well,' he said, tapping his foot on the polished floor and looking at me. 'I have to say I'm not surprised. Are you, Bridge? I never saw this "marriage" working.' And he made two little dots in the air, to frame the word marriage, as though it were indeed afloat in front of us, insubstantial and untethered. 'Now, whatever are we going to do with you?'

*

A week later, Joseph came to the house, to take me for a drive. Robert was at work, he had been spending a lot of time at work during the last week, grateful to be out of the house, but Bridget was there, shadowing me, and she came to stand next to me at the

French windows in the sitting room, watching Joseph's car come up the drive and grind to a halt.

'Who's this?'

'His name's Joseph, he's a friend of Paul's.'

'But I've never seen him before.'

'Nevertheless, he's still a friend of Paul's.'

'What does he want?'

'I don't know.'

We watched Joseph climb out of his car, look about him, and then come up onto the stoep. He looked nervous. He was wearing a white Aertex shirt and suit trousers, he was unshaven.

'He doesn't look very clean,' Bridget said, sucking her teeth.

'No, I don't suppose he is,' and we exchanged a look of something approaching warmth.

Joseph stood in the dappled light of the stoep, his arms hanging loosely at his sides. He lit a cigarette, he was waiting, he didn't intend to come over towards the front door.

'I'd better go out,' I said, looking around for my shoes, 'Stay here, Bridget. I'll see if he has any news of Paul.'

As I walked across the stoep towards him I was aware of Bridget's moony face pressed against the window, her flowery dress in full bloom, and of her terrible anxiety.

'Want to come for a drive?' Joseph said gruffly, without looking at me.

There was something unattractively boyish about Joseph, awkward and insolent, as though he were always uncomfortably straddling the cusp of adulthood but lacking the skill, the panache, to jump right into manhood. He made me feel quite grown up and sensible.

'Paul's mother's watching us.'

'So?' He threw his cigarette down on the lawn, 'Come on, let's go.'

I turned round and gave Bridget a little wave. I'm not sure what it was meant to convey but it was the best I could muster, and I quickly followed Joseph to his car.

We drove in an awkward silence. I sneaked the occasional look at Joseph, who was gripping the steering wheel very hard and looking steadfastly ahead of him. I wondered whether Joseph had ever taken a girl out for a drive before. Looking at his scowling face, and feeling the lack of conversation, I decided probably not, I hoped not, for her sakes anyway. She would have had a terrible time, with him barking questions at her and smirking, and saying things like, 'Well, what do *you* want to do? We *could* go to the pictures if you really wanted to,' and she'd have spent the whole time thinking to herself, 'But *he* asked *me* out, why is he so cross?'

'He's gone,' Joseph said eventually, without looking at me. He reached forward and picked a packet of cigarettes off the dashboard and threw them into my lap. 'Have one,' he said, and then more gracefully, 'if you want.'

'Where's he gone to?'

'Jeez, you're calm. Last time I saw you, you were, well—' and he shook his head, as though still shocked.

'Last time you saw me, I had just stitched up a man's stomach,' I said tightly. 'How is he anyway?'

'Moses? All right, I think. He's disappeared for a while too.'

We drove on in silence.

'Where do you want to go then?'

'As far away from here as possible.'

*

'This is what happened,' Joseph said, sitting behind his desk and putting his hands behind his head. He had driven us to the university, and invited me up to his room. I suspected that he wanted to be around his own things, and I was right because when we walked into his room — masculine, book-lined, piles of paper heaped on his desk and across the floor — he visibly relaxed and seemed more at ease with himself.

He and Paul, he told me, leaning forward across his desk, were in the process of forming a white liberal pressure group interested in 'direct action', he called it a 'Johannesburg operative', explaining that the Communist Party of South Africa had decamped to Cape Town, they were also 'sort of communists'. He whispered that last word when he said it. That night he and Paul had gone to Sophiatown, to a shebeen, they'd been drinking and trying to chat to the natives. 'We were trying to gather information,' Joseph said, pompously, looking pleased with himself.

'Was it the same place we went to?' I asked him.

He was irritated by the interruption. 'What? No, no, somewhere different. You wouldn't know it, lots of journalists go there.'

Joseph said everything had been going fine but then there was the sound of shouting and screaming outside, and he and Paul had gone out to see what the noise was. A truck, full of young white boys, was driving slowly though Sophiatown, the boys were leaning out the windows, out the back of the truck, shouting and jeering, they were drunk and shooting rifles into the air. The street had emptied, emptied except for Paul and Joseph standing there, staring. Paul had wanted to leave, he'd pulled Joseph away and they had run back down through the alleyways to where Joseph's car was parked. Just as they were about to get into the car, the truck had turned a corner and come bumping down the road towards them, still with the boys shouting and firing shots into the night air. Joseph got in the car and started the engine, but Paul had stood, caught in the glare of the truck's headlamps. Then the truck had slowed down beside them; there was a group of eight or nine boys in the back, they threw a bottle of beer at Paul, who caught it. 'They wanted us to go with them, they said they were just riding through the streets, looking for some sport.' They were beery but genial, singing songs, shouting out into the night. Joseph thought they were harmless and waved at them, letting the engine turn over and over. He had guessed that they were a Broederbond group, he thought they looked young.

'Who are the Broederbond?'

'Oh,' Joseph said lightly, 'they're like an Afrikaner Boy Scouts group or something.'

I didn't tell him that I had never seen, and didn't imagine I would ever see, Boy Scouts in the back of a truck, drunk and firing rifles in the air. Joseph then looked uncertain for the first time. He started to fiddle with papers on his desk in front of him.

'Paul panicked, he reached into the car, and got our pistol out—'

'You have a pistol?'

'Yes, it's in the car. He took it out and then he fired it, I don't know what happened — it all went crazy for a moment. I was yelling at him to get in the car, but they all jumped out of the truck and started running over towards us, and I was trying to reverse the car, but Paul was shouting, he was scared, man, really scared, and then he ran. I didn't know what to do.' Joseph looked up at me, hostile and uncertain. 'I started to drive away.'

'You left him?'

'Well, I was planning our escape route,' he coughed, unconvincingly. 'I saw Paul running down one of the alleyways, and three or four of them were following him, so I drove around to the other side. I couldn't see him, the place was empty, deserted. I didn't know what to do, I was frightened too.'

And then Paul had run towards Moses's house, he didn't know what drew him there, perhaps it was just that Moses was the only person he knew in Sophiatown – he had been to a meeting once at the house – and these boys had followed him, and when Moses had come out of his front door, to see what all the fuss was about, one of these boys had produced a knife, and ignoring Paul they had stabbed Moses, then and there, on his own porch, and then these others had laughed and whooped and run off back down the alleyway towards their truck.

'Paul came to find me,' Joseph finished, having the decency to look a bit sheepish, 'he knew where I'd be. We didn't know what to do, so we put Moses in the car and brought him to you.'

'To me?'

'Yes, Paul said you would know what to do,' he said, with his now familiar sneer.

My personal loss was nothing to Joseph, he lived for the cause, a cause anyway. He told me, with some relish, that he believed radicals shouldn't have families or love affairs, that it was patriarchal and bourgeois – had I ever heard of the concept of free love? He thought Paul soft for marrying me, had suspected his commitment, had been surprised and appalled by Paul talking of love having a place in the world.

'He said that, did he? That he loved me?'

'Well, we were talking on larger issues, Laura, metaphorically, do you know what that means? We were considering the bigger picture.'

I hated him. He loved the sound of his own voice, didn't care that I had only the slightest idea of what he was talking about. I wanted us to talk about Paul, where he was, how he was, when he'd be coming back – but he only wanted to sit back and share his thoughts on historical determinism with me. Later, much later, when I knew Moses Mvubelo better, he told me that nobody took Joseph seriously. He said he was a schoolboy. Moses taught me more about politics in one afternoon than Joseph ever did.

'Tell me about Paul,' I insisted, 'that's all I want to hear about. I need to get this straight. It was an accident? You were in Sophia-town having a *drink*?'

Joseph looked uncomfortable and shrugged his shoulders and nodded.

'Paul's gone away. We know people.'

'But—' I faltered, 'that wasn't very heroic, was it? I mean the accident, the running down the streets, the being there to have a drink?'

And in spite of myself I knew I was pleading with him, though perhaps I didn't want him, just then, to give me the truthful answer to my question.

'Laura,' he said, 'the revolution must require that we give ourselves in a variety of ways.'

I waved my hands in front of him, more irritated than upset. 'So I can go to Paul? I'll go and join him.'

Joseph coughed, annoyed to be talking about this, and probably by my impudent hands.

'No, I don't think so. He wants to be away for a while.'

'I'm going to join him.' I was making Joseph nervous but I didn't care. 'I will not stay here and live with his parents.'

'Do you want to go back to England?'

'No, Joseph, I do not want to go back to England. Mr and Mrs Lovell ring the Union Castle offices every day to see when I can book a passage, they want me out of their house. I just want my husband back, I want to be with my husband. That's all I want.'

I started to cry, which terrified him. He searched about on his desk for a tissue which he knew didn't exist but it gave him something to do with his hands.

'What am I going to do?' I was panicked in a way I hadn't been for a week, I had held myself together in front of Robert and Bridget, but now I was unravelling, fast, I wished it were not here with Joseph in his study, but I couldn't help that. 'What is going to happen to me?' I shouted at him.

'I'm not really responsible for that,' he said, playing with his papers again.

I looked at him through my tears. Here was the sum hope of any possibility of a free life, little-boy-Joseph who sat behind his big desk, talking about politics and metaphors.

'Listen up, Joseph, I will not leave this room until you find me somewhere to live. I will camp out here. I will not go back to that house with those people who hate me. I will not. So there. And if you don't find me somewhere to live, somewhere *on my own*, I will go to the police and tell them everything you have told me. Is that quite clear?'

Two weeks later he found me a house.

PART THREE

Gay's Diary

July 1947, Durban

I think my parents behave like poor people now. My mother goes to work at her blasted dry-cleaner's every day, and she and the other women have to work these big machines, and the whole place smells of steam and of the chemicals they use. She likes it, she says to me, 'Come on in with us, Eileen, we have a good time. The other women are so friendly,' and she's there with her sleeves turned up, working in the dark, night and day, loving it all. She's always wanting to work, to pretend we're poorer than we are. It's perverse.

What a one-horse piece of shit this place is. The port is tiny compared to Liverpool, but seemingly still full of sailors. There are plenty of ports in South Africa, they say. There is an esplanade with palm trees and a long, wide golden beach, with white surf. The wind is always up here.

I have tried to contact the man in Johannesburg I sent my telegram to. His secretary says she doesn't know who I am, and then my money started to run out, because I didn't have much, I was using a public telephone in a bar, and I said, 'Oh, the line is very bad, I'll call you back.'

I have a life of daytimes and a life of night-times. Sometimes they meet in the middle. We are staying in a flat the size of a storage cupboard, it is bare and squalid. My mother is so happy! She and Dad are out a lot at work, and he is working strange hours, so sometimes we pass when one of us is on the way out and the other on the way in. They are humiliating me. They said, 'We won't give you any money, Eileen. You can stay here with us, but we won't pay for you. You must work. That's all there is for you, work.'

In my daytime life I read newspapers left on cafe tables and look for acting work. I like to wander down Grey Street, it's a strange buzzing place, with buildings like temples with columns and colonnades. There's shops selling every kind of Indian thing, dresses, vegetables, bookstores, jewellery. You can walk about unnoticed, it's busy and smelly and colourful. I half close my eyes sometimes and just wander about, bumping into people, feeling the ground beneath my feet, looking at the piles of spices and dried herbs, the dark women with their pink veils and necklaces and jewellery, all busy with baskets and the deep husky smell of things.

In the night-time life I wander through the bars, getting drunk with sailors, they are always happy to buy me a drink. I tell them I am like them, I too have served in the army or the navy or whatever, and they fall about laughing and push their hats up on the backs of their heads. 'I have been in France and Germany,' I tell them, but then I stop, what's the point, what do they care, they don't buy me drinks to hear my war stories after all, do they? We drink beer and sing, and sometimes I let them put their hands up my dress, just for the fun of it, just to feel something happening against my skin.

Tuesday
Tried to get through to the man at the South African Broadcasting Corporation again. I spoke to his secretary again, we hate each other now. 'I've told you, Miss Gibson, he's very busy. Send in your photograph and CV, then we'll be in touch.'

'My photograph?' I shouted down the phone at the prissy bitch. 'I thought it was RADIO.'

Wednesday

I went to a photographer's studio today. He was a young man, nice, with an easy air about him. He had a potted plant for me to sit next to, and some old rocking chair to sit in. 'Oh no,' I told him, 'I don't want that. I want Hollywood,' and he laughed.

'Are you an actress then?' he asked.

'Yes. I'm going up to Johannesburg, but I need to take some photographs with me. I haven't any money to pay you, but when I get to Johannesburg I'm going to work on the radio, I can wire you the money then.'

'I know a man here in Durban, he's looking for actresses,' he says. He turned most of the lights out, and I could feel my eyes getting narrower and narrower as his flashgun goes off in my face, cracking and breaking into little exploding parts. 'Do you want to do it like that then?' he says eventually, his voice thick and tired in the blackness. 'Agh, you need to take something off, dear, nothing is ever for free. Your top, your skirt, I don't mind which.'

Thursday

I'm being followed. I'm sure of it. I walked along the promenade today, feeling the salt in my hair, watching the waves whip up and crash down below the wall. I could feel someone behind me, sense them, following my footsteps, I could feel them on the hairs on the back of my neck. I spun round a few times, to catch them out, but when I turned, there was nobody there. I did this all day. I wandered, I could feel it, for sure, somebody, but then when I stopped in the park in front of the town hall, or on the corner of West Street and pretended to pause by a shop window, to catch a reflection, there was nobody there. But I know he is there. I can feel him.

Twelve

There was a note on the hall table, it sat on top of a school exercise journal, and an old damaged book, whose pages were falling out the sides, browned and frayed. The note was written in brown ink in exquisite Edwardian copperplate handwriting. '*Read this book*,' it said. '*I have built my garden on Thunberg and Masson's botanical discoveries. I believe a gardener has been found – watch him like a hawk. Spare keys are in the kitchen. Everything works as you would expect. Yours, Mrs C. Richardson. PS Leave everything as you found it. I will be in touch.*'

My cardboard suitcase was in my hand, the door was open, I had come straight in. Joseph had brought me to this house, but he hadn't wanted to come in, in fact he'd wanted me to know that I was wasting his precious time, and that he was worried about his car, as he hadn't many petrol coupons, and hadn't been planning on ferrying me about the suburbs. There were shadows and damp patches on the walls in the hall, I looked about me, it was grey and quiet.

*

I spent a day sitting and holding my toes. I had to prove to myself that I was real, that I could feel my own body, because nothing I touched seemed solid, as though everything was fluid and changing, dripping. I sat on the floor in the kitchen holding my feet and staring at a yellow corner cupboard, and then I went to the bedroom and wrapped myself up in Mrs C. Richardson's old-lady sheets, listening to dogs barking far away in the night. I wore my clothes in bed, it didn't seem to matter whether I changed or not. I lay in bed and waited for the sun to come drifting in through the old faded curtains in the bedroom. Then I went back to the kitchen again, and boiled the kettle. I loved the smell of the gas, the clinking of one old teacup in a saucer. I took my tea outside and sat on the front-door step and surveyed the garden, this extraordinary, terrifying garden. I closed my eyes in the pale light, opened them again, watched the birds gather at the bottom of the garden. Sometimes I thought I saw Paul, walking up the garden towards me, marching his way through the thick, green undergrowth, and I had to blink quickly to see if he was real and then, in a second's passing, the image of Paul dissolved away, back into the shadows of the day. It was very quiet.

*

It was a widow's bungalow, creaking with emptiness and old age. Mrs C. Richardson had simple tastes – all plain linoleum floors and heavy, dark European furniture and bare, stained walls. It smelt of soil, damp and neglect. The next afternoon I picked up the school exercise journal and the book off the hall table; the gold lettering on the spine had almost rubbed off, but the title page declared itself as *Travels at the Cape of Good Hope* by Carl Paul Thunberg. Mrs

229

Richardson's handwriting covered the margins – I could barely read what she'd written but the journal was more legible. On the first page was a detailed plan of her garden; on the following pages descriptions of plants, hopes and expectations for each, and a code marking their whereabouts. I took my first walk through the garden – a double plot, terrifyingly full – and all her descriptions and classifications made me quite dizzy. I could barely make head nor tail of any of it; euphorbia, agapanthus, clivia miniata, Amaryllis belladonna, Amaryllids. The Irids: gladioli, freesias, crocosmias, ixias – next to this last she had written: 'Cuttings of the *Ixia viridiflora* brought from W. Cape. Turquoise-green flowers. Not yet flowered.'

I had never seen plants such as she had before, some were tall and sleek, with overhanging branches, a whole area of 'succulents' in the middle of the garden where the lawn should have been, some tiny little ones, like pebbles, lots of knobbly and threatening-looking cacti, and then a couple of taller trees with candles hanging off them – the *Euphorbia grandicornis*. I followed a small path through the garden, dense with plants. I couldn't see the house once inside the plants, everywhere were strange, huge bushes, heavy verdant leaves, and then something abrupt and alarming would appear; an old gnarled plant reaching out across the path towards me or vines hanging down near my neck, trees whose branches stretched across the path towards one another, darkness.

Back in the kitchen, I sat on the chair that creaked when you rocked it from side to side. I had stopped crying, I thought I had cried myself out. Night after night at the Lovells' house, I had wept and thrashed about the bed, I had cried at breakfast and at the supper table. Robert had been impatient and cross, Bridget had slapped me once, across the face. 'You must pull yourself together,' she'd said. 'This won't do. You need to make some plans.'

This had been a plan, I suppose. I had insisted Joseph find me a house, and he had come back triumphant one night, sitting in his car outside the house, waiting for me to come out to him.

'I've found you somewhere. Someone at Wits knows a Mrs Richardson. She has to go overseas on urgent business – called away by her daughter or something. You can house-sit for her – apparently she's something of an amateur botanist.'

It didn't seem much of a plan, sitting in this strange house in a suburb I didn't know. I had no plans, I had no idea what to do, what would happen, what to expect. Where was Paul? Was he coming back? I could hardly even ask myself these questions. All was foreign and I was abandoned.

★

When he arrived, I didn't recognise him through the window. I could only see a black man in gardening overalls and I didn't go out because I was too nervous. I watched him from the kitchen window, and eventually he stopped hammering on the door and went out into the garden. I could see him at a near bed, squatting down, not moving. At noon he came back to the back door and banged on that. I didn't have much choice but to open it.

'You know me,' he said. 'Don't be frightened. It is Moses Mvubelo, Mrs Lovell. I am to be your gardener.'

'Oh Moses!' I wanted to hug him, I nearly did, but he took a few steps back away from me. 'How are you? How's the—' and I nodded at his stomach.

'Doing just fine, Mrs Lovell. May I have a drink?'

'Yes, yes, of course, come in, come in.'

Moses followed me into the kitchen.

'What would you like? Tea? Coffee? Beer?'

'A glass of water will do fine.'

He was an unsmiling presence, awkwardly standing near the table, not wanting to touch anything. I fetched a glass for him and filled it at the tap.

'Here we are then, back in another kitchen! We must stop meeting like this,' I said too loudly.

'I am staying in the boy's room, over there.' He pointed out the back of the house.

'The boy's room?' I passed Moses the glass, ashamed to see my hand was shaking slightly. 'Is it all right? Would you rather stay in the house?' I don't know why I said it, I knew there was only one bedroom in the bungalow, I didn't want Moses sleeping in the sitting room. He frowned as he drank the glass of water. 'I mean, is there anything I should be doing? Do I need to pay you your wages? Get food or anything?'

'No, I have my wages sorted out with Joseph. He got me this job.'

'He did? He got me this house too. He has been busy.' I was laughing, trying to be friendly.

Moses wiped his mouth and set the glass down on the table. He stroked his beard for a moment, and picked at the cuff of his fraying shirt, poking out from under the overalls.

'You must not trust him, Mrs Lovell. Joseph is not to be trusted. He is a bad man, up to no good. We do not trust the English. You are different because you are ignorant of this country. I will tell you what we say, we say the English smile at you with their front teeth but chew you with their back teeth. Why are you here, Mrs Lovell? You should be with your in-laws, showing your husband what a good wife you are by looking after his parents.' He frowned again. I wasn't sure where to put myself, I didn't know whether I should

232

ask him to sit down or not. I was pleased to know he would be staying but unsettled by the idea too. I could feel his skin on my fingers, smell his blood and the brandy curdling together, hear Paul's heavy breathing and the sharp jag of the needle pricking my thumb when my grip slipped. I thought that perhaps Moses blamed me, for everything, blamed me because Paul was not there to blame. I was frightened by the idea that we were living here together, and that he was angry with me.

'You know that thing you said about the English? Well, that is rather how I feel about Bridget and Robert.' I sounded faint and weak, it was my attempt at a joke, to lighten the atmosphere.

He shook his head, looking down at the now empty glass on the table, folding his arms across his chest.

'Why shouldn't I trust him? Not that I do, not at all, I've never liked him, he sneers when he talks to me. Do you find he does that to you? Sneer, I mean.'

Moses looked at me and smiled quickly, gravely. 'I must get back to work now,' he said. 'Thank you for the water.'

People come in the dark, at night, to see Moses. I think I can see them trudging up towards his hut at the back of the house, never more than four or five, they are quiet and always come very late, in the early hours of the morning sometimes. They never disturb me and I never mention it to Moses.

*

For the first week I saw nobody but Moses and then Joseph turned up early one evening, offering to take me out for a drive, as though I were a dog or a spoilt child who couldn't entertain herself. He drove very slowly, saying he had to save on petrol, and he kept the headlamps turned down too, putting his arm across the back of my seat and driving with one hand. I couldn't tell him he had to drive with two hands because he drove so damn slow. We never got out of the car, we just chuntered along though the northern suburbs, Sandton, Bryanston, Sunninghill, smoking cigarettes.

'Have you heard from Paul? Where is he? When is he coming back?' But he didn't have an answer to these questions, he just shrugged his shoulders and shook his head.

'As soon as I know, you will know,' he said.

But then he started to ask me questions too. He wanted to know if people were coming to the house to visit Moses, if I ever saw strangers in the garden. I told him that I hadn't seen strangers, no, but he wouldn't be deterred.

'Did you know it's against the law for more than twenty miners to be in a room at once? That's why I think they might be coming to your house, it would be the last place anyone would think to look. You can tell me, I got Moses this job, I got him the pass. Paul said you cared about our cause Laura, he said you were *surprisingly* interested, he would want you to tell me.'

'I think I'd know if I had twenty miners in my kitchen, wouldn't I?' And I wound down the window to smell the sweet autumn air and to turn my face away from Joseph.

*

After two weeks, two weeks of eating all the tins in Mrs Richardson's cupboards, Robert and Bridget had a fit of conscience and arrived on the doorstep. On the morning I left their house, defiant in coat and with cardboard suitcase, I had given them my address. 'You don't have to come and visit me,' I told them, 'it's so you can forward any letters from Paul, please, if they come.' I had been measured and calm, but all hell had broken out, Bridget had grabbed my suitcase and tried to snatch my hat off my head. 'Where do you think you're going?' she'd shouted. 'You can't just waltz off out of here.' I'd stamped on the floor and told her that I knew I wasn't wanted, and that I had made 'plans' as she had suggested. The daft thing was, I'd then walked out of the house, but Joseph wasn't due for another hour and I'd had to hide down the bottom of the drive, behind a hedge, until he came.

Bridget had brought a chocolate cake with her, she fussed about Mrs Richardson's kitchen, wiping down the table, and looking nervously at the sink and the plate cupboard. She said their house felt very strange with 'no children in it' and wasn't I a 'lucky girl' to have landed on my feet this way. She didn't say she was sorry for having slapped me. I cut up the cake into big slices and we sat at the table eating them, while Robert prowled around the room, asking me if I was happier now I was living here, in this, well, this, he waved his arm around and couldn't finish his sentence.

'Yes,' I told them, 'I think it's for the best.'

'It's just we realised, Laura, that you're not old enough,' Bridget said, sucking some of the icing off her finger, 'I mean, we keep forgetting how young you are.'

'I don't feel very young,' I told her, but I lied. I did. I was pleased to see them for all that I pretended I wasn't. I very much doubted my chances of success living here in the widow's house, watching miners walking across the garden late at night to visit my gardener. Bridget said her friends had been asking after me, and she started to cry, she said that this situation seemed 'so wrong' to her and that people were saying wasn't it just a little bit eccentric for me to be living here alone. She said she felt 'responsible' for me. I was sitting on the creaking chair, rocking it from side to side, listening for the bends and cracks in the wood.

'You never liked me,' I said to her. 'You put us in separate bedrooms. You never believed in Paul and me.'

'Oh, now that's not true,' she retorted, reddening slightly. 'But we did just wonder whether you'd changed your mind. We're still happy to buy you that ticket home, Laura, first class if you like?'

'No, Bridget, I'm not going. I'm going to wait for Paul.'

'But he's gone, you told us. He's gone.' Bridget started to look tearful again, and Robert came over and handed her his handkerchief. 'We should have told you, I feel bad that we didn't tell you, we didn't know what to do.'

'You should have told me what?'

'About Paul,' she said, the handkerchief over her mouth, stealing a look at me. 'It wasn't just Robert being mean, the separate bedrooms, he wanted to give you time to change your mind.'

'Let's take a walk around the garden,' Robert said hastily.

In the garden Robert pulled me to one side and said, 'I don't want you to suffer, Laura. I told you Paul was useless and this is his mess to sort out, but in the meantime I've set up an account for you at Thrupps, you only need to ring and order your groceries and the boy will deliver them here.' I started to thank him, but he interrupted me with an impatient shake of the head, then he leant in closer and whispered in my ear, 'I will be expecting something in return, Laura.'

'What did she mean, "We should have told you"?'

Robert looked me up and down slowly; he was considering what to say. 'You can guess,' he said eventually, 'he's a bit, you know,' and he tapped his finger against the side of his polished head and smiled at me, knowingly.

'*Mad*, do you mean?' My hands were flat against the sides of my legs; I felt a chill run across my neck and down the insides of my arms. It seemed to settle under my elbows. I blinked at Robert in the pale sunlight.

'Well, not mad, no. Just well—' and he shrugged and started to walk away from me, but before I could defend Paul against this latest accusation, Bridget screamed.

'What are those?' She was standing next to a monstrous-looking plant in the succulents area, all big and brown and gnarled, covered with peduncles and raised red areas – like sores. She was peering at it, horrified, her mouth wide open, her face itching with revulsion. I looked it up on the plan.

'It's a *Euphorbia filiflora*,' I told her.

'Well, I think it's horrible. Whatever is Mrs Richardson doing having one of those in her garden?'

At that moment I resolved to like the garden more. I decided that it reflected Mrs Richardson's independence of spirit, and I was sorely in need of some of that.

*

Joseph had come on another of his visits. He stood in the kitchen, looking out the window towards Moses's hut.

'Is he in there?' he asked impatiently.

'How do I know?' I was sitting at the table, a bottle of beer in front of me.

'Have you seen people coming here?'

'Why do you keep asking me that? Joseph—' I picked up the beer and took a swig. I had never drunk from a bottle before, it felt rebellious and masculine, I liked it. 'Is Paul a bit?'

and I made the same tapping gestures against my head that Robert had made.

'What? What do you mean?'

'Is Paul, a bit, well, *simple*?'

Joseph laughed and shook his head. He picked up his jacket from the chair he'd thrown it over. 'I've got to go. This place can do funny things to you, Laura, I've seen it before, it plays with people's heads.' And he stared at me while he was putting his jacket on, 'If anybody is a bit,' and he tapped his head, 'it's *you*. You do know that, right?' and he laughed again, and strode out the house, banging the front door after him.

*

I wonder at myself always sitting in houses and gardens. I wonder at how restricted I seem, how incapable of breaking out into the wider world. I accept that I am young, that I gave up my parents' home for some other parents' home, I handed myself over as a wife before I'd even had the vaguest glimmers of who I might be, the me that should be fully realised, mature, capable, functioning on all levels, all the parts fitting together and coloured-in. But still I am here, in another house, ring-fenced by another garden, yet another road at the bottom, and no means to get on it and embrace the world. I decide I will walk down the road, it is my first step towards freedom. I fancy that I will go out of the garden on to the road and find a neighbouring house. I will walk up to that house and introduce myself. 'Hello,' I will say, 'I am house-sitting for Mrs Richardson. I thought I'd pop in and say hello. Oh yes, I am from overseas, I am in a foreign country now, I find I do not know myself.' And they will be very pleased to see me, very impressed by my maturity and poise. It will be a friendly and successful thing to do, neighbourly, sociable, something my mother never did. It is a normal thing to do.

I stand outside on the road, looking up and down. I do not know this road, I understand that it joins another one further up, as I remember how Joseph turned down this road when we went out for our cigarettey drive. It is a narrow road, not wide and house-lined like the Lovells', but I know there are houses here, just more spaced apart. I turn left, I walk purposefully along the grassed verge. I can only see bushes and high trees either side of me, the road is deserted, the sky low and cloudy, it is quiet. I reach a high white wall, behind this I suspect there may be a house. I follow the wall, running my fingers against it, waiting for it to break into a gate or a door. I wonder who lives behind this wall. The road is dusty, and my feet are beginning to hurt, but I like the feeling of my fingertips bumping against the wall. And then there it is, the grass verge dips down to nothing, to make way for this driveway. There are two huge iron gates, closed shut. I peer through them, I can see a grey, slated rooftop behind some trees, it looks like a big house, a vast Victorian mansion. I try the gate but it does not open, it must be locked on the other side. I look for a bell but cannot see one, though there is a postbox built into the side wall. I wonder whether I can climb over the gates, I might just be able to, though the top of it has tall spikes. I try one foot on the bottom part, grip my hands above my head, wonder whether it will be possible to pull myself up and get my foot up by the lock and handle. The gates feel secure, the space between the bars is narrow, and it hurts my foot already, squeezed in there, the side of my foot bedding down into the iron. With one mighty heave I pull myself up, grappling to pull myself higher, finding the lock to balance my toe on, now suspended in air, clinging to the bars, wondering how I will manage to go further and vault over the top.

'Excuse me, but what are you doing, Mrs Lovell?'

Still hanging on tight, I tried to turn my head, and caught sight of Moses below me. He was wearing his gardening overalls, a brown pullover and a knitted hat, stamping his feet and blowing on his hands.

'Oh Moses,' I said, 'I thought I'd visit the neighbours, but the gates were locked.'

Moses looked up at me, frowning, he didn't move. 'He doesn't want to touch me,' I thought. 'He is appalled at the idea of being near me.'

'I just thought it would be a normal thing to do,' I told him, trying to smile.

'Normal? Come on then, I will help you down if you like.' He stepped forward, and held up his arms. Was I supposed to fall into them? I wanted to, very much. I wanted to let go of the iron bars, and fall back, without a thought or a care in the world, to fall freely through the air into his strong, overalled arms. In the end, Moses had to pull one of my feet out from between the bars, where it was stuck, and sort of hold it while I tried to lever myself down, sliding and burning my hands on the gates. He should have supported me by touching my bottom, but of course he wouldn't have done such a thing.

We walked back towards Mrs Richardson's together. I felt foolish and I could tell he was annoyed with me.

'When I first came out here, to Johannesburg I mean, me and Mrs Lovell, the other Mrs Lovell, went to a luncheon at the club, and this old woman there, a Lady Someoneorother, told me this place was poisoned, that's what she said, the ground is poisoned. Do you think it's true?'

'No,' he said quietly, without looking at me. 'It is a beautiful country. But at this time, there is not another white woman walking along the road talking to her African gardener, like we are. That is the poison in this place, Mrs Lovell. You should know, I am not a gardener, I am a lawyer,' and he looked over at me then, sternly, measuring my response.

'Oh.' I wasn't sure what to say.

'Does Joseph ask you many questions about me?'

'Yes.'

'He is spying on me. I have taken this job because it is necessary and useful, and because I think I know what he wants. I work for an organisation which is non-European. Joseph and his friends are very interested in our organisation, they would like to be a part of it. They think they should be involved, this is how it is with the white communists in this country, they want to be at our meetings, they want to be in our trade unions, they think they know the best way forward for the African people in this country.'

'Why? Why would he do that?' I said this with a laugh, but I did not feel light inside.

'Your husband should have told you more, I think. I am surprised at him, I would not involve my wife in this way.'

'Are you married, Moses?' It had not occurred to me that Moses might be married. I am curious and, alarmingly, a little jealous.

'No, I am not married, but if I was, I would worry for my wife if she were here alone, without any family around her. We should go inside, I think, and talk, Mrs Lovell, I think I should tell you some things, so you can protect yourself.'

'Oh really, Moses! You do say such melodramatic things.' He sighed, and looked at me. I sensed I was a burden to him, an annoyance.

I felt suddenly cold in my summer dress. 'I'm sorry, Moses, I don't understand. Why are you here?'

'Joseph got me the pass, so I can work and live here. It is better for me, for the time being. We agreed I would come. He wants to keep an eye on me, and we want to watch him too, him and your husband.'

'Oh, I see.'

Moses gave me that kind, pitying smile again.

'Come, let's walk on. I will tell you something. There is a big thing going to happen soon, in early August. It is a strike at the mines along the Reef. You will not feel the impact here in your garden, Mrs Lovell, but if anything should happen to me, they will come here and look for me, they will bang on your door and want to search my room, and perhaps your house too. You are just to say that I am your gardener, you are looking after the house for the old lady, that is all you know. I do not want you to be in any danger. And you must remember that Joseph will want to know things too, he will ask you questions, take you out for more of those drives he likes. You must not tell him what we have discussed today. Can you make me an oath on that, Mrs Lovell?'

'Yes, of course. But Paul would like to be here for that, Moses, he really does believe in all — all this. He wants to free the workers from their chains of oppression, he didn't mean for what happened to you to happen, you know.'

Moses stopped then and looked at me.

'It is good that you believe in your husband, Mrs Lovell, it is fitting.'

'What do you mean by that?' I asked him hotly. 'He does believe that, he wants to be a hero, I mean, he believes in — the ideals.'

Moses paused, wondering whether to continue, then he spoke

to me quietly, without lecturing me, without the wild, unbalanced enthusiasm of Joseph — or indeed Paul.

'Excuse me, Mrs Lovell, but this is not the time for heroes. Do you know why the miners are going to strike next month? Shall I tell you? Because people are starving, Mrs Lovell, all they require is a living wage. Is that so ridiculous? The Chamber of Mines preserve a cheap labour system — of the sort that you have not had in your country since they sent children to work up chimneys. Mrs Lovell, this is the struggle to live as a human being. Do you see that? These miners, these men, have left their homes in the reserves, their children naked and starving. All they ask for is a living wage. It is pragmatic politics of the most basic kind. I mean no disrespect, Mrs Lovell, but your husband and Joseph? They are schoolboys.'

I stared at him, my skin pricked with shame, I was blushing.

'Will it work, Moses?'

'Many will die, the resources of this racist state will be mobilised. But, Mrs Lovell, it will educate a nation. It will be the end of begging and compromising. Enough politics now, we are back at your house. I will go into the garden, and you should go and see if you can find the telephone number for your neighbour's house,' and then he looked at me and laughed.

*

I don't sleep much. I lie in bed listening for footsteps, murmuring voices. I fancy I can hear them outside, in the garden. I imagine hordes of African men squatting down among the succulents, whispering to each other over the spiky leaves. I think I can hear laughter sometimes, I wonder whether Moses is telling them tales about me. Sometimes I get out of bed, to try and drown out the voices, to remove the fear, and I look around the edges of the curtain, expecting to see them, all out there, and perhaps Joseph too, skulking down near the fig tree, his pale face lit by the moon, hiding. But there is nothing, just a darkness and silence. A never-ending unpunctuated silence.

Some nights I think of what is beyond that dark, growing garden. I think of the straight suburban roads I have seen, of the Central Business District, of Sophiatown, the koppies. I think that there is no 'there' in this nowhere city, it is a place that lacks a proper centre, a magnetic heart. I think of the old lady at the club, jabbing me with her fingernail and telling me that there is no room for love here. I think she is right. It is an abject place, without a heart, spiralling out towards the heaps of earth rising up by the mines, peopled by the workers who have left their wives and children, naked and starving in some far-off dusty unknown town. And then Paul, always Paul. What had Robert meant, tapping the side of his head? Did I have to rethink it all, everything? I replay our meeting, our courtship, our sudden marriage in my head, over and over like a tired newsreel, alert for signs of – what? Vulnerability, madness? What? Why had I blushed when Moses had spoken to me about the miners? Because I felt such shame on Paul's behalf? Is that right? Where is he now? I can't see anything any more, or only one thing that this place, this city, is a place for commerce only, a terrible, empty, ungovernable place, which will eat me and spit me out if it can, will defy all intimacy, and then I turn over to find a cool spot on the pillow.

Gay's Diary

July 1947, Durban

I'm sitting on the esplanade, late in the evening, trying to stop my skirts from blowing over my head, looking at the dark sky, thinking and making plans. Mother is on the hunt every day now with her 'telephonist wanted' advertisements and 'shorthand secretary required, apply within' and her 'Oooh, Eileen, I've just seen the thing for you – look at this, they want a personable young lady of excellent reputation to work in the Fisheries Board Office.'

I had a huge set-to with Father last night. He came back from his shift, just as I was going out, and he looks about the flat and says, 'This place is a dump,' and I says, 'Telling me,' and he says, 'You should be looking after it. Your mother and I are working all hours, and when we're not we're down at the Mission, and what are you doing? Nothing, nothing at all,' and I say, 'If you give me the money to get to Johannesburg then I can get some work, there's a job in radio for me there,' and he says, crashing his hands down on the table, 'I don't believe you, I don't believe a word you say. We're not giving you any money. We've made that quite clear. Get a job, make your own money.' And I quite lost my temper with him, what with the banging hands and his raised voice and all that. 'This isn't Banbury Road, you know, I'm not a little girl you can tell what to do any more,' and he says, his teeth all clenched together and the tip of his nose going white, 'Oh no? Is that right, miss? All we want is for you to get out of here, to stand on your own two feet and stop bleeding us dry night and day. Get out, get out of my sight.'

So out I goes, and I'm sitting on a bench on the promenade and I get that feeling again, in the back of my neck. Like I know, I just know there's somebody there, following me and watching me, the same person. I can feel them, like cold fingers running up and down the nape of my neck. So I says loudly, 'You can come out of wherever you're hiding. Come out where I can see you.'

I don't feel nervous or scared, I fairly shout it into the wind. And then I can hear these footsteps behind me, hesitant ones, a few steps then stop, then a few steps more.

'Come round here where I can see you.'

And I keep looking straight ahead, at the moon on the charging high sea, and I think I can hear more steps, but the waves are a noise too, and the wind. And I'm still looking ahead, with one hand in my hair to stop it blowing all over the place. And then this figure comes round the side of the bench, I can feel it before I can see it, and it's dark, he is a shadow or a presence rather than a person. And when I know this person is standing there in front of me, I look up, and it is him.

'How are you finding Africa, Miss Gibson?' he says. He is in a dark overcoat, holding it around him, I can just see the curls on top of his head, dancing in the wind.

'This place seems more like India than Africa, and I should know, I was born in India,' I says. 'I am not finding it all that well, as it happens.'

He walks over to the railings, keeping his back to me, so that all I can see is the outline of his overcoat. He is leaning forward against the railings, both arms out by his sides like he's going to take off. I get off the bench and walk over beside him, there is the moon in front of us, and clouds. I can hear the rasping sound of the wind in the palm trees. The waves crash and break below us on the black sand.

He takes me to a place I've seen but not been in before, he says it is the most famous restaurant in Durban. I don't much want to go there, but when he says it's famous, I think perhaps it's the sort of place I should be seen going to. It's on the corner of Grey Street and Victoria Street, it's called Kapitan's Balcony Hotel. It's a lively place, we sit in the restaurant upstairs, it has painted red walls and little wooden chairs. I'm not hungry, I drink Martinis, but he eats all this Indian food. 'It's delicious,' he keeps saying, trying to push this weird-smelling food at me, 'only vegetables,' he adds, as if that will make a difference. We are the only white people in there – oh no, except for a couple of other men on another table – which is all right, Nobody seems to mind.

'So tell me all about Miss Gibson,' he says, eating fast. I can't be bothered to tell him my life story, it's too long and too complicated, and his attention does seem to wander all the time. I think there's something a bit unglued about him, he keeps drifting off when he's talking, like a wind-up toy winding down, and then he'll turn his hands over and over in front of him and then he'll stroke the top of his head, forgetting what he's talking about. He looks different than I remember him at the Professor's. He looks more lived-in, less enthusiastic and clean. I am a bit disappointed for some reason.

'Why have you been following me?' I am very upfront about it, but I smile when I say it and cross my legs so he can see, and take a sip of my Martini, raising an eyebrow at him.

He looks flustered. 'I needed to get the package.'

'You could just have come right up and asked for it.'

'I was going to – but then – I, just – well –'

'Then you just couldn't stop yourself from spying on me.'

'Yes.' And he looks at me in a slightly pleading way.

Hah! Isn't that curious? Imagine that, just following me about all over Durban, night and day, skulking behind trees and hiding in shop doorways. It's rather flattering when you think of it.

Afterwards, he is suddenly full of energy. He has all these ideas. 'What would you like to do? Have you taken a rickshaw ride yet? Shall we get one? Where do you want to go?'

I tell him I am going to go home for now, but he says he'll come and see me tomorrow. 'I could show you around,' he says. I tell him, 'No, I don't want to look around. I want to get out of here, you can help me do that if you like. What's your name anyway?'

'My name is Paul Lovell,' he says slowly, as though it might mean something to me. I laugh at him and say, 'My name is G-a-y G-i-b-s-o-n,' like that. He doesn't like it when I laugh at him.

Tuesday

He is waiting for me when I come out of our apartment building, over on the other side of the street, reading a newspaper. I stride right over. 'You don't have to follow me about any more, you know,' I says. He is embarrassed, he blushes and looks down at his feet. 'Come on,' I says, 'let's take that rickshaw ride then.'

We get one down near the esplanade and we sit in the back of a sort of chariot, while this African, all dressed up with feathers on his head, picks up the long wooden handles and pulls us along. He can go at quite a pace, running barefoot down the streets, like the dogs of hell are after him. He takes us all the way down West Street, past the huge Victorian buildings, past the hideous town hall, where we see ibis on the grass outside, and then into Albert Park. I like it. I had a bad night, my chest was very tight and I ended up having to sit up straight next to an open window, desperate to suck some of the cold air in through the windows, though in truth it only made me cough more.

'Are you cold?' he says. 'You're a little blue.'

I laugh and say. 'Oh no, I go this colour sometimes.'

And he's sitting beside me in the rickshaw, with his thigh all pressed up beside mine, staring at me.

'You skin is almost transparent,' he says quietly and he reaches over and takes my hand. I let him hold it. I don't know what he's thinking, there's something a bit desperate about him. He's nice-looking, but he's got this watery faraway look in his eyes, he's weak, I think. I can't be doing with his wet eyes and his hand-holding just now. I've got to get something out of this.

We spend the day together, just wandering and talking. I find him quite irritating after a while, he's a bit jumpy, jerky, like I said, unglued. He wants to talk about himself all the time too, I keep yawning and staring off looking at the horizon, but he doesn't seem to notice. He's going on and on about the Indians and something called 'pegging' and meetings he's going to go to, and how he feels more useful down here in Durban than he did in Johannesburg. He's been here for six weeks or so 'trying to establish contacts,' he says. Not that he's actually got anything to do of course, or people to see, he just wants to hang around me and tell me how important he is.

'I need to get to Johannesburg' I tell him eventually, shutting him up. 'There's work for me there at SABC, but I don't have any money. How am I going to get there?'

He just shrugs his shoulders and says, 'I don't want to go back.'

'Did you save that schoolgirl then? The one you made the detour for? The one I wanted you to save?' and he looks at me, very sullen and like he's been caught doing something he shouldn't.

'Yes,' he says slowly, 'but it didn't work out.'

'She didn't want saving then?'

'Yes, but she didn't make the transition very well.'

This makes me laugh, I fairly throw my head back. I slap him on the arm. 'You men,' I say, 'I bet she didn't. Not if she had to put up with you talking on and on about pegging and meetings you never go to and you not even knowing why you married her. I feel sorry for her, I can't see you saving anyone very well.'

'Well, you shouldn't be sorry,' he says, cross.

'Did you run off then? Where is she?'

I feel sorry for the schoolgirl being seduced by him, when he's clearly a bit loose up top and probably a little underdeveloped down below. But then I told him to save her, didn't I? I wanted him to. He doesn't answer me though.

'I tell you what, you take me to Johannesburg, Paul, and I'll give you the package. How about that? It's a trade.'

'But that wasn't part of the agreement,' he says, looking scared.

'You can fuck me too if you like, I'll throw that in for free.'

Thursday August, Durban

Kissing in the wind, pressed up against a wall, desperate. It's like Chalmers all over again. Like he wants to fall inside of me to forget it all, like he can't control himself. He can't talk or think or anything, he just wants me up against the wall but he doesn't know where to put his hands, he doesn't quite know what to do with anything. He thinks this is love, or so he says, beneath the palm trees, and people walking past looking shocked and amused. He couldn't stop himself following me, he said he knew he was meant to get the envelope but he didn't want to approach me. He said, 'I've seen you with the sailors and in the cafes, I followed you to the photographer's and watched you all the time you walked about the city.' He can't believe that he can touch me, he can't stop himself, he says he's never seen a woman so beautiful, he used to look at my neck in the wind, or see the outline of my legs in the breeze and he wouldn't be able to breathe or move for ages after and now he can't believe he's allowed to touch me like this, against the wall.

Oh, for God's sake, I want to tell him, you're not the first and you won't be the last.

'I need to go to Johannesburg. I need to see a man at the South African Broadcasting Corporation. Can you take me there?'

But he's all lost with his hands in my hair. I want to scream at him, just stop it. Answer my question.

'I'll take you anywhere, anything,' he says, 'but not Johannesburg, I can't go back there.'

Friday

Paul is staying in a little hotel on Grey Street. I've moved in with him, I've got to get away from my parents. I said, 'I'll tell you what, we'll spend the weekend in bed, how about that? Then after that we'll go together and buy a train ticket to Joburg.'

I'm writing this in the hotel room now. It's a little steamy place, run by an Indian. Paul has a nice enough room, with two windows looking down on the street below, old wooden floors which smell of polish and shine, an old wardrobe, a big ceiling fan and a little battered desk in the corner. I didn't say anything to Mother or Father, I just packed up my stuff this afternoon and left them a message saying SABC were so keen for me to come, they've paid for my ticket. I said, no hard feelings, I'll contact you as soon as I'm settled.

Paul is nervous around me, but pleased too. He keeps saying, 'Now I know what love feels like, this is love, Gay, between you and me.' And though I should set him straight, I don't, I don't know why he says it, he must know it isn't true. Why say it?

I say to him, 'What does it feel like then? Tell me.' He sits down on the edge of the desk, he looks a bit nervous again, a bit lost, running his hand through the air. I want him to be specific but he can't answer me. Now I've moved into his bedroom at the hotel, he doesn't know where to put himself. He says. 'I haven't that much money, Gay, I live off an allowance from my parents,' and I say, 'Well, that's more than I've got.'

Saturday

Have crept out of the hotel and down to a bar to write this. I had to get away for a bit. It's so bloody simple – he gets to fuck me, he buys me a ticket to Johannesburg. What could be more straight-forward than that? But no, oh no.

I was getting dizzy in the room, feeling nauseated. I couldn't breathe proper. I've got to move him on to Johannesburg, he's got to stop crying in the night. Why does he do that? I don't want to comfort him, I don't want to know about the mess he's made of his life, or how he doesn't seem to see things straight, can't quite organise himself properly, how frightened he is of his father, or how guilty he feels about the schoolgirl he left back at his parents' house. I can feel new beginnings though, I can feel them on my skin, my hair, in my bones. Sometimes it feels like my legs are swelling.

I ask him lots of questions about the schoolgirl, and he thinks I'm jealous and is cagey. I can't imagine being swept off my feet by him. What sort of a person would have traded in her life for him? Why did she trust him in the first place? Did she know that I'd told him to do it, did she know about me? 'What's she like? What does she look like?' I asked him, and he said, 'Not like you. You're beautiful, you're so beautiful I feel like I'm being eaten up on the inside,' and he looked tearful and naked when he said it. He says he is overwhelmed, he doesn't know what to do with himself, he says he thinks I look ill, he thinks he's in love with an ill person. Hah! He's the one who's a bit ill. He is making me be cruel, I can't help it. I can pick him apart bit by bit, it's almost as if he wants me to, is getting a thrill out of it. He cries a lot. Way too much. It's tiring. He goes on about how he is responsible for somebody getting stabbed, how he had to run away from everything. We've been drinking too much, in that sweaty bed, clinging together in the face of it all. He never goes to meetings of course, knows nobody. The hotel receptionist told me he'd been here for over a month, just sitting in his room, she asked me, 'Was he waiting for you then?'

The air gets colder by the day, the wind more ferocious. I take walks in Albert Park when I can, wearing his coat in case Mother or Father see me. I am like a shadow now.

I went along the esplanade today, stopped by the paddling pools they have in front of the sea. I wanted to take all my clothes off, I wanted to jump in them and freeze myself to death, in the water, and the choppy, choppy seas.

Monday

I have missed my monthly. I cannot remember when I had my last. I said this to Paul, just like that. I was getting dressed at the time, sitting on the side of the bed, my back to him. 'I missed a monthly.

I might be pregnant.' There was a silence, I could almost hear him taking in this information. I looked over my shoulder at him, he was standing there looking terrified. 'I really need to get to Johannesburg if I'm pregnant.'

He went on a bit about how we'd only been together for a little while, and how did I know, and I told him I knew exactly when my monthly should be, which was a bit of a lie of course, because I never do know for sure.

'Why else might they stop? What other reasons?'

I looked at him, standing by the window. I almost felt sorry for him, he looked that frightened, that trapped. I just said to him, 'We have to leave this hotel. We have to go to Johannesburg and sort it out.'

'Yes,' he said. 'Yes. We should. Let's go to Laura, she'll know what to do.'

How loopy is that? Anyway, I have my ticket at last.

Thirteen

There is somebody outside the house, no, there are people, many people banging things outside the house. It is night, or very early morning perhaps. I throw back the sheets and sit up, I can hear voices now, and a hammering on the door, the front door. A man is shouting out, he is shouting in Afrikaans, I don't understand what it is he's saying. I am too muffled and clumsy by sleep to put on the light. I find a cardigan at the bottom of the bed and put that on. I can't find any shoes.

Are they trying to break in or are they shouting for me to come out? A dog is barking, insistent, hysterical. I come through to Mrs Richardson's hallway, I find the light switch and turn it on. I can hear banging and knocking — but that is too polite a word — on the front door. A man is shouting loudly, hammering on the door. I come up the other side, he is quiet for a moment, he has seen the light, he knows I am nearby now. I place my palm flat against the door and press my face close to it.

'Who are you? What do you want?'

'It's the police, madam, the police. Open this door.' He answers me in English, but his accent is thick and heavy.

'Just a moment,' I say. I stand back from the door in the hallway, on the little grass mat. I don't know what to do. The policeman is banging on the door. They have come for Paul, they have come to arrest Paul.

'Open up! You, open up, or we'll break this door down!'

He'll huff and he'll puff. The carriage clock on the hall table tells me it is five o'clock in the morning, I can see pale watery light coming in through the sitting-room windows next door.

'You're frightening me, shouting like this,' I say. 'I can't open the door.'

There is silence on the other side. I see the letter-box lid flip open, can just see a stubby finger poking through the slit.

'Madam, we will do you no harm, but you must open the door or we will have to break it down.'

Perhaps he is attempting, in his odd-sounding English, to sound reasonable and unfrightening, but he does not. I can hear footsteps outside, they are walking round the outside of the bungalow, three or four men and a dog, they are banging on the windows. I think they are heading towards the kitchen door. I take two steps forward to unbolt the front door.

'We must search your house.' He is a big man, burly, his face closed, pressed by the responsibility of this task. He is holding a large stick in his hand.

'Why?'

What a flimsy response, how flighty and insubstantial, how like me, in my flannelette nightgown and cardigan and bare feet. My mind is trying to wake up, I am trying to think of a story I might tell them about Paul, about where he is, about his innocence.

'We have orders.' He pushes past me, refusing to be embarrassed, and calls out behind him into the early-morning air, something harsh, an instruction. Or perhaps he is saying, she's opened the door, she is in her nightgown, she is all alone. In the light of the hallway, I think he looks tired, his eyes are red, the skin on his face patchy and rough.

'My men are going to your maid's house also,' he tells me looking around the hallway, banging the stick against his leg.

'I don't want the dog in here,' I say, leaning against the wall, my eyes on his stick. I don't know why I say this, I have nothing against the dog, I am just trying to find a way to resist, to stake my claim on this house, on my rights as a person not to have policemen come barging in the house so early in the morning. Perhaps he will believe the Kenya line, have they already been round to the Lovells'? Will Robert and Bridget appear any minute at the bottom of the drive, or out of the police car looking reproving and self righteous?

'Who is here?'

'Nobody. Just me, and perhaps my gardener in the outhouse.'

'Your gardener? What is his name?'

'Moses.'

'Moses what?'

'I can't remember.'

He accepts this – why would I remember? Another policeman comes in the front door. He looks me up and down coldly, then addresses himself to the first one. He nods, listening, then he turns to me.

'We must search your property, madam.'

'What for?' I can't decide whether I should put up a fight or not – what would there be for them to find? Mrs Richardson's back copies of *South African Country Life*, my cardboard suitcase and a sink of dirty dishes – I am wondering what he might already know about Paul.

'Don't you know what has happened this week?' He looks at me out of the corner of his eye, he is uncertain whether to carry on, but he does in his thick halting English.

'The Kaffir miners have tried to revolt, they have walked through our streets thinking to collect their passes and go home! They thought to walk on the Native Commissioner's Office. They have been beaten, put down, policemen from all over the country have come, they have gone down the mines and beaten the men up to the ground, stoep by stoep. We have crushed this Kaffir revolution, we have put them back in their place. Now, they are in our prisons where they will be tried for treason and sedition. It is a great week for the Union. Now we come for the trade unionists and the communists.' He is looking at me intently, he truly does believe this is a great moment.

This must be why he looks so tired, he has been on duty all week, hitting workers with his stick, raiding their homes, dragging them out into the street and beating them.

'But,' I say quickly and triumphantly, 'my husband has not been here this month. He is away on business. How could he have had anything to do with this?'

The policeman frowns at me, he leans in closer, knocking the stick against his legs.

'Your husband? Who is he? Why would we be here for him?'

I stare at him, I shrug my shoulders, but he has noticed something wrong, he is standing very still, frowning and narrowing his eyes.

'We have come for your gardener,' he says, slowly, watching me.

He continues to watch me. Such a stupid mistake, of course — hadn't Moses warned me? — and now I have to warn him somehow. I know he is here, I saw a candle lit in his room last night, the first time in a week. I don't know what is the best way to do this. I decide to speak very loudly,

'What do you want with him? He isn't a miner. He's not anything, he is just my gardener.'

'You think so? He is a revolutionary. Perhaps you are a *Kaffir boetie?*'

'I don't know what that means.'

'It means you are a Kaffir lover, a lover of the Kaffirs,' the other policeman says, trying out his English too, prompt and proud with this translation. They look at one another and laugh. They are excited to think about me in this context.

'Perhaps you think the blerry native deserves to be well treated? That is like the English, but then you come to us and say,' he adopts a whining, plaintive tone, 'oh my house boy has stolen from me! My native girl has taken my things! You don't understand the Kaffirs as we do, you must keep them down in their place and they will be grateful for it. Agh, you make me sick, man.'

The other policeman nods in agreement – clearly I make him sick too.

'Search the house if you have to, you'll find nothing here. I'm going to make a cup of tea.'

I walk away from them towards the kitchen. I need to get out the kitchen door into the yard and over to Moses's hut before they do. I close the kitchen door after me and run across towards the back door. In a matter of seconds I have unbolted the door and am out in the yard, it is cold and the concrete feels shockingly hard against my bare feet.

But I am too late. Another policemen is there leaning against the far wall, smoking a cigarette, the dog at his side. He looks up at me in surprise. A black policeman comes out of Moses's hut, he has a big stick in his hand, then the white policeman goes over to him, they whisper something to each other, then the black policeman goes back into Moses's hut and quickly returns dragging Moses out along the ground. He drops him in the yard at the feet of the other policeman, who gives Moses a quick, disdainful kick.

I rush over to Moses, kneel down and try to turn him over onto his back. He is unconscious, his face almost unrecognisable from swelling and bruising. I can see a thin line of blood appearing on his shirt across his stomach, it is the old wound, it must have reopened during the beating, I want to sew it again. I look up at the two policemen. The black policeman will not meet my gaze, but the other one, with the cigarette and the dog, is frowning at me.

I don't know what to do for Moses. I pat his cheeks, I want to bandage that old wound. Somehow I think this is all because of Paul, all because of me and Paul and the poison of this place which has ruined everything, I am hysterical, I think I am shouting in the cold yard, I don't know what, I think my words are bouncing off the walls around me, I am crying, I can't let them take Moses, if they do I will be all alone and I will not survive, not here, not alone. Somehow that stomach wound, which we tried to sew up, is important, I don't know why, but it is significant, it was a good thing, it was an attempt to put right Paul's mistake, and Moses had been brave, he had been gracious, he had thanked me even though I had done a bad job.

The policeman from the front door arrives in the yard, with his sidekick. They sent four men and a dog to beat Moses? The men stand around staring at me, on my knees, by Moses's side. I press my hand across the old wound, I can feel his blood between my fingers, thick and warm.

'We are taking him to the van,' the sergeant says.

I want to stop them taking Moses, I wanted to stop them beating him. I do not want to be alone here in this strange house, I want Moses to have succeeded, more than anything I want Moses to have done something good, something which will have made sense of Paul, and this place, and me. I try to fight them off, wildly hitting out, crying, feeling my feeble wrists bouncing off their uniforms, but one of them pushes me aside, hissing at me, and I stagger over by the wall.

When they drag Moses by his feet towards the van, his head bumping on the concrete, I think I see him open an eye, just for a moment, and that his dark eye meets mine, and that his look is hostile and accusing.

Fourteen

I couldn't think of anyone to call, except Robert. I fairly hissed at him over the telephone.

'You must come, Mr Lovell, please, come today. And Robert, I need all the newspapers from this week, please can you bring them?'

'What's that?' he said. 'The line is bad. You want some newspaper? Yes, I was planning on coming over this afternoon. I have something for you.'

Robert brought me a car. It was outside on the driveway, large and obstinate, shiny grey. I could see it from the window as we sat in the kitchen. Robert was dangling the keys from his fingers. He told me he knew someone at work who'd bought his wife this car, but she had refused to drive it on the grounds that she didn't ask for such a thing, and where, in this godforsaken country, did he expect her to drive it *to*? He told me the story with some relish, he enjoyed this tale, perhaps much repeated around the office, of this foolish women and her nameless, hapless husband who must have been attempting to placate his wife somehow, to make up for this new life she has, the insects, the black servants who swig her sherry behind her back, for having been so rudely pulled away from her family and the familiar streets of where? – Sheffield perhaps, or Plymouth.

'I don't know how to drive.'

But Robert was excited by the plan; his face flushed, he waved his hands in the air.

'You can learn, I'll learn you. It's not difficult. Even Paul could drive by the time he was fourteen.'

I was filled by the nauseating thought of Robert teaching me anything.

It was a gloomy afternoon, wet, grey and cloudy, and the kitchen was shadowy cold. The windows were dirty and I hadn't washed up my cups and plates for at least a week now. I was working my way through Mrs Richardson's china cabinet. I had washed some of my underthings though, in hot water, banging them against the sides of the basin, swirling them about in the warm water and scrubbing them with face soap. They were draped around the kitchen, over the backs of the chairs, trying to dry off.

Robert had brought a bottle of whisky with him, as well as the car and a newspaper, which I was looking through, searching for even a small article on the miners' strike. It was unnerving having him in my kitchen, bringing me presents.

'Do you know anything about a strike at the mines, Robert? About what has happened to the people they've arrested?'

He looked at me, surprised.

'No – was there a strike? Oh, hang on, there was something at the start of the week, about how they'd tried to strike but the union had been broken. Bloody good thing too, everything got too relaxed during the war, the state has to put these people in their place, you know. What are you so het up about?' He produced a packet of cigarettes. Robert was in his office clothes, a black suit

263

and pale blue waistcoat. I thought he looked sleek and villainous, his hair creamed back and his awful forced smile. 'I brought these too.'

'While the cat's away,' I said vaguely, remembering the time he had said it to me, when we sat smoking on his stoep, but then regretted it immediately because it came out wrong and sounded flirtatious. 'There was a huge strike, a policeman told me. He said that police had come from all over the country, that it has gone on all week. If someone has been arrested – an African – where would they take him?'

'What? The Fort I should think. Why?' and he narrowed his eyes at me a little, sitting very still again. But something stopped him from pursuing it.

'Yes, exactly, while the cat's away, eh?' he said smiling and changing his tone, pleased with me in a predatory way, as though I were saying these things to flatter him. 'Are we going to have a drink then? Fetch us some glasses, there's a good girl.'

As I stood to fetch the glasses from the yellow cupboard I could feel my heart hammering in my chest. My only concern had been for Moses, but then I suddenly thought of all the times Robert had looked me over at his house, of how he liked to sit up close to me in the evenings and ask difficult questions. Fear and nerves washed over me like a cool wind, that look on his face, the presents, the loosening of his tie – Robert had come here to seduce me.

'It's a funny business this,' he said behind me, 'you here in this creepy garden. Are you sure you're happy? You don't look quite like yourself, you know.'

What to do? Would Robert take no for an answer? Would anyone hear if I called for help? No, not now that Moses was gone. I reached down as slowly as I could, and opened the drawer below, beside the yellow dresser, where I knew Mrs Richardson kept her sharp knives.

'Hurry up with those glasses then. Been getting the groceries from Thrupps all right, have you?'

I could hear him taking the bottle out of the brown paper bag and unscrewing the lid. I reached down into the drawer and grabbed the first handle I could feel, I brought it up and out very carefully. It was a long, large carving knife. A lucky choice. I slipped it inside my cardigan, and trying to hold it securely in place by clamping by arm against it, with the tip of the knife pointing upwards, a mistake, I turned round and returned to the table.

'They sent me this month's bills. You don't seem to get very much, you're not to worry about it. I can always claim it back off Paul, with interest.' He laughed at this, but nervously. 'Really, you don't need to budget. Are you having some? I know it's early, but what the hell.'

I sat down opposite him, trying to appear natural and relaxed. I took a big swig of whisky. I thought of Moses's blood outside in the yard, and then of my own father, back at the Grange, of how Robert would disapprove of him, would find him disturbingly dreamy, how Robert would make snide judgements, and of how my father would smile at him, painfully, and mumble something and go and find somewhere to hide, in his best tweed jacket, just as he had worn it for Paul when he'd wanted to show him his gun collection. I thought I should have written to my father, how if I'd tried more he would have responded better to me. I wished he were here now, aimlessly wandering from room to room, sighing, and turning his palms upward all the time. Here to look after me, on this day, when the world was rocking on its axis, unbalanced and without laws or sense. I wondered whether Robert would rush me, or whether he would ask first. Robert further loosened his tie and undid his top button. I looked at his brown muscular neck; he smiled at me.

'Bridget wants to know whether you've changed your mind about going back home.' But he didn't say this with any sincerity, he pulled a face, as if to say, 'Look, I'm just going through the motions.' I shook my head at him. I sat quite still but I was as alert as an animal waiting for its prey. Robert had drunk down his glass already; he refilled it and ran his hand across his creamed hair.

'All family in the end,' he said, flashing a smile at me. 'No need to beat about the bush, Laura, I might as well just come out and say it. Everything is not as it might be with Bridget and me, in the bedroom, and I need to find an *outlet* from time to time, a physical outlet. You're a married woman, you'll understand what I mean.'

I uncrossed my legs, I was prepared. I let the knife drop down a little within the security of my cardigan – the blade had been digging into my upper arm – I tried to sneak one hand down under the table, to catch the knife when I needed it. How could Paul have abandoned me to this, to this awful seduction by his terrible father? Robert had run out of words, he stood up and flicked his ash into the sink. He turned and walked towards me, purposefully. I leant back in my chair, eyes wide, frozen, watching Robert with his pantomime-villain hair coming towards me.

'How long am I expected to wait out here? Bobby? Are you in there?'

Her name was Ruby. She erupted into the kitchen, impatient at having been left outside in the new car for so long. She walked around on faulty high heels, running her fingers through the grime of Mrs Richardson's kitchen tops and saying she thought this was a 'dear little house'. Ruby had dyed blonde hair, I could see it popping out from under her purple turban, she was wearing lots of rings and a heavy wooden necklace. She picked up the bottle of whisky and swigged it back, neat. She weaved about the kitchen like a sprawling, overgrown rose bush.

'I'll just show Ruby around the house then,' Robert said, leaning against the kitchen door frame smiling broadly at me, and with that they disappeared into Mrs Richardson's bedroom.

*

Sex. Moses was lying beaten in a police cell, the miners had been beaten, quashed and the newspapers had not even bothered to report it. All was well in their world. Order had been resumed. Business as usual. Nobody cared, nobody knew. Robert and his mistress in my bed, drunken laughter and lechery, the sound of a slapped buttock and a cry of mock outrage, sordid things, sweaty bedsheets and smudged lipstick, the powerful reek of whisky – Robert playing at power.

Fifteen

Weeks passed. At the time I don't think I even knew how many, I stopped counting. I had no desire to count off the passing days except in the garden, tending the cacti, the bizarre succulents, the flowers which had started to appear again as the weather warmed slowly towards its spring. Carrying the heavy metal watering can slopping with cold, green water up and down the garden path.

Lonely, dazed and slightly dirty, ordering my groceries, frowning at the earth. I rang the police station, and the Fort, countless times, though recently when they heard my voice they just hung up on me, or swore at me in Afrikaans. Joseph had disappeared too, I'd even tried ringing him at the university, but nobody had ever answered. I ordered a newspaper now with my groceries. Read it carefully each morning, painstakingly, trying to work out what was truthful and what was not. There were occasional, brief articles — hemmed into tiny news round-ups — about the Indians' campaign in Natal, their resistance against being segregated and denied the opportunity to buy land. Though of course it didn't put it in those terms. I read these snapshots especially carefully because I thought that was where Paul must be, in Durban, working with the Indians. It made me feel warm to think it, to believe it, to imagine him down on the coast, trying his best.

Until one night I was woken again, by another banging on the door, another voice shouting out to me through the darkness. I lay rigid with fear, I thought perhaps it was those policemen returning for me, that poor, mad, simple girl in her nightdress who cried about her gardener – do you remember her? Let's go back, she'll be some sport, they would have said to one another, let's go back for her, stop her from ringing us once and for all eh? Agh, she makes me sick. I pulled the sheet up over my face, only hearing the sound of my breathing, fast and hot, closing my eyes, willing myself to be far away, left alone, to not have to be frightened any longer. Then I heard it.

'Laura, Laura, open up. It's me, Paul.'

*

I didn't know where to put myself when he walked in the door, I wanted to do a million different things at once. I wanted to kiss him, to hit him. I was struck by a quickening in my stomach, like the lurch of love, as I watched him walk in Mrs Richardson's front door. He smiled at me; I thought I could see guilt surround him, like a heavy inky cloud, hanging low in the hallway. He looked different to me, sticky with experience and new discoveries, thinner. He was not wearing any clothes I had seen him in before, I thought he might be a ghost; my body went slack and I leant against the wall. Did I look different to him? I felt different.

'Are you really here?'

'Yes really, Laura, I'm real,' he said quietly.

We didn't move towards each other or cry out or run over to hug one another.

'Hello,' I said, a big foolish grin sweeping my face. Paul took a few tentative steps into the cool, shadowy hallway; he looked about him. Unspoken words were filling my throat, like butterflies, and I was worried that if I opened my mouth I wouldn't know, or be able to control, which ones came flying out. He held out his hand to me and I took it. There was a new pale scar running across the top of his right hand, like a garden path; he was looking at my hand – it looked different to him, I think – it was rough from the gardening work; we were examining the maps of our different experiences. I traced that scar with my finger, but he pulled his hand away from mine and gestured towards the open door.

'There's someone else here, Laura,' he said. 'Come on in, Gay.'

We sat awkwardly in the sitting room, well, Gay sat and Paul and I gauchely stood either side of her. There was no focal point to this sitting room, so none of us knew where to look, it wasn't even much of a sitting room. Mrs Richardson probably didn't go in for entertaining very often, this was the room where she kicked off her outdoor shoes, or sat in one of her two armchairs, slung in the middle of the room, to thumb through *Country Life* before dozing off, or where she might have sat with her plans spread around her, the gardening notebook on her knee, pen in mouth, organising her planting and propagation for the next year. It was just the room she walked through to get to the kitchen, it smelt of earth and old cigarette smoke, stale and dark.

Because there was only one other chair in the room, neither Paul or I were comfortable taking it. Though we didn't acknowledge this and the situation was too strange for some elaborate comedy act between us to keep gesturing to the other one to sit. Paul had urged

270

Gay to sit down, though, he'd even picked up one of the cushions on the chair and plumped it up a little.

I was looking at Gay. I had never seen a woman who looked like Gay before. I had known English schoolgirls – pink, hearty, their breasts covered in sensible jumpers – and middle-aged Johannesburg matrons, I had never known a woman who looked like Gay. She was long, delicate, pale to the point of translucency, her red hair was tied back but tresses fell down beside her face, she was wearing something flimsy, a silken dress, ivory or pale green. An evening dress. I thought she was a creature, not a person, a sea creature. On the ends of her impossibly long legs were delicate satin slippers, they looked like satin, though I could just see a dark rim of faded mud around the bottom which had spoilt them. Her skin was tinged with a ghoulish green undertone, though perhaps this was just the reflection the dark walls gave off, she had pink spots high on her cheekbones, and was breathing quick, shallow breaths, a little wheezy. I thought I could see her breasts, small and pert, rising and falling inside the satin dress. It was dark in the sitting room, it was a dark room, and we had only put on one light. Gay did not look at me.

'Paul,' she said, 'be a darling and bring me some coffee, would you? I'm pooped.'

I looked over at Paul, who was responsible for bringing this sea creature into the house, this person who said 'pooped'. He looked back at me, smiled a little apologetically, but there was something in the set of his mouth which was serious, he was not prepared to laugh at her.

'Yes, can we, Laura? Make some coffee?'

Yes, I wanted to say to him, yes we can, let's go now, you and I, into the kitchen and make some coffee, but he did not mean this of course, he meant for me to go and make them coffee.

Seeing Paul had made me blurry, I was sluggish in the kitchen, and forgetful. I forgot to put the coffee in the pot, then I forgot the teaspoons, the correct amount of saucers. Something was washing over me, I was not sure what it was. I half-heartedly ran my fingers through my hair, wishing I had made some effort with my appearance, wanting to appear delightful, crisp and capable to Paul. While I was waiting for the kettle to boil, I thought how familiar all this was, other people being around when all I wanted to was to be alone with Paul, for us to have the space and time, to renegotiate, to circle each other, to have the luxury of empty afternoons together in bed. We seemed always to be surrounded by strangers.

When I came back into the sitting room Gay and Paul were whispering, he was sitting on the arm of her chair, and she had her pale face turned up towards him. She was smiling, a little washed-out kind of smile. She was sitting very still. Paul was looking concerned, he was frowning and kicking his foot against the chair leg. I saw then how very tired they both looked, how wasted. I had the sense that they were trying to control themselves, but I didn't know why or from what, but there was an undertow in the room, something murky and unsayable, something pulling and pushing and forcing Paul and Gay together. They both looked round as I came nearer, Paul smiled at me and stood up.

'Marvellous. Coffee, this is what we need.'

I placed the tray on the floor, because there wasn't a table, and knelt down to pour the coffee out.

'Where's Joseph? Do you know?' I asked, to fill the silence of the room. 'I need to talk to him about Moses.'

'About Moses?' Paul shot a look at Gay and then back at me. 'What are you talking about, Laura?' he said with a little, nervous laugh.

'He was taken by some policemen. It was awful, Paul, they beat him up and dragged him along the ground. Did you know about the miners' strike, Paul? Did you hear about it? That wound, you know, the knife wound, it had reopened and—'

'Laura!' Paul's voice was loud. 'That is all forgotten now.'

'No, no. They took him away. Joseph has to help him. The policemen said they were taking all the communists and trade unionists. I wondered if they'd got him too. Do you know about it? Don't your people know about it, Paul? We must find Moses.'

Paul looked awkward for a moment, staring at me with something close to disbelief, then he coughed and said, 'I don't know anything about any of that any more, Laura. I've moved on from all that.'

He'd moved on? I looked over at him. Here was Paul. Here were his curls lapping over his shirt collar, here his kind smile, his wide blue eyes, my husband. What did I know about what he'd been doing? Perhaps he couldn't talk frankly in front of this sea creature. I was grateful he had come back to me. I wanted to touch him so I could claim him as my own, and in so doing banish the echoes and shadows in the room, that strange edgy nervousness, their tiredness, their whispering, their coming here together.

'Did the policemen frighten you, Lala?'

He was being sincere, but I found the question, this nickname, patronising; it struck me as childish, babyish even, the name, his question should have been for a nervous sickly child, one who is haunted by random and foolish fears, the dark, barking dogs and beasts under the bed.

'No,' I lied, 'no, I wasn't frightened. I am worried about Moses though.'

'Hmmm,' said Gay, 'this coffee tastes good.' She leant back in her chair, smiled at me. 'Tip-top. Thanks, you are a doll. I need to sleep, can I sleep?'

I showed her to my bedroom, embarrassed at the sight of my underwear strewn on the floor and the unmade bed. I quickly pulled the sheets up and ran my hand across the pillows to flatten them and tried, surreptitiously to kick my dirty things under the bed. She yawned and stretched her arms up above her head, they were long and pallid, I could see wavy blue veins running up the insides of her arms. She stood there with her arms up in the air, and I half wondered whether she expected me to grab the shimmering hem of her dress and pull it off over her head for her. She kicked off her shoes and crawled into the bed, pulling the sheets up over her. She lay her head on the pillow, her glowing hair steaming across the pillow.

'This is nice,' she whispered, 'this is nice. Thank you.'

I turned off the bedside lamp, so she could have the peace of darkness; I don't know why but I sensed she needed this, and then, for some reason, I picked up her satin slippers and placed them together at the foot of the bed. Her breath was uneven, too fast, a little rasping even. I tiptoed towards the door.

'Don't go. Stay with me. Please, I'm frightened. Won't you just stay with me, until I'm asleep?'

I sat down on the side of the bed, her hand sneaked across the top of the blanket, found mine and wrapped itself around; her fingers were cold, clammy, she squeezed mine tight. Eventually, Gay fell asleep.

Sixteen

'Who is she, Paul?' I had been so long on my own that the sound of my own voice was surprising to me. My jaw felt tense, aching, my tongue furry and slow.

He was in the kitchen, opening one of Mrs Richardson's dusty wine bottles. He poured us both a large glass.

'I had to wash them up,' he said. 'It's got a bit messy in here, hasn't it?'

It was bright in the kitchen, after the sitting room. I narrowed my eyes a little, as I moved over to sit down at the table. Paul sat opposite me, he wasn't looking at me, he was swirling the wine around inside his glass, then he drank it suddenly and quickly in one huge gulp and then refilled the glass.

'Your father brings a woman here,' I said.

He looked up then, frowning.

'That's a horrible thing to say. What are you talking about?'

'He has a mistress. Her name is Ruby, she wears strange clothes and dyes her hair. What do you think to that?' I was tired, sipping on the wine, flushed.

Paul stared at me across the tabletop. He picked up the wine bottle and refilled both our glasses. I looked over at him, he seemed wobbly on his chair. I thought of Robert tapping his finger against his head but Paul didn't look mad to me, he never had.

'Why are you telling me this?' He sounded aggressive.

'Oh, I don't know!' I smiled at him, I didn't know why I was saying it. 'I thought it might amuse you. I've had a terribly strange time.'

He frowned at me.

'I met Gay in Durban. She's a contact of Joseph's, she brought some papers out here for him. I went and got them for him, that's all. She's an actress, she has some work here in Johannesburg, so we travelled up together. She didn't know where to stay, so I brought her here.'

'Oh I see.' I smiled at him again, hopeful. I wasn't sure why he was so cross with me. 'I'm so pleased you're back.'

'You have been good, Laura, very game.'

'Game?'

'Yes, you've been so—' He let his sentence hang in the air between us, unfinished and unsaid. I felt suddenly angry with him, resentful and heavy with the wine rolling about in my empty stomach, drunk. I reached across the table taking his hand, holding onto it to stop the ground rising and falling beneath my chair.

'Tell me what you've been doing in Durban, Paul. Let's have some more wine.'

'I – in Durban?' He picked up the wine bottle, quickly taking his hand out of mine. His face looked thin and pinched, new worry lines had appeared across his forehead. He shut his eyes for a moment.

'Yes. I know about the pegging movement. I've been reading about it – or trying to anyway. I know that they passed the Pegging Act

276

to stop Indians buying their own land, and that now the Indian community are launching a campaign against the attempts to segregate the Indians. Is that right? One paper said there had been violence and imprisonment, but the others skimmed over it. I guessed that was what you were up to. They don't report things here though, do they? The miners' strike, I mean I couldn't find anything on it. That's outrageous, isn't it? Tell me about Durban. What did you do?'

'What?' He opened his eyes again then and glared at me across the table, shifting a little in his seat. He looked away, fixed on a point behind my shoulder. 'What do you know about the bloody Indian pegging movement, Laura? Jesus. You ask all these questions, and you don't know bloody anything. You're so critical, eyeing me up all the time. You're so bloody suspicious.'

His eyes were bloodshot and unfocused, he would not look at me.

'You don't understand how this has been for me.' My anger came out quickly, violently, surprising us both. 'You asked me to wait for you, you said you'd come back, and I have waited.' I could feel hot tears in my eyes, I did not want to cry. 'You wanted to marry me, and I *believe* in you. Why do you always forget that?'

'I should have known better, really, than to bring you here. I don't know what I was thinking.'

'We did the right thing.'

'Did we?' He was challenging me. 'It seems a lifetime ago, doesn't it? Charlotte's party, the wood, the Grange. All that?'

'No, it seems like yesterday to me.' This conversation was dangerous, I wanted to take a wet cloth to it, smear it away. 'I'm pleased you're back. It's been utterly horrid without you. Moses said that the fight wasn't about freeing people from chains, he said it was about asking to be treated like a human being. At the mines they were asking for a decent wage, a liveable wage, that was all. To be treated with humanity. I understood it then, when he put it like that. I felt ashamed actually, of myself, of how stupid I was about it all.'

Paul took my hand, we both looked down at our hands on the tabletop, our fingers interlaced, the whiteness of my knuckles as I was gripping him so hard.

'I want to go now, Paul, I want to leave this place. We need to give ourselves a chance. We need to be together.'

'Not yet, no, I can't go yet.' He wouldn't look at me, just stared at our hands and my gleaming wedding ring, caught under the kitchen light, the tiniest spark of gold. I looked at the top of his head. I could feel that stick in my hands, the one we had both held on the koppies, when we'd tugged at the ends of it, when it had been so hot and dusty, when he had said I was lucky to have been saved by him, and where was home? I wanted to tell him that I could not trust myself in this place alone, I felt ungrounded and uneasy, as though likely to be swept away by the first force I met, a sudden wind or a downpour of rain. I was affected by the changing nature of all around me, by the poison in the ground, by all that was perilous and risky in this city.

'Paul—'

'I can't do this now, Laura,' he said softly. 'I'm sorry, I'm just — there's a lot on. I know—'

What was I doing in this house, in this country? It was all for him, it had all been for him. I was lost, bewildered, hanging on by my dirty, bitten fingernails, trying to piece together my days. I was full of the misery of the last months, full of paranoia and loneliness and fear. I wanted to tell him how very much I loved him, how I always had, from that moment in the centre of the frozen wood, when the branches of the trees had seemed to creak with frost, and the ground had been hard under our feet and the light of the torch our only guide. I didn't care if he was mad or simple because I half suspected I might be too.

'I'm so sorry,' he said, sounding near to tears himself. 'I can't do this now, it's all so futile. Everything. The politics is futile, after what happened with Moses, I − we − I . . .'

'No it's not,' I said quickly, 'None of it is. I thought it was, but it's not. Moses is right, you are right, it is important. Something's not right with this country, it's sinister. Those policemen, the way they hit Moses, the way Moses looked at me when they dragged him to the van.'

Paul looked at me, unblinkingly. He seemed not to understand what I was saying.

'I can't do all this. It's too much. I don't understand. I thought—' and he stood up, knocking his chair over and wrenching his hand out of mine. He looked about him wildly, turned on his heel and left. I ran after him, but was too late, the front door was left swinging open, I couldn't see him through the bushes and the dark forms of the garden. I rushed down towards the gate, but he wasn't there, nor on the road. I ran out looking up and down the lane, the pale moon in the sky, the whispering trees.

He was gone.

PART FOUR

Seventeen

In downtown Johannesburg women are shopping and stealing looks up at the black thunderclouds gathering overhead. Everyone is grimly determined, eager to get home before the rains start to fall. They do not wait for the lights to change, they cross the roads wherever and whenever they please. When the rain comes it does not come casually or gracefully as it does at home, it is sudden and threatening, accompanied by claps of thunder and bright streaks of lightning. As with everything else in Johannesburg, the weather is all or nothing.

Gay was wearing a sundress and a large hat; she consulted the piece of paper in her hand, holding on to her hat as the heavens opened.

'Kirk Street, she lives on Kirk Street,' she told me for the hundredth time as the first fat raindrops fell on her piece of paper, blurring the ink.

We were on our way to a singing lesson – Gay had proven to be a keen taker of courses and lessons – she had told me that she needed to work on her stagecraft, and that she had heard that Mrs Franton Taylor was the best teacher in town. Where she had heard this from I didn't know, perhaps from one of her actors at the radio studio, where she had been every day that week for rehearsals of a play called *The Silver Cord*. We had already that week been to Dr Ina Schoub's gymnasium for a class in 'physical culture' in preparation for an upcoming audition. It had been tiring watching Gay do those painful, contorting exercises, driving herself to the edges of exhaustion, dressed only in her French knickers and vest. She was driven by something more than a desire to reduce the size of her hips, which weren't wide at all, as narrow and brittle as sparrow bones in fact.

I didn't know where Kirk Street was, but I didn't tell Gay this, I didn't imagine it mattered, I suspected that Gay did know, that she would find it herself and that I would just tag along behind, drenched and dazed.

*

'What are you doing, kiddo?' she'd said coming into the sitting room the morning after Paul had left, rolling her eyes heavenward, looking about the room as though she'd never seen it before.

I'd fallen asleep in the armchair; I gingerly stretched out one leg, testing for cramp. My neck and head hurt, my eyes scratchy-red with exhaustion.

'Has he gone away, that man?' She stretched her arms above her head, interlacing her fingers, I could see her nipples through her slip.

'Which man? Paul?'

'Oh, is that what he's called.'

'Yes, he's gone.'

She looked about her and then down at me; she smiled. I squinted up at her, surprised by her smile, surely everything was dark and grievous that morning, I didn't think I could smile, I didn't want to smile.

'You look terrible. I'll make us some coffee,' she said. 'Now, where is the kitchen?'

I watched her, slumped in my kitchen chair, sliding about, pale and ethereal, it seemed strange that such a creature should do something as commonplace as fill a kettle or spoon coffee into two cups. The wine from last night was still out on the table. I picked up Paul's glass and ran my fingers around the top of it, I thought I could still see his fingerprints, ran my finger through the puddle of wine on the tabletop, it must have spilt when he'd jumped up so quickly.

'Where did he go then?' Gay asked, putting the kettle on the stove, her back to me. 'Have you been crying?'

'I don't know,' I said, 'I don't know where he's gone.' My words sounded fat and plain. 'I don't know anything.'

'Have you been crying? I never cry. Do you think that queer? I can't remember the last time I cried.' She was staring out the window, her hands on her hips, lost in contemplation. Her shoulder blades looked as sharp as knives. 'Do you live here alone then?'

'I'm house-sitting. I am, was, waiting for Paul to come back.'

'Oh, I see,' she said airily, turning round, narrowing her eyes at me, almost glaring. 'Do you have a servant? She should really see to these dishes. I can't bear housework. Don't you find it a terrible tedium?'

I blinked at her, disbelieving, in the pale light. She peered out the grimy kitchen window, ran her finger down the inside, and sighed.

'You've been living in an old-lady house, haven't you? Well, we're going to have to make some changes now, Laura, if I'm going to stay here with you. I think I should stay here, don't you? Just for a few days of course,' and she laughed her glittery laugh, 'I'll move out when I've got things sorted.'

And though there was a question in there, I knew that no answer was required and so, I imagine, did she.

*

Gay thought it a sensible arrangement that we share the bed. She certainly wasn't going to sleep in an armchair ('My looks are my profession, Laura') and she didn't want me to either. She took a tour of the bungalow, coffee cup in hand, picking her way through the dark and earthy rooms.

'I suppose we can make something of it,' she said, sniffing. 'We could have parties here, couldn't we?'

Though what of Mrs Richardson's house persuaded her to this point, I could not imagine. I followed her about the house, feeling shocked and heavy.

In the bedroom, she said I wasn't to waste too much time thinking about Paul, trying to guess his motives. 'Men are an enigma,' she said, taking off her slip, not embarrassed or ashamed in the least that I should see her naked. She patted her cheeks with her hands, her fingers were a strange blue colour, her mouth ringed with the same bruised blush. I sat on the bed, looking at her, moving about that dark, austere bedroom, listening to her breathing, high and low, pitches of sound and silence, a slight wheeze, her breasts rising and falling, she was a column of white, iridescent light.

'Are you all right? Your mouth is a funny colour.'

'It's the light,' she snapped and slapped herself harder across the face.

I was dazzled by the whiteness of her skin, it was a fine, delicate sheath barely covering her bones. I felt dizzy, reached out a hand to steady myself on the bed, looking at those fine blue lines which ran up the backs of her legs, her pert bottom. She picked the green dress up from the back of the chair and slipped it over her head like water. Then she sat down on the bed beside me and started putting on make-up, a little powder, pencil on her eyes, looking this way and that in her compact mirror. She wasn't cross any more, she was getting on with her business.

'We're not so different, Laura,' she said, smacking her lips together as she smeared on her red lipstick. 'I've got a feeling, we're not so different. We shall become firm friends, I just know it.'

And she snapped the compact closed, and looked at me. I suddenly thought of all those late-night conversations in the dormitory about 'presenting oneself' and how the girls had slid about under their blankets and sheets and whispered to one another about secret unknowable things to do with their mother's face creams and lipsticks, and how little they'd really known, and what would we all have done if Gay Gibson had turned up and snapped the lights on and spun about the room with no clothes on.

'How do I look?' she asked me.

'Beautiful.'

'Good, right, first stop is South African Broadcasting Corporation. Where do I find them then?'

'I don't know,' I said weakly. She turned to me, throwing her long red hair about, and frowned.

'You're not to go about with that long face. It won't do at all.

Not at all. I'm going to look after you now, we've got each other now, haven't we?' She was most emphatic about it.

Gay said we were two 'orphans of fortune' thrown together, making house and sharing a bed. She used that phrase repeatedly that first morning, pursing her perfect mouth at the first syllable as though she were kissing the air. I, on the other hand, wasn't sure what to think about anything. Not of her, or Paul, or any of it. I was in shock, but also oddly grateful that she was there, making presumptions, and I think she must have known this. I couldn't stop staring at her, I kept apologising for the state of the house, for the creepiness of the garden, for my lack of servants. She asked me to drive her into town to find the radio station, and I had to explain that I had the keys to the car, that Paul's father had given it me, but that I didn't actually know how to drive.

'Oh, *driving*, it can't be that hard, can it?' she said crossly. 'Come on, I'm sure one of us will be able to work it out.'

'I don't know the way.'

'Well, all roads lead somewhere. We'll just get in it and drive until we see a signpost.'

And so we did, sitting side by side in Robert's car, Gay driving fast and then slow and the engine coughing and spluttering at us, her with the window down and the wind in her hair, driving up pavements and off again, hooting at trucks and stalling the car at every crossroad we came to.

When she came back out of the radio station she jumped in behind the wheel and leant over and kissed me on the cheek. I'd waited in the car for her to come out. 'Yes! I got a job!' She laughed, opening her mouth and throwing her head back so I could see the insides of her mouth. 'Isn't this marvellous?'

And as she roared off into the traffic, without a thought as to the correct direction we should be travelling in, or even what side of the road we should be on, I curled my hands up into fists, and blinked back the tears. I wanted Paul back. That afternoon she insisted we get drunk, tipsy in the armchairs, my head throbbing and Gay singing snatches of songs to herself. I wondered at her being here with me.

'Why are you here?' I said, my voice sounding like a weak echo in my head. 'I want Paul back. It doesn't matter that he wasn't a hero. I understand.'

'Oh, we'll get him back for you,' she told me confidently. 'Don't you worry about that.'

Gay's Diary

Johannesburg, August 1947

I knew we would be friends, in the same way I knew Seda and I
would be friends all those years ago. I knew we would have things
in common, I mean more things than just Paul. Though I don't
suppose a stranger would see it, not really. She is plain, younger
than I thought, her hair, I noticed, gets quite matted at the back,
like she forgets to brush it sometimes, and she's not very directed
as a person. I wonder at Paul thinking she needed saving. I do see
it, I suppose, but I wonder at her thinking that Paul could save her.

Paul ran off, as I thought he would. We are both orphans of fortune,
Laura and me — isn't that a wonderful phrase? I thought that up.
When I said it to Laura, she frowned as though she didn't know what
it meant, but really I don't think she liked being called an orphan
because of being married to Paul. I think he has a habit of bringing
his problems to Laura and then running off, that's what I think. It
can't be a coincidence, her in this house all on her own, abandoned
and needing someone to live with, someone to be with. And me,
just arrived, ready to take the city by storm, but needing somewhere
to live. Just for a while. It can't be, can it? It was written in the stars,
we needed each other and now we have found each other. Banged,
collided, fallen over and picked ourselves up, apologising, dusting
ourselves down and laughing, shooting little looks at one another
under our fringes, surprised by this stranger in front of us who
might seem oddly familiar.

I have work, at last. It is a radio production of *The Silver Cord*. I knew it would happen. The first morning Laura and I drove into the city, we were both excited, like we knew it was the start of Everything. I walked straight up to the bitch receptionist sitting behind her desk, playing with the switchboard and pushing her hornrimmed spectacles up on her nose. 'I am here,' I told her. 'We have spoken a number of times on the telephone, Now I am here, would you please take me to meet Mr Silver?'

The cast seem very impressed with me, and I have been very professional at the radio studio. 'Oh yes,' I told them, 'I'm really quite an experienced actress, I've played at the Liverpool Empire.'

Yesterday when I came back from a rehearsal Laura was sitting outside in the garden, even though it was quite dark and cold. I asked her what she was doing out there and she said, 'Shh. Robert is in there with Ruby. I have to wait outside until they've finished, otherwise I can hear their noises.'

So I sat down next to her. She said that Robert was Paul's father and Ruby was his mistress. I said it was a bit of a cheek coming round and using our bed, wasn't it? She shrugged and looked a bit upset and said she didn't see there was much she could do about it because he paid for the groceries. I said, 'Well, there are other ways of getting groceries, you know. Do you think they put a towel down first?'

She thought that was very funny and started laughing, a bit hysterical, and that made me laugh too, and so there we were sitting on the ground with our backs to the wall, laughing and crying like we were seven years old and the best of school friends.

'Hello, who's this then?' says Robert, coming outside, and I swear he was doing his flies up as he came out, looking all pleased with himself and running his hand across his head, just like Paul does.

'I'm Gay Gibson, pleased to meet you,' I say, standing up very tall.

Laura gets up then and goes over to Robert. 'Is Paul at your house? He came back and now he's gone off again. Is he with you?' and I think, for God's sake, Laura, have some pride. Robert looks a bit uncomfortable and then this Ruby comes out. She looks me up and down too.

'Are you staying here with Laura?' she asks me, tucking her hair up inside her turban, very matter-of-fact. 'Are you a friend? Bobby, who is this person?'

'So, Bobby,' I says to Robert, 'you'll be fine with us adding champagne to our groceries, will you? We've been thinking we might need a few little extras too.'

And I could see him peering at me, and I stick my neck out and stare right back at him through the dark night air.

'Oh, and Bobby,' I says, 'you can find somewhere else for your afternoon fucks now.'

'Come on, Ruby, let's get you home,' he says, quick as can be and they fairly ran off to the car.

I thought it was funny, but Laura was cross with me. 'Why did you say that? I wanted to know about Paul,' she said.

Wednesday
I fainted yesterday, quite unexpectedly, crossing the road outside the studio. I saw out the corner of my eye a tiny black spot, it covered the shopfront on the opposite side of the street, a tiny blot out the corner of one eye. I looked the other way, but the black spot came too, and then it got larger and larger, and I knew the moment when I could see nothing but the blackness that then I would pass out, and it happened in seconds, though it felt like years, getting larger and larger and only the very vaguest edges of light

around the sides, shrinking and darkening, and then nothing.

A man picked me up off the street – well, he said he did – and took me into a cafe. When I came to he was sitting next to me, holding a glass of water.

'Are you new out here, madam?' he says, raising his hat. 'You are unused to the climate and the thin air, I suspect.' And he reached forward and gave me a sip of water. It took me a moment to come round, to gather myself. He was sharply dressed, pinstripe suit, handkerchief, the works.

'Thank you,' I said to him, 'I'm so sorry for the trouble.'

'Not at all. Where are you staying? May I take you home? I couldn't help noticing you're not married, are you here with your family?

'No,' I told him, 'no. I'm working here. I'm an actress. I live here with my good friend, my very good friend, Laura,' and then he gave me his card. 'In that case, may I buy you dinner?' he said.

His name is Charles something, he's a fur trader. I took his card anyway, and thanked him for the trouble.

Friday

Yesterday after the recording, Henry Gilbert, the producer, asked me out for a drink. We went to a nightclub called Ciro's, it was very busy, very fashionable, very glamorous. Lots of people came up to say hello to Henry, and then of course they wanted to know who I was too.

I drank cocktails and sat in a cubicle, smiling at them all, knocking back the drinks. We soon had quite a party going. I can't remember so much of it now, I remember wishing that Laura was there. I'd have liked to have had her there with me. I know I danced a lot, with everyone, with anyone. The room was dark and crowded, thick with cigarette smoke, used-up air and American jazz music. It was like floating, but thrilling too, getting high on cheap imported champagne, giddy, tripping about the place. When I was dancing with Henry he said, 'I want you to be in the play I'm doing at the Standard. I have the perfect part for you.'

And then how nice to come home to Laura. It feels like coming home, for the first time ever. To sneak into our bed, to hear her breathing and sighing, I fancy she smiles when she feels me slipping into the bed beside her, and I can fall asleep and know in the morning she will be there, and we will have coffee together and I can tell her about the play and Henry Gilbert and all about the nightclub and the people that were there, and that she will smile at me and make breakfast.

Eighteen

I tried calling Paul at his parents' house many times. Sometimes I would get Bridget or Mary, and when they heard my voice they quickly hung up, except once when Bridget whispered, 'Nobody wants to talk to you, Laura, go away, he's in a terrible state, my poor boy, oh Laura,' but mostly the telephone just rang and rang. I could see it, I could picture their ebony-black telephone on the table in the sitting room, jumping and trilling, demanding to be answered, while the floor was gleaming down below and Robert and Paul were studiously playing draughts and Bridget was sewing in a corner, humming to herself, and all the time the telephone was ringing and screaming, making the table shake, sending reverberations around that immaculate room. And I was standing in Mrs Richardson's dark, earthy hallway, leaning against the wall, looking out the open front door and into the bright garden, just listening to the endless ringing of the telephone, feeling it bump around my empty head. Anger was growing in me, but not of the hot, fiery kind, no, it was cold and chilly, sharp as a November wind, the cold tendrils of injustice about my skin.

*

If Gay were in the house, she'd come and take the telephone out of my hand and lay it in the cradle, and yawn, put her head on one side and say, 'I want to do something, what shall we do?'

I found her intense and flighty, vulnerable, demanding, so certain and yet needy. How she drove into town wheeling up the pavements, screeching the brakes, the car juddering and smoking and filling with the smell of petrol, how the air around us filled with exhaust and her talking all the time. How she'd say, 'We're going to Eloff Street, we're going to Margaret Squire's Dance Academy, come with me,' and then she'd abandon the car on the side of a street in central Johannesburg and look at me, accusingly and say, 'Where is it then? This dance academy?'

And she wanted to drink champagne at breakfast time too, or at any time – she had added it to our grocery list from Thrupps, had told Robert one night when he and Ruby were here, she'd marched up to him and shown him her long neck and collarbones and frozen him with one of her stares and he'd been dazzled by her. She would suggest we lay in Mrs Richardson's bed and drink, our mouths full of fizz and bubbles, Gay kicking her legs in the air and talking about herself so much. Talking so much and so fast that I felt as though she were eating up the air around me. She had so many plans, so many dreams, such surety of purpose, and she considered herself utterly fit for that purpose too. I thought she didn't see shadows or the grey in the world, wasn't scared by anything, how she seemed unaffected by Johannesburg, not startled by the people or the casual hatred I'd seen in everyone and everything. As though the evil, the evil way this country did business with itself, couldn't influence her. She was unstoppable, her life seemed one of rehearsals, singing lessons and evenings at nightclubs, late parties, Gay always jacked up on drink and dancing.

She was not bound by a perimeter fence, was not content to live within the confines of a house and garden. She liked me, which surprised me. She was very keen to keep me close, she wanted me to go to her after-rehearsal parties with her, the singing lessons, she did not want me to leave the house without her. I told her I had nowhere to go, nobody to see.

'Nobody but me,' she said smiling through half-lidded eyes, 'I need you, kiddo.'

I might wake in the middle of the night and she wouldn't be there, but then by the morning she was, smelling of smoke and stale cocktails, wheezing and pouting in her sleep. When she woke, she would be full of stories and smiles, would come padding through the house in her black silk pyjamas to find me, and I would shake my head at her a little, overwhelmed by her sudden rush of words and affection, wondering why she wanted to talk to me so much. Sometimes she would come back early, swinging in the front door shouting, 'Have you missed me?'

The producer of *The Silver Cord* had given her a part in his play for the Standard Theatre, and she was soon attending rehearsals at a theatre in town and talking about the actors as though she had known them all her life. She said, one night, that a member of the cast, Mike Abel, was madly in love with her. 'How can he be? He barely knows you,' and she'd told me I was 'sweet'.

We were lying in bed, side by side in the darkness. I had tucked my hands under my bottom, and was lying on my back. She was excited, I could feel her kicking and fidgeting next to me, moving my warmed sheet up and down. I was as annoyed at this, as I was at being called sweet.

'I'm not sweet, Gay,' I said, turning my head towards her in the blackness. 'Really, I'm not.'

'I will become consumed by my part,' she declared, ignoring me. 'The character is called Lorna Moon. I'm playing a good-time girl. A gangster's moll. What about that? Can I put the light on? I really can't sleep, it's early. Let's smoke a cigarette.'

'I tried to ring Paul again,' I said, looking at her reaching over for cigarettes and taking the one she offered me, 'I need to talk to him. Gay, what was he doing in Durban? You saw him there, didn't you? I need to know. It's this silence I can't bear. His running off all the time, I don't understand it. I want him to look me in the eye. I want him to explain it to me.'

She became impatient when I wanted to talk about Paul, and I did want to talk about Paul, I needed to think about him, I tried to ease him into the cracks of our conversation, to give him some air and often asked her about Durban. This time, as always, she frowned at me and became restless and irritated.

'Don't you think it's just over, Laura? Over?' she said, tossing her hair about. 'Why don't you let it go?'

I was shocked at how casual she was, how flippant about everything.

'This is my marriage, Gay, he is everything to me.' My voice cracking and splintering on the word 'marriage'. 'I only want to know the truth. I can't let them win.'

'The truth?' This made her snort. 'I don't know what he was doing in Durban, not much anyways, of that I'm sure. I don't know, I told you. Can't let who win?'

And then she jumped to her feet before I could answer and clapped her hands. 'Let's go out, let's go to a party. I know where one is. Come on, get dressed up, let's take you out.'

And they did like to party, Gay and her theatrical friends. They held parties after every rehearsal, impulsive, impromptu parties at different people's houses. Often Gay would insist I come too, she would make someone drive by our house to pick me up, the car would sit purring in the driveway, and she would honk the horn and shout for me out the window. Sometimes I would ignore her, I might hide in the garden or in the kitchen, and wait to hear the car drive off again. But not always, more often I would go. I'd come hurriedly to the front door, and see her leaning out a car window, her long arms waving at me, her hair caught in the evening light, drunk and shouting at me to hurry up, so pleased to see me when I got in the back seat that she'd grip my hand and kiss my cheek.

And so it was, me and Gay in Johannesburg, this person who had moved in, watching me trying to work out my fractured life. I was wary of her, heartbroken, but perhaps more than that, I was feeling the sharpness, the uncompromising light of disillusion fall over me, like a ray through a church's stained-glass window, picked out in red and blue, in my hair and across my skin, how everything around me and inside me seemed for ever altered.

I dreamt of sex, I didn't know why; night after night, when I woke in the morning, I was flushed and disorientated, I would look over at Gay and wonder if I'd touched her or if she had heard me. I always woke first, my eyes opening, my heart hammering and I would clutch at the warm sheets and try to bring myself back to this strange new reality. I dreamt of the red dust on the koppies, of Paul in the back of his mother's car, the smell of him, the feel of his skin against mine, the curls flat with sweat against his neck. I was surrounded by phantom sex. The garden with its phallic structures and knobbly cacti, by Gay and her parties, the echoing sounds of Robert spanking his mistress, by the men Gay spoke of, by all the hostility I thought surrounded me — by the terrible aching loneliness I slept with every night, by my dreams of Paul, the husband I had wanted, who I felt slipping through my fingers, as though he were made of water and pond weed.

*

'Mrs Richardson has sent a postcard from Paignton,' I said, looking at the photograph on the front. Everything looked small on the postcard, tiny white houses and a small grey road, an insubstantial hill and fluffy storybook cloud. 'She says *Daughter had twins. Most time consuming. Daughter not a stoic. Plan to return October. Trust you are still in situ? Have you mulched agapanthus bulbs?* She'll be back in a month. Are you still thinking of getting a place of your own, Gay?'

We were lying outside in the garden on one of Mrs Richardson's blankets. The sky was a chalky blue, the sun pale but warm. Our lunch of ham and hard-boiled eggs and some fruit, which I had prepared, lay uneaten on china plates beside us. She was sunbathing in a green polka-dot two-piece, which she said she'd picked up in Stuttafords, she told me it had cost an arm and a leg, but she hadn't paid for it. One of her new friends was a fur trader called Charles, and he was responsible for the bathing costume, and for the new cosmetics which lined the bathroom windowsill, for the orchids in the kitchen, which she had brought home in cake boxes. She hadn't told me how she'd met him, it was as though these men appeared at the snap of her fingers. I idly wondered whether he was also responsible for the dark purple bruise on her shoulder. Her white skin didn't seem to change colour despite how often or how long she lay out in the sun, didn't brown or redden, her alabaster skin remained impervious, as though she were indeed carved out of stone.

'Hmm?' she said, pretending artlessness, rolling over onto her stomach and kicking her legs up in the air. 'Have you ever missed your monthlies, Laura?'

I looked from the picture of sleepy Devon to the back of her head.

'No, I don't think so. Though when I first came out in January, the climate didn't agree with me, and I might have missed one then.'

'So you think it might be that?' She stretched out one long arm and picked up a hard-boiled egg. She slipped a red fingernail inside the shell, I watched it crack.

'How many have you missed?'

'One or two, maybe three. I lose count. Life's been pretty hectic what with the play and the boys and everything.'

'What does it mean?' I said the words slowly.

'You really don't know anything, do you? I might be pregnant,' she said simply, looking up at me. She was picking the shell off the egg and throwing the bits down on the ground. 'I'd rather not think about it, to be honest.'

'Aren't you scared, Gay? I feel frightened all the time, like everything is a bad dream and I can't resist it but I hate it too. As though somebody has thrown ice-cold water over me and washed everything away, and what was washed away wasn't properly developed in the first place. Do you ever feel like that?' I was running a finger across the British stamp on the back of the postcard.

'No. Well, maybe,' she put the peeled egg back down on the plate. She seemed to have lost her appetite. 'You're not unformed, Laura, you're seventeen. You're dangerous, it's a dangerous age to be.'

'I think you're like that with men,' I went on flatly, 'the way you carry on with them, with Mike, like you're frightened but you can't resist, like every time you have sex you're asking to die.'

Gay was lying on her back, she opened one eye and shot a quick look at me and then closed it again.

'Men have always wanted something from me. When I'm old, they won't so much. I don't want to be old, do you?' she said quietly.

'Yes,' I told her, 'Yes, I do want to be very much.' And then I wondered how it would be if I arrived at the frozen gates to the Grange and walked up the drive, crunching purposefully on the gravel, towards my parents' house like a ghost come back to haunt them and whether I would recognise the memories of who I had been, whether my mother would treat me differently. Whether they would see me as somebody different, somebody who had been on a journey.

'You're not a schoolgirl any more, Laura. You've done something extraordinary in coming here. You are powerful.'

Gay sat up and looked at me, and we stared at one another long and hard, as though we were seeing each other for the first time, understanding something dark, shattered and shining inside the both of us.

'Gay, I have to see Paul. I can't just stay here and let it all go past me any more. I have to talk to him, I have to sort it all out.'

'Go on then,' she drawled, sounding bored and impatient.

'They won't answer the phone. You have to drive round there and speak to him, bring him here, or arrange a time for us to meet. You have to make him. You're my only hope, otherwise I'm just stuck here, not knowing, not doing anything. I don't know who he is any more, who he was. I don't know if I was right or if his parents were right. I think I might be going mad, Gay, can you help me?' And then because I thought that perhaps she might not, that she might just swat me away or be cool and uninterested, I said hotly, 'You *have* to. You have to. You do.'

'Keep you knickers on, Laura. All right, I will, if it means so much to you.'

September, Johannesburg

Paul is still about, following me around. I see him when I come out of rehearsals, when we are going into that cafe on Pritchard Street for luncheon, or when I'm meeting people for cocktails after rehearsals. The other night he popped up in Ciro's, I was there with Mike Abel from the play and a crowd of other people. He came fighting through the crowds, he was half dressed, he looked a bit mad. He was drunk, he leant on the table, and glowered at me.

'We have to talk,' he said. 'What are you doing living with my wife?' and he knocked someone's drink over on the table. He was unshaven, drunk like I say, something a bit wild and useless in his eyes. Mike got quite heavy about the whole thing, tried to pick him up and get rid of him, but Paul fought back, and I told Mike not to make a scene.

'You told me Laura would know how to sort it all out,' I said to him, lighting a cigarette. 'And she has, she does. We're living together, we're friends. We've neither of us got anyone.'

'Issshess got me,' he says, all slurred, and I wasn't sure if he was saying 'she's got me' or 'you've got me'. Anyway, I didn't want to be dealing with him.

'Go away,' I told him. 'You're weak and stupid, go away and leave us alone. Laura and I are doing fine without you.'

And then he got angry, and started shouting at me and carrying on and then the management sent someone over to remove him, and he made a terrible noise being carried out of the nightclub, his feet off the floor, kicking in the air, looking over his shoulder, shouting out my name.

Mike wanted to know who he was, he didn't like the attention. 'You're a dangerous woman,' he said, playing with his tie. 'I'd better watch my step, eh?'

I just shrugged and said he was Laura's ex-husband, that he's obsessed by her, stalking her all the time, and she needed someone to stick up for her. He said, 'You're a good friend to her, Gay, though God knows why. She seems a bit strange to me, that one, if you get my drift,' and he laughed. I wonder if I will fuck Mike Abel at some point, he expects it. I don't care, though he's a bully and a bit ugly. He talks about his wife a lot but says, 'Her name must never be mentioned.' He's not even a proper actor for God's sake, he's a stationery salesman. I'll be with him or Henry Gilbert or Charles the Fur Trader or any of the others at the nightclub, but then I go back home and see Laura, and all is as it should be.

She comes to the parties sometimes, but she just sits in the corner with a sour face on. I don't mind. I like it that she's there even if she doesn't want to have a good time. She needs to get out more, stop sitting around in that awful garden pulling at the weeds and pretending she knows what she's doing. It's a distraction. I don't know if she even knows how to have a good time. She asks me about sex a lot. Not upfront, not obvious, but it's on her mind and I wish I could hold her face in my hands and tell her, 'It's nothing, sex is nothing, it means nothing, it's like falling through the darkness every time, through hoops of fire and through the stars into a black hole. It is nothing. It is nowhere as nice as you and me in our bed, sleeping side by side and holding hands. It is nothing. It is all Charles Chalmers putting his hands down a schoolgirl's knickers and giving her chocolate afterwards, it is Pierre, and Mike Abel, and Paul in Durban sad and lost and only thinking of himself, it is the Professor wanting to touch my legs. It is what is expected, that is all.' But I don't, I can't.

I am not well. I feel breathless and dizzy. I should stop, I should take early nights and exercise more, but I can't. I am pulled outwards, and everything is so busy here, so noisy, so many men asking me things, people turning up and wanting to take me to dinner. At Ciro's I can't keep count with who I've danced with, who's asked me out and when and for what. It is a blur of men in suits with cakes and make-up.

I have been practising my lines in the garden. Saying them over and over. I wanted to write these lines from the play down in my diary. It's when Lorna is talking to Joe on the bench, and he's all cut up about her being with Moody. And he wants to know WHY she is, and she says 'with sudden verve' – that's what it says in the script, 'with sudden verve' – 'Would you like to know? He loved me in a world of enemies, of stags and bulls! . . . and I loved him for that. He picked me up in Friskin's hotel on 39th Street. I was nine weeks behind in rent. I hadn't hit the gutter yet, but I was near. He washed my face and combed my hair. He stiffened the space between my shoulder blades. Misery reached out to misery—'

Isn't that great? 'He stiffened the space between my shoulder blades. Misery reached out to misery. A world of enemies.' I wrote it out on a piece of paper, changing 'he' for 'she' of course, and left it on Laura's pillow. I don't know if she saw it though, she never said.

Monday

I keep this diary hidden in the rehearsal room at the Pre-View Theatre. There is a prop cupboard here, and I always volunteer to help put away the chairs and tables, and then I pop this diary in last minute, on a shelf down the back which is empty and dusty. I don't dare keep it anywhere else.

I saw Paul again today, as I was crossing over down near President Street. He was on the street corner, waiting for me, I suppose. I'm getting a bit fed up with this, I have a lot on, what with my part and everything. I went up to him, because I'd told Laura I would.

'Laura wants me to talk to you,' I said, very upfront like that.

'No,' he said, shaking his head. 'No, I can't see her. I don't know what to say to her.'

'She doesn't want to see you, Paul. She wants me to tell you it's all over, you and her. She wants a divorce. She doesn't want you to see her again. She wants you to stop following me around all the time too. She wants you to leave us both alone.'

I was talking loudly, and some people on the pavement turned and looked at me, standing there talking so fast and loose. Sometimes I can't breathe on the pavements.

'Have you told her?' he said, looking quite pale and beaten up. 'My parents don't want me to speak to her. They won't answer the phone. They just want her to go away, but I don't. I don't know what I want. What about the baby? Have you told her?'

'About what? About you and me? No, I haven't, but I will if you keep hanging around. And the minute I tell her that, well, it will break her heart. Why would we want to break her heart? She'd never talk to either of us again.'

Paul sunk down to his knees, he did, right there on the pavement, and he hugged his knees to him and rocked a bit, shaking his head. I had no patience with him.

'I think I love her, Gay, I think I do still love Lala. Is it too late to tell her? Oh Laura, oh Laura,' like that, with tears on his cheeks and not caring that people were looking at him. I kicked him with my shoe.

'For God's sake, get up,' I said. 'Did you hear what I said? She doesn't want to see you, neither do I. If you ever see her and tell her that you love her, I will tell her everything, Paul, everything about you and me in Durban, about you following me and seducing me, about all those afternoons in the hotel and you saying you loved me and about my being pregnant by you. I will tell her everything. You have to let her go.'

It will be much better when Paul is out of the picture. We don't need him. I will tell Laura everything, one day, but not now. I want to tell her the truth, I nearly told her about Paul's baby the other day when we were out in the garden, but I didn't, I couldn't bring myself to. I don't even know if I am pregnant, sometimes I imagine I am, but then other times I feel quite hollowed out, as if I am just a dark space where nothing could live, nothing could grow.

Thursday

Doreen from the play told me a story today, we were sitting outside the rehearsal room waiting for our rehearsal. She's South African, Doreen, very proper, quite shy, we haven't spoken much before. She said, 'Do you want to know some gossip, Gay?' only she pronounced it 'goh-SEYP' and I couldn't understand her for a moment. 'Well,' she said, putting her glasses on the end of her nose, 'Mike and Henry told me they were at a party the other night over in Sandton and the man who's been going about in the white suit – do you know who I mean? he's been saying he's a Polish count – well, at this party someone from London was there, they said they knew him, they told everybody, he's no Polish count, he used to run the vegetable stall on the Mile End Road. What do you think to that?'

I told her I thought that was marvellous. I told her I knew I would like it here. I said this is just my kind of place. But then she tsked and looked serious and said, 'My ma says it's gone to the dogs now this country, with all these Europeans coming over, and nobody knowing who anybody is. She says they were bus conductors in London but by the time they come here they're directors of transport. She says, how can we build a country on lies?' and Doreen looked at me, all sanctimonious and disapproving. I says to her, 'How can you not?'

Nineteen

Gay and I, in the Doll's House, a little coffee shop which sold strong European coffee in little white cups and German pastries dusted with icing sugar. She had taken a great deal of effort with her appearance that day, even though she was not needed for rehearsals, and had spent the morning drifting about the house and garden, tetchy and argumentative. It was her idea that we go out somewhere together, first to the Doll's House and then to see the afternoon picture at the Twentieth Century Theatre on President Street. Gay was rolling little bits of pastry in her fingers and then popping them in her mouth, while I was taking greedy bites of mine, smearing sugar across my upper lip and chin. The coffee was hot, sweet and strong. She stretched her arms up high above and looked about her. I could tell she was bored and wanted to think of something to entertain her with.

'Is Mike rehearsing today?'

She snapped her green eyes onto mine and frowned. 'Why do you ask?'

I shrugged.

'Oh, what does it matter. I don't like him anyways, he's a bully.

And a thug. Honestly, it's like Amateur Hour when he's around, I can't believe they couldn't find a proper professional actor for his part.'

She lit a cigarette and passed it to me, which I took gratefully. I could feel her looking at me, appraising me; I was a little frightened to be so much in her sights, unnerved by this quizzical gaze.

'What are you doing, kid?' she said softly, reaching her hand across the table to flick her cigarette in the ashtray but then touching mine on the way. It was a little gesture, but a kindly one.

'I'm just waiting to find out about Paul.'

'Find out what?'

'Have you spoken to him?'

'Well, that ain't much of a life, is it? Yeah, I spoke to him.'

Those Americanisms were beginning to annoy me – she claimed they were important, Lorna Moon must have a convincing New York accent, she had been working hard on it, I could often hear her about the house, standing in the kitchen saying lines I now knew by heart, trying for twangs and slurs, running the taps at the sink saying loudly to herself, '*I'm not much inter-ested in myself. But the thing I like best about you . . . you still feel like a flop. It's mysterious, Joe. It makes me put my hand out, makes me put my hand ahht.*' I'd even found a bit of paper in the bedroom, where she'd tried writing her lines out, her writing all sloping and difficult to read. Gay Gibson was annoying me, sitting there with her red nail varnish and long white neck, sitting with her legs crossed, dangling one shoe off her foot. She was wearing a wide hat and white gloves, I wanted to put that shoe back on her foot, and to tell her to sit up properly with both feet on the floor.

'You spoke to him? What did he say?'

This was news to me. I couldn't understand why she would so

casually slip it into conversation like that, why she wouldn't have steamed home and told me all about it one night. The sun threw bright slants across our table, it was hot and I was regretting the two cups of strong coffee. I could smell the street outside and could see the sun bouncing off the dusty grey, blank pavement. I wished I'd never agreed to come out on this trip, I wanted to be back in the garden, lying under the shadows of the mimosa tree or even better weeding up the far flower bed which had become overgrown with weeds this last week.

'You need to take some control over your life, kiddo. Make some decisions, you can't carry on like this. You can't trust men, Laura, now that much I do know,' and she laughed a little to herself and shook her head.

'I think I can trust Paul, oh I don't know, I want to trust him.'

'Oh yeah?'

I couldn't account for why I felt so angry with her, a knot of fury built up in my throat, I didn't want to cry. I could feel rings of sweat under my arms, and the backs of my knees were damp, my hands shook. I put my cigarette out so I could put them under the table. Gay was being very cool but she looked nervous too, she looked away from me and stared out the window, stretched her neck a little. I could see her eyes following a car which was gunning up the street emitting vast plumes of black smoke out the back. When she did speak she did so softly, quietly.

'We should go home, Laura, don't wait around for him. I'll come back with you, after the play. I have to get myself sorted out.' She looked over at me, 'Paul said that he was not coming back to you. That is what he said. Look, I'm just telling you, I don't know how to say it, he says it's over, he thinks it was all a mistake. And from my point of view, Laura, he doesn't deserve you. He's not a real man, Laura, that much I do know. That's it. I don't fancy a movie anyways, I'm going to walk down Commissioner Street and look at the shops, I might catch the others coming out of rehearsal. I'll see you later.'

And she threw a handful of coins onto the table, without looking at me, and picked up her bag.

'He says it's all over, he's not coming back to you.' I watched her crossing the road outside the Doll's House, the self-conscious wiggle of her bottom, her long legs, floating, up above the tarmac. 'He thinks it was all a mistake.' On the other side some men raised their hats to her and she waved to them. Then she stood wondering whether to turn left or right, made a decision, and then soon I couldn't see her any more, though I stood up to be closer to the window, to try and catch sight of her red hair bobbing down the busy street.

*

Kneeling on the scratchy grass, pulling odd yellow vines out of the ground, I watch the dry earth moving and, pulling upwards, grab hold of the soil in my fingers and feel it running through my hands, shifting, dry and hard, trying to find the root of this vine which has spread across the ground, pulling at it, seeing it snap in two and then burrowing down again, deep into the dry ground, small shards of stone snagging on my fingers, making them bleed, and still running after this vicious vine which has made itself at home in my flower bed. My knees are hurting and I can feel the sun beating powerfully on the backs of my legs. I lurch. I fall, face down into the ground and start to cry hot terrible tears, opening my mouth into the earth, crying for the sake of it, crying at what has

313

become of me, the earth is like this place, I cannot get a hold of it, I cannot control it, I am hot and wasted and miserable, I have done my best. I can't stand the blank sky any longer, this loneliness and homesickness, I can't stand this house, Gay Gibson, I can't stand myself any longer. I am frightened by the hot blank streets, the angry blacks and smug whites, by making-do and fighting my corner and by sitting and waiting for Paul. I was foolish and lost, I should never have married him, never come out to this place and allowed myself to be abandoned. I cannot pretend to be a grown-up any longer. I cannot bear how everything is shadows and light, trying to follow the subtleties of conversations, how in the dark I am, how alone, how utterly alone.

I lie face down in the soil for a long time.

*

I heard the door bang shut. It must have been early morning. Gay came in and lay down beside me on the bed. Her breathing had not improved much, and when I turned to look at her I could see traces of blue all around her mouth. I reached over and touched her lips.

'Are you all right? You're a funny colour.'

She nodded, screwing her eyes tightly shut, reaching out her hand across the pillowslip, trying to find mine. I gave it to her.

'I'm not tired,' she said, 'I just want to lie here with you.'

She moaned and squeezed my hand even tighter.

How things seemed to spiral and shift and change in that room. I thought, Gay is sick, in her head as well as her body. She is untrustworthy, flighty and dangerous. I wish she'd never come into this house. I wish she didn't think she needed me so. I have been too long around Gay, I feel light and uncertain. I cannot say why I am here, who I have become is no longer clear to me. This place, it is this place, Johannesburg, that has done it.

'Gay, I want to go and see Paul now. You can drive that car. I've been thinking, I know Paul. He won't contact me, he'll be feeling guilty, overwhelmed.'

'I need to sleep. He doesn't want to see you.'

'No. I must see him, you must take me to him.'

It was still early, before their breakfast time, and the Lovells' house was all shuttered up and closed. It frowned down on Gay and me as we parked the car on the driveway.

'Are you going to wake them up?' Gay yawned and rubbed her eyes.

She had been quiet on the drive over, which took longer than it might, as neither of us were absolutely sure of the way and ended up going in the wrong direction along Melrose for about a mile. The roads were empty save the odd truck, blank grey stretches, pale sun, closed-down houses. The Lovells' house looked old to me, like a memory, I couldn't quite believe I'd ever lived there, or that I was the same person who'd stepped out of the taxi, fresh from the boat, raw with innocence. As we sat in silence inside the car I'd never driven, I thought I could see myself sunbathing on the Lovells' lawn, wearing the bathing suit Paul bought for me, my chilly white English legs slowly crisping in the sun. I saw myself trying to relax, to enjoy the sunshine, I saw myself waving away a fly, jumping up because I'd heard the ring-ding of a strange insect, casting suspicious glances behind my back at the house, wondering whether Bridget was watching me, where she was, why I was out there all alone, burning up under the hostile sun.

'Well, are you going in?' Gay yawned again. She leant over the steering wheel, her hair tied back behind her ears. Her skin looked paper-tired, new freckles had appeared on her arms, she rubbed one hand up and down her arm, to give herself comfort perhaps.

The seats in the car were squeaky hard, and it smelt of smug, sanitary living, polish and overheating. I had become infected with this place, I couldn't see straight, couldn't see what was in front of my eyes. I thought of Elms Wood and how I cycled through it to Charlotte's party, elated with daring, the cold on my face and fingers, streaming through the trees, I was nerveless. I would rather have been on a country lane, with high edges, which ribbons past hills and copses, past streams and fields. I understood the contours of those places, but not this upstart city with its suburbs and sunburn, skyscrapers and shanty towns.

Gay nudged me with her elbow.

'We can't sit around all day, kid. Do you want me to come with you?'

I looked over at Gay and she looked at herself in the mirror.

'I look awful,' she said, slapping her cheeks, trying to get some colour in them.

'Don't do that. You hit yourself too hard.'

She grinned and slapped herself some more.

'We gotta suffer, kid, that's the point. Come on, let's go and make some noise.'

Gay banged on the front door, and shouted loudly, then she found the door knocker and gave that a couple of bangs. 'You in there, *Bobby*,' she hollered, winking at me. 'Stop it,' I whispered, I wanted her to get back in the car.

There was a shuffling on the other side of the door, which I knew to be Mary. I heard her unlocking the door, could imagine her displeasure and disapproval.

'Oh, it's you,' Mary said when she opened the door. She was in her pink housecoat, her hair tied back in a scarf. She had already been up for hours, probably polishing that parquet flooring and picking up Robert's newspapers. She had her hands on her hips, her lips pursed in disapproval.

'Hello, Mary. I need to see Paul,' I said, stepping inside.

'He's asleep, they're all asleep.'

'Well, go wake him.' Gay leant against the door frame and yawned again. She was so long and languid, casting her eye around the hallway, taking it all in and looking bored.

'Yes, it's important, Mary.'

A flash of interest crossed Mary's face, like the glimmer of a fish in shallow waters, but she did not move from her spot.

'I cannot do that, Mrs Lovell. I have been told not to let you in.'

'But he is here, isn't he?'

She looked me up and down, and nodded.

'Oh yes, here.'

'What a couple of creeps.' Gay sidled in past Mary and leant against the hall table, her red hair shining in the early-morning light. 'How ever did you survive here so long, Laura?'

Mary looked at us both in the hallway, and she shifted slightly on her slippered feet, considering a course of action. Then she decided.

'You want a cup of coffee. I shall make you one,' and she shuffled off towards the kitchen.

'Smart woman. Come on, let's find him,' Gay said. 'Where's the bedroom?'

But I needed to go somewhere else first. She followed me through the hall and into the study under the stairs. My camp bed had gone, but that little pink cushion was still here, propped up on the windowsill.

'They made me sleep in here, when we first came out,' I said to Gay, looking around the room.

'Nasty.' She walked over towards the desk and opened the top drawer and then the next. I was still stuck in the middle of the room, looking around. I could see the dents in the carpet where the camp bed had lain. I must have pressed down heavily upon it.

Gay was sitting on the corner of the desk, her leg kicking against the side, she was idly picking up the pens from Robert's pen tray and examining them.

'Come on then, let's go see lover boy,' she said, 'before Bobby wakes up.'

On some strange impulse I rushed over and grabbed the 'sweetheart' pillow off the windowsill, and stuffed it under my arm. As we were coming out into the hallway, Mary appeared again.

'You came and asked for coffee. I went to make you coffee. That is all I know.'

I felt a wave of gratitude for her, went over and hugged her, but she did not return the hug, she merely endured mine.

'Go quickly now upstairs,' she said, tapping me on the bottom. Affection at last. 'I am making the coffee, I do this for Moses Mvubelo.'

'But Mary, where is he? How is he? I did try looking for him, I rang the police stations and the Fort but nobody would tell me anything.'

'He is in prison, but he will soon be out. They will all soon be out, and the trouble he will make . . .' She smiled at me, I think it was the first time Mary had ever smiled at me.

'Remember me to him, will you, please? He was very kind to me. Make sure he knows that, please.' She nodded and smiled again.

'Now go, go, quickly, upstairs before the master hears you.'

I crept slowly up the stairs, I would not deny myself the truth, I would not be like all the immigrants, who lived in the suburbs and refused to accept they were in Africa, that not so far away Africans were living in shanty towns and burrowing down under the ground, mining it out from under their feet, so that at some point this whole made-up unjust city would collapse in on itself. I would know the truth.

Twenty

The curtains were drawn, it was still and musty in our bedroom. The light coming through the blue curtains was comforting. Paul was asleep in the bed, I could see the hump of him under the blankets. I walked slowly across to sit down on the side of the bed. Pulling the sheet back, I watched his sleeping face. He looked peaceful, kind, plumper and more rested than the last time I'd seen him, his hair flat against the pillow, the warmth of his body, his nose and the curls around his ears and neck. He was snoring a little, his mouth slack and open, red and inviting. I didn't know how to wake him. I almost didn't want to, I wanted to lie down with him, to curl up next to him and to feel his arms around me again. I could hear my own breathing in the dark room, I tried to regulate it to join in with his. It was shocking to be with him again, to have him so near to my touch.

'Paul.' I leant in close and whispered in his ear. 'Paul, wake up. It's me, it's Laura.'

He stirred slightly, moved over onto his back, a slight smile sneaked upon his lips.

'Darling Lala,' he said, and I smiled at him, hopeful, but then realised he was still sleeping. He was wearing a pair of pyjamas I hadn't seen before, they were blue-and-white-striped, with buttons, I could feel the hand of Bridget about them. The top had risen up, I could see a small dent in his skin from one of the buttons, I wanted to touch it.

'Paul,' shaking him more roughly this time, urgent. I wondered where Gay had got to, whether she was causing any trouble downstairs, I didn't want her to wake Robert and Bridget, not yet.

Slowly Paul uncurled, his eyelids flickered, he frowned. I saw his tongue flick out and lick his lips.

'Paul, will you wake up?' I shook him quite roughly and this time it did the trick, his eyes sprung open, he looked at me, closed his eyes again, and then sat suddenly bolt upright in the bed.

'Laura,' he said, looking at my hand on his arm.

'Yes.' I smiled at him.

'What are you doing here?' He was rubbing his eyes and yawning. He pulled the sheet up over his stomach, which was difficult because I was sitting on the end of it. I didn't move though.

'I needed to see you, Paul.'

We looked at each other for a moment, staring at one another like a couple of children, with round eyes but no words, vulnerable and all-seeing.

'Well, here I am.' He smiled back at me, blinking his eyes. He looked as though he were trying to make decisions, as though everything had run away from him, as if he'd arrived at a party just as the fights had started and was trying to guess what was going on, who he should endorse and who he should turn on.

'We need to talk,' I said lamely.

I wondered at him looking at me like this, I wondered at why this was all my responsibility, at how he could have slept so peacefully in a bed when everything is so unresolved between us. Was this why Robert thought him simple?

'I've missed you. Why did you run off that night, Paul? I don't know why you won't answer the phone. I don't want it to have been a mistake, Paul, it wasn't a mistake, it was us in the wood, and oh, Charlotte Locks, and us at Madame Dupont's and my mother in the sports car, and oh, Paul! I told you that I believed in you, didn't I?'

I loved the sound of my voice then, I wanted to talk and talk. 'I think about you all the time, and the things we did, and how at the Academy Mrs Frobisher had always seemed so disappointed in me, and when I met you I wasn't disappointing, and we ran away together and it was just the best thing that had ever happened to me, but then coming here, and I don't know about families or foreign things but I am learning.'

He looked upset, he *was* upset. He blinked at me a little, uncertain where to put all my words, then he rubbed his eyes, with two balled-up fists, like a five-year-old.

'But you shouldn't believe in me, Lala,' he said yawning. 'When you were talking about pegging and about Durban and – Moses –' he had difficulty saying his name – 'I had to leave. I'm not the man you think I am, Lala.' He said this last part simply, smiling at me. 'Everything just got in a mess, didn't it? Everything was a mess. I'm so glad you came, I do love you, I thought you didn't want to see me any more.'

And I looked down at him.

'Oh Paul.'

And then the door banged open, and Gay appeared in the bedroom, wheezing slightly from walking up the stairs so fast.

'So this is where you both are,' she said, running her hands through her hair. 'I couldn't take it downstairs any longer. Not with Mary staring at me, and worrying that Bobby would appear any moment. Is this your room then?'

We both stared at her.

'Go and wait in the car, Gay,' I snapped at her but she ignored me and came over and sat down on the foot of the bed. I felt Paul's arm tense on my leg before he pulled it back and crossed his arms in front of him.

'Gay,' he said. I turned to look at him, he looked pale and frightened.

'Have you talked then?' she said, crossing her legs over and smiling at us both. 'Have you told her the truth, Paul?'

'The truth?'

'About how you feel of course, silly. Oh, and of what you really got up to in Durban.' She stood up and went over to the window. 'It's dark and smelly in here,' she said pulling the curtains back, 'we need some light.'

Sunlight poured into the bedroom. I blinked and put my hand up to shield my eyes. Gay stood in front of us both with her hands on her hips, pale and silky, immovable.

'Gay, we need to be alone,' I said quietly, but she didn't move. She pursed her lips and looked from Paul to me and then back again.

'I told her, Paul, what you said. How you thought it was all a mistake, how you didn't want to see her again. I told her. She wanted to come and see you though, to hear it for herself. She deserves that much, doesn't she?'

Paul said nothing, he sunk back against the pillows, staring at Gay. He shivered slightly, I felt the bed shudder, I heard a small noise escape from him, like a frightened animal running for cover.

'He wasn't doing any politicking or whatever in Durban, Laura. He was on the run, weren't you, Paul? I bet you always are, I know your sort. You were probably on the run when you met Laura. You wanted to save her, you wanted to save *somebody* because you couldn't do anything else. You are a coward, chronically incapable of doing anything at all. He's a weakling, Laura, everyone knows it, everyone can see it. Even his own parents. How can you not see that?'

'No, it's not like that, Gay. He loves me, he said it. Don't you, Paul? You love me still?' and I didn't know why I had to make him tell her, how I needed to hear it from him, hear him say it, define it, make it large and loud and sayable, and not something whispered to me in the darkness within the warmth of his childhood bed. I needed Paul to say it out loud to Gay.

'I don't know,' he said slowly, faltering. He wasn't looking at me, he was looking at Gay, as though mesmerised by her in his bedroom. Sounding out the words carefully, bewitched.

And then it happened, as though the light in the room were caught inside a Johannesburg diamond, and the three of us were caught in it too, inside a crazy room of mirrors and sharp angles, the room studded with a million different pieces of blinding light, fractured, iridescent, each reflecting off one another, sharp and beautifully cut, and I felt myself swinging on the side of the bed, dizzy, unclear and everywhere around me pearls and shards of rainbow light, blinding me, and I could see the fire and ice, the red hair and pale white skin reflected in the shards of glass, could hear Gay's voice coming at me as though through a mist, 'Well, that's all sorted out then. You had to hear it from him, Laura, now you know. It's all over.' And a million different pyjama tops surrounding me, my hands refracted around the room, Gay's legs, the three of us caught inside this terrible crystal bauble, bouncing and turning, cut up into a million pieces each caught and mirroring the other, our body parts, separate and discrete, spinning. And it was clarity, but also a disenchantment, like everything sweet and good fell away, and I had lost the fight to make Paul the better version of himself. His parents had won, Gay had won, and I had lost. I half knew it all about Paul, of course I did, that night in the kitchen when I was mopping up the blood, when I knew it was Paul's fault and that he was no hero, when he was tearful and jumpy, trying his best and failing, but I hadn't minded. I felt that icy rage again, in my finger-tips, I thought I could touch those shards of brilliant glass with my cold fingers, hold them, see myself turning into stone.

And I forced myself to look over at Paul sunk back in his bed, I tried to focus my eyes to find him, but it was too late, I couldn't, I saw only the face of a feeble stranger.

It was over. All of it.

Twenty-one

Sex. Power. Weakness. A party.

Gay and I were at a party at a house in one of the northern suburbs, a long ranch-like house with long windows and a big garden. Gay and her theatrical friends were drinking American cocktails and dancing. It was late, and the house was steamy with drink and music. It seemed a very modern house, very fashionable, with strange square-looking chairs, and little steps in the sitting room, small lamps and bright white walls hung with odd black-and-white paintings. I didn't know whose house it was. They were a vain and quarrelsome group, Gay's 'friends', grasping for attention, self-consciously calling for 'more highballs' as though these cocktails were some shorthand for the high life, glamour and easy living. A group of them were singing around the piano, ostentatious, showing off and draping themselves over the keyboard and piano player, singing loudly as though to outdo one another. I found their fulsomeness embarrassing. Rehearsals had finished and the play was due to open at the Standard Theatre the following evening. I was sitting in the corner, being awkward and dark, I was feeling very dark that night. I hadn't dressed up, despite Gay going on at me and offering to do my make-up. I was feeling scratchy and thin, permanently frowning, staring at Gay, trying to make sense of what had happened to me, what had happened in Paul's bedroom. I could feel those shards of diamond inside me still, at odd angles, reflective and cutting, I was waiting for them to fall back into place so I could see all things clearly.

Mike Abel was there, throwing his weight around. He was a large man, clumsy and unattractive. I knew him but had rarely spoken to him, only exchanged a word from the back of his car, or sometimes when he came to pick up Gay he might try out a line on me in the hallway. But that night he made a point of coming over to sit with me. When he sat down, he loosened his tie a little. He had too much hair, Mike Abel, it erupted out of his shirt collar, crawled up his arms and out of his ears. He was a man built for different climes. He rubbed his eyes and crossed one plump leg over the other, gave me a nod and wink, and drank down his cocktail in one go.

'How are you, Laura?' he said, running a hand across his filmy brow. 'I wanted to have a word with you, a chat, just the two of us. How is she?'

'Who, Gay? I don't know, I haven't seen much of her.' I was sitting on a beige sofa under a standard lamp, he had trouble squeezing in beside me. Mike smiled at me, a flash of white, perfectly measured teeth. I had forgotten that he was a salesman by trade.

'She's one helluva girl, isn't she?' he said, looking over at Gay. Gay was dancing in the middle of the room to the music from the gramophone player, she had her eyes shut, was dancing in a dreamy, somewhat daft way, swaying and pouting, rolling her arms up above her head. She looked very drunk. I didn't answer Mike.

'The thing is,' he said, putting his arm across the back of the sofa, pretending confidence, 'she's been acting a bit odd recently.'

'She's always odd.'

'Yes, but more than usual. I mean, I think she's really crazy.'

I shot a look at him, to see if he was joking, but he was leaning in towards me looking serious, and a little scared. I crossed my arms and my legs. I was prim and conscientious, I could feel the heat of the party on my body.

'She's a line-shooter, Laura, you know what that means? A liar. She's told all the cast that her parents were killed by a V-8 bomb. But she also told me that her mother works at a dry-cleaner's in Durban. And now she's saying,' and he dropped his voice to a whisper, '*that she's pregnant.*' Mike sat back a little then, and looked inside his empty glass. He prodded a fat finger at the slice of lemon in the bottom. He was much too big for the sofa, he seemed to be spilling over the sides of it.

'Is she?' he went on, because I hadn't answered him. 'I thought you might know, as you're her best friend and everything.'

'Best friend? We hardly know each other.'

'She said you went back years, Laura. That's what she told me. Look, that's not all of it either,' he said, suddenly getting back into his stride. 'She says I'm the father of this baby. She's crazy. I mean, I'm a married man, Mrs Lovell, I can't be involved in all this. It's a medical impossibility that I might be the father of her child, if you see my meaning.'

I wanted to stand up and go outside into the garden, I could see groups of people wandering about outside the windows in their evening dresses, I wanted to get away from sweaty Mike Abel and his whispered conversations and cheap suits.

'I can't have her saying things like that, I'm a married man, I've got my business to consider. And it's not true, but nobody will believe that. And what about my *wife*, Mrs Lovell?'

I looked over at him again. 'What do you want me to do about it, Mike?'

'Well, you've got to get her out of here. She's got to do something about it.'

'About the baby, you mean? Perhaps she means to have it.'

'No, no,' he laughed, or tried to and wiped his forehead again. 'Don't say that, not even in jest. Of course she can't have a baby, a woman in her position for God's sake.' He looked quite shocked.

'If you give us some money, I'll take her back to England,' I told him, this idea coming to me quite suddenly. I blinked a little as I said it, surprised to hear myself saying these words, as though now, slowly, a perfect shard of diamond had fallen into place beside another. 'We will leave here. Together.'

'Yes, yes,' he said nodding quickly. 'Not that it's my baby of course, but I'll be willing to help.'

'Very well then. I'll talk to her. We will leave as soon as the play has finished.'

'Oh thank God,' he said, leaning back and looking around the room. 'I'm going to get another drink. Gay said your marriage was over, I suppose there's nothing here for you now either.'

I shrugged, I had no intention of discussing my private affairs with Mike Abel. He heaved himself slowly up from the sofa, but then didn't walk away immediately. 'Oh, just one last thing, she's never mentioned a diary, has she?'

'A diary?' I looked up at him then.

'Yes, she told me she kept a diary, since she was sixteen or something. She said she writes everything in there. She was being silly at the time, emotional, saying she was going to show it to my wife.' He pretended to laugh again, but he was looking at me intently.

'No, she's never mentioned it.'

'Ah well, probably just said it to frighten me, eh? What a girl! Thanks for the chat, Mrs Lovell,' and with that he walked away from me and back to the party.

*

Two hours later, when I was tired, bored and wanting to go home, when I couldn't bear sitting there any longer on my own, staring at the strange paintings and having these thoughts clinking in my head like broken glass, I went looking for Gay. I wandered through the garden, and back up towards the house. I heard someone shouting my name, urgent and frightened. It was Mike Abel, standing by his car in the driveway, beside the driver's door which was open.

'Laura, Laura.' I ran over to him – only on coming closer did I see, with shock, that he had his trousers down near his ankles, and that he was standing half naked under the bright outside light.

'It's Gay,' he said, 'quick, help me.'

I peered into the car, and there was Gay on the back seat, her legs up against the windows, one little breast exposed, a rip in her dress, her dress gathered up over her pale, thin stomach and her legs spreadeagled exposing the surprising sight of red springy hair between her legs; one arm hung off the back seat, and the other was thrown back over her head. Her eyes were wide and glassy, she saw me, she tried to say something, but couldn't, she reached out one of her arms towards me.

I thought he'd tried to kill her, that was my very first thought, that Mike Abel had ravaged her and then tried to murder her in the back of his car. There was something so dramatically appropriate about her pose.

330

'I don't know what happened.' Mike was speaking quickly, quietly panicked. 'We were just – you know – and then she suddenly stopped breathing, she went blue and, well . . .'

It was difficult squatting in the front door trying to reach out to Gay. I looked sideways and could see him through the windscreen, how ludicrous he looked in his dinner jacket with his bare thighs trembling in the moonlight.

'For God's sake, pull your trousers up,' I snapped at him.

I climbed on the driver's seat and reached through to pull Gay up to sitting, and told Mike to open the other car door to let more air in.

'Breathe,' I said to her, 'in and out. Slowly, come on, Gay.'

And she did, staring at me with those huge green eyes, listening to my every word, trying to get some air back into her, in and out, following what I was saying, hanging on to my hands for all she was worth, her mouth half open, her breasts rising and falling, the rattling sound of her chest, wheezing and gasping. I am dangerous, I thought to myself looking at Gay in front of me fighting for air, following my mouth with her eyes, she was right, I think I might be dangerous. I could feel things moving inside me, moving towards symmetry. I suspected Gay of sleeping with Paul, I didn't know if she did, but I knew that in some indefinable way she was responsible for all the bad things that had happened, her very presence seemed threatening to me now. I wanted to tell her that doesn't she see that I was right, that every time she has sex it is as though she is inviting death, that the two are joined in an evil dance, just as distrust and envy are built into the pavements of Johannesburg, just as the abject and miserable burn here under the same unrelenting sun as the glittering and powerful. Everything was joined together in my head, coming to me slowly, as I started to breathe in and out, to show Gay, one, two, three breathe, made comforting noises towards her, and all the time thinking of Joseph, the gin, Moses lying beaten in the yard, of the sprawling emptiness of Johannesburg and the mounds of earth, of Gay's small satin slippers, the dry dust on the koppies, Robert and Bridget, and of Paul shrinking back on his pillows, always of Paul. This place had disturbed my mind, I wouldn't understand anything until I had left it behind, as I saw I must. 'We need to leave this country, Gay,' I said to her softly. 'Let's leave.'

*

I could not account for the rising feelings of panic and sickness I felt as I searched the bedroom the following afternoon, it spread across my prickly skin like a livid, allergic rash, though I could not find the diary. I thought, I know all her hiding places, all of them, but I couldn't find it in her suitcase or under the mattress or in the drawer where she kept her underwear.

*

The opening night of the play was considered a great success by everyone and each morning of the following week Gay came into the kitchen and sat at the table, humming quietly to herself, trying to shake off the excesses of the previous evening by pouring herself coffee from the pot and pretending to leaf through the newspapers only to be struck with delighted wonderment at 'stumbling' across her name in the entertainments column. The *Rand Daily Mail* said Gay had made an 'admirable job of the part of Lorna Moon. There was hardly a false note in her conception of the easy-going girlfriend' and the *Sunday Times* said that hers was a 'harsh, metallic but convincing portrayal'. The *Sunday Express* wrote that apart from 'sharp delineations by Gay Gibson, Doreen Mantle and Michael Abel' – this last name making Gay splutter – this crisp little play had a ragged stamp and descended into melodrama'.

'What a terrible thing to write,' Gay said, peering loftily at the *Sunday Express* once more, 'don't you think so, kid?'

I shrugged and poured us some more coffee, because no, I didn't think so. I thought her harsh and metallic in person, I watched her every move with caution and fascination, I was sure that soon she and I would descend into melodrama, it would be a Victorian play and she would scream and shout as she was tied to the railway track, her legs kicking in the air, her eyes wide open, her mouth pursed into an adorable little 'o'.

When she was out in the evenings, I went like a fool, like a glutton, searching for the diary, I was sick with shame and jealousy. I lay on the bed, twisting my legs around each other, smoking cigarettes. I was hot and shivery. I couldn't find it anywhere.

*

In the garden, touching the succulents, feeling their thorns prick against my skin, I breathed the musk of the flowers, I rolled on the grass. I was making decisions, I was waiting to see what might happen.

I stared for hours at the *Cotyledon orbiculata*, at the bunches of upturned green and yellow pods with red tips, they looked like they had been kissed, they were obscene and exciting. I sat next to the *Euphorbia tuberculatoides* with their scaled green dry fingers, I rubbed them against my cheek until it hurt.

I decided to take extreme action with the orchids. Mrs Richardson had said in her notebook that she had done her best with them but she couldn't get them to flower. Moses had told me that she must have brought them back with her from one of her tours, and that they would only flower after a veld fire, so I decided to make a fire of my own. I found a tin of gasoline in the shed and marked out the area where the orchids were with little white pebbles, and then I slowly poured the gasoline around the outside of the pebbles. It was my ring of fire. I bent down to light it, wondering briefly what I'd say to Gay and Mrs Richardson if I ended up burning the whole place down, but I placed the match and jumped back in shock as the flames rose up before me, angry and ravenous, gold and orange and blue with petrol. The fire burnt across the circle, quick and impressive, scorching the flowers on the ground, but it did not catch anything else, and soon the flames turned in on themselves, argumentative and mad, trying to leap outside the pebbled circle, and then I heaped loads of earth on top of the flames, burning my fingers in the process, until there was nothing, nothing, nothing, just blackness.

Twenty-two

After *Golden Boy* had been running for ten days, and Gay had been living with me for five weeks or so the cast received devastating news. The Municipality of Johannesburg declared the Standard Theatre a fire risk and ordered the play to terminate its run; the theatre was to close with immediate effect. Henry Gilbert, their producer, ran around for two days, his beard steaming with discipline and ambition, until he finally, triumphantly, secured them a new theatre in Pretoria. Gay was excited by this prospect, and agreed immediately to his suggestion that she, and the play, transfer to Pretoria. I had to act quickly.

I sat her down at the kitchen table and said, as sternly as I could manage, 'You can't, Gay, you can't go to Pretoria. You need to deal with this pregnancy.' I remained cold and resolute. 'We must go back to England and get it sorted out. There are people there. I know people,' I lied, suddenly reminded of Cissy. 'We both need to leave this place, I can't stay here any longer.'

'Is that what you think best?' She looked up at me, her face run with pale tears, her skin mottled, red hair falling down across freckled shoulders, her pretty sundress. 'Isn't there someone here?'

'You can't trust the doctors here. Most of them are vets. I'm going to book us two tickets home.'

'You'd do that for me? You'd take me back to London?'

'Of course. You need a friend and there's nothing here for me now. What did you call us, orphans of fate or something? Like you said, we only have each other now.'

I got a notepad and a pen out from the kitchen drawer.

'Who's the father?'

'I don't know,' she said in a small voice, 'I'm not sure.'

'Well, who are the main possibilities?'

'Mike Abel, the fur trader – Charles Brown, the guy who runs SABC, you know the one who gave me the radio jobs – I can't remember his name, isn't that awful?'

'What about the Man in the Suit?' This was the nickname we had for one of her admirers, the one who came to every performance of *Golden Boy* and sent lilies backstage each night.

'No, I don't think so.' She looked uncertain.

'You don't *think* so?'

'Why do we need to do this?'

'Well, how much money have you got? I've not got anything. I can't magic two tickets out of thin air.'

'What about Paul?' she said abruptly. 'He owes you something.'

'I'm not asking him. He's gone again, he's in Durban, Ruby told me the other night.'

'His parents then?'

'Gay,' I said strictly, 'this isn't about me, it's about you.'

In the end I rang every one of the men on my list. Sitting at the telephone table in Mrs Richardson's hallway, trying to sound diplomatic but assured. Some of them hotly denied the fact they'd slept with her – the fur trader said, 'Who is this? Are you kidding me?

Since when do you make a baby by buying a girl dinner and taking her to a music lesson?'

Mike Abel was delighted. 'You're off then? I'll send you some money to help you out.'

It was a bad line and I had trouble hearing him.

'It's to help Gay out, Mr Abel,' I shouted.

'How much?'

I told him I didn't know and added, enigmatically, he should send as much as he thought advisable.

'What's that?' he shouted back. 'I'll bring you the money.'

Mike sent us quite a lot in the end, and the man from SABC whose name Gay couldn't remember was a perfect gentleman and said that while it was a physical impossibility that he could be the father he was happy to give us some money if we were in trouble, and he included a letter of introduction to a theatrical agent he knew in London, saying he hoped it would help Gay find work back home.

*

Four days before we were due to depart, I went round to Robert and Bridget's house, ostensibly to say goodbye, but also to see whether I couldn't wangle some money out of them too.

It was a difficult meeting. We sat on the stoep and the sun was low behind the trees, sending wide blue shadows across the lawn. These shadows looked like henchmen, standing shoulder to shoulder, their hats pulled low over their ears, waiting to hear what would be said. I looked at the spot on the lawn where I'd sunbathed and read, oh so intently, about pickling and preserving, remembering Paul in that sparkling sunshine lying at my feet and showing

337

me the swimming costume he'd bought me. I remembered the camp bed in the downstairs study.

'We did our best, you know,' Bridget said, 'it's not been easy for us either.'

'I know. It's not been easy for any of us.' I was being reasonable.

'It's been easy for Paul,' Robert said, 'he's gone back to Durban. Did you know?'

'Yes, I heard, Ruby came round to collect an earring, she told me. When I get back to London I'm going to sue him for divorce,' I told them, 'on the grounds of abandonment.'

'Who is Ruby?' Bridget wanted to know. I could feel Robert's eyes on me, I decided to be kind.

'She's a friend of that man Joseph, you know that one who came here that time after Paul ran off the first time?'

Bridget decided to cry so Robert fetched us more strong drinks, and we sat in silence for a while.

'You'll pick yourself up again, dear,' said Bridget, 'won't you? You're still young. Perhaps there'll be another man out there for you,' but she looked as though she very much doubted that this could be the case. 'At least you didn't – I mean, at least there aren't any children involved.'

She was smiling – her overcrowded teeth rushing forward like so many bossy matrons to wave me goodbye – so I put my hand on her knee and said, 'You've been like a mother to me, Bridget. I won't forget you.'

We sat in silence, contemplating this unlikely exchange of pleasantries.

Robert went into the house and came back with an envelope.

'Robert went to the bank this morning,' Bridget said. 'We wanted to give you something, Laura, we hope you'll accept this gift.'

I protested a little, just to please Bridget, and then took the envelope in both hands and put it on my lap.

'Well,' I said, raising my glass, 'let's drink to old times.'

'Old times,' we all said in unison, without a hint of irony.

*

Robert drove me back to Mrs Richardson's later that evening.

'I'm sorry you're going,' he said as we turned out of his driveway, 'I've come to almost like having you around.'

'What will you and Ruby do?' The envelope of money was still on my lap, I'd been trying to guess how much there was in the envelope, what Robert might have considered an appropriate pay-off.

'Christ knows.'

'You won't leave Bridget though?'

'I don't know,' Robert murmured, 'perhaps we all need a new start from time to time.'

'But then you'll be like Paul.'

'No, darling, no. Not like Paul,' and he reached over and took my hand and squeezed it. 'There's £450 in there.' He nodded at the envelope. 'I know you've been wondering.'

Robert and I sat in the car in Mrs Richardson's driveway for a long time. Gay was out and the house was dark. I felt small and frightened suddenly, overwhelmed by the complicated path, with its precipitous dips and curves, ahead of me. Feeling, for the first time, the slackening of my spirit. Tired. I thought of my father taking his weekly shuffling tour of his priceless timepieces, the careful laying out of the clock keys, the muttering, the way he ran his hands lovingly across the tops of the clocks as he bent towards them. 'Here we go, it's your time now.'

'My father gave me some money when I went to London to marry Paul,' I said to Robert. 'Have you got a cigarette?'

'And now you've got some more to divorce him with,' he said, passing me one. 'What are you up to, Laura?'

'How do you mean?'

'How come you waited so long for Paul but now you're off in this great rush? Did something happen? Ruby says she's seen that woman at your house out and about in town. She says she's getting something of a reputation.'

I shrugged and wound down the window a little to blow the smoke out.

'Must have come to my senses,' I said.

'You really thought he'd come back to you, didn't you?'

'Yes. I blamed you for a long time, Robert, did you know that? I thought you bullied him, were denying him the opportunity to be himself. I still think that. I think he does want to do things, to make a difference, find his place in the world — he just can't shake you and Bridget off.'

Robert laughed, a short barking sort of laugh. 'So who are you going to blame now?'

'When you said that about Paul being simple, what did you mean?'

Robert coughed, and looked over at me. He didn't speak for a moment.

'He's not very *sound*, he's feeble-minded, weak, impulsive. Bridget thinks it's because we came to live here. She thinks he went mad when we brought him here, something about moving him at a vulnerable age. He's not ill, Laura, he's just not "quite right". He should have told you before he married you. We should have told you, but we didn't dare. I suppose we were optimistic, but of course he couldn't cope with being married, it was too much for him. I thought he was provoking me in marrying you, he wanted something to show for himself.'

I thought about this for a while.

'That's not a bad thing though. I wouldn't have minded. It could have worked,' I said softly to myself, 'it could have, if we hadn't come out here. I think this place has done something to my mind too. Would you like to come in, Robert?'

He shook his head. 'No, darling, I don't think so, kind offer though,' and he kissed me hard on the mouth and then leant over to open the door for me. 'You've had a helluva time, I'm sorry about it all. Goodbye, Laura – oh, and good luck.'

One week later, having packed my possessions into the cardboard suitcase, I was waiting for the taxi to take me to the landing strip, and I took a final tour of the garden. I saw it then – a tiny head above the soil, a delicate white flower, touched with pink, arising out of the scorched earth.

The orchid had flowered.

Norman Mead Hotel, Winchester

March 1948

I have taken some notes from the trial today – they talked so fast it was difficult to get it all down. Of course there has been much talk of fibres found on the window, urine and saliva stains on a pillowslip and much, much discussion about her missing black silk pyjamas. The jury heard Camb's claim that during consensual sex Miss Gibson suffered an asthmatic turn, or perhaps a heart attack – the experts were unclear – and how in a fit of terrible panic, he fled the cabin only to return resolved to destroy the evidence, and this was how he arrived at the bizarre, impulsive decision to push her out the porthole. But, as is so often the case, the truth did not bear up to close scrutiny, it cannot account for the illogical, improbable or bizarre. Judge Hilbury clearly considered him to be guilty from the off and had been assisting the prosecuting counsel as best he could, and Camb's smooth, cold, movie-star turn in the witness box did nothing to help his cause. Today he was found guilty of the murder of Gay Gibson and sentenced to death. I watched him carefully during the sentence, he did not cry out, he did not even flinch.

But these are the exchanges which have interested me the most, the ones that seem most worthy of inclusion in the diary:

Mike Abel was cross-examined by Mr Roberts, Winchester Great Hall, 2.45,
Saturday 20 March 1948

You told the jury that this dead girl clutched you by the arm and
said, 'I love you, Mike'?

Yes.

You are sure you're not romancing?

No.

A girl of twenty-one said that to you?

Yes. I told my wife about it.

Henry Gilbert, theatrical producer, was examined by Mr Casswell for the defence.
What sort of temperament had this girl, Miss Gibson?

When I first met her she was a charming, nice, well behaved
young lady. During the process of my production she showed a
temperament of a peculiar type. I found her often distraught and
highly strung.

Was she reserved, or did she speak of her private affairs?

To me, she readily discussed her private affairs. She found at
first the part of Lorna a rather difficult part, as it had many facets
to the character, and of course, I did my best to guide her, as the
producer, to enlighten her as to the type of part it was. As time
went on her behaviour became peculiar towards one of my cast,
Mike Abel. First of all she told me she was in love with him.

Did you see any signs of that?

No but one evening at rehearsal for no apparent reason she kicked
him, got hold of him and sort of mauled him about. Naturally, I put
a stop to that.

Was that an isolated instance or did you see her attack Abel again?

I didn't see her attack Abel again, but I was present when he came out of my own drawing room. He showed me his legs, and both shins had been kicked.

Do you remember an occasion in Commissioner Street?

Yes. We were at the Pre-View Theatre — a private film preview theatre belonging to African Consolidated Theatres — about two and a half weeks before the opening of the show on 10th September. The rehearsal terminated at 10 o'clock at night, and the greater percentage of the cast walked across the street. She went into a dead faint in the middle of Commissioner Street. We picked her up and put her into a parked car which belonged to one of my cast.

What would you say with regard to her health?

When I first met her she told me she had come to South Africa because of her health. She said she had asthma.

Did you hear or see any indications of asthma?

Only when she complained to me that she had to stop taking her singing lessons.

Did you hear her coughing?

I did, but I didn't pay too much attention.

What about her appearance?

She had the most beautiful white skin I have ever seen in my life. White like alabaster. It was the most striking thing about her. She said she was an unhappy human being. I said why. She said, 'I cannot love like other people.' I said, 'What do you mean by that?' She said, 'I am not like other girls.'

Laura Lovell — cross-examined by Mr G. D. Roberts KC for the Crown.
Mrs Lovell, you say Miss Gibson came to stay with you at 10 Mimosa Drive, Auckland Park, and that you shared the house for roughly two months?

Yes.

Had you met Miss Gibson before that time?

No. My husband was working in Durban, he met her there and he escorted her to Johannesburg, where she had hope of finding theatrical work.

Did you know her well?

No, not very. She rehearsed a great deal and I was busy a lot of the time with my gardening. She was my lodger.

Did you ever see her suffer any fainting fits?

No, a couple of times she was short of breath and she did look a little blue around the mouth.

Did she cough?

Not much, but like I say, I didn't see much of her during that time.

Was your husband also staying with you at the house?

My husband? No, he was working in Durban, and visiting his parents. Why do you ask?

Did you ever see Miss Gibson behaving in an indiscreet or hysterical manner?

Sometimes. She was a complicated person.

And then you decided to return home together?

Yes. I was due to come back to England to see my parents, and Gay wanted to leave after the play so we decided to travel together.

And you found money for the tickets?

Yes, people were very generous. They wanted to support Gay in her career.

On the night in question, Mrs Lovell, did you see much of Miss Gibson?

No, she wasn't feeling well. She retired to her bed for the afternoon and then early after the dance, and I returned on deck and chatted with Mr Hopwood and Mr Bray and a few others. Then I went to bed, and slept through the night. It was very warm and muggy, it made me feel sleepy.

Had you ever seen Miss Gibson talking to Mr Camb? Paying him special attention?

Yes. He was very attentive towards her, he found her very attractive. A lot of men did.

Do you think it likely or possible that Miss Gibson died of natural causes during the sex act with Mr Camb?

Natural causes? I'm sorry. I don't understand the question. That would be natural for her, I think, sex and death, yes, I suppose so.

Mrs Lovell? You'll need to speak up, we can't hear you. Do you need a glass of water?

Twenty-three

Did I intend for what happened to happen? To this day I don't know the answer to that question, and I have asked myself it often enough. As Gay and I stood side by side on the deck of the *Durban Castle* looking at the flat top of Table Mountain, and as the buildings gathered around the curve of the bay and slid down towards the long stretches of white sand, the clear dark blue seas and the busy activity of the port, I don't believe I had a set plan in my head. A child with dark skin but a shocking mop of red hair sat in the back of a truck near a warehouse, I thought he was looking at me, I half raised my arm to wave at him, but he didn't respond. I saw, from the deck of the departing ship, how beautiful that country was, how Cape Town seemed vibrant and alive to me, an airy place, how unlike Johannesburg. And though I was grieving with the failure of leaving Paul behind, gripping the wooden rail with Gay beside me in her fur coat, complaining about her mother and trying to link her arm through mine, I did see it. I saw what Moses had meant when he had said it was a beautiful country, that the poisons that ran through it were those of division; I saw with a shock that it was a place where I could never have belonged, that I never had belonged anywhere,

347

except perhaps one place, the crook in Paul's arm, his other around me, his cheek balanced across the top of my head. And that I had changed from the schoolgirl who'd stepped off a ship just like this one, only ten months before, that I was dangerous and capable now, that I understood what power meant, and what the consequences were of having no power.

*

The *Durban Castle* had been refitted and this was her maiden voyage in her new guise. Gone were the troops and the march of their feet, the damaged passageways, the saloon rooms ripped apart to make space for armaments and frightened soldiers, the maps that must have hung on the walls and the kitchens turned in to mess halls and the smell of frightened boys. Now it was all chandeliers and brass fittings, bleached wooden decks promising evening games and light refreshments, new carpets in the Long Gallery and saloons, attractive fixtures and finishings; gone was the battle-ship grey, she was lavender once again, smelling sweetly of possibility.

I saw an inevitability to what would happen the first time I saw James Camb, the following morning out on the deck. I was standing outside the stateroom, taking the air, and I could see him moving smoothly down a line of deckchairs to my right, tucking blankets under the feet of the more elderly passengers, stooping to pass an old man his reading glasses, lingering beside two ladies who giggled at something he said and batted their geriatric blue eyelashes at him. There was great vanity in his obsequious service, and I could imagine him preparing himself each night for this performance on deck, sleekly priming himself for the delights of excessive courtesy.

348

How they adored him, how patiently he attended to their every need. He was a handsome man – even I could see that – there was something of the matinée idol in his well-cut features and dark eyes; but underneath that cool exterior I could sense both his weakness and his vanity. He reminded me of Gay. A sudden burst of nausea erupted in my stomach, and I had to put my hands over my mouth. I shut my eyes and felt the sun on my face. I fancied I could hear Gay humming to herself somewhere nearby; everywhere there was weakness and vanity, I was afloat with it, drowning in it, on our ship of fools.

*

There were set places in the small first-class restaurant, with its shining white tablecloths and silver cutlery, and at dinner on the first night Gay and I were seated with two gentlemen who introduced themselves as Mr Frank Hopwood and Wing Commander Bray. Gay made a fool of herself, leaning in too close to Mr Hopwood, who must have been at least forty-five and looked inexperienced in the ways of women. She kept putting her hand on his arm, which unnerved him and he had to shrug it off by pretending that he needed to pour himself some more water. Mr Hopwood told us that he was the catering manager of the Union Castle line, and then Bray told us that he was returning home to Chichester after a long bout of illness following the war. He hadn't seen his wife or children since 1943 and that as far as he was concerned, the ship couldn't sail fast enough. Then they both looked at Gay and me, waiting to hear our reasons for returning home. I was stuck, I didn't know what to say to these clean, conscientious men. I looked at their polite, expectant faces and frowned, I was having trouble holding the glass because of my burnt fingers, and I sloshed water on the white tablecloth. Bray went to great pains with his napkin to soak up some of the spillage.

'I'm returning home having taken the leading role in *Golden Boy* at the Standard Theatre in Johannesburg,' Gay announced loudly. 'I have been given the opportunity to perform at the Abbey Theatre in Dublin, are you familiar with that theatre?'

They both told her that they were not, but Bray was polite enough to ask her how she found the audiences in Johannesburg.

'Oh most receptive' she answered airily, looking over her shoulder and around the room. Though if she hoped to see more interesting and exciting people than Hopwood and Bray, then she was going to be disappointed. I had already noted that Gay and I were by far the youngest on board, by quite some distance, the respectable, greying heads and the hum of middle-agers making polite conversation surrounded us. This was why, inevitably, her eyes would eventually fall on James Camb.

'The *Durban Castle* has just been refitted,' Mr Hopwood told us. 'She had a marvellous war, but I must say it is a pleasure to see her back in service again, and looking just as splendid as she ever did.'

'Extraordinary food, Hopwood, well done,' said the Wing Commander. Mr Hopwood flushed with pleasure.

'Thank you, yes, we're not restricted by rations on the line, you see. Lots of ox tongue, turbot and curried prawns here, and I think there will be Pudding au Malaga with almond sauce to finish off with.' He smiled at me.

There was a buzzing in my ear, I think it was the effort of all this polite conversation, I could not think of a time when I had been with such sincere and honest people, or when they had sought to engage me in conversation. I was not giving a very good account of myself, and Gay was bored, I could tell. She was frowning.

'So you are both returning home,' said the Wing Commander.

'Yes, I suppose I am,' I murmured, giving him a vague smile which I hoped indicated a resistance to further enquiry.

'Yes, together,' said Gay. 'We're *together*. I don't suppose there will be much to keep me entertained on this trip, do you?'

Mr Hopwood looked startled and mumbled something gentlemanly about how he hoped himself and the Wing Commander would do their best and Gay stared at him and asked if anyone minded if she had a smoke.

Gay and I took a brief stroll along the deck after dinner that night, the wind was up but it was warm and airy. I loved the feel of the wind in my hair, the ship plunging through the seas towards the darkness. Gay leant against the railings, looking down at the dark waters below.

'Home' she said to herself, and she shivered and ran her hands up and down her arms. 'Funny idea that, isn't it, Laura? Home.'

*

The first week we meandered gently on our course, and I soon got to know the other passengers. There was General Albert Osborn of the Salvation Army, who every morning marched along the decks singing hymns before breakfast; John Butler, a Rhodesian tobacco farmer, and 'Sport' Pienaar who was always much in demand at the bar and at dinner because he was the president of South African Rugby and hence something of a social catch, albeit a shaky seventy-year-old one. Gay intrigued the other passengers, because she was so pretty, I suppose. I overheard two elderly women discussing her, one described her as 'tarty' and the other sniffed disapprovingly and said, 'That other girl she follows about the place, she looks a bit odd, doesn't she? Don't you think?'

Gay wasn't being very tarty though, she was conducting herself in a rather modest, almost dreamy way. She did follow me about a lot, that was true. I kept trying to find places on the ship to avoid her, I couldn't think straight when she was with me, she seemed to fill the cabins up with her long legs and her hair and her talking all the time. If I sat down in the Long Gallery for a coffee, she would appear within a minute and stretch out on the chair beside me.

'Where do you keep getting to, kiddo?' she said, looking around her. 'Is that deck steward about?' Then James Camb had come over and bowed in front of her with mock courtesy; hovering, his eyes met hers and he winked.

'What can I get you Miss Gibson?'

'A coffee,' she said, looking him up and down, 'just a coffee, for now.'

When he came back, I saw her looking at him more carefully. He was very well turned out – his buttons and shoes gleamed with the same sheen as his oiled hair. He slid up to her and ostentatiously poured the cream from a silver jug, making a great show of checking for drips.

'A pleasure,' he said smoothly. 'Is there anything else?'

'Yes,' Gay told him, looking out the window, the sun falling on her legs, 'I'd like afternoon tea in my cabin. Can you bring a tray down?' And with that he padded away. 'I don't feel so well, Laura, I'm tired. I feel so tired, can you hold my hand?'

And I took her thin bird-like hand in mine, and squeezed it tightly, looking out at the horizon. I thought about the night I had met Paul, and how he had seemed to step out of the shadows and drag me towards the light, how he had told me what sort of a person I was, and of how readily I wanted to believe him.

*

At lunch, a week into the voyage, on the Friday, our resident martinet Captain Patey announced that there was to be a dinner-dance that evening, he told us that we could all look forward to Mr Innocent and his band delighting us with some dance numbers. A small cheer went up when he said this, it wasn't a sincere cheer, it was polite. Gay, unusually, hadn't appeared, so I went down to her cabin, hoping to find it empty. I tried her door and was surprised to find it locked. I knocked.

'Gay, it's me, open up.'

She opened it a little, her green eye levelled at mine through the crack in the door.

'Let me in, Gay.'

'What do you want?'

'Oh come on, I've got news.'

She reluctantly pulled the door back wide enough for me to slide in next to her. Her bed was still unmade, and she was in her black pyjamas.

'You came to find me then? Did you miss me at luncheon?' she asked, sliding back into her bed. 'I'm not feeling right, Laura.'

'It's hot in here — why don't you open the porthole?'

'Can you do it?' She leant over to get a cigarette from her bedside table, and then back against the pillows. The porthole was above her bed, it was difficult to squeeze myself between the bed and wall to try and open it. I saw a pen on her pillow.

'Guess what,' I said, trying to ease the catch on the window, 'there's going to be a dinner-dance tonight.'

'Is there?' she said, lighting her cigarette. 'Where do you keep going? I can't ever find you. I'm not feeling very well.'

'I don't go anywhere, don't be daft. There isn't anywhere to go. I came to find you, didn't I? Because you missed lunch.'

'James said he'd arrange a tray to be sent down for me.'

'James?'

She shrugged and smoked her cigarette.

'I'm pleased you came, Laura.'

I sat down, tentatively, on the side of her bed. And then I saw it, her diary, open on the bedside table underneath the ashtray. A large book, the pages curled at the sides, slightly grubby, I could just see her spidery writing through the glass.

'Give me one of those cigarettes,' I said, and she threw the packet at me. I could feel her eyes on me as I fished one out and lit it with her lighter. As I hoped she would, she picked up the ashtray and placed it on the bed between us. There was the diary, in full view, open and inviting.

'I've got drink, kiddo,' she said. 'James got it for me.'

'He does seem to have singled you out rather,' I said, filling my mouth with smoke, trying not to stare too hard at her diary.

She leant over and brought a bottle of rum out from her bedside locker; as she leant down, the diary shook a little. It was tantalising, having it there, so close. Gay also produced two tooth mugs, then she measured the rum out in equal portions. I took the mug and had a sip. Her face looked flushed and her hands were a little shaky.

'Do you like him?'

'Who, James?' she snorted. 'No, Laura, I don't like him, I don't like any man all that much. I like you though. So who are you going to dance with tonight? Will it be Mr Pienaar for the geriatric shuffle or the Wing Commander for a slow respectable waltz?'

We laughed, and she drained the last of her tooth mug with a flourish. She was breathing quite heavily, and put out a hand to steady herself on the bed.

'I feel quite queer,' she said, in a small faraway voice.

'Probably the rum.' I took her long, pale hand in my dry one and stroked the top of her fingers. 'Gay, your fingers are a very strange colour.'

The skin under her nails was a strange mud-brown colour, and the tips of her fingers were pale blue.

'I feel dizzy.' She was very pale now, and those familiar traces of blue had begun to appear around the edges of her mouth.

'Are you going to faint? Sit back against the pillows.'

'Everything is swirling, Laura, always swirling.' She screwed her eyes shut and was breathing even harder now. I could see the rapid rise and fall of her breasts, the strain in her neck. I lay one hand on her soft hair and stroked it.

'Take a minute, keep breathing, in and out.'

She was grasping for air now, shallow and fast, her fist clenched up by her side.

'Shall I call a doctor?'

She shook her head and curled round on her side, taking my arm from her head and holding it under the side of her face. This was my moment. Shooting a quick look at Gay, folded over and slack like a damp towel, I reached down and snatched up her diary. Moving slowly, I tried to tuck it up inside my dress. When I turned back again, I thought I caught a flash of green, her eyes snapping shut, but I told myself I was imagining it.

'I'll let you rest then, Gay,' I said, pulling my hand out from under her face. 'Try to get better for tonight. We need a party.'

'James . . . is coming to see . . . me . . . tonight,' she said in a light, breathless voice, as though the very words themselves were being squeezed out of her.

I walked slowly from her bed towards the door, clutching her diary near my stomach, almost bent over. I could feel her eyes on my back all the way out of the cabin.

Gay's diary

October 1947, the Durban Castle

Laura and I are sailing home. It was all decided quite suddenly, quite dramatically, as though Laura suddenly woke up and saw around her, like the scales fell from her eyes, and she saw it all clearly, like now she understands how it should be, how it must be. And perhaps I see it all truly now too.

I am near to telling Laura that I slept with Paul, that he went a little mad over me, or perhaps that he was a little mad already. Because it's all about possession, isn't it? And belonging and knowing where you belong and where you should escape from and where to. When I saw Paul in Oxford and I told him to save her, well, that was the start of it all, wasn't it? That he should save that little person, and that I should come and ultimately be with her.

All this acting and pretending and making do with boys, the falling through the blackness, seeing the stars and the golden hoops of fire, the broken-up earth in Europe, the wide streets of Johannesburg, the Empire, the cocktails and the smoke and the money and men in their suits. All of it. And Laura sees all that, she knows all that. She thought that place was one that was taken over and changed, that it had no heart, that the earth moved and that nobody can truly own a made-up city, that she wanted Paul to own her, but that he wasn't capable, not really. She sees it all now. I could tell her about Paul and me, about how we made love in Durban and how he cried, and how all I wanted was to get to Johannesburg, yes to act, but also to find her. Because we were both lost, both needful. She will understand that I had to tell him to send her home, that he wasn't worthy of her, that I told her lies to keep her away from him, because they weren't meant to be. Not as Laura and I are meant to be. And we can bring up his child, the two of us. Which is a funny turn of events however you look at it, because she's not much, Laura Lovell, she is like Paul said, a little person, a funny, squitty sort of person, not like me at all.

Twenty-four

It took me the whole afternoon to read Gay's diary, from the beginning to the last entry, the entry where she described me as 'squitty'. Sometimes my reading was interspersed with her coughing on the other side of the wall. At one point, when she was in France with Pierre, I had to get away from the diary and I abandoned it on my bed and went up on deck, opening my mouth wide, wanting to be filled with air. But it was tropical and muggy, everything filmy with warmth and wetness, a few passengers looked over at me heavy and sleepy, elderly men shuffling by in their wide shorts, and I knew I had to return. I read it slowly, carefully, urging myself to take in every line; sometimes I smiled or laughed, in spite of myself. I read on and on, as the afternoon light faded to evening, making myself know the truth. Though I had 'known' in some hidden strange way about Paul and Gay from that moment when the three of us were all in poor Paul's bedroom, caught in the shafts of reflecting light, our lives intersecting, reflecting one another and casting strange lights into the corner of his bedroom.

*

I lean back against the wall of my cabin, imagining I can hear Gay moving about on her bed next door. I close my eyes. I can see Gay and Paul on the promenade, kissing and sweaty, can see Paul's open face, pleading with her as she twirls around him, always just beyond his fingertips, her painted mouth, the windy air laced with salt, Paul laughing and needy, captive. My head is hot and I feel the sudden lurch of nausea in my stomach. I rush to the loo just in time, and violently vomit, lurching with pain, pressing my head against the cold steel door, down on my knees. I place both hands on the floor, feeling the coldness in them, and knowing that coldness is now in me too.

I sit for a long time on the floor, pushing my hair behind my ears and crying. I have stopped being sick now. This despair, this desperate, pitiful grief. I cannot hold it any longer. I think of Paul and I on the Melville koppies, him so proud and carefree, my picking my way carefully behind him, getting scratched by the thorns, the sun on my head, and then Paul taking my hand and helping me through. We could have survived, he and I. We could have beaten that place and made a life, I know I could have, before Gay arrived with her long legs and sinister know-ingness, her paranoia and carelessness, her desire to possess and take over, to be powerful and to be hurt, to be both victim and persecutor.

I get dressed quickly, wipe my face with a cold flannel and apply some lipstick. I know that James Camb uses the cupboard on the Promenade Deck as a kind of unofficial office, and I go straight there to find him. I see him on the deck first though, dancing along bringing people cocktails, stopping just long enough to charm them and then moving off leaving them wanting more. I see Frank Hopwood hot in his evening suit, and he waves at me

360

and I raise my hand back at him. I wait for James Camb to finish serving and then follow him as he goes down the empty Long Gallery.

'I've got a message for you,' I call to him.

He turns in surprise, runs his fingers through his hair, puts the silver tray under one arm.

'Sorry, Mrs Lovell, were you speaking to me?'

'Yes.'

My skin pricks, I can feel the hairs standing on end. It is a hot, still night and I think he looks like he is wading his way through the air as he walks back up the Long Gallery, towards me. This is how it is meant to be – isn't that what Gay wrote in her diary?

'I have a message from Miss Gibson,' I say. 'She says she hopes you will remember your arrangement, for tonight. She is expecting to see you in her cabin after the dance.'

He coughs, pretending embarrassment, and shoots a beady look at me, but he looks pleased with himself too.

'Whatever I can do to be of service,' he says with a smirk, and gives me another of his ironic half-bows, wanting me to feel and understand his power. Yes, this is right. James Camb and Gay Gibson, I do not think she will refuse him, I know her well now, all that I might have guessed about her has been made certain, truthful, whole. It is right that they should come together, and I am certain that she will not survive him.

I turn round and walk quickly out from the Long Gallery, back onto the Promenade Deck, wondering whether Gay knows this also, and knows I have read her diary, is expecting it all to end tonight, and join Mr Hopwood by the railings.

'Are you all right, Mrs Lovell? You don't look quite right. It's hot, isn't it? Can I get you a drink?'

I nod, holding tight to the rails, feeling my blistered fingers squeeze painfully against the wood.

*

We are a useless bunch, huddled into the dining room, any sense of expectation that this will be an evening of festivity quickly dispelled by the sober reality of our own limitations. Dinner is quickly eaten and dispatched with, and Mr Innocent and his band start their first number. The dance floor is empty and looks destined to remain so, people are edging their chairs away from it, as though it may be contaminated.

Gay has been quiet and pale during dinner, but I notice that she's drinking a lot. She talks casually to Bray about his children, and he seems surprised to find her so easy and accommodating. Mr Hopwood and I talk amiably enough about very little at first, but then he becomes persistent, battering me with questions, 'So you were in Johannesburg for a year, is that right?' and 'Where is Mr Lovell? In England? Are you going back to see your mother?' I look at him, spooning prawns into his mouth, and I smile at him. I cannot answer these questions, I don't understand them, I have no answers.

Old Sport Pienaar comes shuffling over, adjusting his tie, and asks Gay to dance. She accepts and takes his proffered arm. We all watch them turning around the dance floor, him proud and resilient, but Gay doesn't look at him, she looks like she's folded over in his arms, a wisp of a thing, there to do his bidding. Another couple follow them onto the dance floor and assume very correct postures, their unsmiling faces turned away from one another; as they start to dance we can all see that they are rather good. They must have felt the sight of Old Sport grabbing folds of Gay's dress around her waist one sight too far, and felt the need to correct the balance somewhat.

Bray steels himself and asks me to dance, with a shrug of his shoulders and a grimace on his face which suggests that he'd really rather not, so I pat his arm and ask if he wouldn't mind if I sit this one out. I tell him I feel a little hot and walk out onto the deck, prettily lit with lanterns for the dance, and hope for a breeze to cool me down, to stroke away this hammering in my head. Gay follows me out, carrying her glass.

'He kept trying to press himself against me, the old goat,' she says, leaning against the railings and looking down at the water.

I glance over her shoulder into the room. 'He looks exhausted, he's had to sit down.'

She laughs and drains the last from her glass. 'Let's go in and get drunk, Laura, shall we?'

Mr Innocent manages to keep playing, somewhat against the tide of the passengers' wishes, until eleven o'clock. Gay is smoking a great deal, her lips look paper-thin and there are still those telltale traces of blue around them. She throws herself into the party well enough, laughing easily and listening obediently to John Butler's tales of the surprising things his natives get up to on his tobacco farm. Someone suggests a midnight swim and Gay is enthusiastic about the idea and tells everyone that she's going down to her cabin now to find her swimsuit. I follow her out onto the deck, she is weaving her way unsteadily in front of me. Camb appears, from his cupboard, stretching an arm out to stop her, and I can see her look up in surprise. I run over as quickly as I can, and as I approach I can hear Gay saying, 'I'm going for my swimsuit, there's to be a midnight swim.' Her voice is high and wild-sounding, and Camb murmurs something back to her, leaning in, his head dipped in the low shadows.

'All right, Gay?' I say, as heartily as I can manage. 'Did you get your swimsuit?'

'I've got a bone to pick with her.' Camb is looking straight at me, his arm still barring our way forward. 'She's not been eating the food on her trays,' he says, smiling at me.

'Oh well.' I am breezy and take Gay's elbow. 'Come on. Do you know where you put it, Gay?' And I push past Camb, escorting Gay down the steel steps towards our cabins.

'I'm not sure I'm really up to it.' Gay has one hand on her door, and she leans her head heavily against it, giving no impression of wanting to go in. 'I might just turn in, Laura. I still feel a bit off.'

'Yes.' I open the door for her. The stewardess has been in and remade her bed. I take her black silk pyjamas out from under the pillow and lay them out for her.

'Off to sleep then,' I say.

She sits down, defeated, on the end of the bed and slowly slips her shoes off and rubs her feet.

'I'm so tired of it all,' she says quietly. 'Men are so demanding, I find.'

'Promise me, Gay, that you won't lock your door tonight? Please? Just in case you're unwell.'

She nods, not looking up at me. She is rubbing her pale feet. I think she wants to ask me something, I wonder whether she has noticed her missing diary.

'Goodnight then, Gay,' I say at the door, 'hope you feel better in the morning.'

But she doesn't answer.

*

The party is breaking up, nobody but Gay had taken the idea of the swim seriously, and people are saying goodnight to one another. Hopwood, Bray and John Butler are sitting together on the deck smoking cigars, so I go over to join them. They aren't particularly pleased to see me, but they struggle out of their deckchairs and Bray offers me his.

'Has Miss Gibson retired for the evening?' Hopwood asks, the rim of his spectacles catching the thin strips of light from the saloon behind us.

'Yes, she's tired.'

They have been talking about us, I can tell, and because I've interrupted them we sit in silence while they all puff on their cigars. I stay for a bit and then tell them I'd better be off myself and they are suddenly charming to me, liking me in the instance of my departure. I walk back down the deck, which is deserted, and stop outside Camb's cupboard, which looks locked up for the night. Then I go down to my cabin, without checking on Gay.

I hang my dress up, slip off my underwear and pull on a night-dress. I sit on the edge of the bed, it is hot and still, I can barely hear the sound of the ocean outside my porthole. Everything seems peaceful and calm. I wrap my arms around my legs, stare straight ahead of me at the cabin's blank wall.

There are footsteps outside in the corridor. I quickly lean over and turn off my bedside lamp, then creep over to the wall and press my ear against it. I can hear Gay's voice and then Camb's, he sounds insistent, drunk perhaps, but Gay isn't shouting or protesting, she sounds light and sleepy. I wait to hear their sounds. I know Gay, though sick, will not want to refuse him, that he will want to take her, as ill and injured as she is, he will heave himself on top of her and tug and rip at those black pyjamas and she will surrender herself to him, tensing that neck as he pulls apart those silly skinny thighs. Excited now, but frightened they will hear my beating heart, I press myself, palms open against the wall, spread my legs, close my eyes, will myself to see and hear everything. I see Gay there with Paul, her teeth digging into her bottom lip, an arm thrown casually out to her side, pink nipples erect, her pale stomach, breathing in and out, up and down, one pale hand wrapped around Paul's neck, pulling him closer, his astonished face, her red hair, her running a hand now across her own body, tickling the sides of her breasts, showing Paul how best to excite and please her. He with one hand cupping her trembling bottom, trembling himself, whilst pressing his other hand against the side of her face.

I am breathing heavily, when I hear with a quickening Camb shout out, a cry of shock rather than ecstasy, and I lean closer against the cold wall, hearing the sound of Gay's door opening and closing and then Camb's footsteps creeping past my door and up the corridor. Too soon, he is gone much too soon.

I open my door and sneak into Gay's cabin. She is lying on the bed, naked, and her hair a flame spread out above her head and across the pillow. She is lying quite still but then she turns towards me, her green eyes glassy with panic. She cannot breathe, her hands are around her neck. She sees me and tries to speak, delicate spittles of brown phlegm are collecting at the corners of her mouth. I creep closer. She reaches out a hand; I can only hear the faintest rasping sounds of her pathetic attempts to breathe. I take one step closer, a splinter of hope swims across her face and her eyes lock into mine. She is trying to tell me something, she needs help, she tries to move but she can't, her mouth is wide open now, flapping, desperate for air. As I bend down near her I can smell her sex, and Camb's, can see red, raised marks on her knees, has she been on all

366

fours? Her eyes are wide now, scanning across my face as though trying to read it. I reach out to touch her, bending closer, looking into her terrified bulging eyes. Her body is giving little spasmodic kicks, tensing and gasping, she is still looking into my eyes.

'I read your diary, Gay,' I whisper in her ear. 'I know everything.'

I stand by her watching her body fight for breath, I reach up my hand and place it over her mouth and her nose. Within seconds her body takes one last spasm, a violent tensing, and then collapses.

There are footsteps outside again, matching my own heartbeats, it must be Camb coming back. Perhaps he had gone to fetch a doctor or the Captain. I panic, I look around wildly, and then decide to hide myself in the clothes closet. I trip over her pyjamas on the floor, I stoop and gather them up into my arms, and squeeze into the closet. I leave the door a tiny bit ajar and through this crack I can see Camb come back into the room, alone. I see him walking over to the bed, bending over the body, checking for a pulse. He swears, panic and fear are rising up inside his body like a bad injection, he flaps his hands against his body and stamps his feet like a moody schoolboy.

'You stupid bitch,' he mutters. 'Fuck.'

He moves out of my eyeline, round the bottom of the bed, but I can hear him swearing and grunting. I wonder what he is doing, is he rolling her up in the bed sheet perhaps before going to fetch someone, or is he trying to dress her? I open the door a tiny bit more. Peering out I can see Camb heaving poor Gay's body up over his shoulder. He is standing on the bed, facing the porthole. He raises her up, feet first, and then with one sudden lunge starts to push her body out of the porthole, but she is long and difficult and he has to heave and push her to get her hips through. She is a desperate mermaid trying to climb into the ship's cabin, trying to find refuge. Camb pulls her arms out long, he stands behind and shoves her by the head, one quick lunge and then she is gone, sliding out into the darkness. Do I hear, or do I imagine, her soft and sudden splash?

I am frozen still, looking at Camb still standing on the bed. He flaps his hands again, as though trying to rid himself of all they have just done. He jumps off the bed, pads past the closet door, standing only an arm's length from me, and looks about him. I don't care if he sees me, I want him to, but then I hear the click of the cabin door closing and I know he has gone.

I step out into the cabin, the place where only moments before Gay had existed. The bed is still warm from her, I can feel her lips against my palm, her pyjamas still in my hand. I have seen the passing moment, I have caught it between my fingers. I look out of the open porthole, see the stars in the night sky, hear the faintest sound of the waves easing against the ship as it ploughs on its course, leaving Gay behind in her dark watery grave with the fishes, sharks and seaweed.

Epilogue

June 1948, London

There is one last entry to make before I destroy this diary. I am in the kitchen of my flat in London making tea. It is cold for June; from the window I can see grey slanting roofs shining in the grey slanting rain, and everywhere I am surrounded by broken, ruined buildings waiting to be reborn. It is raining and cold, the kitchen is grey, small and dusty. The kettle is on the gas hob, not boiling. These are cramped living conditions; my neighbour across the landing is an old woman who shuffles in her bedroom slippers to the corner shop each morning, she wears her husband's old raincoat and a woollen hat on her head. Her name is Mrs Midges, she says she has lived in this building all her life and nobody, not even the Nazis, could destroy it, even though they had bombed the whole street; this one house remained untouched and still standing. She strokes the wall as she tells me this and smiles at me. 'It's a survivor,' she says, 'just like us.'

Gay has no grave, they never recovered her body. There was a report a few weeks ago about a body washed ashore in West Africa, but it was incomplete, it had been savaged by sharks, and nobody could even tell whether the body belonged to a man or a woman. I shudder of course, just thinking of it all, I try to shake it out of myself. After this I won't think of Gay Gibson again, won't allow myself to dream of her on her bed in the cabin, or remember how she looked in Mrs Richardson's bed, believing she had found a home.

No, I am here now. I am somewhere I understand, a place I feel I can move, a place where I am learning confidence. I have learnt there is so such place as home. When I placed my hand across Gay's already dying mouth I was in possession of myself, I knew what I was doing, and it was revenge, of course it was, I cannot claim it were anything grander or less venal and commonplace than revenge, but it was a sort of kindness too, a releasing of her desire to be free from it all, knowing that she had anticipated it all along, that everything had to close. The last entry of her diary, where she thought we both saw the world as a place of possessiveness and power, of wanting to belong and not, of departures into the dark, the unknown, of returning home again, was right in a way, I suppose. But we couldn't have lived like that together, and I proved to be the survivor after all. That is the graft of our stories, here in this diary, our girlish voices like echoes across the seas and the flat lands of Johannesburg, that quiet collision of our silent fears in a strange land.

The trial brought me one surprising thing: Paul. He appeared on the street in the rain outside the Norman Mead Hotel in Winchester, on the last day. I spotted him as I stepped out to go to the Great Hall — he was leaning against the building opposite, his hat pulled down across his face, the rain dripping onto his shoulders. He looked up at just the moment I saw him, and he ran across the street, jumping out the way of a car, and came across the wet pavement towards me.

Paul stood in front of me and pushed his hat to the back of his head. We looked at one another in silence. Because it is awful, knowing things and having to hold the small, hard seeds of truth, secrets and certainty between your hands. It's unnatural. I don't think other people do. I think they go about their lives, making messes and having triumphs, muddling along and hoping for the best. I think their hands are usually open, their fingers splayed, fingertips running over tabletops, bumping along iron railings or trailing across the edges of a lover's face. I envy them their casual, faulty relationship with the world.

'Laura,' he said.

He was brown and tanned, out of place in Winchester's wet medieval streets. He held out his hand to me.

'I thought I'd find you here. I came to find you.'

I looked past him at a woman and her child, a girl, with tight blonde curls and white socks pulled up over her chubby pink legs, on the pavement opposite. They were turning slow circles with their heads down, searching for something dropped on the grey, wet pavement. I suddenly wanted, very much, for them to find it. The girl thought she might have spotted something and she ran back up the street, away from her mother, and then bent down and picked something up and held it above her head for her mother to see. The mother rushed over to her and knelt down to take the small, gleaming object from the girl, and then they were both laughing, wide smiles of pleasure and relief.

I told him everything, how I had read Gay's diary, had read about their affair, everything, how unfair his parents had been, how shifting and uneasy I'd found the ground, the hostility of the place, it all came spilling out without reason or design, I threw it at him, all the facts I had at my fingertips, everything, even how I had put my hand across her mouth because I'd wanted her dead.

He'd stopped me then, and pushed me up against the wall.

'Laura, she was a fantasist, a loon. She was crazy. Never mention it again, it happened like they said, she died with James Camb. How do you know if anything in her diary was true?'

I told him that something bad had happened to me there, that I wasn't the same person as the one he had married. I told him what Bibi Bathurst had said about an apple never falling far from its tree, that perhaps I was as cold and chilly on the inside as my mother. And he'd laughed and hugged me, as though he thought I'd said it to be endearing. I told him I'd thought he was my one chance, my one hope of escaping the chill.

'Why,' he'd said, 'I hardly knew who I had married. You hardly knew yourself. It was my fault –' and he waved his arm in the air – 'I was messed up about everything. It has to have been worth something, doesn't it?'

Still the same optimistic Paul. Traipsing through the old streets of Winchester. It was there on the tip of my tongue, the question, 'But was it all true?' and then I realised that I didn't need to know, or even want to know his answer.

*

Paul has appeared now at the kitchen doorway, holding up a newspaper. He has come to take me out for lunch, we are taking it slowly, being polite and solicitous of one another, wary but kind and open to suggestion. I like how wet it is here, how broken-down; we will go to the bistro round the corner, wrapped up in our summer jackets, where it is dark and the food not good, small congealing bits of meat in gravy and grey potatoes, but we like it because it is quiet and we can sit opposite each other at our little table in the corner, and try to make amends.

'Look at this, Lala,' he says. 'They won. The Nationalists won the election.' He scans the paper, a pen between his teeth, *When arriving in Pretoria by train, Mr Malan was greeted with a tumultuous welcome. "In the past," he*

372

said, "we felt like strangers in our own country, but today South Africa belongs to us once more. For the first time since Union, South Africa is our own. May God grant that it always remains so."' They're going to do dreadful things, Laura, now they've finally got power. I know it.'

I will go over to Paul and stand next to him, by the crook of his arm, and read the newspaper he is holding.

'Yes,' I will say to him. 'They thought they were strangers in that country, they will do dreadful things with power. I know they will too.'

Right, that's it. It finishes here, this is the last entry in our diary.

Acknowledgments

The events and persons surrounding Gay Gibson's murder are largely truthful, as are the bare bones of Gay's life as shown here in her fictionalised diary. James Camb was convicted of her murder but doubt remained about his guilt. He was sentenced to death but escaped the gallows when a House of Commons vote suspended the death penalty in 1948 for a trial period of five years. He was released in 1959. I have used the names which appeared in the trial transcripts, with the obvious exception of Laura Trelling, and whilst their names are factual, I have characterised and coloured all characters and facts for my own imaginative purposes.

In the course of researching the Gay Gibson murder I read numerous books and websites. I am particularly and enormously indebted to Denis Herbstein's *The Porthole Murder Case* and to *The Trial of James Camb* edited by Geoffrey Clark, which is part of the Notable British Trials series. Many thanks to the staff of the British Library newspaper archive and to the wonderful and informative website South African History Online, sahistory.org.za, which proved invaluable, as did the ANC's website at anc.org.za. They are in no way responsible for the fact that I have dated and placed the miners' strike in August 1947 when in truth it took place a year earlier in August 1946. Many thanks also to Judy Heath for telling me everything she could remember about post-war Johannesburg and for being an inspiration.

My very great thanks go to my agent Peter Straus and to Caroline Gascoigne and her team at Hutchinson, to my husband, Stewart Harcourt, who read, cajoled, ignored and suggested at all the right times and who makes everything possible. Thank you to my children Benjamin, Thomas and Molly for being themselves and for being funny and patient when I was disorganised and vague. Thanks guys, you rock.